CHANGE OF HEART

M PROCTOR

# FriesenPress

One Printers Way
Altona, MB R0G 0B0
Canada

www.friesenpress.com

Copyright © 2023 by M Proctor
First Edition — 2023

All rights reserved.

No part of this publication may be reproduced in any form, or by any means, electronic or mechanical, including photocopying, recording, or any information browsing, storage, or retrieval system, without permission in writing from FriesenPress.

ISBN
978-1-03-914708-9 (Hardcover)
978-1-03-914707-2 (Paperback)
978-1-03-914709-6 (eBook)

1. FICTION/OCCULT & SUPERNATURAL

Distributed to the trade by The Ingram Book Company

Chapter 1

OBLIVIOUS TO THE vibrant spring flora dominating her surroundings, Karen Shorn frantically carried her eight-year-old daughter into the local hospital emergency area and rushed straight to the reception desk. Awkwardly balancing a very distressed Sway in her arms, while simultaneously attempting to unearth the necessary medical documents from the depths of her cluttered purse, *and* keep from falling apart completely, Karen explained to the intake nurse that Sway was experiencing the exact symptoms that had plagued her during the nine previous emergency visits. The nurse mercifully bypassed the already long lineup of patience waiting for care and motioned to follow her directly to an available bed, quickly checked and recorded Sway's vitals, and then informed them that a doctor would be with them shortly. Karen sent a silent message of gratitude to the Universe that at least, this time, they didn't have to remain, for hours on end, in those impossibly uncomfortable waiting room chairs. What Karen did not know was her child had been red flagged as a child at risk which immediately place her as a priority.

Karen forcefully stifled the rising panic that was threatening to drown her and held back the tears in a valiant attempt to mask the fear from her daughter. It seemed like forever before a doctor appeared and she was just about to lose her composure when the curtain finally opened.

"Hello, I'm Doctor Hamilton – who have we here?" His pleasant demeanor and kind expression provided a thread of calm to the situation. As he spoke, he checked Sway's vitals. "How are you feeling young lady?" Sway seemed less anxious with his attention.

"I think I'm feeling better now."

Dr. Hamilton regarded her with measured, yet relaxed scrutinizing gaze – he was good at this, and Karen's spirits lifted just a little...maybe this time?

"I'm glad to hear that, Sway," he responded as he glanced at the chart. "How were you feeling before, when your mother first brought you in to the hospital?" Sway looked up at him with huge trusting eyes and Karen winced from the jab to her heart.

"Well, I just wasn't feeling well," Sway reported, confusion written over her features.

"Can you be more specific? Where exactly in your body did you feel this discomfort?" The doctor gently continued his examination as he prodded Sway for more information.

"I had pains in my chest," Sway's lips quivered. Karen interrupted the doctor's exploratory questions with, "Check Sway's medical file. You are asking the very same questions that my daughter has responded to the previous nine times I rushed her into this emergency facility, so why are you torturing her with the same repetitive questioning?" Why is it each time the medical staff found no abnormal results in any of their tests. The doctor took a long hard look at Karen. Tears of frustration welled up in Karen's eyes.

"Please Mrs. Shorn, would you come with me so we can talk privately?" His tone was quiet, and he turned to Sway with a reassuring glance. "I just need to talk to your mom for a minute – a nurse will come to keep you company until we get back." The words had barely been spoken, when a smiling uniformed young lady breezed into the cubicle, her blond ponytail cheerfully bobbing back and forth, with each bounce of her gait.

"Hello Sway, my name is Hope," she gently squeezed the young child's hand. "I'm going to keep you company for a bit, is that OK?" Sway smiled shyly and nodded. Karen's unease at leaving Sway's side abated a little, and she reluctantly followed the doctor to a small meeting room, just down the hallway. She managed only until the door closed behind them, and they were seated facing each other, before she burst into tears. "What is wrong with my daughter?" She agonized, visibly shaking in her agitated state.

Dr. Hamilton held his professional composure. Cases like this one he found to be difficult. This child had been flagged due to evidence building that the mother may have Munchausen Syndrome by proxy, a mental health condition in which the caregiver makes up or causes an illness or injury of a person under their care. Yet, they did not have enough evidence to call child services, God forbid they falsely accuse the mother but at the same time God forbid they don't intervene in time and the child is permanently harmed. All the tests for poisons or drugs to create the child and mother's description of the child's symptoms have come back negative.

Dr. Hamilton was thankful they had a new child psychologist who had recently joined the hospital team. Finding health specialists willing to live is a small remote area in northern British Columbia with limited back up resources was challenging. Dr. Faith Kerr was highly regarded in her profession and a legend in the number of documented successes with traumatised children. She claims her success comes from teamwork with everyone involved in the child's life. Dr. Kerr's calls her sister Hope Burnett, who is a nurse, her secret weapon, who is a critical component of her team. No one bonds fast with a child than Hope, which is why they have her caring for Sway at this very moment.

Dr. Hamilton had heard a rumour that Dr. Kerr had lost her own child to the acts of a mentally ill patient who had stocked her. Maybe someday in the future he would be able to ask her about it, but now the focus was on this patient, Sway and her mother.

Dr. Hamilton hoped Dr. Kerr would arrive soon as he took a deep breath before explaining to the mother on next steps in this process. "We can find nothing wrong with your child. In your past emergency visits, we have run every test in the book, and have found nothing physically wrong with her." He then straightened and added with a look of resolve, "In circumstances like this, our only option left, really – protocol - is to undergo a home evaluation to determine what might be going on in the child's household what may be contributing to the problem."

"There is nothing going on in our home," The flow of tears increased as Karen broke down, sobbing uncontrollably, and screamed emphatically, "you are missing something in your tests!" She looked like she was broaching her limit – a point of no return. She became startled at the sudden rap on the door, which swiftly opened, and Dr. Kerr entered. Dr. Hamilton displayed his professional admiration and respect as he stood for the introductions.

"Mrs. Karen Shorn, I'd like you to meet Dr. Faith Kerr, who is a psychologist that specializes in cases such as Sway's - she will be taking Sway on as her patient." He afforded a brief smile that did not quite reach his troubled eyes, and then abruptly left the room. Karen tried to stop the flow of tears as she turned to Dr. Kerr, and feeling increasingly out of control of the situation and thoroughly fearful for her daughter's welfare. She closed her eyes, took a deep breath and gathered her wits.

"You people are clearly missing something," she stated unequivocally, regarding the doctor warily. "My daughter is experiencing chest pains and nausea – yes, it abates randomly, but keeps coming back, and you need to find out what is wrong with her!" With an assessing glance, Dr. Kerr sat down in the chair, reached out across the table and firmly took hold of Karen's hands. Clasping them gently, she spoke softly.

"I understand that you are worried about your child and believe me, we will do our very best to sort this all out." Dr. Kerr assured her. The doctor's quiet, soft-spoken demeanor, together with the solacing warmth radiating from her hands, provided a measure of calm – a soothing balm to Karen's frayed nerves.

"No one believes us," she whispered softly – almost indistinct. But the doctor was listening.

"Who is 'us'?" Dr. Kerr inquired in the same whisper and tone as Karen," sustaining firm eye contact.

"Sway and I,"

"I believe you," Dr. Kerr assured her, increasing her hold, in tight affirmation. It felt like a promise – a commitment and Karen collapsed in renewed weeping, with her head on the table, maintaining her grip on the doctor's hands. Dr. Kerr slowly disengaged one of these from Karen's grasp and gently stroked the top of her head, patiently waiting for the wave of teardrops to subside.

"What is your greatest fear?" Dr. Kerr softly probed. There was no mistaking the compassion in this woman's eyes and Karen resolutely wiped her tear-ravaged face and blew her nose with a tissue Dr. Kerr had offered, before answering.

"Losing my daughter, because the doctors have missed something – that a mistaken diagnosis could threaten the life of my little girl," Karen explained. Dr. Kerr once again enfolded Karen's hands within her own and looked directly into her eyes.

"I promise you; we will figure this all out - you, I, Sway, and any other people and resources we need to pull into the mix to solve this mystery." At the look of solid conviction in Faith Kerr's eyes, Karen relaxed, and her fears dissipated, feeling reassured by this doctor's promise.

"Oh God, I behaved awfully with Dr. Hamilton!" At Dr. Kerr's dismissive shake of the head, Karen tucked away a mental note to offer him an apology at some point in the near future.

"You wait right here – I'm going to go gather up Sway – I'll be right back." When Dr. Kerr rose and opened the door, Karen's heart leapt in alarm at the sight of a security guard, standing just outside. Dr. Kerr politely informed the guard that his duties would no longer be needed.

"I don't think so doc, these patients with Munchausen syndrome can be dangerous." The guard stood his ground, seemingly not the least intimidated by her.

"What medical school did you attend?" Dr. Kerr snapped – her tone deadly cold.

"None," the guard responded tentatively, having enough sense to drop the arrogance in his previous tone.

"I never want to hear you deliver a misinformed medical evaluation about a patient ever again - now get out of my sight before I have you removed from your job *and* this hospital!" Dr. Kerr hissed.

"Yes ma'am, sorry ma'am," the guard stammered hastily, visibly quaking in his boots, and with lightning speed, scurried out of the doctor's view. Dr. Kerr came back into the room and Karen closed her jaw which she was sure had dropped fully to the floor after witnessing the astounding admonishment that the previously gentle doctor had just administered onto that man.

"I am so sorry you had to hear that." Dr. Kerr stated, then with a speculative look, went on to ask, "Do you know what Munchausen syndrome is?"

"Yes, I think so," Karen replied, then went on to clarify," it is where a parent makes their child sick, in order to get attention." She fought down her defensive compulsion – she really didn't believe Dr. Kerr was seriously going anywhere with this.

"That is correct," Dr. Kerr concurred with a conciliatory smile, "but that is *not* what I believe is going on in this case, so pay no attention to what you've just heard." She sent an affirmative glance Karen's way. "Now, I will go get your daughter," she concluded as she left the room. Karen let out a deep shaky sigh – releasing some of the pent-up anguish, worry, stress and fear. And trauma – yes trauma, she silently acknowledged. Her next breath was deep, steadying and blessedly hopeful.

Just moments later, Sway bounced into the room with a gigantic smile plastered across her sweet face. It was like a breath of fresh air!

"I am feeling better Mommy," Sway announced joyfully as she jumped up onto her mother's lap.

"I can see that," Karen quipped in return, as she squeezed her daughter in a loving embrace. Both the nurse and Dr. Kerr followed Sway into the room.

"This is Hope," Sway announced, regarding her newfound friend with an adoring grin, "she is a nurse and I really like her." Hope reached over and shook Karen's hand warmly.

"Nice to meet you and I must say that you have a beautiful daughter," Hope commented.

"Thank you," Karen responded kindly, but cautiously, as she was a little unsure of where this was going and what would happen next. The two women sensed Karen's apprehension and quickly offered reassurances - that at this point in time, Sway showed no symptoms for immediate concern, but there would most certainly be further and thorough investigation toward a resolution.

"Part of that process would be for us to visit your home for further evaluation," Dr. Kerr explained. Karen squared her shoulders staunchly.

"Please believe me, there are no issues in our home, but you have my full support to investigate whoever and whatever you need to, in determining what is making my daughter sick," Karen professed.

"I asked Hope to come visit me and see my room while she's there," Sway chimed in excitedly.

"Of course, it would be on your schedule and convenience – thank for your support – I know how hard this is for you!" Hope smiled warmly, in an obvious effort to inspire confidence and further put Karen's mind at rest.

"I appreciate what you are doing for my daughter." Karen conceded. "If you don't mind, it is late and both Sway and I are tired, so I would like to get her home - that is - if there is nothing else you need?"

"That is an excellent idea!" agreed Dr. Kerr. "If and when Sway's symptoms recur, I would like you to bypass Emergency and call one of us. Both of our numbers are on here." She handed Karen a card that provided their credentials and specialties, as well as contact information, and Karen nodded gratefully when she noticed options listed, in case of emergencies. She gathered up her daughter, offered her thanks and said goodbye. Sway ran over and gave both the doctor and the nurse enthusiastic hugs before she bounced out of the hospital, as if she'd never been in distress. Karen, on the other hand, felt as if she'd just been tossed out of a giant twister.

She was grateful they were able to finally leave the hospital with an open line of communication with professionals that, for the first time, had offered a viable plan to address her daughter's problems. She'd been contemplating her options – where available medical resources just too slim, in their small northwestern B.C. community? It was no wonder that the medical staff believed she was crazy, Karen pondered, as she watched her daughter skip down the sidewalk, humming merrily to herself, while taking great pains to avoid stepping on the cracks – such an amazingly speedy recovery! The hospital security had stood watch as Karen had rushed her daughter out the doors, like a thief in the night.

Chapter 2

DR. FAITH KERR turned to Hope Burnett, as she cleanly gathered her notes and Sway's file. "Is it what you think?" she asked, in a tone that suggested absolute trust and comfort in their relationship. Hope nodded her assent.

"Then we don't have a lot of time," Faith concluded.

"How is our dear mother faring?" Hope inquired.

"She is expecting us," Faith grinned affectionately. Hope smiled back, obviously sharing the sentiment.

"Yes of course she is, so let's get these reports done - then tuck her in." Hope suggested. Faith nodded her corroboration. They finished their paperwork on Sway and headed to their mother's room. Both women were lost in thought – would it be possible to save this little girl, and her family?

They had lost count of cases they had worked on. It was their mother's crusade they had joined at birth. Developing their gifts so they could work closely with their mother saving children from the darkest evil planted on this earth. Their mother is a seer, which means she has the gift of seeing into the future. What baffled them was how their mother could see some things coming and other things she was blocked from. Like the murder of Faith's child, Rose.

They both had the gift of healing. Faith's gift was healing the mind and soul, whereas Hope's gift was healing through energy. Their mother had encountered the evil up close and personal when it sought out Faith and Hope when they reached the ages of 5 and 7. Fortunately their mother was able to intervene. But with every intervention there is unforeseen consequences, so every move must be carefully thought out.

Dr. Hamilton's voice was a pleasant sound to their ears as he called out their names, "Dr. Kerr, Ms. Burnett, can I have a moment of your time?" Faith turned to her colleague with a bright, warm smile and replied, "of course." Dr. Hamilton motioned to an available meeting room to which the sisters followed.

Dr. Hamilton closed the door behind him and the three settled comfortable in their chairs. "How can we help?" Faith asked in a soft tone. Dr. Hamilton responded with an infectious smile and stated, "first I want to apologies for not welcoming you both to the team in a more formal way, like a team dinner, but as you can see, we are all stretched to the max and just getting a few of us together at one time would be difficult. We have so many short-term health professionals in the north, we truly value those who sign on full time."

Dr. Hamilton started to say, "Ms. Burnett, when Hope interrupted and said, "please, call me Hope." Dr. Hamilton's smile got even more infectious, "OK, Hope, you can call me Gary." He stood up and reached over to shake Hope's hand, then Faith's. As he took Faith's hand she responded, "and I am Faith."

Gary cleared his throat then went on, "now we are onto a great start, I want to discuss the Shorn child. I just ran across a visiting physician that saw the child on a previous visit, Dr. Crowley, and he is adamant that we should keep the child here for observation. He also wants to take over the child's file as her family physician, which of course raises concerns. I know her family doctor is away at this moment, but she holds all that family's medical files. It isn't normal protocol to move a child to another G.P. without the parent's request."

"Thank you for the heads up," Faith responded, "as for now there is no evidence of the child being in danger. We have already gotten permission from the mother to start home visits to investigate the possible causes of the child's temporary symptoms. I agree that the child is not transferred to another family doctor. This is how we lose we lose vital medical history and this doctor you stated is a visiting General Practitioner. I am new here so I do not have a huge patient workload so I will ensure all basis of Ms. Shorn's health is covered and will meet personally with her family doctor when she returns."

Gary nodded in agreement, then enquired, "your mother, does she have a family doctor assigned to her yet?" Both Faith and Hope shook their heads. Hope chimed in, "we are working on that." "Well how about I take over her case?" Gary offered. Hope and Faith rose from their chairs and shook Gary's hand and promised to run it by their mother and thanked him for his kind offer. Gary assured them that it was his pleasure and offered to meet for coffee soon. The sisters agreed as they left the meeting room. Gary felt all warm and fuzzy as he watched Dr. Kerr, - Faith – leave the room. He was looking forward to coffee.

The sister's minds where back on task. Part of the plan for their next case included admitting their mother, Susan Burnett, into the hospital for observation a week prior. She was quite the charmer, when she chose to be, and aside from being somewhat seasoned, she seemed quite healthy. None of the team questioned her presence, respecting that the two sisters must have had good reason for concern. Their colleagues were top notch and highly valued one another – in short – they had one another's backs. Well, most of them...As they left the emergency area and entered the Patient Care wing, both cringed at the grating sound of Dr. Crowley's incredibly annoying voice.

"Dr. Kerr, one moment please." Hope hissed under her breath, inaudible to all but her sister. "God, I hate that man, I cannot wait for his day in hell." Faith shushed her sister and turned to respond to this incorrigible man that they thoroughly despised.

"Yes, can I help you?" Faith asked, there was a sense of evil about this man, she was not afraid of him, but knew to never let her guard down.

"Where is the Shorn child that was admitted this evening?" Dr. Crowley queried.

"Oh, she wasn't admitted," Hope corrected the doctor, with a cool smile.

11

"I wasn't asking *you, nurse*" Dr. Crowley snapped, his distain obvious with the pointed emphasis of her position.

Faith turned to her sister and stated, "I will deal with this, and meet with you after I am finished with Dr. Crowley." The latter observed Hope's departure with a smirk.

"These nurses just don't know their place," Dr. Crowley chuckled pompously, an unspoken challenge in his eyes, "*you* managed her well."

"Don't you ever talk to any of my health team in that manner again - not the nurses or any other team member at this hospital." Faith's tone inflected a calm chill. Dr. Crowley stepped back in shocked surprise, but quickly recovered.

"You don't have any idea who you are dealing with, do you?" His chest puffed out with indignation.

With clear intent, Faith shifted closer to Dr. Crowley in an intimidating gesture then snapped, "I know exactly who I am talking to – now, why are you wasting my time?" Dr. Crowley squared his shoulders in obvious distaste, more than little outraged at what he clearly considered to be her insolence.

"The Shorn child is my patient from a previous emergency visit - I believe her mother is the cause of her illness, and the child should not have been discharged into her care!" he spouted, no longer quite meeting her burning gaze head on.

"You are wrong on both counts," asserted Faith. "First, there is no substantiation to that preposterous claim - it is just one remote possibility from any number of variables - and second, without evidence to support your theory, the mother is within her full legal rights to remove the child from this hospital at any time of her choosing." A determined Dr. Kerr then went on to contend, "Let me assure you - this case has all of our attention, especially because it involves a child's welfare!" she bestowed a formidable glare upon this egoistical man, "Furthermore, you are a visiting physician who does not specialize in pediatrics, and therefore, no child being treated in this hospital will *ever* fall under your scope of practice, effectively deeming Sway Shorn *not* to be your patient."

"Don't you see you are missing something which may result in this child's death?" Dr. Crowley sputtered angrily. Faith's contempt was well-grounded, and she didn't bother to hide her derisive smirk.

"I am more than aware of my responsibility to my patient, and right now, my attention is needed elsewhere. I suggest you focus on your own patients as I will on mine," she concluded, stepping away from Dr. Crowley. "Now if you will excuse me, I am extremely busy!" She departed without a single backward glance and headed off in the direction her sister had gone. She tried in vain to disregard the cold shiver snaking through her body, and the unsettling sensation of physical assault by Dr. Crowley's rage - the sharp, dark energy barbs stabbing into her back. If looks could kill, without question, she knew she'd be a goner. She willfully shook it off and focused on the next task at hand. There was never enough time and so much to do.

Faith found Hope sitting on their mother's bed engaged in a quiet conversation. "Hello Mom" Faith greeted her mother warmly as she kissed her upraised cheek. Glancing out the window toward the picture-perfect scenic backdrop – low mountains in the distance and the mighty Skeena River silently snaking through the city, she gloried in the fiery sunset, and pondered their fate – hers, Hope's, her mother's - how could anything sinister possibly touch this majestic paradise?

"Hello, my darling Faith," her mother returned. "Hope has just been filling me in on the child, Sway Shorn." Susan shot her a knowing look.

"From what I have seen so far, as Mom predicted, every timeline is moving into place." Hope assured them.

"Then we need to work quickly" Susan insisted emphatically. All three women nodded in agreement.

"Dr. Crowley is not far behind us," Hope interjected.

"Yes," their mother acknowledged, "that cop that has been following you from our last three locations, has he showed up yet?"

"As you foretold, Mom," Faith heaved a troubled sigh. Susan reached out to pull her oldest daughter into her arms.

"I am so sorry honey, out of all of this you have sacrificed the most, and I feel your pain." Susan held on tight. Hope reached over and rubbed her sister's back in a comforting gesture – the two women were rocks in supporting Faith through this ordeal.

Time was always at an essence, but there are painful moments in the reality that not all results included a better future, so it was critical that they tread very carefully. The ultimate consequence came with one of their interventions to save a stranger's child, resulting in the murder of Faith's own child, Rose. Their mother's comment regarding Faith's deep sacrifice was the epitome of an understatement. Faith retreated from her mother's embrace and wiped a solitary tear from the corner of her eye, standing tall as she regained her determination.

"What is the plan mom?"

"Save the child," just as both sisters knew Susan Burnett would say, as fear crept into their souls. This was always a dark journey with very little light. What would it cost them next?

Chapter 3

AFTER FINALLY TUCKING her daughter in, a flood of exhaustion assaulted Karen and she ruefully acknowledged that they were both totally spent from their hospital ordeal. Hell – how much could they be expected to endure? It was frightening, to receive no diagnosis for her episodes, without the added insinuated accusation that Sway's illness could somehow be caused by something Karen may have orchestrated! The very idea broke Karen's heart and she felt the weight of that heavy ache in her chest now.

If one were to ask, Karen would describe her life as ordinary – predictable at least, if lacking a little excitement. She considered herself to be average – relatively run-of-the-mill; garden-variety female, by society standards - married to Tom for eleven years, with two children; Sway – eight years old, and Zac, their nine-year-old son. Oh man, how did that happen so fast? Their golden lab, Daisy and a cat named Key-key rounded out the traditional family structure. They bought their house just after they were married, in the picturesque home-town community of Terrace, British Columbia, and took out a thirty-year mortgage. They weren't going anywhere soon – both born here and determined to raise their family likewise.

Karen once aspired of buckling down to law school – earning that prestigious degree that would add initials after her name – a career to take pride in, where she could make a difference. For a time, she engaged in fueling that passion through her work at a local law firm, but when the kids came along the dream was reluctantly set aside - Tom was adamant. "Our children will not be raised by strangers!" He would rant at her every time the subject came up. He'd stayed with his job as a mechanic at the local car dealership, just a ten-minute drive from their home – kept him solidly in his comfort zone. The work he found enjoyable, the compensation generous and he genuinely liked the people on his team. Yep – predictable. She shouldn't complain though – it put food on the table and provided stability.

In truth, full-time homemaker status suited her. Karen's routine was key - dinner prepped daily before the children got home from school so that there was very little left to do, save for putting in front of them. Other than a quick table swipe and storing away food that might spoil, Karen saved other household duties until after the children were in bed. This allowed for quality family time (at least her and the kids), along with jetting them back and forth to their after-school activities. Karen never missed a game or event! But tonight, was different. Sway's symptoms had started just after their meal, and they'd rushed to the hospital…she now surveyed the after-dinner mess that normally would have been handled an hour ago and tackled it with a determination and energy she hadn't known she still possessed.

Karen wearily flipped off the kitchen light and checked on the kids. A quick peek revealed Zac, still positioned upright, thoroughly engrossed in the latest Percy Jackson novel that he'd saved for and bought at a recent school bookfair. Daisy was spread-out in horizontal comfort, on the opposite side of the bed, her head on the pillow. She never strayed far from Zac. When they had gotten her as a puppy, she was intended to be the family dog, but these two had instantly bonded like superglue, so the remainder of the family were graced with her attention only when Zac was not at home.

"Zac honey, it is time to put your book away," spoken for their ears only. "You should have been sleeping a couple of hours ago." There was more affection than admonition in her diction.

"Awe mom," Zac whispered, not willing to risk his father overhearing, or that last bonus chapter his mom always caved in to, would be a goner for sure. "Just one more chapter, *please*," Zac drew out the word for effect with relative confidence in the outcome.

"Ok," Karen conceded, affectionately ruffling his hair and placing a kiss on the top of his head. "I suppose it's not your fault Sway and I were so late tonight…one more, then lights out Mister!" she retorted with mock sternness. Smiling, she pulled the bedroom door closed softly. Zac was doing so well in school, and she couldn't deny that his avid love for reading was an influencing factor. Many of his friends were hooked on video games - thank God that was not Zac's passion!

Sway's door was fully ajar with all lights blazing. Karen flipped the ceiling light off as she entered. Sway's head bobbed drowsily – determinedly awaiting her mother's customary good night kiss and tuck in. Karen gently snugged the blankets up cozy around her neck, ran her fingers through the sweet thick dark hair, then bent down, extending the lip caress to her little girl's brow for just a moment longer than usual.

"Mommy, I'm sorry about getting sick" Sway apologized drowsily, with a mammoth yawn.

"No worries, sleepyhead, just get some shuteye," Karen whispered, brushing the back of her hand against her cheek.

"I like Hope," Sway declared groggily. Karen smiled, instinctively aware that the two had forged an instant bond. She had to admit to an immediate comfort with the pretty nurse too.

"She seems very nice, now off to sweet dreamland."

"You too mom," Sway responded, her voice trailing off as she was already drifting. Key-Key leisurely strolled in and leaped onto the bed with supple feline grace. She nestled into her favourite spot molded to Sway's hips, purring and kneading the soft blanket as if to lull her young mistress into slumber. It was a given - Sway's breathing slowed into an easy rhythm as she drifted into a dream state. Karen switched off the bedside lamp and illuminated the room with the Little Pony nightlight her daughter loved, leaving the door partially open as she exited, with one more troubled backward glance at her sleeping child.

Making her way wearily to the shower, she sighed in frustration as it was necessary to backtrack to the linen closet to retrieve her body wash. Tom was very particular about the scent of the soap she used, adamantly declaring, "no girlie soap for me!" Oh, the warm water cascading over her body felt divine – she could quite happily stay there forever, allowing her worries and stress from the long day to flush down the drain with the steady stream.

Instead, she rushed through her routine - it was getting later, and Tom would become increasingly irritated. She hastily dried, slipped into her night clothes and wandered into the bedroom. Tom was flicking grumpily through the TV channels when Karen climbed under the covers.

"Nothing on TV anymore," he grumbled, a derisive frown revealing his current mood – *only* mood these days, it seemed, with *her*, anyhow. "How is Sway?" Tom was still focused on the TV.

"They found nothing that would cause the chest pains," Karen sighed, her expression troubled – not that he'd notice as he hadn't yet given her so much as a sideways glance.

"Told you she would be fine," Tom cracked condescendingly.

"Yes, you did," Karen agreed sagely, choosing to avoid an argument.

"Lots of clean up tonight?" Tom inquired.

"It was fine," Karen responded. What was the point of retorting that her day would have ended a lot sooner if he had partnered in all the responsibilities? Nor would she ask if he'd checked to see how their son's day had gone – his shrugging response would just stab that painful shard into her aching heart even deeper. She knew Tom hadn't even bothered to ask.

"Kids, ok?" Ok, go ahead and make a liar out of me…

"All good for now," Karen replied, feeling remorseful for the resentful thoughts – in his own way, he surely did care.

"You sure took your time," Tom grunted testily.

"I am sorry honey," Karen apologized, glancing at the clock - 10:15pm. Even with the trip to the hospital it was not any later than usual, but as always, it was all about Tom. Karen curled into her favourite fetal position, her bum inadvertently brushing up against his thigh.

"Get your fat ass over on your own side," he snapped testily. More often than not, these days, he was adamant about mattress territory. Ouch – that familiar slice of pain from deep-seated emotions that resurfaced every time he berated her in this manner. She couldn't deny she'd expanded a little in size every passing year and felt the warm flood of shame – inadequacy as a wife; a woman, and instinctively internalized the blame and accountability. She shifted over to her edge of the bed dutifully. But cooking was her great passion – and to *eat* those creations…where had she heard, "we consume our pain" – at Weightwatchers? Yeah, that was a bust these days. In truth, Karen was still a very attractive woman, wearing her weight well - evenly distributed over her curvy frame. It was the sparkle in her sea-green eyes that caught people's attention whenever she smiled – Tom used to say her gorgeous smile always stopped his heart – it had been too many years now.

"We have a staff meeting tomorrow," Tom informed her; "can you make sure I have some extra cookies to take to work for a snack? Greg loves your chocolate chip cookies." Yeah, she was right there with him, unfortunately. "You do have some right?" It was a demand more than a question. She would not be the least bit surprised if the man insisted, she get up and bake them before she was allowed to sleep for the night!

"Yes – in the freezer." she reluctantly climbed out from the cozy covers, and padded out of the room to retrieve them, to thaw by morning. She kept a good supply of baking in the freezer, as there was always some type of function going on – Tom's work, school, etc. Everyone loved her goodies so there was an ongoing rush of requests for samples. It warmed her heart to know she was revered as one of the best in their social group, consistently winning contests at the local fairs. Her recipes were liberally published in the church cookbook – "Lordy Karen, there wouldn't even be a cookbook without all your submissions," Debbie Owens had professed. Karen supposed it signified a success for her – a skill to take pride in, but deep down she knew it fueled a much subversive inner need – to feel valued, loved and adequate – that she was 'enough'. A single tear rolled down her cheek – how she craved that from her husband!

Completely exhausted now, she was in full automation mode, placing the bag on the counter – couldn't miss it right next to the coffee pot – timer ready to go with Tom's favourite travel mug in place. This time taking great care to stay on her side, she nestled her head into the soft eiderdown pillow he had finally allowed her to purchase last month, and promptly slipped off into sleep as Tom continued to flip through the channels, griping his disgust before settling in on one program.

Karen awoke gasping desperately for her life's breath and fighting panic. It felt like someone was sitting square on her chest. She struggled to a sitting position, and suddenly noticed Daisy in the room, staring intently at her. Their beloved canine released a deep-throated growl that set the hairs on the back of her neck straight up. "Daisy it's me, what's wrong?" her voice betrayed fear. Fully alarmed now, she quickly reached over to Tom and shook him, her eyes locked on Daisy. "Something is wrong!" she turned to him and prodded harder. "Tom, wake up, there is something wrong!" But Tom didn't move a muscle. She could hear his deep breathing and felt hysteria rising. Daisy gaited out of the bedroom and Karen sprang out of bed in pursuit – her children – were they safe? A deep chill in the room seeped straight through Karen's night clothes, permeating her entire body and she began to shiver. Her thoughts immediately sought logic - how did she miss an open window? Following Daisy directly into Sway's room, her heart missed a beat – her little girl was whimpering, in distress. Oh God, another long night!

Daisy growled again; her piercing gaze focused sharply into one corner of the room. "It's ok girl," Karen attempted to soothe their beloved dog, with far less confidence than she felt. This room as well, held a foreboding glacial bite, and she moved to check the window – firmly closed and locked. She pulled a spare blanket from the closet and draped it over her moaning girl. A sudden hiss and growl from Key-Key snapped Karen's attention to the feline's razor-sharp glare – the eerie green luminous stare drilled into the same corner. "It's ok, there is nothing there," Karen could hear the tremor of fear in her words and knew they were solely for her own benefit!

Plucking every ounce of courage she could muster, Karen moved over to the corner and shoved aside Sway's toys – nothing. In hasty retreat, she curled up beside Sway on the bed - a soft caress of her fingertips on Sway's shoulder – just enough so her sweet girl could sense Mom's comforting presence. Karen wondered what in the world was going on with the family pets. Daisy never left Zac's side, unless she needed to go out for a pee.

One of Sway's toys must have shifted, right? A feeling of looming dread overcame her as this did not at all explain these events - Daisy's presence in her room and the suffocating weight on her chest! She eventually drifted off into an agitated slumber with those troubling thoughts running amok in the background.

Karen snapped awake to Tom's bellow, "Karen, get up, for God's sake, the alarm did not go off, didn't you set it?" Disorientation stalled her response. Tom always set the alarm – what was he going on about. A sudden realization that she was back in her own bed brought her jumbled thoughts immediately to the previous night – was it possible she had dreamed it all? But the ominous feeling persisted.

Gathering her wits, she promptly jumped to her feet dashed to the kitchen to start breakfast preparations. Through the wall she heard the faucet turn on for Tom's customary morning shower. Karen couldn't fathom his insistence that she shower at night and he in the morning. The only exception was when he'd return from a night out with the boys. He claimed that a couple of them smoked cigars at the poker games and explained "I hate smelling like smoke all night." Karen often wondered about that – she'd never noticed it, when he strolled in the door.

"Get up kids, we are running late!" Karen called from the kitchen, as she put the final touches on the fare of fried egg sandwiches and juice.

"Ok," Zac called out, "Mom, did you put Daisy out?"

"No honey I didn't," Karen replied, and then remembered her dream, "Maybe check Sway's room."

"Why would she be there?" Zac puzzled, and a moment later continued, "Mom, why did you close Daisy up in Sway's room?"

"I didn't," Karen replied, with an odd feeling in the pit of her gut. Zac ran ahead of Daisy to open the door for her morning bathroom ritual – Thank God that dog had the bladder of an elephant. "Did you wake your sister?"

"I tried, but she is not getting up," Zac replied nonchalantly, sitting down to attack his plate of pancakes.

"No problem, I'll handle it," Karen was more than a bit surprised as both of her children were morning people - must have been her late night. Tom came barreling through the kitchen and hastily grabbed his toasted egg sandwich and coffee. Karen packaged up another one for Zac and asked Tom to drop him at school.

"Will do, as long as he is ready to go now," Tom imposed. Karen felt a stab of remorse over her resentment toward him. It was supposed to be give and take, wasn't it? After all, she was not the epitome of perfect!

"I am," Zac said, as he headed out the door with his breakfast, lunch, and schoolbooks in hand.

"What about Sway?" Tom asked.

"She isn't quite up yet – I'll get her off to school," Karen replied. Spotting the cookies still on the counter, she rushed out the door to catch him, just as he was pulling out of the garage. She tapped on the car window - his initial frown of annoyance changed to a warm smile as he rolled down the window and grabbed the cookies.

"Thanks babe," he gushed, before speeding out of the driveway. That grin had melted her heart many times when they were dating – so many years ago it seemed now. Dang, I wish he still looked at me like he does at those cookies. Or Jean at work…a consuming sadness swept over her. What was happening to her life? She went back in and decided to take a little extra time with Sway this morning – make her favourite chocolate chip pancakes for breakfast. The theme of the day – chocolate – food for the soul!

Before waking Sway, Karen started the decadent chocolate sauce that she dribbled liberally over the pancakes - the secret success to the recipe! She scooped some batter into the pan to test. Half of the fun of cooking was the tasting – nummy, she sighed as the fluffy creation, dripping with warm chocolate, melted in her mouth. Licking her fingers, she abandoned that heavenly escape - it was time! But hey - she could still bend the rules a little and allow Sway to dress *after* she ate, right? She was almost at Sway's door when the heart burn hit her like a brick. She thought it wise to reroute to the bathroom medicine cabinet for antacid medication. Wow, chocolate in the morning with coffee is clearly not the best choice, she mused. Those did little to help as a cold sweat hit her, and she sank down on the edge of her bed. A wave of nausea assaulted; it seemed almost certain she might vomit - what was the matter with her – normally she had a cast iron stomach?

Daisy bounced into the room in a state of frenzy, barking like crazy - that feeling of panic from the previous night set in – was she having anxiety attacks? "It is ok Daisy," Karen murmured assurances, but every cell in her body screamed the exact opposite. The dog paced incessantly from the bed to the door, unnerving Karen further, and she forced herself to follow Daisy to Sway's room. Upon entering the overwhelming nausea immediately passed.

Standing in utter confusion, the same cold chill hit Karen as it had in her dream the previous night. The cliché, "someone walking over your grave", passed through her mind. A sinister fear crept through her soul. Sway had not moved from the position she was in when Karen had checked her. "Sway, wake up honey," Karen called and gently shook her daughter – they had to get out of this room!

Had a mouse or rat gotten into the house? That would surely rile up the pets. The cat was pacing back and forth on the bed, mirroring Daisy's focus. Karen's alarm increased with her inability to rouse Sway! Ok, deal with this mouse or whatever it was - that made sense. Advancing into the corner, she slowly moved toys, watching for any trace of movement. It was soon evident there was not a thing in that corner, and her trepidation recurred two-fold.

The barking transitioned to extended low growls. Glancing over at Sway, she noticed the visible mist of her baby's breath, as if on a frosty morning. Karen moved slowly toward her, and the dog jumped between, teeth bared menacingly, intent on creating an impossible barrier between mother and child. Karen yelped - her senses on full alert. What could be wrong with their dog – the gentlest family pet anyone could dream of – never in a million years could she have imagined this? Had the dog been bitten by something – perhaps was rabid?

"Daisy please stop," She looked over at her beautiful daughter, "Sway wake up, sweetie!" An increasing tightening in her chest robbed her of breath, rendering her barely controlled fear into complete terror. She heaved a breath, trying to suck up as much oxygen as she could, and frantically backed out of the room, hoping the still growling dog would follow – each inch she moved back the dog moved forward – that's it - keep coming girl! She was beginning to feel lightheaded and dizzy.

As she backed completely out of the room, Karen looked around wildly in search of a spot to coax Daisy toward. Theirs was a modest home and all rooms had only one entrance/exit. She wondered if it really was possible for her heart to pound right out of her chest! If she could just lead the dog into the kitchen, would she be fast enough to dash down the hall to Sway's room, before the dog caught her? She surmised that there was no choice – something was very wrong here and she needed to protect her little girl!

Karen placed all her focus and energy on creating distance between her and Daisy, walking backward and making the loop around the island directly across from Sway's room. Through her fear and panic, she rationed that no matter what happened now, she would be between the dog and Sway. But she needed distance to keep it that way. Thud! Her shoulder hit the side of the fridge and she hastily pulled it open, fumbling along the shelves in search of something – anything to throw at Daisy as a distraction. She threw a hunk of cheese as far she could, to the opposite corner, and as Daisy flung around to investigate, Karen backed up, and deftly reached out to snatch the handheld in an iron clad death grip. "Run!" she heard herself scream in her head, as she sprang into action!

Hysteria rose as her mind registered the dog closing in behind her, growling ferociously at her heels. She flew into the room and rammed the door half on the animal's head. As Daisy howled in pain and pulled back, Karen slammed the door shut as hard as she could, and leaned back against it, with her heart pounding wildly. Oh, my dog – had she hurt her? But this wasn't her Daisy – rather some sort of demonic mad beast!

Karen renewed her effort to rouse Sway as she rushed to her side – her skin was so icy cold. Now the cat was upon her, scratching and clawing ferociously. She managed to snatch the scruff of its neck and fling the animal, air born across the room. As Key-key rose and commenced a feral stalk, Karen scrambled to grab the laundry basket with one hand and reached out to open the closet door with the other. She miraculously managed to swoop in and capture the crazed feline, just as it pounced, and with one swift hurl, threw both into the closet, slamming the door firmly shut. Oh My God, this is insane! Amid the background horror of a snarling dog and berserk feline wailing, she shakily picked up the phone and managed pluck out 911. There was undoubtedly terrible danger around them – no way could anyone sleep through this terror! Sobbing, she slid down to the floor like butter – her body shaking - fierce tremors that sent her teeth clattering together so violently, she was fearful of losing them all.

Chapter 4

IT WAS THE usual run-of-the-mill mix for Toby Eastman at the Emergency 911 Centre. A steady flow of calls came in and when Toby answered Karen's, there was no mistaking the customary panic in the voice on the other end. He started out with the usual script, "911, what is your emergency?" He made a mental note of a dog barking and growling furiously in the background, as he strained to listen.

"We live at 922, Elm Street, I need an ambulance, I can't wake my daughter!" It was obvious this woman was struggling to keep hysteria at bay. Toby checked the caller I.D. confirming the provided location of the address. Experience taught him that when a caller is in panic mode, they can often provide incorrect information – house/street/phone numbers, or the dispatcher can completely misunderstand the caller's words. It was imperative that he follow strict protocol to avoid a possible tragic mistake. He focused on keeping the caller as calm as possible by providing reassurance.

"We are dispatching an ambulance to you right now, ma'am," he then calmly and clearly asked for her name. The caller's voice was shaky as she replied.

"Karen, Karen Shorn."

"OK, Karen, are you on a cell phone?" In adherence to training, he kept his tone low and steady.

"No, it is a land line, I have a handheld." Toby then asked her if it had a speaker option.

"Yes!"

"Karen, listen carefully - I want you to put the phone on speaker, so you can place it down near you and still hear me. Do you understand?" At her affirmative reply, he continued, "if we lose our connection at any time, I will call you back, alright? Karen, you are doing great! Just stay with me - I'm going to help you." He paused for a second, giving her a chance to take a breath. "Now, where is your daughter right now?"

"Right here beside me, I am in her bedroom." The break in her voice betrayed her fear. Toby stayed on script.

"Ok Karen, this is important - is your daughter breathing?"

"Yes, she is breathing, I just can't wake her!" She sounded a bit calmer now.

"What is your daughter's name?"

"Sway, her name is Sway." She began to whimper a little, and Toby pushed on.

"How old is Sway?" Karen informed him that she was eight years old. "OK, Karen, I need you to do something for me - can you turn Sway onto her side and position her head, with her neck straight, so as to keep her airway open?" Karen said she could do that, and Toby heard her pleading with her daughter to wake up. The canine's increasing agitation posed a distraction. "Karen, listen – I'm having trouble hearing you clearly, is there a way to put the dog outside the bedroom and close the door?"

"The dog *is* outside the room." Karen began to cry softly. Toby considered the volatility of this menacing complexity in their rescue efforts and now the transition to low growls served only to fuel his concern. He continued to gather critical information.

"Has Sway been vomiting - does she feel warm at all?"

"No, if anything, she's a bit chilly – it's ice cold in here and I'm not sure why," she trailed off, "and she hasn't vomited."

"Has Sway been ill at all recently?"

Karen started crying again and explained, "Yes, I've had her to emergency several times and again last night, but no one would believe me when I told them that there's something wrong with her, and now I can't wake her!" Karen was weeping harder now.

"OK, Karen, the ambulance has just arrived and is parked outside your house. Is the door unlocked?" She replied affirmatively through hiccupping sobs. Toby moved to full alert, at the sound of a loud crash. The growling increased and then abruptly halted. He listened intently. "Karen, can you tell me what is going on right now?" Then the line went dead. From that point, Toby lost direct contact with the mother, but already had the call linked with the ambulance, so they could all communicate. He explained the situation to the First Responders and advised the team to take full cautionary measures when entering the unlocked home, due to a possible canine threat. He couldn't relate details such as the size or breed, and in line with protocol, attempted to re-establish the telephone connection with Karen.

Toby redialed the number on call display. It rang several times before he heard a child's voice on the line, "Hello?" the child's inquisitive tone relayed confusion.

"Who am I speaking with?" Tony kept his demeanor friendly and cheerful in an effort to gain immediate trust with this child. The situation was becoming increasingly convoluted, and a sixth sense had him instantly grateful that there were no inclement road conditions hampering their arrival.

"Sway," the child replied after a brief hesitation – he assumed that she'd been cautioned about giving her name out to strangers and thanked his lucky stars that she'd offered this to him. Clearly, she'd woken up, and he needed to assess their predicament - quickly.

"Hi Sway, this is Toby, and I am a 911 operator. Your mother called me, and I am going to get help for you. Can I please speak to your mother now?" Sway's quick response was that her mother was sleeping.

"Your mother is asleep?" the sense of impending danger tweaked his intuition.

"Yes, my mom is asleep, and she won't wake up!" The girl began to cry, and he knew they were on borrowed time here. The First Responders were also listening intently to this call – it was critical to be armed with as much information as possible, going in.

Toby asked slowly, "Where is your mom right now?" Sway hesitated for a few seconds.

"On the floor - beside my bed."

"Can you try to wake her up, Sway?" then added, "She just called me on your phone a few minutes ago." Toby heard the child calling to her mother.

"Mom - Mommy, wake up, there is a man on the phone for you. Mommy, wake up!" Then into the phone, "my mom is not waking up, you will have to call back. I will tell her you phoned." Toby responded instantly, worrying that the child may hang up.

"Listen to me Sway, it's important you stay on the phone, there are some nice people coming to your house, to help you and your mom. It's OK - your mom called and invited them, so don't be scared when they come into your house." Toby heard the child again call out to her mother, "Wake up Mommy, the nice people are here and want to come in." Toby continued to engage the child, "just stay on the phone Sway. I know this is scary, do you feel sick at all?" Sway quietly relayed that she did not. "Has your mom been sick at all?"

"No, just sleeping." Toby instructed her to stay on the phone while he talked to the good people who were coming to help her and her mother.

He communicated by way of the radio, out of her earshot, "I am unsure what has happened to the mother - the child is speaking clearly now but be prepared for a possible gas leak or a similar hazard and keep the canine danger in mind." He knew they had protective gear ready to use, when necessary, but it was always best to know what they were walking into. Toby turned his attention back to the child on the phone and asked, "Sway do you smell something unpleasant in your house, Sweetie?" Sway replied that she didn't. He intentionally changed to a conversational easy manner.

"What is your dog's name, I heard him barking when I was talking to your mom?"

"Her name is Daisy - she's a girl," she returned cheerfully. Toby paused for a moment, listening for the dog but heard nothing.

"Where is Daisy now?"

"Right here with me, aren't you Daisy?" He could hear the love and affection in her tone. At this point, Toby was entirely perplexed with the dog's disposition. Had Sway's mother been somehow threatening her own daughter? Was the behavior protective in nature?

The radio crackled as the First Responders reported that they were in the house. "So far there seems to be no issues with the dog; the girl is walking and seems fine." Toby wanted to reach through the wires and give that woman, whom he knew as Gayle, a huge hug – he'd gotten a bit invested into this young girl's welfare – who ever managed to stay objective and aloof? "No strange smells," Gayle continued, "nothing registering on the meter. Hey Toby, keep the kid on the phone while we check on her mother." He could hear them speaking to the mother, "Hello Karen? Karen! Wake up Karen!"

Toby tried to keep Sway distracted while gathering as much information as possible, "Where is your dad Sway?"

"At work," she answered easily. This was good – likely employed full-time.

"What is your dad's name, and do you know where he works?" Sway paused for a second.

"Tom – Tom Shorn, and he works for a place that sells cars – I can't remember the name." Toby would have given his right arm to be able to see her face - expressions and body language were key. They often miss a critical nod or shake of the head. He was grateful the team was there with them now.

"Does your dad have a boss? Do you know their name?" She informed him that Mr. and Mrs. Thompson were his bosses – likely the owners of the car dealership, he deduced. Toby deciphered the background chatter and knew things were about to escalate.

"The patient is not breathing – I've got no pulse! Start CPR and get the child out of the vicinity – now!" Toby's attention was fully with the little girl.

"Sway, I need you to take the phone into the bathroom and close the door so we can talk quietly while they look after your mom – can you do that?" Sway started to whimper.

"What's wrong with my mom?"

"We don't know yet, but the paramedics will take good care of your mom, I promise." Shuffling noises assured him that she was doing as he'd asked, and the frenetic chatter faded. Toby kept an ear on the radio network as the First Responders worked on Karen.

"We've got a heartbeat!" Toby knew it was crucial to move Karen to the hospital ASAP. "Toby, we have no time to look for a purse or her phone – we will have to take Sway with us," Gayle again – regret and concern in her tone. It was not an ideal situation and would likely result in trauma to the girl, but Toby held full trust in their judgement. "Could you please prep her, and try to see if you can reach her dad?" He was already onto that.

"Ok Sway, listen to me carefully," his tone was gentle but firm, "They are taking your mom to the hospital to make sure she will be OK," he paused a second to let that sink in. "Sway, the paramedics are going to take you with them in the ambulance. Have you ever had a ride in an ambulance before?" He managed to intone a hint of excitement. She replied that she had not.

Toby went on to carefully explain, "When you get to the hospital, we'll arrange for your dad to meet you there, OK?" Sam, one of 9-1-1's amazing investigative team members had already tracked down his place of employment. His heart lurched at her soft, sad affirmative – "OK". While he knew it was critical to honor age-appropriate intervention strategies, there was equal value in open and honest communication when dealing with children – their fear is elemental and it's a tricky balance. He knew he had already established a fair measure of trust with this little girl.

"It is normal and totally OK to feel scared right now Sway – this may be the absolute scariest time you'll ever have to go through in your life!" he let that sink in, "I promise you that we are doing all we can to keep your mom safe and she has the very best paramedics helping her – super smart and they know exactly what to do! And Sway? These good people will also be there for you – all the way!" His heart melted at the sound of her hiccup whisper, "K."

"Sway, honey, it's time to say goodbye and hang up the phone – we're going for a ride, OK?" Gayle was an angel with kids and Toby knew she would stay glued to Sway's side until they got to the hospital. He continued to listen to the call until he was sure they arrived at Emergency safely. Toby finished his day with several more calls – one turning out to be a child hiding under the bed, watching horrific screaming YouTube videos at full volume! Toby made a conscious decision to check into Emergency later. A million questions bounced around in his head, and he knew the Paramedics had been equally confounded - they get a call from a mother who can't wake her child, only to end up in life threatening medical distress herself; no pulse; not breathing – CPR and all. How does that happen? Toby knew as well that Sway's experience in the ambulance would be traumatic and terrifying. He wished he could meet this little girl, but simultaneously hoped there would be no further need.

They had situated her in the front middle jump seat between the driver and Gayle, who had a firm protective arm around her, but with neck craned, Sway's attention was firmly glued to her mother - horizontal on the stretcher with tubes and machines attached everywhere it seemed. The Paramedics worked intently - Sway was certain she could hear her mother's heart pounding within her own mind. She tried hard to block the resounding booming in her head but could not. The fact that her mother's heart *was* beating provided a measure of reassurance – a peaceful calm in the jumbled mix of emotions she was trying bravely to negotiate. Even if it was not beating as efficiently as it should…Sway did not know how she knew that, but she did, and that knowledge scared her.

After what seemed like forever, but in reality, was only minutes, the ambulance finally pulled into the emergency bay and switched off the blaring siren and bright flashing lights. Sway stayed in the vehicle, shaking and feeling abandoned and lost, until they had her mother unloaded onto a gurney and swiftly transported inside to a place that Sway knew only too well. A feeling of impending dread washed over her – she was terrified! The ambulance passenger door opened; rivulets of tears were pouring down Sway's face as she turned to the person outside the vehicle. At the sight of Hope standing there, she immediately leapt into the kind nurse's arms – only now, feeling safe enough to open her heart and sob it out.

"I've got you now Sweetie – you are safe," Hope whispered, enwrapping Sway snug into her arms. She held the precious child closely until her little body was completely drained of tears. The nurse gently led her into the hospital, headed directly to her own mother's room and laid Sway softly on the bed. "Shh, don't be afraid, you are completely safe, I promise!" Sway looked into Hope's gentle gaze and felt instantly calmer. She turned her attention to an elderly woman standing nearby – kindness radiated from her smile. "This is Susan, she is my mother," Hope explained. Sway peered into Susan's eyes and afforded a tiny smile. All the fear and sadness seemed to drain from her body, as if a plug had been pulled. She felt whole and safe again, with absolutely no compulsion to question this.

"Will my mom be, OK?" Sway instinctively directed this question at Susan, who rewarded her with a tender grin that made her eyes crinkle delightfully.

"My dear, every measure possible is now in place to help your mother." Though not an expected yes or no response, it was enough for Sway at this moment in time.

"I am going to leave you here with my mother and go check in on yours." Hope leaned down close to her, "is that ok?" Sway nodded easily and a sudden exhaustion overtook her as she curled up snuggly with Susan and drifted off into a deep sleep – farther submerged into this subconscious space than she'd ever experienced thus far in her young life.

Susan held the child close and turned to her daughter. "Go do what needs to be done," Susan instructed, "I will protect her - you protect the mother." Hope nodded her agreement and departed. Immediately afterward, an icy cold permeated the room. Susan nodded sagely, as if to acknowledgement something invisible in the room – a moment of resigned acceptance, and vigilantly increased her tight hold on Sway.

Chapter 5

TOM'S MORNING MOOD had been exceptionally cheerful. Spring was in the air, and he breathed deeply. Normally, the added time out of his way would bug the hell out of him, but tonight was card night – and hot sex with Jean. He chuckled inwardly. His extra nice favor this morning for Karen earned him an advantage. Karen would be less likely to bitch – she wouldn't dare! Although, he conceded good-naturedly, it was not in her character anyhow. Tom's rendition of *her* bitching consisted of nosy questions, concerning where and what he did on these nights out. The less inquisition – the less risk of exposure!

"Dad, what is so funny?" Zac appealed, eager to reap the advantage of his dad's current jovial disposition.

"Nothing at all son," Tom replied, "just looking forward to my card game tonight."

"Can you teach me how to play poker Dad?" Zac implored.

"Maybe someday, Zac," Tom promised evasively. The answer was not unexpected but hurt, nonetheless. Tom pulled up to the school and Zac jumped out. "Don't forget, straight home after school!" Tom ordered.

"OK, Dad," Zac replied dutifully. He much preferred his mom stepping in when they were running late – she was not near so rigid. Zac couldn't figure his dad out – it wasn't like the man was home anyhow at that time of day. Exiting quickly, he made a point of closing the door just a tad more aggressively than normal – not a slam – oh no, he wouldn't dare that, rather just enough to assuage his bruised feelings. Maybe Mom would let him go back to his friend's place after he got home, he mused, knowing that would necessitate a lie by omission, otherwise she'd back Dad up for sure. It was so annoying! Thoughts of his mom brought a rush of affection – he was missing her. Usually once he was at school, she rarely entered his mind, but today, for some reason, he couldn't stop thinking about her.

Tom arrived at work, whistling merrily with sweet thoughts of Jean, who just happened to be the boss's wife. The pure inappropriate naughtiness was entirely too enticing, and he moaned with the renewed tightening in his groin. He customarily left the poker game early and parked a block from Jean and Doug's home, which bordered an expansive green space. A nonchalant saunter through the park to stealthily access their house through the back yard – ingenious! Doug had arrived home earlier than expected on more than one occasion, and Tom was not overly comfortable with these heart-stopping close calls. It did, however, ramp up Jean's lustful excitement at almost being caught, rendering her a wildcat and resistance was frankly futile! She was also co-owner of the company and its top salesperson – not too shabby a catch to stroke his ego. Not that he entertained any notion that he was her sole fling. She loved screwing the local help. Tom did not have to wonder at her staggering sales records with many repeat male customers. He supposed that her "supplementary compensation package" to the purchase agreement did not attract nor impress most women. Although from what Tom knew of Jean, he had no doubt that there were one or two female prospects who received the same level of service as the men.

This morning's monthly staff and safety meeting guaranteed an hour of casual hangout with work buddies before his head became permanently stuck under a vehicle. Tom predictively slid into "Mr. Entertainment" routine, generously doling out Karen's cookies and reciting the latest jokes. Doug intervened, calling the staff meeting to order – time to get down to business. With the phone's insistent ringing in the background, he figured they were in for a busy day! Voice mail handled the calls while they plowed through the meeting agenda items. Tina from accounting, left first, to attend to the front. The rest lingered a little longer to savor the treats.

Tom paid little heed when she came rushing back to the lunchroom calling out his name. His first assumption was that some customer with a lame excuse was insisting that their vehicle be serviced first – there was always one or two of those in the daily mix! It was Jean who finally grabbed his attention with urgency in her tone. "Tom! Tina just said that there are numerous messages left from Emergency - Karen has been taken by ambulance to the hospital!"

Tom offered a placating eye roll, "No, that will be Sway. With the slightest cough or complaint, Karen turns into a raging hypochondriac and rushes her to emergency."

"Tom," Tina emphasized, "all the messages relay that it was Karen."

"Did they say why, or what happened – an accident?" Tom inquired. He knew Karen would have driven there.

"Tom," Jean interrupted, "it is just as fast for you to go to emergency and see what is going on, then to call the hospital. Work will wait. Take all the time you need."

Tom pondered this for a moment. "I'm sure it is fine – something simple – I'll be right back."

Heading out to his vehicle, he felt confident that it was a simple mistake. Boy, was he going to have it out with Karen! She had to stop molly-coddling Sway! All those times to the hospital emergency room – all the drama, and not *once* did they find anything wrong with the kid. This had to stop – *now*! Resentment flared - he had no intention of forfeiting tonight's pleasures, all in honor of this little stunt!

He marched through the Emergency automatic sliding glass doors, certain that the staff would be eternally grateful to have him put a stop to these useless alleged catastrophic plights - compromising valuable time and attention that should be spent with people who were *truly* in medical distress, as opposed to repeatedly dealing with Karen's delusions regarding their daughter's health. Proceeding to the reception desk, he prefaced his inquiry with a straight-up apology for yet *another* of his wife's unnecessary crisis visits for Sway, and staunchly assured them that he would be dealing with this situation once and for all.

"I'm not sure I understand what you mean Mr. Shorn?" the receptionist puzzled.

"You left a message at my place of employment that my wife and daughter were brought here by ambulance," Tom patiently responded.

"Yes, I left a message that your *wife* was brought in by ambulance." the receptionist stated.

"It's my daughter, Sway - the wife is always bringing her in."

The receptionist's pleasant demeanor faded a tad, as she realized there was no point in arguing with this man and interjected, "Just a moment sir, I will have one of the nurses speak with you." A minute later, an emergency nurse approached, and Tom wasted no time.

"I understand that my wife and daughter are here?"

"Yes," responded the nurse calmly, "your daughter came in with your wife in the ambulance because there was no one else at home to look after her," then quickly continued, "Sir, your wife suffered a heart attack - she is stable now, and we are running tests to ascertain the cause." Tom was momentarily rendered speechless. "We will keep her until we are able to diagnose her condition." Tom pondered this.

"So...she will be here a couple of hours - then I can take her home?" Tom offered.

"We can't say yet. Why don't you come with me to get your daughter? I suggest that you take her to school – familiar is good and she's had a scare, but she's considerably calmer now. Then come back in a few hours – we may know more then, and Karen is resting now." Tom nodded his agreement, recognizing his lack of options in the situation. He allowed himself to be shepherded through a set of double glass doors, his emotions oscillating between a burning resentment and a confusing niggling of fear for his wife. The nurse stopped and motioned him into a room where he found his daughter sound asleep in the arms of an elderly lady, who greeted him with a sharp gaze and a soft smile, introducing herself as Susan.

"Your daughter has been resting comfortably but has endured a rather traumatic morning! Rest assured, she's been very well cared for and has weathered this like a trooper! You have a very brave and resilient little girl here." This was not at all the description Tom would have afforded his alleged sickly offspring. Two young women entered the room.

"Dr. Kerr," Faith introduced herself warmly, hand extended toward him, "I am in charge of Sway's care." At his confused expression, she clarified, "of course, not from today's incident – rather Sway's multiple admissions with recent troubling symptoms of her own." Tom stayed uncharacteristically silent, more than a little out his element as he instinctively gauged his outsider status.

"I am Hope, Sway's nurse." He offered them both a conciliatory handshake. "Shall we chat a bit about Sway? Your wife is in good hands, undergoing cardiac testing for the next while and we have some time to bring you into the loop." Tom cleared his throat and sat stiffly on a chair that Hope motioned him towards. Faith took the lead.

"Hope and I are part of a crisis team that specialize in working with children. Sway's numerous emergency care admissions have raised concerns. One of the team's goals is to closely monitor recurring undiagnosed health issues in children." Tom felt his hackles instantly rise, and astutely treaded carefully, politely expressing his gratitude for their care and attention, before continuing.

"I firmly believe there is nothing physically wrong with my child, other than excessive pampering on my wife's part – it's frankly enabling behavior and is very likely causing Sway to manifest her ailments." Tom was emphatic. "She's been here at least ten times in the past couple of months with the same symptoms. This clearly constitutes full justification for a lack of diagnosis." Please don't misunderstand me – I know my daughter is not pretending or at fault. This is all on Karen!" The conversation was interrupted as Sway sighed and stretched, instantly seeking Susan's eyes.

"Is my mom, OK?" Susan squeezed the child gently and reassured that her mother was being well taken care of.

"Hi Sweetie," Tom rose, and Sway hesitated a second, then moved into her father's outstretched arms. "May I take her home now?" Faith agreed under the condition that he contact her or Hope immediately if any issues arose, handing him the same card they had given to Karen a day prior.

"Thank you for looking after me," Sway hugged them all enthusiastically. Hope crouched down and gave Sway another card with her phone number on it.

"You can call me day or night – twenty-four seven, if you don't feel well or just want to talk." Hope peered intently into the little girl's eyes – sending a silent but clear message of comforting commitment. Tom thanked them cordially and promptly left the hospital with the contact information burning intrusively in his hand. He didn't like this at all! He also didn't believe for one minute that his wife was ill. Hell, she hadn't had more than a minor tickle in her throat for years! Heart attack, his ass! His indignation was rising without check now – having no outsiders to dictate temperance. Indigestion was his guess – all that food she was constantly stuffing in her mouth! Damn, this woman was a pain in the ass! He quickly chauffeured Sway to school and explained the situation to the school receptionist.

Back at work, he fielded his buddies' concerns. "Karen is fine - they think she may have had a heart attack, but I am sure it is just indigestion. They are doing tests and Sway is at school - all is good!"

Jean motioned him into her office. "What is going on, Tom?" she imposed. The haughty demeanor enhanced her naturally sumptuous pouty lips and had him anxiously wishing the day away – tonight could not come fast enough!

"Like I said, no big deal," Tom responded.

"What did Karen say?" Jean persisted, breaking the spell. He sorely needed to move off the topic of his wife!

"Nothing, I didn't see her, she was having a bunch of tests done and I needed to get Sway to school," Tom stated logically. He was becoming more than a little agitated with this constant barrage of questions. "They told me to check back later."

"You're an ass, Tom! Your wife had a heart attack. You should be with her! If it should reoccur at the hospital, don't you think you should be there?" Jean admonished, her voice escalating.

"Fine!" Tom exploded and stormed out of Jeans office. She had *no* right to dictate to him about how he should deal with his own wife! For the love of God, she had no qualms about screwing the brains out of that same woman's husband, on a weekly basis! Tom could not fathom the root of her anger. An uncomfortable churning assaulted his gut. Was she seeking a reason to ditch their clandestine meeting – someone else in the queue perhaps? An instant bolt of indignant rage surfaced, along with a moderating inner reminder that he and Jean were far from exclusive! Jealousy he could ill afford, and he ruefully acknowledged her transparency regarding the "others", if not their identities – *that* was forbidden territory. Cruising around town, brooding over the way Jean had dared to chastise him, he conceded that she was *his* only diversion – hence creating the imbalance in their so-called relationship. He considered the idea to branch out, experiment, if you will. But the thought of becoming a philandering playboy cheating husband did not sit well with his ego, aside from Jean of course. It did not even occur to him that his fling with her fit *that* bill to a tee.

His thoughts now on Karen, he wondered if she'd be upset at his absence. It wasn't his usual mode of operation – pacifying his wife. This was an impossible situation, and Tom scowled in frustration, marring his natural charming features. He quickly swung into the drive-through lane at Dairy Queen, intent on treating Karen. One large chocolate milkshake - she loved to indulge! Tom completed their meal-deal orders with cheesy bacon burgers and fries. He'd eat lunch with his wife - and *not* because Jean had coerced him to do so. He reasoned that the gesture would likely lend a positive impression upon the staff too.

Armed with Karen's favourite eats, he arrived feeling proud of himself for affording her this generosity. The Emergency Unit Clerk directed him to Karen's cubicle, where he found her resting on the bed, next to none other than Susan, seated in a chair nearby. He dismissed the budding implications, determined to carry out his mission.

"Hi honey, look what I brought you," Tom announced jauntily as he displayed the tempting fare. Karen thanked him with a weak smile. A nurse, manipulating the IV line in Karen's hand, shot a piercing bulleted glare directly at him.

"You do know that your wife has just suffered a heart attack?" She turned her gentle attention back to Karen, effectively rebuffing his presence.

"Yes, the apparent diagnosis," Tom replied silkily," Bolstered by the absence of a reaction, he forged on, "but far likely a case of indigestion."

"Are you a doctor by any chance, Mr. Shorn?" the nurse asked with mock genuine interest and continued without affording him the chance to respond. "I can assure you that your wife did indeed, experience an episode of cardiac arrest, and unfortunately will not be allowed to ingest liquids, let alone this unhealthy feast." She rose to face him. "*Nothing* is to be provided to your wife without pre-approval from our staff, until we have her health issue resolved. *Do* you understand Mr. Shorn, that this is profoundly serious? Your wife is extremely ill!" Though paling beside Tom in stature, this fiery practitioner was not the least intimidated by him.

Tom felt a bit of a fool. Could it be true? He placed the food on the tray, out of Karen's line of sight. Reaching out to take her hand, he was assailed with an array of conflicting emotions, with no idea how to process them. His accustomed rigid control was currently under bombardment, and he hated this feeling of helplessness!

"It is OK, we will figure this out and I will be fine." Karen squeezed his wrist weakly. He sat quietly beside her, maintaining a firm grip on her hand, watching her with growing concern, as she drifted in and out of awareness. With increasing alarm, he took notice of the gray hue to her skin, cold hands, and feeble voice. A flooding fear clutched his gut, taking hold his senses. Could it be possible she might die? What would he do? Who would look after the children? He was self-aware enough to admit that he was a piss poor substitute!

Time ticked by slowly – agonizingly so, and nurses came and went, administering dosages of medication into Karen's IV, recording vitals. Tom glanced at the clock, cognizant of the fact that he needed to make arrangements for childcare. Karen seemed in a peaceful slumber, and he placed a gentle kiss upon her forehead, whispering that he would be back as soon as he could. As he reluctantly left her side, he was assaulted by the painful reality that he couldn't recall the last time he had bestowed such affection on his wife.

Tom entered the house to find Daisy firmly positioned at the door. Turning, he almost tripped headlong over the cat, parked rigidly under his feet. Strange, he mused, as the cat *never* came anywhere near him – probably sensing his intolerance for annoying feline creatures. He opened the door to let them both out, but the cat remained rooted to the spot, her gaze firmly affixed just past the entryway. Key-key refused to budge and hissed menacingly, when he nudged her with his foot. "What the hell!" he hollered and forcefully pushed her outside. Still spitting and growling, she stayed glued to the doorstep. Shaking his head, Tom wondered what in the hell was happening in this household.

Moments later Zac and Sway raced up the driveway from school. "Is mom, OK?" Zac demanded, a worried frown marring his smooth young face.

"Can we go to the hospital to see her?" Sway chimed in.

"Mom is going to be fine and yes, we can," Tom responded. Both pets barreled through the door and planted themselves securely beside Sway. Dismissing the eerie nudges that were poking his senses, Tom directed the children to put their belongings away. "Homework and dinner first – then off to visit Mom!" Sway raced to her room with both pets in close pursuit.

"Hey Daisy," Zac called out, but the dog never looked back. Zac was puzzled. This never happened! In fact, Daisy was indubitably all over him when he got home from school. Today it was like he was not even there. He shrugged it off for now – he had to tackle his homework. His teacher had assigned a pile of it today and he wanted desperately to see his mom. Besides, Sway was spooked, and he didn't want a fuss over Daisy to cause her more angst. Sway had relayed the details of her ambulance ride with Mom. It sounded scary! As they had walked home, Sway had wavered on the edge of tears. Zac had shifted immediately into big brother mode, trying to assure her that their mom would be OK, but it was difficult to hold back his own fears and threatening tears. Mom was never sick - had never gone to the hospital for herself as far as he remembered. He determinedly perched himself at his bedroom desk and dove into the homework. Sooner finished, the sooner he saw Mom.

Tom checked on the kids - Zac immersed in schoolbooks – good job son! Sway was seated on her bed, talking to the cat and dog. His heart lurched when she mentioned her mommy. He made a conscious decision to loosen up on the homework rule – she'd clearly had a rough day. Monitoring the kids was rare for Tom - Karen's department, and he found himself yearning for her parental input – was this pet thing normal? He wasn't really in tune with the routine, but he had the clear sense that something was off. Tom sighed and turned his focus to dinner – what in the hell would he make? The sooner he got them fed, the quicker they'd get on with the evening, and he would be off to the poker game and Jean. Normality was essential now, despite his concern about Karen. Besides, he reflected, a man needed release – even more so at a time like this, and it had been longer than he could remember since he'd found sexual satisfaction with Karen – if ever. Who could blame a strong virile man with primal needs that only another woman could satisfy?

Ok, grilled cheese sandwiches, easier than drive through scenario and he did not want to risk a further confrontation with the snotty pompous nurse who had challenged him earlier. "Supper's ready!" he bellowed. Sway sat down with Daisy and Key-key both at her heels.

"Sway, you know the rule - no pets near the table when we are eating," Tom declared. "This is ridiculous! You've probably been feeding them at the table," he growled. Zac promptly denied this, coming to his sister's defense. "Get them out of here!" Tom hollered. Zac called to the pets but neither responded. Sway calmly climbed down from the table and both animals immediately trailed behind her. Closing them in her room, she returned to her chair with sad sigh. Zac sat in shock wondering what in the world was going on with his dog - Daisy always listened to him over Sway.

She threw him a knowing look and soothed, "Don't worry, Daisy is just fretting about Mommy."

"If there's any worrying to be done it's my job!" Tom riled testily. "As for your mother, she should not be burdening anyone with this hospital stuff. Maybe if she had not gotten so damn fat, she would not have had this supposed heart attack!" Tom snapped. "Snap to it and stop this nonsense, or there will be no visit to your mom!" At their look of distress, he felt a niggling remorse and softened his tone. "C'mon guys, we have to get a move on."

Zac considered his father's words. Mom had always been there as a buffer with their father's anger. In that state he was unpredictable, so the best course of action was to keep quiet – avoid escalating his rage. Both children choked down sandwiches that may as well have been sawdust. It was obvious their father had lost his patience and they were alone with him on thin ice. Zac sent Sway a private look and they both got up to clear the table. A sudden chill permeated the air – they all felt it and Tom moved away to check windows and doors – was one open? Finding nothing amiss, he picked up his light summer jacket and proceeded to the door.

"Shut up!" Tom thundered at Daisy's persistent growl behind the bedroom door. "Let's go, kids!" he hollered, not even bothering to check if they finished eating. Both children hurriedly followed. Zac thought how weirdly surreal it was – a perfect spring day and the whole world around him seemed to be alive and healthy in its rebirth. Yet, nothing about this day seemed right! He placed his hopes on the sight of his mom's blossoming tulips – on impulse, he plucked one and stuck it securely in his coat pocket. The embers of resentment burned inside at his father's words – unfair criticism of his mom.

Chapter 6

SPRING IN TERRACE, BC is a welcome retreat from a wintery wet spell in the Skeena Valley located within the province's northwest region. Typically, this feeds into warm dry summers and it was a gorgeous evening, full of promise. Not one of the Shorn family members took any notice of this, as Tom negotiated traffic to the Mills Memorial Hospital. Their minds were on overdrive with concern for Karen.

Karen was sleeping peacefully upon their arrival. The nurse directed them to a larger, shared room in a general care ward, and Tom's nose wrinkled in distasteful reaction to the strong antiseptic odor. He was surprised to see Susan, comfortably propped up reading, in the neighboring bed. He entertained briefly the identity of this woman, and what ailment had befallen her – made a mental note to investigate this later. Turning his attention to Karen, Tom was unsure if he should wake her, and instead tried his best to noiselessly drag an ancient metal folding chair beside her bed, settling in as best he could – damn seats were so small and uncomfortable. He took her hand in a gentle caress, momentarily oblivious to his two frightened children, hovering behind. After all, it had always been Karen who worried about their needs.

Sway was drawn directly to Susan, and promptly climbed onto her bed, trying in vain not to cry, her quivering lips betraying fear. The anxiety was warranted - her mom had not woken up yet and her dad seemed terribly upset and out of sorts. Susan enfolded her in a warm hug and whispered soothingly that her mom would be fine. The kind matronly woman smiled at both the children, motioning for Zac to move closer.

"Your mom is going to be just fine – here's what she needs from you," Susan continued in a hushed voice, and they both listened intently, wide-eyed and eager. "Think only good thoughts for her now and show her your very bravest smiles when she wakes up. Can you do that?" They both offered solemn nods. Susan patted their heads in encouragement.

"Will my mommy wake up or will she go live with the angels?" Sway whispered.

"Your mommy *will* wake up and she will have lots of time with you before that happens," Susan smiled reassuringly, "your mother is young and strong, and will be given a newer heart, to help her. You have no need to worry, just try to be brave now - she needs you."

Zac moved to stand back from everyone, watching and listening to what was going on. It was like his father had forgotten they were even there. Mom needed a new heart – holy smokes! He kept an ear on the conversation between the elderly lady and Sway. He hoped she was right, but Zac was a little confused – how could this woman know all this about his mom? He was not as trusting as his little sister and perceived instinctively, that there was more to this than she was sharing.

Karen began to stir, immediately catching everyone's full attention. Her eyes fluttered open to the sight of concerned faces - her husband on the chair, expression somber and holding her hand – wow; her son rooted a little distance away, like stone – the apprehension evident, and Sway perched on the bed opposite to hers, safely enwrapped in Susan's arms. "Hi," Karen muttered softly to her family, bestowing a weak grin. "I am sorry, I apparently gave you all quite a scare," she apologized.

"You sure did," Tom agreed, then kissed the back of Karen's hand. She immediately flushed at this unfamiliar attention from her husband, knowing she wasn't exactly in presentable form – monitors and tubes; hair messed akin to a rat's nest she was sure, and this less than alluring hospital gown! God – she was tired – a wave rushed over her.

"It's OK Mom," Zac professed, wide-eyed, and Sway chimed in.

"Mommy!" She slid from Susan's bed and sped over to her mother's. "You're awake! I was so scared!" Her brave smile lingered, but her bottom lip trembled. Karen's heart melted and threatened to crack in to a million pieces over what her precious children had just endured on her account, and she motioned for them to come over for a hug.

"It is OK Sweetie, I am going to be fine," Karen reassured. A doctor had already explained to Karen about the condition of her heart and the events leading up to it. Although Karen only remembered bits and pieces, she was fully aware of the grave situation she was in. Reassuring her family was all she could do at this point. Weakness washed over her, threatening to drag her under.

Tom was anxious to get a full account from the doctor as well – all he had to go on was Susan's explanation to the kids that Karen was going to receive a new heart – transplant? That was pretty damn serious! It was obvious to everyone that Karen needed rest. They each moved in to bestow hugs and kisses just as a nurse's arrival signified the end of visiting hours – she advised his return to attend doctor rounds early in the morning. Tom promised the kids that they would come again the next day. Giving Karen another kiss, he murmured, "see you tomorrow - I love you." But Karen was already soundly asleep. He reflected on the awkward feeling that the mere uttering of those simple three words had evoked.

Tom marshaled the kids into the SUV and headed home, relief flooding his body, as he left the discomforting stress behind. He had arranged for Mrs. Jones, the next-door neighbour, to come and look after the children while he was at the poker game and then - off to see Jean! Tom had quickly relayed to the woman his plans to be with Karen at the hospital. This, he deduced, sounded far better than going off to a poker game, less than twenty-four hours after his wife had almost died. He allowed the thrill of anticipation to drown out the niggling shards of guilt. Karen was in good hands – resting – and there was nothing he could really do for her anyhow, he reasoned. He lingered just long enough to settle Mrs. Jones in, and make sure the kids were in bed. Zac had been wrestling with Daisy to come and sleep in his room, but the dog was not budging from Sway's side.

49

"Dad, can I sleep with Sway tonight? Zac pleaded, fearful that his father would not allow it.

"Sure," Tom responded - less chance of their neighbor needing to summon him because one or the other child was unsettled. Tom left his house with the comforting image of his children curled up together with the animals comforting and keeping guard. Things were good – all under control. He decided to skip the poker game – his need so intense and headed straight over to Jean's. The boys would not be expecting him anyway, given Karen's situation, and the extra time with his sexy mistress would provide an extended haven. Tom pulled into his customary spot and strolled catlike into her back yard. The rear deck light was off, affording better coverage to sneak through the patio door at the back of the house. The sweet smell of evening scented stock permeated his senses, adding to the sensual allure. He found Jean in the living room watching TV with a glass of wine dangling in her hand. An immense wash of gratitude flooded his senses when he realized she was alone – no other visitors. At the sound of his entry, she jumped and turned in surprise. The very sight of her raised his blood pressure a notch.

"I thought you wouldn't make it tonight," she responded in a throaty whisper, revealing her inner pleasure at this turn of events. He reached out to effortlessly uproot her off the comfy couch, locking her firmly against him.

"I wouldn't miss this for anything Jean," he murmured, seductively and softly nuzzling her neck. Her little moan set his heart to racing and he rewarded with a sharp, provocative nip. Jean struggled to extract herself from the heat that was him - he was fully cognizant of the delicious waves of pleasure his caresses were evoking and it drove his senses wild!

"Where is Karen?" Jean struggled to come up for breath. She was one determined lady and he wanted to throw her on the sofa and kiss her breathless – that was a regular occurrence, but he sensed the need for caution – he was not about to blow this session – his need was all-consuming.

"Sound asleep at the hospital for the night and no visitors allowed until tomorrow," Tom replied smoothly, expertly pulling her back to him, deliberately molding her to his hardness. "I may not have a lot of time," he breathed silkily, between feathery kisses and nibbles to her already swollen lower lip, "the kids are having some trouble settling in, and the neighbour is watching them."

"Where does the neighbour think you are?" Jean gasped, her breathing ragged.

"At the poker game," Tom fabricated easily. In short order, things boiled over into a torrid scorching blaze and they stumbled, impatient in their desperation to rip off clothing. They careened into the spare bedroom, toppling wildly onto the mattress in perfect unison, fully consumed by their weekly shared ritual of salacious steamy pleasure. Jean's voracious appetite fueled Tom into top form as he worked hard to satisfy. Her inability to resist, even while he knew without a doubt, that she'd had full intention to shut it down, spurred his excitement to a blazing fury. After expertly drawing her twice to fevered explosive orgasms, he lost own control in a mind-blowing release. The ring of his cell phone vaguely registered in his brain – with the throbbing beat of his heart, and he let it go to voice mail. Jean wiggled vigorously underneath him, only serving to further rouse his hunger and he groaned. When the phone continued the incessant ringing, she forcefully pushed him away from her, breathless but determined.

"Tom, answer the damn, phone!" she snapped, "It must be urgent, or they wouldn't keep calling." Tom took the call on the next ring, half out of breath.

"Where are you, Tom?" Mrs. Jones was clearly anxious.

"At the hospital," he continued the deception, ignoring the sudden questioning lift to Jean's eyebrow. "What is the problem?"

"No, you're not Tom, the hospital has been calling - Karen had another heart attack," Mrs. Jones said in an accusatory, yet concerned tone. This instantly served to cool his passionate ardor.

"I am on my way," Tom shot back, and flipped the cell phone closed, frantically fumbling into his clothes.

"What happened?" Jean was searching around for her own.

"Karen had another heart attack," Tom replied hastily. "I have to go – now!"

"Jesus Tom, you said Karen was going to be fine!"

"That's what I thought, damn it!" He was almost at the door now. Tom rushed out the back and sprinted through the park to his car, Jean's words of admonishment ringing in his ears. He sped only two blocks before passing a police cruiser, and glanced at the speedometer – 100 in a 60 zone – damn, he didn't have time for this! The police car deftly spun around with lights flashing and caught up to Tom just before he reached the hospital. Tom pulled into the parking area and waited impatiently for the officer to reach his car window as he rolled it down - the gravity of this situation was beginning to take over. It was his duty to be with Karen now.

"I am sorry Officer, I am aware that I was speeding," Tom got directly to the point, "my wife just had a heart attack and I need to get to her. Is it possible that I come to the station and get the ticket from you tomorrow?"

"Where were you coming from Mr. Shorn?" the patrolman asked in seeming casual interest, as he took Tom's licence and registration and studied him closely.

"I'll explain tomorrow," Tom said, "I need to get to the hospital." Peering up, he recognized Jim O'Reilly, one of Jean's recent customers.

"OK Mr. Shorn," Officer O'Reilly looked down, with intense regard, "I hope your wife is going to be OK, I will trust you to be at the station sometime tomorrow. Have them page me when you get there." Tom offered his thanks, as he gratefully retrieved his documents from the constable, who tipped his hat politely and sauntered back to the cruiser.

The hospital was quiet with lights dimmed, so the patients could sleep. Tom hastened to her room, but Karen was not there! Tom's blood ran cold at the implication. Was Karen dead? Had he spent these last few hours with Jean instead of his dying wife? A ball of fear gripped his insides, the threat of tears glistening in his eyes.

"Are you OK?" The concern in Susan's voice snapped him from immobility.

"Do you know where my wife is?" Tom inquired.

"I believe they rushed her into O.R.," Susan replied gravely. "You're best to ask the medical staff," she advised. As if on cue, a nurse spotted Tom sitting on Karen's now vacant bed and approached.

"Come with me Sir," she directed, and led him into a private room that Tom considered to mirror all the others – clinical and impersonal. Engaging direct eye contact, she explained "Karen had another heart attack. She's in the O.R. undergoing emergency surgery as we speak. It could be a while before you can see her as she will also be in recovery for some time." The nurse offered the option to stay until she was out or wait for the hospital to call. Without hesitation, he informed her that he would remain there. With a dismissive nod, she scurried out ahead of him and navigated him to the waiting room with blessedly, both a coffee and snack machine. It would be a long night, and he quickly called Mrs. Jones, who assured him she would stay with the kids. With a steaming cup of hot coffee now warming his hands, he reluctantly settled into one of the well-used couches in the sparse waiting room. His mind registered that there wasn't even a single child's toy visible. With thoughts whirling from the day's events, he spotted Susan ambling toward him, nimbly pushing her IV pole out front.

"Rough day," she affirmed, settling herself down beside him. Tom nodded. "I hear your wife is going to be in surgery for quite a while." She paused. Tom met her sharp gaze. "Tom, do you love your wife?" Tom felt his blood come to an instant boil at her entitled inquisition. How dare she?

"Not that it is any of your business," he snapped, "but yes, I *do* love my wife very much. What the hell kind of question is that?" his anger was escalating, with extreme annoyance at this woman's repeated intrusion concerning his family.

"Well Tom, may I call you Tom?" Susan did not wait for a response, "your actions do not reflect those of a loving, concerned husband." She let that sink in, noticing the heated flush on Tom's face. "My guess is that most devoted husbands would never choose to leave their wife's side in such a critical state." She continued, "Most husbands, I surmise, would not choose to show up at the hospital, reeking of sex and perfume…not to mention sporting a liberal dose of lipstick on his face and collar." Susan concluded, her eyes pointedly roaming over him. Tom glanced over to the disheveled man reflected back at him through the vending machine glass, with - yes, clear traces of Jean's lipstick smeared on his face.

"No, it probably *isn't* any of my business," Susan offered "but I do care very much about Karen, and the last thing I would want her to see when she wakes up from her surgery, is the tell-tale signs of infidelity, glaringly apparent all over her husband," she scoffed, distain clear in her tone. Tom had enough decency to hang his head in remorse. "It is fairly clear to me that Karen was not the partner in your recent dallying, or did I miss some wild activity in the next bed that may have been a contributing factor in her heart failure?" her tone softened slightly. It was not in her nature to pass judgement. "I suggest, Tom Shorn, you mosey on home and clean up your act, before you face your wife again."

Tom didn't utter a word – what was there to say? He rose abruptly from the couch and headed out the door for home, feeling the stinging barbs in his back, from those steely gray eyes. Now, he wondered, had Officer O'Reilly also figured out where he had been? His heart sank. A deep heated shame flooded his body. This was a tight community, and leaked gossip of this magnitude would spread like wildfire. Tom intrinsically valued other people's opinions of him – it mattered, at the core of his being, the essence of his ego.

Oh, he had already considered the consequences, if Karen had ever caught wind of his cheating, and wasn't overly worried. He knew that she'd believe his adamant claim that it was simply idle gossip – a lie, as Karen too, was privy to the same rumors as he. Jean, on a regular basis, carried on with almost anything in pants. Yes, he rationed, Karen had a kind heart – she loved him and would come to his defense. He could always count on that. But this…this was an entirely different level of deception. If it circulated that he was spending his time philandering with another woman – a married woman, no less, while his own wife was in the hospital, possibly dying – well, that was something that no man could ever live down! He would be permanently branded as a cad! And his kids - what would happen if they found out? Of course, they would hate him forever. Tom's stomach tangled into knots, as panic set in - deep to the core of his being.

Before entering the house, he'd managed a decent job of erasing Jean's deep pink lipstick from his face, with the aid of a tissue he'd moistened with stale water from the bottle in the console. He heaved a sigh of relief, as he spied Mrs. Jones, snoring softly on the couch. "Thank God," Tom offered silently, as he furtively crept by and made his way to the shower, wasting no time. Refreshed and donned in clean clothes, Tom stopped by Sway's room to peek in - Karen's job – a hollow echo in his brain. What if she could never again check in on their children? Get those thoughts out of your head, Tom chided himself. Daisy gave a low growl when he ducked his head through her half-open door. Zac looked up; anxiety written all over his features. "What the hell is this dog growling about?" Tom snapped.

"She is just doing her job in looking after us dad, while Mom isn't here," Zac responded reasonably, in defence of Daisy. "How is mom doing?"

"Fine," Tom snarled testily, "go back to sleep. Everything is fine," it was a whopper of a fib, but Tom felt it best until he knew more details. Zac put his head back down and closed his eyes. Outside, the chorus of frogs chirping somewhere in a nearby ditch or pond lent a sense of normalcy as he climbed into the SUV and felt the sudden compulsion to stay put – to join them in a carefree frolic. With a troubled sigh, Tom Shorn resigned to his fate, rolled up the window and put the car into reverse. Making his way to the hospital, he sent up a silent prayer of gratitude that Mrs. Jones had seemed oblivious about his coming and going to and from the house. The absolute last thing he wanted was a conversation regarding his previous whereabouts – enough judgemental female chastisement for one day! It probably should have been a point of concern to him that the sitter had slept through it all, and normally he would have questioned that - or maybe not. How often was Karen out of the picture – if at all?

Chapter 7

"HEY…EVERYTHING IS GOING to be OK," Tom was by her side as the sedation slowly wore off. Karen did not feel OK. The pain was intolerable and the exhaustion – she was truly frightened she may not survive! She craved escape - to slip back into drugged oblivion, where there was no thinking, no feeling, no pain, no fear. The trauma from two consecutive heart attacks was debilitating and the fact that she was frankly terrified, pushed her to overwhelm! Karen did not know which was worse, the terror or the pain. She surmised it was the fright – it was an all-consuming reality she never wanted to revisit.

The nurses bustled around her with IV lines, heart and blood pressure monitors and never-ending medication. "You must wake up Karen," Nurse Nancy coaxed, bombarding her with questions. "Open your eyes now. Karen, can you please tell me where you are?"

"I'm in the hospital," she murmured testily. Violence was not a part of her make-up but at that moment she was sure she'd have face-punched that nurse if she'd been capable of it.

"On a scale of one to ten, Karen, what is your pain level?" Nancy was pushing it now. "Ten," she feebly snapped, truly not wanting to open her eyes. "Time to wake up Karen - come on now, you can do it," the caregiver continued to prod. Karen tried in vain to comply, but pain ruled, and her body, despite her utmost effort, opted for blissful oblivion from the abominable discomfort.

"Come on now honey," Tom encouraged, "they are saying it's very important that you wake up." Nancy had explained that the longer she was down, the higher risk of water accumulation in her lungs, which could lead to pneumonia. This could create dangerous pressure on her already compromised heart. She advised Tom to give his wife tiny amounts of water and slivers of ice to ease discomfort with any possible throat swelling and tenderness that, without exception, would occur from intubation during surgery.

Karen focused all her energy reserves on dealing with the pain, as she slowly forced her eyelids to move. Oh, Lord! She looked around sluggishly and spotted an elderly woman regarding her solemnly, from the next bed. Karen recalled her name – Susan – she'd been exceptionally kind to her and Sway during their last emergency visit, her words reassuring. As if thoughts could summon, the gentlewoman spoke, "I know it is hard right now Karen, but it's important to be strong for yourself and your family. You will get through this and soon feel infinitely healthier!" Tom couldn't quite squelch the well of resentment – what the hell did this woman know? Where was her own family, to fuss over her?

Karen attempted to draw strength from the woman's advice but could not pull one thread of courage through the tangles of her inner turmoil – couldn't see past the incessant physical agony. Clutching Tom's arm, she pleaded for him to urge the nurse for more pain medication. Half listening to his conversation with Nancy, she recalled a hazy moment - the doctor's words struck her - "you are lucky to be alive, young lady." Karen did not feel so lucky, or young.

The nurse advised Tom that she would consult with the doctor but until she received different orders, Karen was already getting the maximum prescribed dosage. "It's critical right now to keep Karen as alert as possible," Nancy relayed gently. "I know this is tough, but the best you can do for her now is to keep talking to her - provide comfort and encouragement – squeeze her hand, stroke her hair, ask her easy questions - anything that will help her surface from the anesthetic. The ice chips are a key strategy." Tom nodded compliantly. This entire situation was pushing him far out of his comfort zone – he almost *never* spent any energy or time on catering to Karen's comfort or needs – she was always just there – tending to their home and kids, as it should be. A little niggling inner voice spouted resentment for the predicament she was presently placing him in, but the guilt drowned it out – he had cavorted wantonly in another woman's bed tonight while Karen had undergone emergency surgery. The ultimate rub? His secret was in danger of exposure. Oh, he'd considered the affair harmless – actually beneficial to their marriage, as his primal needs were being met in a way that Karen could never hope to fulfill. She simply wasn't the sensual woman that he found in Jean. And truly, he reasoned, Karen had checked out willingly when she stopped taking care of her body – had let herself go. Besides, she was tired all the time, and perpetually 'not in the mood'. This way, he supposed, she didn't as often have to put up with his unwanted attention and realize her failure as a wife. The rationale supporting this theory, had a hollow ring right at this moment. He decided it prudent to dive into support mode now – he *did* love his wife, after all.

"Hey honey," he prompted. "Can you hear me darling? The kids are at home sleeping but will be here after school tomorrow to see you. Once you wake up, you will start to feel better. You want a little sip of water or some ice?" Karen was aware of Tom holding her hand and stroking her cheek – it was just such a damn struggle to open her eyes. It dawned on her that the raging burning in her throat signalled an intense thirst.

"Yes," Karen was incredibly parched - her lips crusty and dry. "Yes," She felt like she could down a gallon of water but would settle for the ice. Tom slipped a frozen sliver into Karen's mouth. She was blessed with an immediate refreshing relief from the blazing throbbing sensation, as the melting ice tricked down her throat. After Tom was sure she'd finished sucking on the ice, he picked up the paper water cup from the bedside tray, and put the straw to Karen's mouth, urging her to take a sip. Karen felt increasing appeasement as she surrendered to the bliss.

"Let's have a chat – keep you wakeful," Tom insisted, "ask me about the kids." Karen peered at him through one eye, wondering who this man was and what had they done with her husband?

"How are the kids?" Karen acceded softly.

"The kids are good - just worried about their mom and wanting you home," Tom replied. "Now ask me about my day today," Tom spurred her on.

"How was your poker game?" Karen whispered. Tom's heart leapt into this throat as he realized the folly of that particular line of focus.

"I didn't go to my poker game," he supplied. "I have just been hanging out between here with you, and home with the kids," Well that was partially true, but the churning in his gut spoke to his significant omission. She immediately offered her apology.

"No need for sorry, this is not your fault and could have happened to anyone," Tom assured her reasonably. "Yes, Mrs. Jones is with the kids," he confirmed her predicted next query, then added, "she sent her well wishes for your recovery and will visit when she can." The memory of their phone conversation burned in his mind - Mrs. Jones was one person who could reveal his absence from the hospital for sure and had accusingly questioned his whereabouts! He speculated that the neighbor was unlikely to share this with Karen because she was the type of woman that would not choose adding to her troubles - no, she'd prefer to let him stew in it all. He relaxed a little – his mind put at ease. Karen would not find out from that source.

Tom was thankful that Karen was currently not aware of his agitated preoccupation, but as the moments slipped by, he noticed her becoming more alert - drinking a little more water and a semblance of colour returning to her cheeks. He considered the doctor's prognosis that Karen would need a new heart. Tom did not quite believe it. Didn't they say she'd be able to return home in a few days? He was sure it wasn't near as serious as they were insinuating. Medical professionals always overreacted in an attempt to prepare their patients and families for the worst. It was clear to him she would be fine – look at her now! Yes, everything would be back to normal soon.

He suddenly noticed Susan in the next bed - was she scowling at him? Damn, he'd almost managed to forget about her! Tom shifted his body, out of her line of vision – and that all-knowing stare! He had to reluctantly concede that her advice on erasing traces of another woman before facing Karen, was smart and he supposed - appreciated, though he was under no illusion that she'd imparted it for his benefit. Would Karen have noticed? Tom liked to think not. Countless times he'd reluctantly emerged from Jean's bed, and immediately slipped into their own – albeit, after a cleansing shower. This served as a reminder that he needed to practice more caution in future.

"Honey, isn't it time to get the kids off to school?" Her words jarred him awake, and he was momentarily disorientated. How long had he been sleeping? Karen now recommended he go home – drive them to school and assure them that she was fine. Ok, so he'd slept here all night! "Mrs. Jones will be tired and need a break too." Karen offered a brave smile. "Don't worry – I'll be fine. I'm feeling much better and thank you for being here with me." Tom agreed, kissed the back of his wife's hand, and assured her he would be back soon, Tom was oblivious to Susan's keen regard as he exited the room. Checking in at the nurse's station to see what time doctor rounds would be, he was told that the team had left them to sleep this morning. The head nurse assured he could consult with Karen's doctor during evening rounds.

Karen was much more alert now and her regular regime of medication had kicked in, rendering the horrid pain to a throbbing dull ache. She was relieved to see Tom go and relaxed considerably. She was aware of his discomfort in hanging out at the hospital with her. So, she'd let him off the hook – Mrs. Jones had left a message that she'd walk the kids to school. Tom was, after all, a good provider. Karen sighed in sad reflection. In Tom's world – it was all about him. Her heart attack, she acknowledged with anguish, would be a major inconvenience for Tom. Her introspection was abruptly interrupted by her roommate's compassionate voice.

"How are you feeling now my dear?" Susan asked gently.

"A little better," Karen replied. "How are you?" She offered a customary polite response - really appreciating this woman's care and comfort. With an ache in her heart, she realized it preferable to her husband's attempts. Oh, he offered all the right words and gestures, but it was in his eyes – the look of a frightened trapped animal.

"I am doing well." Susan smiled, "just an old lady in an ancient body," she chuckled. Karen guessed there must be something seriously up with her hospital room mate but did not feel it polite to pry. She hadn't noticed any nurses hovering over the woman, nor did she seem to be hooked up to any monitors – then again, who was she to talk? She'd been out cold!

"I've met your daughter already of course, when Sway was last into emergency, and I know you have a son as well. So lovely, I believe they call that the million-dollar family, one of each – boy and girl," Susan offered warmly. Karen was compellingly drawn to this woman with the instant smile and mischievous sparkle in her eyes. To be so positive and happy in a place like this, Karen contemplated, was amazing.

"How many children do you have?" She was curious about this mystery lady and recognized an unquestionable trust in her.

"Well, you've met my two grown girls, Faith and Hope," she smiled and laughed. "I named them aptly, as they both remind me on a daily basis to embrace those virtues in this crazy world. They are my sole two blessings in terms of offspring."

"Do you have grandchildren?" Karen asked, instantly alarmed by the wash of sadness evident on Susan's features.

"No, not anymore, I did have a granddaughter." Susan softly replied but offered nothing further. Karen sensed the woman's sorrow and immediately apologized for prying.

"No worries," Susan assured - her demeanor switching back easily, with a friendly smile, "and at my age I am not so very far away from reuniting with her." Susan smiled and Karen noticed an undefinable glow about her. Through the sadness of that brief moment, Karen could not help but grin at this delightful woman's faith. She briefly closed her eyes and placed her hand over her heart. Would she live long enough to see her children have children of their own? As if Susan were reading her mind, she softly offered solace.

"Do not worry, my dear, everything will work out and you'll soon be home, cuddling your babies and getting back to normal. It is not yet your time."

"Thank you!" marvelling at the sense of well-being this evoked within, Karen couldn't contain her burning curiosity, "How do you stay so positive?"

"Oh, my dear, it is not hard," Susan assured, "nothing happens without reason." Not for the first time, Karen was struck by Susan's seemingly inherent wisdom and recalled details from their former interaction. "Case in point – I've been blessed to meet you and your lovely family. Now that would never have happened if circumstances had not placed us here together." Yep – an old soul – Karen determined.

"Good morning, Karen!" A nearing middle-aged doctor breezed in, defined by the typical stethoscope wrapped loosely around his neck. He was accompanied by one of the nurses Karen recognized from the previous day. "How are you feeling?"

"A little better," Karen responded politely, noticing the distinguished spray of gray sprinkled liberally at his temples and perfectly groomed hair. Ok – this is one exceptionally attractive man. Lord, I must be recovering nicely, she giggled inwardly. What was his name? Dr. Edwards – that was it!

"Good, good," he was pleased. "I promise, you will be feeling even better once you are up and about. You definitely needed a little repair work." He grinned broadly while listening to her chest. "I was able to clear a ninety per cent arterial coronary blockage, by threading a stent through your femoral artery. You should benefit with a little increased energy, and symptoms should start to improve immediately. With this in place, you should be relatively safe until we can find a suitable donor heart – you are on the transplant list, through the Fraser Health Authority. However, on the interim, it's vital that you take diligent care of yourself. Ready for my sermon?" He reached out and gave her shoulder a brief squeeze. Wow, that charming, crooked grin was a heart stopper. "This includes healthier diet and exercise. You will have a wealth of support through the Health Authority's Cardiac Care program, but the work is all up to you." He paused, allowing that to sink in. "Sound doable to you?" At her quick nod, he continued.

"Three things – nutrition, exercise, and rest. We develop habits over our lifetime that can impact negatively on our overall health. Right now, your heart is depending on you to make changes and adopt new habits. Eating is not just about food consumption; it is about fueling your body with proper nutrition. Exercise not only enhances the metabolism efficiency, but also serves to keep the body in top operating condition – physical, emotional and mental. There also needs to be a balance between observing adequate sleep patterns and engaging in activities you look forward to doing every day – that nurture that work/life balance. This is not an easy journey," the doctor concluded, "but it is one that you need to commit to, Karen, if you want to increase the odds of maintaining your health, both before and after the transplant." The doctor squeezed Karen's hand gently. "OK, OK! I'm a real basket of cheer – I know." He winked at her, "I will check on you tomorrow and hopefully we can send you home in the next few days." Karen murmured her thanks as the doctor left the room. A flood of exhaustion hit her – this was all so overwhelming!

Susan's watchful gaze followed their exit from the room, and she pointedly craned an ear to hear the nurse vocalize her doubts about Karen's ability to follow through – the odds were slim with a less than supportive husband in tow. "Well, it is in her hands," Dr. Edwards imparted, "all we can do is educate and support." The surgeon's response spurred Susan to survey Karen's reaction, but she had drifted off to a deep slumber. As their voices faded, Susan Burnett was struck with a deep empathy for Karen. Oh, she knew exactly where the nurse had contrived her opinions from - the musky odor of fleshly delights he'd brought along with him this night, still clung to her nasal passages. The man was either having an affair or habituating prostitutes. He'd rushed into the hospital thoroughly disheveled, straight from the source of the unchecked lipstick smears. Wow, you would think cheaters would observe greater caution – but wasn't that the draw - the thrill of escaping dangerous brushes with exposure? He may finally just have plucked the short straw on that one. Actions speak louder than words and the low regard for his wife rang loud and clear. He demonstrated little to no patience for Karen's situation and exhibited a manipulative posturing to convince everyone of his caring. Susan knew that Karen was not fooled by it – puzzled perhaps! She wondered if the man's refusal to take his wife's condition seriously was a product of narcissistic indifference…or was he truly that naïve?

Susan was abruptly awoken by the sense of her two daughters' presence – hadn't she just closed her eyes to rest? She regarded them both affectionately, as they fluttered around her. Flutter was an apt description - their movements carrying the grace of a hummingbird or butterfly, and most times she pondered whether their feet actually touched the ground.

"How are you, Mom?" Faith bent down and kissed her forehead lovingly.

"I am doing fine - no need to fuss," Susan smiled back affectionately at her two daughters – her most precious gems, who'd effortlessly brought so much joy to her life, just in their very essence. She marveled at their resilience, as they consistently met every challenge head on - together. Hope glanced over at Karen's bed. "Don't worry, she is sound asleep," Susan reassured them." She reached out to take their hands – in a gentle command for immediate attention. "We have to start the process tonight - our timelines are tight."

"Are you sure mom? Look what happened to Rose." Faith's concern clutched at Susan's heart.

"I know my girl, but we must consider the alternatives. If we do nothing, they both die or worse – I have thought this through." The girls recognized that iron-clad determination – once she'd made up her mind, there was no negotiating. "This is the best…and…only possible scenario."

"I have to agree with mom, we are lucky to have found Sway before they did," Hope interjected.

"What about the boy," Faith countered?

"The same, without our intervention, he will die as well." Susan stated.

"Will we find him in time?" Hope asked, a troubled frown marring her beauty.

"I am working on that." Susan assured them. "Now, get some sleep, you two are surely going to need it with what lies ahead." Hope and Faith kissed their mother goodnight and resigned to the wisdom of trying to catch some much-needed shut-eye. Only moments after they had departed, Susan heard Karen whimpering in her sleep. She moved over and took her hand in a warm and comforting squeeze, wishing that she had access to the source - to her thoughts at this moment. Karen's eyes suddenly flew open.

"Fire- save my daughter!" Her crazed stare sent a chill up Susan's spine.

"I can help but only if you let me." Susan kept her voice to a calm whisper. Tears welled up into Karen's eyes – she was frantic. "I know," Susan said, "this is all new to you – I can help, and you can trust me – I am aware of your vision." Karen slowly nodded her head.

"Please, please help us!" Karen's head drooped down to her chest, racking sobs shuddering through her body. Susan held firmly to her hands.

"Do I have your permission?" Susan asked. Karen's hiccupping cries started to calm as Susan held her firmly within a locked gaze.

"Yes," you have my permission," Karen whispered, then collapsed into unconsciousness as her body turned frigid. Susan concentrated – commanding the warmth of her hands to draw the cold out until Karen's skin was again warm. The hospital room, however, carried an unmistakable icy threat, as Susan crossed to her own space. She pushed the call bell and struggled back into bed. Momentarily, the nurse scurried in to see what Susan needed assistance with. "I am cold, Susan relayed in a shivery whisper, "could I please have one of those heated blankets?"

"Yes of course," the nurse whispered back and left to retrieve the blanket. The cold sensation had now seeped into every cell in Susan's body, and she began an uncontrollable, violent shiver. By the time the nurse returned the whole bed was vibrating. My goodness, the nurse wondered how this patient could possibly have gotten this cold. Could she have somehow wandered outside? At a touch, she found Susan's skin to be ice cold as if she'd been submerged in freezing ice water. The nurse wrapped a heated blanket around her and reached for the thermometer. The shaking did not abate. "How did you get this cold?" the nurse inquired as she inserted the thermometer in Susan's ear for a reading? At the electronic beep she removed it. Her routine scrutiny turned to incredulity - this could not be possible! Ninety-five degrees Fahrenheit! "Susan were you outside?" the nurse asked, alarm evident in her tone. "No," Susan responded through clattering teeth. "I'll be right back," the nurse assured, and rushed from Susan's bedside to the nursing station.

Just minutes later, she returned with Dr. Hamilton and second nurse. Susan's skin was now warm to the touch and her temperature was back to normal, but when they tried to rouse her, she was totally unresponsive. The medical team jumped into action, checking Susan's vitals. Her heart was strong, and all else was normal. The team shook their heads in puzzlement and the doctor quietly informed the nurses that this patient, for reasons he could not define, had clearly become comatose. The attending nurse felt a permeating shiver invade her body and she could have sworn she saw a shadow move across the room but didn't dare voice it. Everyone would believe she was losing her marbles! Instead, she quickly shook it off - God she needed sleep.

"Nurse Vicki," he instructed gravely, "please page Dr. Kerr immediately and advise her of the urgency of her mother's condition. Order an emergency cranial CT scan as well." Dr. Hamilton sighed. "Keep her warm and comfortable, that's all we can do for now."

Chapter 8

TOM MADE IT home in time to get the children up for school and relieve Mrs. Jones from her post. When she inquired, he assured her that Karen was doing well and would be home in the next day or so.

"I thought she had a heart attack," her look of astonishment convinced him a further explanation was in order – no need to get onto this woman's bad side!

"Yes, she actually had two heart attacks, but they've unblocked a heart artery and she's come out of it marvellously. She will require a heart transplant down the road, but they have this under control." He smiled and opened the door in a clear invite to leave. "Thank you for your concern and for watching the kids, I'll pass it along to Karen."

Mrs. Jones left the house shaking her head in disbelief – not one, but two heart attacks - needs a new heart, but is just fine? Wow, the man was in denial, she presumed. Poor Karen - she would make a point of visiting as soon as she got home. Her heart went out to the children - what would they do if things went from bad to worse and they lost their mother? She pushed that thought firmly from her mind. Better not invite trouble with dwelling on the negative! Picking her way through the newly sprouted dandelion stems sprinkled over the lawn, she pondered on the most beneficial help to offer - babysitting, cleaning, and anything else they may need, she supposed. First things first – call Karen at the hospital and offer to cover off for Tom, with his work and whatever else the man had on the go – clearly there was at least one thing that he was unwilling to share. Well, he wasn't *her* husband, thank God!

Before heading to wake the children, a troubled Tom watched his neighbor waddle to her house and disappear around the corner. He thanked his good fortune that she hadn't asked of his whereabouts when the hospital was trying to track him down.

"Sway, Zac, time to rise and shine. We are going to McDonalds for breakfast!" he bellowed. They could use a helpful diversion from the stress and worry over their mom. He was genuinely at a loss to comfort them, and it was highly plaguing. Both children and pets, he found in Sway's room. Zac was curled up on the floor – arms wrapped around Daisy and the cat was regally perched up on the bed, glaring at Tom – accusingly it seemed. What the hell had he ever done to that cat? "Come on, up you get - Zac put your dog outside, you won't have time to walk her before we go." Tom barked the orders.

"Can we go see mommy before school," Sway peered up with a pleading expression?

"No, but I'll pick you up after I get home from work. Visiting hours start in the late afternoon so the patients can rest," Tom explained, not particularly concerned if that was true or not.

Zac headed to let Daisy out the back door, feeling the heavy weight of guilt for not walking her, but he had learned the hard way not to challenge his father's decisions. His heart ached with the absence of his mom - her gentle way of buffering things regarding his dad and whatever else came up, for that matter. Despite his determination to stay positive for her, shards of worry slipped into Zac's mind. He hoped with all his heart that she'd be ok and home soon. Zac ran to his room to get ready – dress, wash his face, brush his teeth, then his hair - in that exact order. A meal at McDonald's - hands down, was one of his absolute favourites but today's prospect didn't evoke the usual anticipation. Too much was awry – his mom ill, Daisy transferring her devotion. Sadness permeated his entire being.

Sway had woken, plagued with worries for her mom. She desperately wished to tell her father about her sore tummy, but she knew what his response would be – the words reverberated in her brain – "off to school you go – you'll be fine once you get there". Mommy always took it seriously when she was sick – heck, even the doctors didn't think she was making it up. They trusted her, even when the pains went away quickly. Sway could feel the breathtaking panic rising within – how would she manage this without her mom? She'd heard their arguments – numerous times – Dad accusing Mommy of babying her when the episodes hit. She'd tried to shut out his angry raised voice – "why do you let her get away with feigning illness?" But Sway was not pretending, and her mom believed her. Mommy also helped her pick out her clothes in the morning. Feeling utterly lost without her now, Sway stood and simply stared at her closet. An overwhelming heartache ensued, and she called out for Zac, who instantly poked his head through her doorway.

"Can you help me find my clothes? I miss Mommy," Sway sniffed, holding back a flood of tears. He instantly went to her closet and drawers and after finding a familiar combination of clothing he had seen Sway wear at least a dozen times; he gave her a gentle hug. In truth, he wasn't in much better shape, but she needed him strong now.

"I miss Mom too – here, put these on and once you're dressed and cleaned up l will brush your hair," he promised. She was clearly feeling calmer, "but hurry - you know how much dad hates waiting!" Zac's warning spurred her into immediate action. She was still brushing her teeth when their father bellowed for them to step it up. Tom tracked them to the bathroom to see Zac hastily but gently running the hairbrush through Sway's dark shoulder length hair.

"Can't she do that herself?" Tom growled. "No wonder she's such a damn baby!"

"Yes, she can – I'm only helping to speed us up." Zac immediately stuck up for his little sister. Tom glowered at the two of them, lending implication to his volatile mood – one that the kids knew they needed to skirt around as best they could!

"I'll be in the car!" They both winced at his snarly tone. Zac rushed to pour the food and water into the pets' dishes, then raced to the back door to release Daisy, who immediately returned and scampered to Sway's side. Zac didn't have time to wonder about that - he scooted Sway out the front door, while expertly blocking Daisy from escape - then, herded his sister lickety-split into the back seat of the running car, where their father was clearly impatiently waiting, fingers tapping wildly on the steering wheel. Zac quickly secured the buckle on Sway's booster seat and ran around to jump into his own side of the car. Normally he'd be overjoyed to have the front seat with his father but today he chose to sit in the back beside Sway. Tom paused for a second to glance back at him but did not say a word. As the car backed out of the driveway, Zac heaved an inward sigh of relief. Ten minutes later, they were at their destination.

Upon entering the restaurant, Tom was taken aback by the greetings from neighbors and acquaintances, aware of Tom's plight - wife in the hospital, full time job and two children to look after. They offered warm handshakes, thoughts, prayers and the odd hug, wishing Karen a speedy recovery and homecoming. Tom felt warmed by the empathy and attention given to him and his children.

He was grateful he and Karen had no interest in moving to a larger city – this is a scene you'd not witness in the middle of Vancouver, or even Prince George. While Terrace's population rightly earned its city status – along with many conveniences not afforded in smaller towns – the residents all valued the same community feel that came with the latter. The people here had common bonds – isolated north-western location; economic ties – logging, tourism, pipeline and mineral development; and Terrace was now considered the Northwest Transportation hub in the province, with CN Rail and the local airport. Its rich history and cultural influences, in large part through First Nations arts, fostered pride within the community. Residents could fondly lay claim to the highest cedar telephone pole ever produced – still standing in New York City, USA. Yes – grown right on their home ground! Great place to call home!

The order line moved quickly and soon they were chowing. Zac wolfed his pancakes and apple slices down while Sway picked at hers, barely eating enough to fill a small bird. Without Mom, Zac took on the role, wrapping her food for later, and encouraging her to finish the milk.

Tom, on the other hand, was oblivious to what was going on with his children. His focus was strictly limited to those compassionate individuals who stopped by their table to share concerns. He verbally denoted the seriousness of Karen's current condition and the odds for surviving the impending heart transplant. The well-wishers listened intently and revered the strong man that he was - committed to persevere through a significantly heavy burden - yet spotlighting a positive outcome. Tom smiled with genuine pleasure – he'd never thought of it that way. The story was simply better told in this manner and after all, people thrived on doom, gloom and drama. His grins and chuckles were mistakenly perceived by others as reinforcement that Tom Shorn was nobly putting on a good show for his children – minimizing worry about their mom. What these kindhearted folks did *not* see, was the growing apprehension within Zac and Sway as they watched and listened to their father regale the frightening details concerning their mother's current health issues.

"I need to go to the bathroom," Zac muttered to his father as he got up and left the restaurant table. Tom barely noticed. Zac escaped into one of the bathroom stalls, put his head in his hands and tried to drown out his father's voice still resounding in his brain. In an effort to calm his body and mind to the fear of possibly losing his mom, he engaged in deep slow breathing – Mommy had taught him this strategy, years ago. Zac was conscious of men coming and going in the washroom.

"Hey George, did you hear about Tom's wife?"

"Yup," responded George, "don't look good. They say the woman is overweight and clearly does not take care of herself. My guess is they will not get a heart to her in time - I have heard it can take years to find a donor match." The man clicked his tongue. "All I can say is, Tom had better get his affairs in order – and soon. He is going to be raising those kids on his own," the man predicted.

"Yes, sad situation." the other man concurred, as Zac heard him wash his hands and go out the door. He waited until the man named George left before hurrying out of the bathroom, not even stopping to wash his hands. Back at the table, his father was urging Sway to get ready to leave. Zac took her hand and led her out of the restaurant to the car. Tom was still relishing attention, waving to people as they left. It occurred then to him, that his father might actually be gaining some enjoyment, at the expense of his mother's current urgent health predicament. An unpleasant ache filled the pit of his stomach.

Sway grabbed her stomach and whispered anxiously, "I don't feel good."

"It's ok," Zac returned under his breath, "we will be at school soon and we'll go see the nurse - she will probably have something to make you feel better." Zac dutifully buckled his sister in, before climbing into his own side. With all his heart, he wished to see his mom - have her tell him everything was going to be fine.

The nurse was fully aware of their mom's predicament, so gave them both a warm hug. "Miracles happen in medicine every day - try not to worry." She administered something to help Sway's stomach and assured that she could stay until she felt better. Perhaps from an intuitive nudge, the nurse offered an invite for Zac to stay with Sway – she would send a message to his teacher. Zac thanked her politely but firmly insisted on attending class. He knew how important his grades were to Mom and how proud she was of his efforts - going to class just seemed like the right thing to do. He vowed to work extra hard so she wouldn't worry - God, that might hurt her heart! Zac felt a niggling feeling of dread spiraling up his spine – was this part of the reason his mom was sick - worrying about him?

Tom's reception at work mirrored his experience at the restaurant. Jean lingered in the background, keenly listening in on the conversation. Once Tom had briefed everyone, they trickled back to their offices and workstations. He now followed as she motioned him into her office. Once inside, with door closed, she directed him to sit and he began to repeat the update on Karen's health, but she halted him with a raised hand.

"I heard it all out there Tom," Jean spoke abruptly. "Why are you even here?" she asked.

"I am fine!" Tom insisted. He couldn't believe she was going to travel this road with him again!

"Well, *you* very may well be, Tom, your wife is not! She could very possibly be at death's door! Don't you think your behavior is more than a little unusual?" Jean snapped.

"No, Jean, Karen will be fine," Tom insisted, "I can't do anything for her at the hospital."

"Oh really," mocked Jean, "you should be her rock right now – she's the mother of your children!" Her look of stern indignation affirmed to him that this conversation would not come to a happy accord. Tom put his head in his hands – he couldn't face the hospital and Karen would be just fine! Work was his haven – it provided commonplace normalcy - Tom *needed* normal. But something inside was nudging him otherwise.

"Tom, we have not booked any work for you today," Jean said softly. "So go - where *are* the kids?" He shook his head distractedly and replied that he'd dropped them off at school. "Are they ok to be there, Tom?" She started firing questions, "They must be having a tough time worrying about their mom, no? How is Sway - wasn't she with Karen when she had the heart attack - that is traumatic for anyone, never mind a child?"

"Oh God," Tom exhaled, "With all that's been going on, I haven't thought of it." But Karen would have, he admitted ruefully. Karen always knew what was going on with the kids - he never paid much attention because he considered that to be *her* job, not his. It was a natural maternal thing, wasn't it? "Yes, Sway called 911. She was there through everything. It must have frightened her."

"Of course," Jean confirmed. "Tom, you are accustomed to having the world revolve solely around *you*. Karen has been the giver - to you and to those kids, her entire married life. Everything she does – her solitary purpose, is for her family – *you*, in particular. Time to put your big boy pants on and go look after your family. I don't want to see your face at work until she is stable at home, do you understand me?" Jean ordered. "Now - out of my office!"

Tom's initial temptation had been to forcefully demand that she mind her own damn business and *he* would decide on how he handled his wife and kids, but the expression on Jean's face - the exact one he had seen only a few times before, aimed squarely at her husband, gave him sensible pause.

It always turned out badly for Doug, so rather than push his luck he wisely deferred to quietly leaving her office.

Back in his vehicle, Jean's words echoed through his mind – she was right, his inner voice scolded. He had not thought much about how his kids were feeling, if at all. He mostly considered Karen's illness to be an inconvenience. Sighing, he dismally acknowledged his shallow satisfaction from the attention bestowed by everyone. While others viewed him as a man putting on a brave face for his children's sake, Jean saw right through him. She was the only other person in this world who knew his inner workings as well as Karen. Hell, he guessed - Jean likely knew him better than his own wife. Of course, it made sense – between work and their weekly bedtime romp, there was ample opportunity to catch every side of him. Yes, Jean *did* come out on top – in more ways than one.

Tom headed the car in the direction of the hospital. As he got closer, he was slapped by the sudden memory of being pulled over the night before by the police. Oh crap, he'd better go check in with Officer O'Reilly! He rerouted to the police station, where he received another round of well wishes. Tom was directed to an interview room to wait for the officer.

Toby was on his coffee break when he spotted Tom request an audience with officer O'Reilly. Pouring a second cup of coffee, he grabbed a handful of creamers and sugar, and followed him to the interview room. "Hi Mr. Shorn, I am Toby - the one who took the 9-1-1 call from your wife – I thought you might appreciate a cup of coffee." He smiled warmly and handed it to Tom. "Do you mind if we chat while you wait for the officer?"

Tom nodded, "Sure, thank you for what you did for my wife – and the coffee. Please, sit down." Tom gestured to the chair across from him, "but what do you mean my wife having called? I was told it was my daughter Sway who called 9-1-1."

"Initially, your wife called, alarmed because she could not wake your daughter, but during the call we lost connection. When I managed to get the call through again, your daughter answered and told me that your wife was, as Sway put it, sleeping. We already had the ambulance at your house by this time and when they entered, they found your wife unconscious and non-responsive," Toby explained.

Tom sat gaping at Toby, unsure on how to respond, other than to voice his confusion. "That doesn't make sense." Just then the door opened, and Officer O'Reilly entered the room.

"I have to get back to work," Toby stood, "I do have the recording of the call. Would you mind if I played it for you sometime later? It might help with some of my questions." Toby explained. At Tom's affirmative nod, Toby gave him his card and shook his hand. "I wish your wife a speedy recovery and please do call me at your convenience." As the young man left for his post, Tom was aware of a fleeting bewilderment – what sort of questions did the 911 operator have on his mind – and why?

"What was that all about?" Officer O'Reilly asked.

"I am not sure," Tom said, still in wonder on all that had taken place on the day of his wife's heart attack.

"Thanks for stopping in to look after your speeding violation, Tom – I know this is a busy time for you." Officer O'Reilly looked him square in the eye. "I have reviewed your driving record and found it unblemished in the past three years. Considering your wife's heart attack and the understandable ensuing stress and distraction, I am going to let you off with a warning. I'm confident that you are not in the habit of such a serious breach in speed laws. If you don't mind my asking though, where were you coming from when I pulled you over?"

Tom felt an instant ball of fear in the pit of his stomach and sat quiet for a moment - needing time to gather his thoughts. Jim O'Reilly knew full well, that his address, along with the well-known poker gathering spot, were in the absolute opposite end of town from where Tom had been coming from. "I was checking out some new corner stores on the newer area of town – my wife loves candy bars and I thought I'd find a better variety," Tom laughed nervously. "I thought it might cheer her up in the hospital. Thanks for just giving me a warning - I really appreciate it."

"We just want to see everyone safe," the policeman regarded him thoughtfully, then offered an indulgent smile. "Just hold on here for a minute and I'll get the paperwork in order." Tom instantly knew that the officer had not bought one iota of his story. After all – candy for a heart attack victim? He'd had time to stop at corner stores but then furiously sped to the hospital. This was lame and Tom felt a fool. He hated to have anyone think of him as naïve, or even more humiliating, less than highly intelligent – even in weaving a web of deception.

"Thank you," Tom repeated, "I hope it won't take too long. I wish to get back to my wife and check on how my kids are doing." Better to leave this meeting with his concern for his family on the forefront.

"No worries, Tom," the officer replied, "this will only take a few minutes - just relax." The officer returned in a moment with the written warning letter. "Please be clear, this is conditional – if you are stopped for another speeding infraction in the next 60 days, this will be amended to a dangerous driving infraction, in line with legal procedure for driving a motor vehicle at 100 km in 60 km speed zone," the officer's tone was polite but brooked fair warning.

"You are correct – it is not my normal driving behavior – thank you for letting me know," Tom responded. "I won't be engaging in any further speeding," Tom promised. The officer showed Tom where to sign in acknowledgement of all that he'd just imparted. Tom took his copy and left the station – feeling somehow like an escaped criminal.

Once in the car Tom was unsure what to do next. He did not feel capable of going to the hospital, school, *or* home. So, he sat there. He couldn't stop the events of the last hour from running rampant in his mind - Jean refusing to let him work. She had intrusively brought up their kids and questioned their well-being – as if he didn't care at all? Hell, he did not have the answers – that didn't make him a bad father! Then the 9-1-1 operator relating that Karen had made the call – well, he had thought that in the beginning. What had happened that morning? Was he doomed to be raising his kids on his own? Tom sat mentally reviewing memory tapes from the last few days. The scene of the restaurant came into view - how his children must have overheard him tell others that she needed a new heart – and he'd told them only that she was fine. My God, what they must be thinking and going through! In a decisive gesture, Tom spun out of the station parking lot, tires squealing. Two blocks later he heard the blaring siren and pulled over. As Officer O'Reilly got out of the car behind him, Tom's head began to spin, and he laid it down on the steering wheel. His entire world was falling apart. God knows he did not dare think what was to come next.

Chapter 9

DURING A PARTICULARLY lengthy lecture from Officer O'Reilly, Tom dutifully signed the speeding violation document which he now assumed would serve as a second violation. That was a hell of a hefty fine! He surmised that now would *not* be the time to bring up the dangerous driving amendment to his first ticket – hopefully the good officer would give him a break on that one. Tom's cell phone rang.

"Ok, this is the hospital calling, may I…?" The constable nodded politely and waited patiently for Tom to finish the call. They were discharging Karen this afternoon after a health team consultation meeting – they were awaiting his arrival to start. Further, they expected both children to be in attendance.

"I don't think that will be necessary for my kids to be there," Tom responded, to which the caller informed him that it was at his wife's request. Tom thanked the person and turned back to dealing with the current crisis at hand.

Officer O'Reilly drilled him with a hard stare and handed Tom his copy of the ticket. "Drive safely Tom," He turned his back and delivered a resounding parting shot, "some guys just don't know how good they have it 'til it is *all* gone." Jim O'Reilly shook his head, jumped in his cruiser and was off, leaving a shaken and frustrated Tom Shorn in his wake.

Those prophetic words rang in Tom's ears as he collected the kids. The situation was swiftly spiraling out of his control – he was not managing this well. He thought back to the message he'd delivered in the restaurant on Karen's dire health situation, and how it must have affected the kids. Karen would have stepped in if she'd been there, to field his thoughtless comments. He pulled up to the curb outside the school and called the office. "I am here to pick up my kids. Can you send them out front please?"

"Is everything ok?" inquired the receptionist, concern evident in her voice.

"Yes, we are picking their mom up from the hospital." What business was it of hers? He had no obligation to spill the family troubles to the school staff – it was frankly none of their concern!

"It would be better if you came into the school."

Tom's tone changed from arrogantly demanding to ass hole in 30 seconds. "Listen, I've had a day and cannot tolerate your inquisition. I am quite capable of doing what is right for my own children! Now, I expect you to get off your lazy ass and do as I ask, immediately!"

Fifteen minutes later, in full boiling over mode, he spotted the kids hurrying toward the car, accompanied by none other than the Principal. Tom did not have time for nonsense and knew at any minute, he was going to lose his shit! Principal Miller stood by the driver's door and Tom refused him an audience by pointedly leaving the window rolled up – no eye contact. The kids got in and Tom peeled out, leaving the man in his wake. These teaching professionals seemed to think their college degree lent them power over parenting – well not this dad!

In the back seat, one could have heard a pin drop - neither child uttered so much as a peep, both hearts pounding with fear. They had watched anxiously, as their father left their Principal standing on the sidewalk. Both had witnessed him in this state many times before and knew it was best to observe absolute silence – become as invisible as possible. Sway reached over to hold Zac's hand tightly. While Zac struggled to hold back the tears forming in his eyes, Sway's flowed freely. But she had mastered the art of crying silently – without so much as a sniffle.

At the hospital, they were quickly ushered into a meeting room where Karen was already seated, - fully dressed and her personal items beside her - ready to go home.

"Mom!" the kids called out joyfully – thick with emotion as they ran to share hugs with her. Karen pulled them tightly to her and showered repeated kisses on their tear-stained cheeks.

"We will be going home as soon as we have a chat with these good doctors," Karen explained. Sway stepped back from her mother. Tom watched her allow Zac access to his mom, who immediately enfolded him into her arms – in a gentle rocking motion, whispering assurances that everything was going to be all right. The tears flowed from Zac. He was clearly terrified and confused, begging her not to die. Karen continued to comfort as he broke into body wrenching sobs. Tom battled a huge lump invading this throat, witnessing his son's emotional breakdown – his first grasp of how absolutely devastating it would be for Zac to lose Karen. It was, perhaps, the first time in Tom's entire existence that he felt immense compassion for someone other than himself. He stepped out of the room for a moment to regulate – his kids didn't need to see *him* fall apart too – not to mention the medical team. Tom was aware of his shortcomings but considered them a copacetic balance with all the good qualities he possessed as a family man. Deep down, he conceded that to forge an inner agreement – walking the pathway to redemption - meant embracing accountability and profound introspection. Tom could not accept ownership of any failures on his part, because that rocked his self-perceived perfection, which kept his ego firmly intact. To mess with that meant change – which unfailingly came with sacrifice – something Tom Shorn had no palate for.

Zac's tears had subsided by the time he returned. It was almost possible to see the emotional pain and tension visibly fall away from his body, enfolded Karen's embrace. As the three of them whispered reassurances and comfort to each other, he felt an instant stab of indignant inequity – why did his family constantly place him as an outsider? He fixed his wife with a brooding stare – she was after all, at the root of it. Things would have to change – and soon. Intuitively, Doctor Edwards cleared his throat. Now it was time to focus on the essential task at hand.

"Well, everyone, let's get to it," Karen's cheerful outburst broke the palpable discomforting energy in the room. "What do I need to do to keep this heart ticking until the new one arrives?"

"Karen," Tom interrupted abruptly, "I think the kids should stay in the waiting room while we have this conversation."

Karen turned to face her husband. "Thank you for that Tom," the response was both respectful and indulgent, "but I have already discussed this with Dr. Edwards and this entire health team – they deem it appropriate for the children. Leaving Zac and Sway in the dark is not in any of our best interests. There will need to be changes in our household which will require all of our buy-in. This involves the entire family, and we need to arm these children with tools to deal with this in a healthy way," Karen concluded. Tom felt his temperature rise - no one, least of all his wife, had his permission to speak to him in such a manner!

The doctor intuitively provided a timely interjection. "That is correct - we have worked with many families in the same situation. Experience and critical evaluation have proven that involving children in this process achieves maximum benefit for all. Are there any other questions or concerns?" Tom glanced around the room and shifted uncomfortably – all eyes were on him. Realizing in this room, at least, he was at a complete disadvantage, he sat back in his chair, offering no further input. "Let's begin," Dr. Edwards nodded to his colleagues. He prefaced by explaining that the optimum outcome of course, was to find a suitable heart donor. Failing this – outline a viable contingency plan to optimize the length and quality of time for Karen's remaining years.

Considerable strategic measures were taken to include specialists on the team, who provided expertise in all pertinent areas of Karen's care - cardiologist, nutritionist, physiotherapist, and psychologist. Each methodically covered the functional logistics of Karen's heart, and the requirements to optimize efficiency with overall health, to ensure Karen's suitability as a candidate for the transplant, which would be performed at St. Paul's Hospital in Vancouver – many key players needed to line up their schedules for that to be possible. There were lifestyle changes that would be critical to the success.

"We can do this - get this body in the best possible condition for that new heart." Karen addressed the underlying issue, and they sat back and gave her the floor – she was clearly engaging in the next steps. "I know what I must do – what I'll need from my family and all of you, for support. Thank you, Dr. Edwards, for the comprehensive talk and shared resources. I will do my utmost to follow the recommendations put forth." All smiled and nodded their approval.

Once the medical team completed their counsel, Doctor Edwards closed the file and stood to shake their hands, squeezing Karen's warmly in both of his. "We've got you Karen – please don't hesitate to call any of us on the team." Turning to address the children he crouched down, with the ease of a well-toned athlete. "Your mother has the best team of doctors possible." He winked and smiled at the kids, who promptly returned the gesture.

"Don't you worry, Dr. Edwards, we are going to help our mom with everything!" The doctor reached over to ruffle Zac's hair.

"Of course, you will. I could tell the moment I met you!" With a parting wink, he straightened and departed the conference room. Karen voiced her gratitude to the medical team who were genuine with supporting her success and efforts to follow through with life changes.

Family now alone in the room, she turned to the children and gave them a fierce hug. "We can do this!" Both smiled and nodded their heads enthusiastically. Tom stood back and offered a resounding grunt. Sway ran over and hugged him "Yes Dad, we really can!" Zac squared up to his father and looked him in the eye. "Yes Dad, we *will* do this!" It was another first - his son challenging him. In part, he was enormously proud of Zac, but couldn't shake off the discomforting feeling of exclusion – the increasing loss of control. How did it get to this – respected as a loving father, husband and provider, to what - the enemy? For a fleeting moment he thought how much simpler things would be if Karen had just died. His heart skipped a beat or two - had he really harbored such a thought? Looking at her now, he was shocked at her cold, calculating regard. Did she somehow read his thoughts? Tom quickly averted his gaze.

"Ok family," Karen said, "let's get this party on the road. First stop - the grocery store." Tom walked ahead of his family to the car. She was acting as if she now were the head of the family – well, she wasn't *his* boss – that was for sure! He pointedly opted not to carry her personal items and announced his intention to go to the house.

"I suggest you get with the program Tom - I can't drive until I have a clear bill of health and you're going to learn how to shop healthy for this family," Karen snapped.

Tom slammed on the brakes, jarring everyone forward to strain against their seat belts. He lifted his hand and for a moment, it seemed like he was going to hit her. "Dad!" both children shouted fearfully from the back seat. He turned to both his children and yelled, "Shut up!" Turning to Karen, he raged, "you will never talk to me like that again, no matter how sick you are!" Karen did not respond – her shock evident. Without a word, Tom drove to the grocery store. With hand shaking, Karen grabbed a cart - Zac took over, saying "I got this Mom!"

"Thank you, Zac," she replied. Sway had taken her mother's hand in support, trying to calm the trembling. Tom saw his daughter struggling to hold back her tears and registered the wave of dread in his stomach – once again, he'd lost control of the situation.

"Karen!" One of Karen's best friends, Aggie, popped out of an aisle to greet them. The Shorn family listened to Aggie go on about her good intentions to visit Karen in the hospital, but she had thought it would be family only. They noticed Karen's odd discomforting reaction. Aggie must have perceived it as well as she stepped back – her initial joviality retreating with her.

"Thank you, but I am tired and need to get home - please excuse me." Karen hastily backed away. Aggie vanished as quickly as she had appeared. Tom attributed Karen's off-normal behavior with her friend being due to his violent outburst in the car. He had never raised a hand to her like that before - especially in front of the kids. With a sick gurgling in the pit of his stomach, he felt his world spiraling out of control, and he quite simply had no idea how to take charge of it.

Sway pulled on her mothers' arm, and Karen bent down as Sway whispered in her ear. "I don't feel good mommy."

Karen turned to Tom. "I am really sorry for my behavior - shopping was a bad idea - can we just go home please?" Tom immediately softened, grasping onto that familiarity – his wife respecting *his* needs and feelings – her apology went a long way to soothing his bruised ego, and of course, she *was* potentially dying.

"Of course, let's go home." He afforded her a kind smile. "Just leave the cart where it is," Zac did not question and followed his family out to the car.

Tom studied Karen thoughtfully. Something was off. Her defiance – she'd never challenged him that way before. In full realization, she never talked to *anyone* like that – not even the kids. Tom decided to make an appointment with her doctor and find out if Karen may have somehow suffered from brain damage? They did relay that she'd needed life-saving CPR. It would certainly explain her odd behavior.

Once home, he followed her to their bedroom, watching her rifle through the closet and drawers, selecting items of clothing. She then moved to the bathroom and firmly shut the door, locking it with resounding click - another first. He found the kids in the kitchen – pets glued to their sides. "Hey, no animals in the kitchen!" he ordered, his tone brooking no argument. Sway sighed and walked out of the kitchen with both animals at her heels.

"What's up with your dog?" Tom observed.

Zac sighed, "Beats me! It started the night before Mom's heart attack."

"Really," Tom murmured, thinking it strange - wondering what may have caused this odd switch in Daisy's loyalties. Perhaps she sensed Karen's overbearing concern regarding Sway's health. Both Tom and Zac stood back and watched the interaction between Sway and the family pets, neither letting her out of their sights. Karen sauntered out from her bath, donned in her favorite robe. Tom sighed and relaxed on the couch as she called the children, requesting help to prepare dinner, and for Zac to retrieve some pantry items. Tom lent half an ear on the bustle of activity, as he flipped through a Sports Illustrated magazine, unconsciously registering the delicious smells wafting into his territory.

Karen called him for dinner and Tom was amazed at the sight before him – the kids placing bowls of food which Karen normally handled without fuss. His astonishment increased, as the kids politely passed dishes and filled their own plates. Grilled chicken, broccoli salad and wild rice completed the meal for the evening.

"Mom, what is this?" Sway queried, referring to the rice on her plate, and Zac echoed her curiosity. Karen explained that wild rice was much healthier due to the whole grains. Tom realized that he'd never given it a moment's thought before. Suddenly, he noticed the pets in the kitchen watching Sway intently. This was seriously getting out of hand and was just about to bark a demand to remove them, when Karen gently motioned with her hand to the pets, who quietly both relocated to the outer edge of the kitchen. Not one word had been uttered by her to achieve this miraculous compliance. Zac was equally flabbergasted and peered over to gauge his father's reaction – had he noticed it too? Tom's reaction mirrored his own, with a raised brow to his son. Zac shrugged his shoulders, feeling an instant bond with his father.

"Why aren't you dishing our plates up, Mom?" Zac voiced his curiosity.

"It's time we all started fixing up our own plates. Sway abruptly stopped what she was doing and looked over at her mother. "What's wrong honey?" Karen put her own fork down.

"Are you teaching us this stuff for when you're not here anymore?"

"No Sweetie," Karen whispered softly, "this is just me helping *you* become stronger and more independent. Now eat this delicious meal you worked so hard to help prepare – and by the way, you did a beautiful job setting the table!" Sway beamed up at her. The children had seen dinner served this way at other people's homes, so this was actually pretty cool, and they were both feeling proud. All eyes were on Sway as she struggled with cutting her chicken. She glanced around the room, but the rush of pride from her newfound independence stopped her short from asking assistance. Finally, she picked up an entire piece and promptly took a bite out of it. Karen laughed, then Zac followed suit – giggling heartily. Sway was not too sure at first whether to be offended or amused, then joined in. There was an infectious buzz of positivity in the air. Tom was particularly surprised that he enjoyed the meal - being a meat and potatoes kind of guy.

"The only thing missing is dessert," he offered hopefully. Karen surveyed the puppy-dog eyes around the table, visibly pondering.

"I know - mom's fruit cobbler that is in the freezer!" Zac jumped up joyfully, not about to give his newly health-conscious mom a chance to kibosh the idea. "We can cut small pieces, heat it in the microwave and put little scoops of ice cream on top." Karen graced him with an affectionate look of relief.

"That sounds fine, but only three pieces Zac." Overall, it was a wonderful meal and in keeping with new beginnings, the four of them worked together as a team cleaning up. When Karen handed Tom the tea towel, he muttered under his breath something about dishes not being his chore, but reluctantly dried the remaining pots. Now didn't seem to be the time to start a war with his family. It had been a long, eventful day, and they all wandered off to their evening routine. Zac grabbed Daisy's leash, fully expecting her to be right there waiting – she lived for those walks with him. Tonight, though, she hung firmly by Sway. Karen paused putting together the kids' lunches for the next day.

"Sway, how about you go with your brother to walk Daisy." Sway enthusiastically grabbed her jacket and headed out the door with Zac, Daisy now trailing between them. Key-Key stood vigil by the door.

"How are you feeling Karen?" Tom turned to face her, the question hanging in the air like some unfamiliar odor. Karen regarded him with what he thought to be a rather odd measuring expression – curiosity? He could have sworn he saw a semblance of a grin as she swung away, before responding.

"A little winded but ok." Tom watched her wander down the hallway to the bedroom, his emotions muddled – waffling between the strong force of denial, concerning the reality of her condition, to the uncomfortable premonition of the high odds against losing her in the near future. A sudden cold draft assaulted him and Key-key growled, peering intently down the hallway where Karen had disappeared. What the hell's going on with your cat? The kids returned and Sway scooped her up.

"I don't feel so well Key-Key." The animal purred loudly in her arms. Tom walked over to check his daughter's forehead. The cat hissed and spat simultaneous to Daisy planting herself between him and Sway, growling deeply – the aggression exclusively aimed at him.

"What the hell!" Tom moved to kick Daisy out of his way but in an instant, Zac placed himself between. A simmering boil began in his gut – this boy was getting just a little too big for his britches!

"Dad!" Zac cried, "They are just protecting her." Sway started to cry, and Karen hurried into the room. "Sway's not feeling well." She reached over to place a comforting hand on Zac's shoulder and inquired as to when this had begun. She gathered Sway up and carried her to the bedroom, as Zac relayed it was right after Mr. Swenson had stopped them to ask after their mom's health.

Tom trailed behind, completely out of sorts with the situation unfolding. "Do you think we should take her to the hospital?"

"No," Karen replied, strangely unruffled, "she will be fine." Damn – how could she be so calm about all this? And what was stopping the emergency visits now? He stood in the doorway and watched as his wife tenderly undressed their daughter. "Would you get her pajamas, please?"

"Where are they?" Tom appealed. Zac rushed to the rescue and retrieved a pair from her top dresser drawer. Tom stood helplessly by, watching Karen soothe their daughter who slowly drifted off to sleep. He barely noticed Zac silently slipping out. "Aren't you going to get her to brush her teeth?" Tom whispered.

"Not tonight," Karen whispered back." Tom hadn't watched over his daughter like this since she was a baby – hadn't afforded the time. He'd also missed the nightly ritual between Key-Key and Sway – cat curled up to her hip – purring Sway to dreamland. Daisy stood by the bed watching all three of them - like a palace guard. The hairs on the back of his neck stood straight out. A cold draft invaded the room – Tom shivered as the dog gave a low growl. Karen rose to gently stroke the dog's ears. "Good girl," she softly soothed, "its ok, not tonight my girl, not tonight." Walking out into the hallway, she took Tom's arm in a soft but firm grip. "She is ok, she will rest now," They met Zac, armed with his blanket and pillow.

"I think I should stay with her again tonight," Zac said.

"Why is that" asked Tom? He was damn sure this was not normal behavior for kids of their age.

"Because that's what big brothers do when their little sisters are scared or sick," said Zac. Not waiting for an approval or reply, he passed them both and quietly entered her room. Daisy – *his* dog - maintained vigil at her side. Zac ruffled her ears and arranged his blanket and pillow on the floor by the bed. Daisy laid down beside him. Zac shook his head – it was the darnedest thing - his dog would not go with him to his room, but here she was, curled up snugly with him by his sister's bedside – for that he was thankful. As he drifted off to sleep the room turned ice cold, the children and pets' breath took rise eerily - a swirling ribbon winding a sinister pathway into the air. Both children shivered – Sway whimpering softly. Low animal growls accompanied as they settled into a deeper slumber. As abruptly as it started, the room returned to its normal temperature.

Chapter 10

"KAREN IT IS garbage day tomorrow, have you put it out yet?" Tom inquired, unbuttoning his shirt in preparation for bed.

"No," Karen responded easily. Tom wandered to the bathroom to find her standing in front of the mirror, critically eyeing up her body - hands tracing a pathway over the ample flesh. "Wow girl, this took some time to put on, but I don't have a lot of time to get it off," Karen mused softly, slowly exploring the spot on her throat from the heart surgery. Tom wondered what was going through her mind, and Karen sent an inquiring glance.

"The garbage," Tom stated.

"So, I would guess since I am a tad under-dressed, you will put it out?" She threw him an amused half smile. Tom shook his head and muttered, "bunch of bullshit," grabbed a sweatshirt, pulled it over his head and paused briefly at the doorway, glaring.

"A little more exercise could rid you of that useless fat," He smirked as he headed out. The utterance of those words felt *so* good - she had a nerve! That will put her back in her place! Gathering the trash from under the kitchen sink, he grimaced at the odor wafting into his nostrils – *so* not his job - then ventured out and dragged the cans to the driveway, mumbling and griping all the way. Now that he had the chore, he was seriously reconsidering Karen's request to invest in bins with wheels – he'd squashed that idea with a sarcastic comment about her laziness costing him an extra $12.00. He figured perhaps he'd indulge for her birthday or anniversary. Distracted by the flashing of bright lights reflecting off the surrounding houses, he scanned the street to find an ambulance parked ominously

93

outside the Swenson's home. Paramedics emerged from the house with Mr. Swenson strapped to a stretcher. Mrs. Swenson followed behind, clearly upset and weeping. A neighbour gently took her arm and guided her into their car, prepared to follow the ambulance as it sped off - sirens blaring. As Tom turned back to the house, he hoped all would be well.

Karen was in bed waiting for him. His mood had not improved in the least – who the hell did she think she was, lounging in bed while he was running around doing *her* chores? "You're really pushing this illness, aren't you?" Tom grumbled as he headed for the bathroom. "Did you lock everything up for the night?"

"No, why would I do that, when you were just outside? Unless of course you were *hoping* to get locked out..." His annoyance piqued with her amused giggle. After securing the doors, he took a quick peek into Sway's room. Zac was sound asleep on the floor, and she was curled up in bed, with Key-Key glued to her side. Fear crept along his nerves at the disquieting thought - what if he had to raise these kids alone? Tom quietly made his way to their room, to find Karen sitting upright in bed, intently lost in a familiar magazine. *His* magazine? What the heck was she doing with that? Tom stripped and reached for his pyjamas, about to crawl in and snatch his property away from her, when Karen inquired about his shower. He thought better of acting on his petulant urge for a nasty retort – thinking of his nights with Jean. A giant ball of guilt spurred him to the bathroom. Her offending soap glared accusingly at him from the shower shelf! Boy - was she pushing the envelope! This was just not like her – too many things were not adding up here! Was her brain was deprived of oxygen? That *had* to be it!

Back in the room, he turned to the sight of his wife for more than a decade - lying stark naked for all to see. "Don't you think you should hold off on putting those pyjamas on?" Karen purred with a seductive smile. So intense the shock, Tom feared it was his turn for heart failure! Words simply escaped him – turning her down may lead to suspicion of an affair. Did Mrs. Jones perhaps out him, and this was a test?

"Are you sure that is a good idea with your heart?" he sputtered.

"Just climb into this bed, and we will see what this heart can manage," Karen murmured with an enticing smile and come-on wink. Thoroughly out of options, he complied, feeling completely out of sorts. Karen wiggled over and began a feather-light fingertip exploration of his body. He nearly jumped out of his skin when she commenced nibbling and gently sucking his earlobe.

"What are you doing?" It was a croak - this was frankly not in his comfort zone – *he* was always the one in control. "This is not something you have ever done." His voice came out in a rasp – damned if he wasn't starting to get a little turned on! Karen laughed low in her throat – alluring and provocative.

"Well Tom, this body has missed a few things – time to catch up."

Karen continued to ravage his well-toned body with her mouth and hands. Both of their temperatures took a flaming leap as she boldly caressed his hardness, glorying in the groan her touch emitted. Lying back, she emitted a soft sigh and commenced a slow fondle of her own body, in places - in ways Tom had never seen before. He was helplessly mesmerized. She then drew his hand to touch her in kind, where he had not ventured for a very long time – certainly never with the heated evidence of her desire in play. Karen softly moaned and evoked the sharp intake of his breath. Tom moved to get on top of her - thick and ready.

"No, no wait!" she insisted and held him back, guiding his hands back. He held his body up with one arm, forearm muscles bulging with the effort, but nevertheless biding her will. Tom closed his eyes, in disbelief – she was hot and wet for him! It was like he was in bed with another woman! At this moment, he couldn't for the life of him, conjure up his sexy mistress, as was his strategy whenever taking a much-needed release with Karen. This was incredibly foreign and completely unexpected – it bloody well excited him! Karen had never even had an orgasm that he was aware of – he truly assumed she had no real interest in sex, so he had expected to get through this briefly, with lurid images of Jean spurring it along. To his utter astonishment Karen had other ideas. Damn if it wasn't getting him hotter by the minute! He felt a sudden need to plunge inside of her now, and expertly forced her thighs farther apart to accommodate – the blood pounding in his ears. Each time he attempted to enter her; however, she held him back. It was driving him insane!

Karen took Tom's head between her hands and pressed her lips against his – nibbling and sucking on his lower lip, teasing him with little tongue flickers. Tom moaned his pleasure as he thoroughly possessed her mouth with his own – his tongue tasting and devouring, hips grinding against her thighs. Karen pulled away and pushed him lower – sucking in her breath as he expertly suckled and teased each of her taut nipples. Still, she continued guiding, toward the junction between her legs. Tom kissed and licked his way down, pausing as he reached the sweet essence of her womanhood. By now he was completely invested in the game.

She needed his mouth on her now and thrust herself upwards into his face. "Let's see how good you are with your tongue big boy," she whispered in a thick, passion-drugged, titillating voice. Tom was no longer thinking with his brain. His other head was nearly exploding with need, but this delightful teasing game was entirely worth the wait. Karen was frantic for release and bucked wildly against him, as he held her firmly – exactly where he wanted her. She finally lost control of the flood of ecstasy. Tom managed a look into her eyes when she came for the first time, thrashing and thrusting, clutching and pressing his head to her source of pleasure. Now she squirmed and slid down the length of him, pushing him back, her hands eagerly exploring his body. She slid seductively on top, and he grabbed her hips, guiding her to sheathe him, and began a slow rhythmic rocking. Now he could freely caress her body, driving her desire to another level with the added stimulation. The look of pure sensual abandon on Karen's face as she reached her second orgasm instantly sent Tom over the edge. Karen continued to amaze him, several more times through the night, leading them on a sexual journey they'd never traveled before. Tom marvelled at witnessing his wife achieve multiple orgasms. Hours later, they were both fully sated.

"Wow," Tom panted, sweating heavily as they laid slightly apart, Karen in an elevated position, giving their bodies a chance to cool down and catch their breath. Tom moved onto one elbow and propped himself up to take a good look at her. She inhaled deeply, allowing her heart rate to slow. She had engaged in breath exercises with a physiotherapist at the hospital. "Are you OK? He looked worried.

"Yes," panted Karen." She still had the irresistible glaze of lustful satisfaction in her eyes and giggled gleefully.

"That was so different, "Tom murmured softly, "your first orgasm, wasn't it?" At her shy nod, he continued. "What do you think happened? Do you think it has something to do with your heart attack?" Karen shot him a look of surprise and a thoughtful expression washed over her flushed features. "What – did I say something wrong?" She smiled.

"I am a bit surprised at your focus – you are not excited to be the catalyst for my very first orgasm? What about the thrill at the prospect of continuing this journey with me? This is something healthy Tom – not a product of my failing heart."

"Hell Karen, "Tom laughed, "you got to know a guy has to wonder how his wife can go from a nice girl in bed to a wild cat - not that I am complaining," he held up his hands in assurance. Karen grinned at him.

"Yes, considering our history, I guess you would. Women have needs too you know."

"Well, I will be damned, the house mouse has turned into a cat," he chuckled.

Karen slid out of bed. "I am headed for the shower - rain check on another go around, maybe tomorrow night?" Karen threw him a beguiling wink and disappeared into the bathroom. Tom lay, deep in thought - she was in there a long time which customarily would have pissed him off, griping about wasted water. But there was nothing normal about tonight. Waiting quietly, his mind relived their love making - well actually it felt more like *hot* sex. Karen's near-death experience and the reality of her uncertain life expectancy was something Tom avoided thinking about. Every time the thought slipped in; he firmly pushed it out. Karen was the kindest, sweetest soul he knew. Her recent sharp-tongued attitude could only be attributed to brain affectation and coping with the fact she was going to die. A fleeting moment of guilt assailed him for being an asshole - then like any notion that did not serve Tom Shorn, he placed it solidly out of reach, to the impenetrable inner realms of his subconscious.

Karen strolled naked back into the room and climbed into bed, propping herself in a semi sitting position. "Do you mind if I take that pillow?" pointing to the one under his head, "I'll trade you for this one," holding out a much flatter version. Tom's first response was a resonant growl, but something held him off. Karen smiled and patiently explained that it is easier on her heart - elevation. What the hell? Karen always attended to his comfort first! He opened his mouth to rage his objection, but then figured that would make him out to be the ultimate cad, so reluctantly surrendered his pillow, doubling up the pathetic replacement and bunching it under his head.

Karen peered at him, "Do we cuddle?" His adamant negative response seemed to amuse her. "Didn't think so," Karen retorted playfully, and closed her eyes for sleep.

"We sleep with pajamas," Tom railed testily.

"Well, maybe *you* do - tonight I am not," she responded buoyantly.

"What if the kids come in?" Tom pursued, still buck naked himself.

"The door is locked," Karen offered merrily.

"When the hell did you do that?"

"Before we started having sex," Karen laughed gleefully. Tom grunted, slipping in beside her, immediately succumbing to post sex drowsiness. Sometime in the wee hours of the morning, he woke to find her sensuously mounting him. He was instantly rock hard, and she took control, riding him thoroughly to a mind-bending orgasm, stopping periodically - just long enough to keep his release at bay – then bucking herself to a second peak. Only when weak with satisfaction, did she allow him to take his release. With the room still dark, Tom closed his eyes and drifted back to sleep, feeling like a well-used stallion. When he woke again, it all seemed an erotic dream, but the evidence was on the bedsheets – where was she? With a satiated calm, he rose and hit the shower – making breakfast he assumed.

Back in the bedroom, the clock glowed 6:00 a.m. Their usual rise and shine are not for another hour - maybe a good thing – an early start to his day. Swirling thoughts led to their intoxicating night together – never had they shared an experience that even came close! A virgin when they'd first dated, Karen was the first *nice* girl he had ever taken out. His usual flirtatious focus was on the fast girls who were notorious for 'putting out'. Rejection was not something he ever faced – built, inherently sexy, rugged, and a very persuasive guy. Karen was a trophy wife, he supposed. Everyone knew, in a small community, which girls were for what purpose – she was a looker but without doubt, a good girl - at least until last night. Confusion took reign now – could be handle this transition? It felt like having sex with a mistress – his wife was not supposed to be wanton, and it seemed almost like this new development was an infringement upon his freedom of pure unrestrained sexual exploits – for his own pleasure – not to be shared with his wife. Yet, there was no denying how hot and steamy the night had proven to be – was it possible to have both? To top it off – the scent of Karen's soap which he despised without exception, now lingered intoxicatingly on his senses – provoking all sorts and kinds of lusty images. The niggling premonition that his life was forever altered weighed heavily in the background as he moved on about his morning routine.

Once dressed, he stuck his head in Sway's room. Geesh, was he developing the habit of checking on the kids – Karen's job? He found them still sound asleep, minus Daisy. He moved forward to check further and the cat growled, her fur standing up on end. What the hell? Key-key was unquestionably a mild-mannered tabby. This just didn't make sense! Tom noticed that Daisy's leash was missing from the hook in the hallway. Karen must have taken her for a walk – another first! In the kitchen, he gratefully poured a liberal measure of steaming coffee into his favorite cup and threw two pieces of bread in the toaster. He was munching on the last piece when he heard Karen and Daisy come through the front door.

"Hi," Karen smiled, covered in a sheen of sweat, as she bent over, gulping air. "Just went for a run," she rasped in explanation to his inquiring look.

"Karen," Tom bit back sharply, "you do not walk, never mind run - aren't you pushing it just a bit?"

"I know," she huffed, "but I have limited time to whip this body back into shape." Karen sauntered past him and effectively silenced any retort he may have had when she smartly slapped his butt. "Thanks for this morning," she murmured softly, "I am off to the shower." Adorned with a smile that had a life of its own, Tom was once again rendered speechless, but he managed to stammer that there was no need to thank him. Karen turned and whispered huskily right into his ear, "you *do* realize how many calories we burned last night?" He was stabbed with pure invitation from her sexy-eyed stare – turning him immobile and breathless. "No? Hmm – might have to work on that," her gaze devoured his lips. "Of *course*, I need to thank you." With that she bounced down the hallway, leaving him in stunned fascination, fighting down the aching bulge in his crotch.

"Ok, Ok, I am *awake*, Daisy!" At the sudden distracting sound of Zac's laughter, Tom shook it off, and walked over to fondly rustle his hair. Still giggling, Zac dragged his blanket back to his own room, his dad in tow.

"How did you sleep, son?" Zac smiled up at him in pleasant surprise.

"Good, I got cold, but Daisy curled up against me to keep me warm. It was weird, Dad - I could see my breath."

"Really, that must have been quite the dream you were having."

"Maybe," a thoughtful expression dominated Zac's features. Tom moved to sit on the edge of his bed.

"I know you're worried about your mom - we all are." He searched Zac's eyes to ascertain his full attention. "You may notice she's a little forgetful. Heart attacks can cut the flow of oxygen to the brain causing memory issues. Plus, your mom is trying really hard to shape up for her new heart so she might be engaging in some new activities," Tom explained.

"Like what? Zac's eyes grew wide, completely alert to his dad's words.

"Like this morning's run."

"She ran?" Zac sputtered in surprise.

"Yup, and you know your mom's limit is to walk somewhere - if she has a reason, and never with Daisy, right?" Tom chuckled, and ruffled Zac's hair again. "Ok, let's get ready for our day!" His tone was jovial, and Zac impulsively reached out and put his arms around his dad's waist in a fierce hug. Tom returned it and whispered, "everything is going to be OK, son." Zac nodded and stepped back, wiping tears from his cheeks. "It's OK", Tom whispered again, leaving the room to check on Sway. He was beginning to grasp the importance of the interaction with his children – for them and for him. In his gut broiled a fear that he might be helpless to protect his children from coming events. Sway was sitting on her bed stroking Keykey, who purred lovingly in her lap. "Hi, hon!" Tom greeted her cheerfully, "are you thinking about getting ready for school any time soon?" Sway responded with an absent-minded nod. "Do you want me to help you find some clothes?" Tom offered – probably a first for him, he acknowledged.

"No thanks Dad, it is time I learned to do it myself," Sway responded matter-of-factly.

"Good for you," Tom encouraged. "How are you feeling this morning?"

"I am good Dad, just a little sad." Her huge blue eyes held too much sorrow for such a little girl and clutched at his heart.

"I know honey, it is hard - I know you're worried about your mom" He gently rubbed her back. This was not easy for him – nurturing was not in his make-up – never had been, and he was a tad out of his element, hoping he was doing the right thing. He sunk down on the bed and pulled her close to him. He was grateful that the cat seemed unaffected. The doorbell rang and Tom heard Karen announce that she'd get it. The sound of Mrs. Jones' voice unnerved him, but he could not make out what she was saying.

"I am not just sad about mom," Sway offered. "I am also sad about Mr. Swenson – he died last night." Tears formed in her eyes.

"Oh honey, I am sure he is fine, like your mom - just because the ambulance took him to the hospital does not mean he died," Tom reassured her, with a squeeze.

Karen had entered the room just at the end of Sway's sentence. "Is everything ok, sweetie? How are you feeling this morning?"

"I am ok, Mom, just really sad for Mr. Swenson."

"I know, honey." Karen gave Sway an empathetic smile and a warm hug. "Tom, please come and help with breakfast while the kids get ready for school." Tom agreed and followed, grateful for the escape. Zac met them in the hallway with Daisy. "How about you take your sister this morning - I think it will help her feel better," Karen suggested.

"Sure mom." Zac held back to wait for her. Tom started to respond but Karen put her hand up to intervene. Zac keenly observed the interchange between his parents. He had never seen his mom shush his dad before! Well, things were weird around here - that was for sure! Shrugging his shoulders, he headed to find Sway and speed her up.

Karen took Tom's hand and led him into the kitchen. "What's up?" Tom whispered, although he couldn't say why.

"Wait until the kids are out of the house," she began requesting items for their breakfast. Without question, Tom did her bidding with the increasing suspicion that their roles were somehow reversed – maybe that was the reason the sexy wildcats were not for marrying! He reflected that it had been a long time since they made breakfast together like this. It hit him that their lives had changed right after Zac was born. In any case, he conceded that he was actually enjoying this, but he surely was not about to announce it to the boys at work. He was proud of his reputation as the man's man. He ruled the roost – no women's work for him, and he felt a strong determination to preserve that image.

Once the kids were out the door, Karen turned to him. "I am going to pick up schoolwork for Sway and have her stay home with me for a while," she imparted casually.

Tom stifled his urge to loudly spout his objection. "Yes, that may be a good idea. I know she's having a tough time," he continued, "she told me that she was sad because she thinks Mr. Swenson died. I think she made that assumption after finding out about his trip in the ambulance - it must have brought back the trauma from her trip with you to Emergency. From what I understand, she likely saw them working on you when your heart stopped" He stopped at her assessing gaze. "What?" Karen slowly walked over and removed the bowl of eggs he'd been enthusiastically whipping from his hand, placing it on the island. He felt a knot forming in his gut. "What!" he shouted from fear more than anger. Karen took his arm and led him to a kitchen chair.

"Mr. Swenson passed away last night." Nausea assaulted Tom. He wasn't sure what to make of it – how did Sway know? The kids were already in bed when the ambulance had come. For a second the room turned icy cold, and he could see their breath. He thought perhaps he'd imagined it as the temperature returned to normal. But his blood went cold with Karen's urgent whisper – "not now, not now." She wasn't addressing him – rather some unknown presence in the room. What the hell?

Chapter 11

TOM'S MIND WAS IN a flurry. How on earth could Sway have known that Mr. Swenson had passed away? Perhaps she'd heard something from down the street with all the commotion – Mrs. Swenson had been surely sobbing loudly enough. Or maybe Sway had woken when the woman returned home last night or early this morning? Tom was just about to voice his thoughts to Karen, when the kids came bursting through the door.

"Boy, are we hungry!" Zac shouted, hanging Daisy's leash as he rushed in. Both children eagerly bounded up to the table.

"We saw a squirrel on our walk!" Sway announced joyfully.

"You did, what mischief was it getting into?" Tom welcomed the timely diversion from his current troubled deliberations, with this blessedly sane conversation. Sway chattered away about the squirrel teasing Daisy, who strained to chase it, but Zac had held tight to her leash.

"Yes," laughed Zac, "she towed me halfway across the neighbourhood after that little critter. I am getting stronger though - I was able to keep her from getting to it." His chest puffed up with pride. "That squirrel was not even scared - just sat there at first watching us and ran up the tree at the last minute."

Sway chimed in behind her brother excitedly adding to the story. "Yes, and then the squirrel sat up there just talking away to us." She giggled at the memory.

"Talking?" teased Karen playfully, "what in the world did it say?" Both children laughed.

"I don't know," Sway twittered, "lots!" Tom considered the significant benefit for the kids to walk Daisy together - it was good to see Sway so happy and carefree over a chattering squirrel!

By now they had finished pulling breakfast together and all four plates were served up. Even with the toast already devoured, he lost his will to resist - vegetable omelette, bacon, toast and freshly cut up strawberries. He noticed Karen foregoing the toast. She was indeed adopting huge changes, Tom realized, but then wouldn't most people in her condition? His mind wandered back to the medical team's shared observation that too often, those changes frankly do not happen. Old habits *were* hard to break, he supposed. It made more sense to him now why they included the whole family in the treatment consultation.

Before sitting down, Karen filled the pets' food dishes and placed them just outside the kitchen entrance where they were both patiently waiting – as if they already knew she'd feed them at this exact new spot. Tom shook his head - foolish thoughts, he said to himself. Karen bestowed a cheerful smile on her family as she sat down to breakfast - then as if she had read Tom's mind, remarked, "Everyone together for breakfast - fur babies and humans. Certainly, we are all family?" Both children nodded enthusiastically as they tackled their food, and peeked up for a reaction from their father, who, to their amazement, chose not to object. Zac was astute enough to reserve trust for now – there was something about his mom – wow – she somehow held this newfound power, and though he wished with all his heart that she wasn't ill, he sure did like this recent development.

Karen reached across and took Sway's hand. "Honey, I need you to do me a favor," Sway gave her full attention, "Stay home with me for a bit to do your schooling - just for a while, 'til I am feeling better." Before Sway could respond, Zac interrupted with an offer to stay home too. Karen smiled affectionately at this, "thank you Honey, but I think it is easier for me to help Sway with her schoolwork than it is for me to help *you*."

"What do you mean?" Zac puzzled, "you are a super good teacher - you help me all the time!"

Tom intervened, "What your mother is trying to say Zac, is that Sway needs some one-on-one attention from Mom for a few days. She's been pretty worried about Mom, and this will give her a chance to maybe feel a little better."

"Oh, OK," Zac responded reasonably. Karen rose to clear the dishes and motioned for the kids to assist with clean-up.

"Don't even think helping with breakfast is happening every day," Tom whispered in his wife's ear, as he prepared to get on with his day.

"I know," Karen whispered back saucily, "some days you will be making breakfast *and* cleaning up all by yourself." She giggled, expertly sidestepping his futile attempt to smack her across the butt. The kids looked on with wide grins. It felt awesome to see their parents playfully relaxed together. It was like their dad was a new man – no gruff grouchiness spurning harsh words and judgement that perpetually impelled their mom into protection mode. Sway stepped out of her comfort zone and bravely tested the new waters.

"Dad, can we have a happy breakfast every morning now?" Tom's heart flipped, looking into her innocent blue eyes - he knew exactly what she meant but couldn't find words in reply. How does one respond to a child whose mother is most likely going to die – this being highly instrumental to his current pleasant demeanor? For sure, Tom knew he was an asshole – he actually *liked* being a first-class jerk. It was elemental to his status – a man's man, the tough guy. That was as necessary to his ego as oxygen is to life. Being the boss in his own home required a rough exterior – that was certainly evident with Karen's cheeky attitude of late – he'd been treating her with loving consideration, and she was milking it!

He was a tad taken aback when she quickened to his defence. "We are all trying to make good changes Sway and that takes time and baby steps. This morning is one of those for all of us." Sway smiled and nodded happily.

"I get it," she agreed, "even for Daisy and Key-Key." Everyone looked over at the two pets sitting patiently watching their family interact.

Tom headed for the bedroom to finish getting ready for work. Karen leaned over to Zac and asked quietly, "How long does it take you to walk to school?" Zac was a bit surprised by his mother's question, figuring she already knew that.

"About fifteen minutes," he supplied – he truly would do anything for his mom, so was not about to question her.

"Thanks, Bud." she murmured and followed Tom into the bedroom. "Tom, can you please drive Zac to school, and I will walk over with Sway a little later to pick up her schoolwork." It was a directive as opposed to a question – she was informing him now on what he would do? This was thoroughly irritating, but he kept himself in check. "Sure," he replied and walked out of the bedroom without another word.

"Zac, I'm driving you to school, so you have five minutes to be in the car!" Tom bellowed. Karen entered the kitchen to the sight of their son, scrambling to put a lunch together.

"Don't worry Sweetie," Karen called out, "just grab some fruit for recess. I will bring your lunch when I pick up Sway's work."

"Thanks Mom," Zac called over his shoulder, hastily grabbing a peach and banana, and rushed out the door ahead of his father, feeling pretty proud of himself when Tom actually had to deploy the remote to allow Zac to get in the car first. Zac climbed into the front seat, and they were soon off, with Karen and Sway waving goodbye at the door.

Tom glanced back with a return wave. So much had changed in the past week. It hit him that he'd never left the house without Karen packing his lunch - ever. Guessing he'd have to grab lunch, which if, by choice, would have been totally acceptable, he couldn't fathom how this had gotten out of his control. Tom felt the stirrings of a bad mood coming on. This was all bullshit, he raved inwardly. A look at Zac confirmed he needed to soften his expression.

"Thanks for hanging in there and supporting your sister with everything going on with your mom," he spoke quietly. "I know this is tough on you - on everyone. Lots of changes with your mom, and for all of us, but we will get through this," Tom assured him and ruffled his hair. Minutes later, the car pulled up to the curb and Zac quickly jumped out. The relief was palpable – it was so stressful talking with his dad whose emotions were up and down like a yo-yo. Zac likened it to a volcano. The momentum from the emotional highs and lows would increase the odds that when his dad *did* blow, it would be a douser – catastrophic in nature. Opening the school door, his guts churned, remembering that yesterday his father had almost hit his mom. There was a good measure of comfort though, to see his mom so much more assertive – somehow unaffected by his father's moods. Maybe part of her knew she had no choice but to be strong to survive the ordeal ahead of her.

His mom had always protected them from their father's volatility, at a high cost for her, but something had altered. Maybe the difference came from the doctors warning for needed changes. Boiling anger welled up inside. No wonder her heart was stressed, with such a poor excuse for a husband! Mom's heart worked overtime caring for everyone, and his father could be so cold and mean at times – never returning the love and kindness he received from his family. Emotions swirled in Zac's head and the underlying fear took over.

"God, please find my mom a new heart or fix the one she has," he mouthed a fervent silent prayer, with such intensity, that he completely missed picking up with his best bud, Ben, standing there waiting outside the office door, mouth agape – they always walked from this point down the hallway together. Pushing back the tears as he entered the classroom, he knew his mom was right - he needed to be at school and focusing on his education. Zac squared his shoulders and got his head back in the game of being an excellent student - an excellent son. No way was he going to be the cause of his mom's worry – her health and happiness was all that mattered to him right now!

Tom thoughtfully watched his son walk into the school before he pulled out of the student drop off zone. There was little to no traffic, so he arrived earlier than usual to work. His first stop was Jean's office. She pinned him with an alluring smile when he opened her office door and got up from behind her desk to enwrap him in a very close intimate hug, pressing all her curves into his hard body. Jean purred in the warm seductive manner that she reserved exclusively for her one-on-ones, "Tom, so glad to see you, you have been missed in more places than one." She ran her hands sensuously down her body.

Tom was riveted in place, as his eyes traced her every move. From out of nowhere, his thoughts flew to Karen and their totally unexpected, shared night of incredible passion, and his pants tightened to uncomfortable proportions. Wow, he could now show Jean something new, instead of it being the other way around. It never occurred to him to credit his wife with the source of his erotic thoughts.

"How are Karen and the kids doing?" Jean inquired silkily – not a trace of sincerity evident in her pursed lipped come-on expression. But he could play that game too.

"Well, she is home - our whole life has changed overnight. Karen is already working hard on herself – she needs to take off a ton of flab and build healthy habits to prepare for the transplant. The kids are worried of course - we all are - but they seem to be hanging in there," Tom related, his gaze wandering hot over her body.

Jean played her fingertips up and down Tom's arm, and he wanted nothing more than to throw her on top of her desk! "I haven't booked anything for you today so how about we both play hooky from work for a few hours and relieve some of that stress I can see building up inside you – poor Tom." He threw a devil's grin in response to her batting eyelashes.

"Time and place," he demanded

"My place in half an hour," It was a teasing whisper – a caress in his ear.

"See you there," Tom promised in a muffled voice. As he headed toward the door, Jean slapped his ass – hard enough to stimulate excitement – God he was ready! Enjoying the pain/pleasure after-sting, he entertained for a fleeting moment, the notion that Karen had introduced that to him during their steamy sexual exploitation – and then he pushed it firmly out his mind – lustful thoughts of Jean's naked supple curves luring him to the exit. He got out of the building unnoticed but none other than Doug caught up with him in the parking lot. They exchanged waves and Tom called out, "got a few things I have to do for Karen, then I will be back."

"No worries," Doug replied and nodded, as he headed into work to start his day. If Doug had any suspicions or reservations, it didn't show in his response. Tom was feeling cavalier – not to mention horny as hell! It was going to be a very good morning! Following his usual route, he sauntered into the back yard. He wasn't concerned about nosy neighbors because the Thompson's oasis was designed for complete privacy – and he sure didn't need to worry about Doug! He hung out in a lounging chair while waiting for Jean to arrive. Contemplating on the steamy night with Karen, his dick stiffened admirably. Jean unlocked the back-deck patio doors and slid them open a crack as a signal to come in. In a flash he was off the patio chair and through the doors, closing them quickly behind him.

Jean had gone directly to the bedroom, with him in hot pursuit. She started with the usual instant warm up ritual, but Tom stopped her in her tracks. "Not today little lady - I am going to show you a trick or two," he boasted. Jean laughed – a gleam of delicious anticipation in her eyes. Tom was reliving his experience with Karen, replaying that hot night over, only this time he switched roles and claimed the driver's seat – Jean would bow to his bidding – would beg for mercy. Like Karen, his goal was to hold his mistress, off – making her wait for the ecstasy of orgasm. It was akin to Russian Roulette – as he slowly teased his way down her body until she was gasping for air. Moving atop, he hovered over, capturing her arms firmly above her head as he entered, thrilled to her shocked gasp. The sensation of ultimate power provided the motivation to hold back his pleasure which required that he cease movement periodically, also serving to drive Jean to a mewing frenzy. He continued this delicious game of cat and mouse until he knew he was soon going to lose control. He never had to wonder when Jean was coming - she always screamed out her passion – loud enough to scare ghouls away he was sure, and it fired him to flames. When he could no longer hold back his own orgasm, he flipped her over and none too gently took her from behind, holding her head down. Fighting to regain his breath, he rolled heavily off of her onto the bed and left her lying face down. Jean slowly flipped over onto her back and lay beside him, unusually quiet.

"Wow, who have you been having sex with?" Jean ventured. Tom laughed out loud.

"My wife," he replied, with some incredulity. She joined in the mirth. The mood was broken by her cell phone - Doug's calls had a specific ringtone and she put her fingers to her lips as she reached to answer. Tom lay there listening, still catching his breath and stunned – Karen's sensual image had intensified his pleasure.

"Hey Darling," Jean cooed in her sweet voice, "I am just downtown, is there anything you need?" Tom clearly heard Doug's voice booming through the phone in a tone rarely used with Jean. "What the fuck are you doing? We have a business to run, get your ass back in here and look after these orders that are coming in," Doug yelled. The phone went dead. Jean lay back on the bed, in all her naked post-sex steamy glory – in utter shock.

"He just hung up on me! The ass hole just hung up on me!" she snarled. At that moment, Tom was grateful not to be the target of her rage.

"Hell Jean, I have never heard Doug talk to you like that, are things OK with the business?" Tom prodded. His gut turned into a tight knot.

"Yes, everything is fine with our business," Jean answered noncommittedly, then started scrambling, picking up her clothes, telling Tom he had better leave - that she needed to get back to work. Stopping for a brief moment, she softly uttered, "You are right, in all of our years together, Doug has never spoken to me like that - something is wrong." Back in action, her tone held a higher pitch, "you have to go Tom," and she threw his clothing at him. He dressed hurriedly while she was in the shower and did not wait for her, exiting quietly the same way he came in.

Jean ran her hands sensuously over her body as she let the spray from the shower cleanse the evidence of the mid-day sexual delight, regretting that she didn't have time for self-pleasure now – she needed to get going. As she dried herself off vigorously and reached for her face cream, she considered their session today – to say it was hot was a glaring understatement. She'd had similar experiences – certainly a lot rougher – but she was not into being forced – be damned if she'd ever travel *that* road again. For a split second when she was immobilized, and he was completely consumed with taking his own pleasure – using her body to suit that goal – she'd felt a glimmer of fear. Oh, she had no doubt that if she'd fought – he would have released her, but still – there was no denying that it turned her on. Oh Lord, she couldn't imagine that Karen would have shared that same experience with him. Jean was confident in her position as his muse – he was totally hot for her – and that suited her ultimate goal to perfection. As a bonus, he turned her to jelly in the bedroom – he was a damn good lay! Jean truly loved sex – everything about it, every day, several times per day would suit her fine! She was hot for experimentation – with both sexes, though she had an incurable weakness for a hard male body. She supposed her life experience had its upside. Freshened and ready, she hastened to the office.

About to climb into his car, Tom lent consideration to the situation. He had seen Doug angry before but never with Jean. This path of reasoning suddenly stopped him dead in his tracks and his blood ran cold. What if Doug suspected them – knew about their affair somehow? In retrospect it was more than a little risky to leave the dealership for the entire morning at the same time. The short burst of a police siren broke his deep reflection. He turned to see Officer O'Reilly pull in behind him. Oh shit – now what? He closed his car door and walked over to meet the policeman who was just climbing out the cruiser.

"Hey Tom, what brings you out to this neighbourhood?" His tone was official.

"Well, that isn't any of your business, is it?" responded Tom testily, feeling his temper coming to a boil.

"Oh really, you say it isn't now," responded Jim O'Reilly as he squared his shoulders and towered over Tom, who detected clearly, the acrid odor of coffee breath when he leaned down to authoritatively press his point. "We have had break-ins in this neighbourhood during the day so anyone here without a good reason *is* my business. I suggest you curb that temper of yours or I will be hauling you down to the police station for interrogation." Tom quickly realized his folly as panic set in.

"I went for a drive to clear my head and decided to get some fresh air in the park – such a beautiful day. I have a lot going on in my life," Tom explained. "I'm sorry Officer – I know I was out of line."

"All right then," Jim allowed, "next time, be sure to check your attitude when speaking to a police officer or you may get yourself into more hot water that you can handle."

"Thank you, I will," Tom apologized again, "I have no right lashing out – taking my frustrations out on you!" The police officer waved his hand in dismissal, got into his car and drove away, leaving Tom standing to wonder where his life was headed. He stayed there for a moment, letting his eyes scan the area he habitually parked in – it was glaringly obvious in the daylight, and streetlights illuminated the park at night. The sick feeling in his stomach grew - small town, everyone pretty much knew everyone. It seemed clear suddenly. How would at least one person not have noticed his car parked there on regular basis? Had someone called the police to have the car checked out? He figured it rather odd that Officer O'Reilly just happened to coincidentally run into him here – was he being followed? He wondered at Doug – what would he do if he knew? Tom was often curious how he and Jean had hooked up in the first place, as the age gap was considerable – hell Doug was almost old enough to be her father, and they somehow seemed an odd fit. Still, he was a man and messing with his woman would not go without consequence – of that Tom had no doubt!

He slowly got back into his car. Where to now? Back to work - home? Yes, he decided, he'd head home. Daisy greeted him enthusiastically when he came through the door. That was a good sign, wasn't it? He called out but Karen and Sway were apparently not there – probably at the school as Karen had planned. He rubbed Daisy's head for a moment then headed for the shower. Dropping his clothes, he stepped into the steamy warmth, taking his time to cleanse the smell of Jean and sex off his body. He paused, with the sudden strange sensation of someone's eyes upon him – watching. He turned slowly to find Karen standing there, her face buried in his clothing. Raising her head, she met his gaze through the clear glass, her expression unreadable – one he'd never seen before, directed at him. Unable to utter a word, he could only gape as she dropped his clothes back to the same spot on the floor and exit the room. His heart seemed to stop - the bathroom turned ice cold and filled with steam from the hot water still spraying from the shower head. In seconds, it was so thick he could no longer make out his hands in front of him. His body began to shake violently - not from the cold that cut right through to his bones – rather from the paralyzing fear that permeated every cell in his body.

Chapter 12

SWAY WAS BEYOND excited to spend an entire day with her mother – just the two of them! They had strolled happily in the warm spring morning air to the school to drop off Zac's lunch and arranged with the teacher to pick up lessons and homework, which they loaded into her backpack. Sway was skipping ahead, humming merrily as they passed the park toward home. Karen reached out to gently stop her.

"Sway, how about after you and I complete a lesson or two, we head back here? We'll grab some sidewalk chalk, a skipping rope, a ball and some cards and I'll teach you some pretty cool games we played when I was a little girl."

"Yes, yes!" Sway squealed in delight, hopping even higher and faster. Laughing, Karen attempted to join her but was not quite able to keep up. When they got to the driveway, they noticed Tom's vehicle parked in the pad. Sway's heart dropped into her stomach. She would never dare voice it, but fervently hoped this would not squash their play plans – she folded and crossed her fingers in a fierce tight interlock behind her back.

Upon entering the house, Karen gently touched the top of Sway's head and instructed her to go find the items they had just discussed. "I need to talk to your father, Sweetie." Sway could hear the shower running in her parent's bathroom, as she happily set out in search of the toys her mom had listed off. Her father had been in a rare, good mood this morning, and she hoped nothing had gone wrong to change that. She knew it was odd for him to be home at this time of the day – normally he'd be at work. Sway scurried to her room and rustled through drawers and toy bins. Daisy and

Key-key were on her heels, seemingly eager to help – Sway giggled and hugged them both. She easily located the first three items but could not find her cards anywhere. Maybe they were in Zac's room. As soon as she neared his door, an intense wave of nausea assaulted her, just like it had so many times before. She stopped dead in her tracks with her hand on her stomach, tears welling in her eyes, praying she would not be sick today. No, no! Not today!

Slouching down on the hallway floor, she fought to calm down – stave off the nausea and fear. Daisy was instantly by her side - licking her tears, as Key-key rubbed back and forth across her legs purring her magic balm to comfort and make it better. Sway gratefully reached out to both of her pets as they poured their love upon her – it really did help, and she knew that somehow – these two were very special. Daisy abruptly stopped the slurping and turned towards her parent's room. It was then that Sway felt the wall of icy cold, and involuntarily shivered. Key-key climbed up into her lap, purring louder, with Daisy releasing a low growl beside her. Sway looked towards her parent's door to see a strange mist rolling out of the room. "Mom," she called out in a whisper, uncertain as to why she was afraid to summon her aloud. She watched incredulously as her mother emerged from the cold mist, almost as if floating in thin air. Karen picked Sway up in her arms, carried her back to her room and put her onto the bed - grabbing up the blankets and wrapping them snugly around her. Sway noticed that her mom was quivering too. "Mom, I am so cold, and I don't feel good," Sway whispered shakily through the tremors, as tears flowed freely – she thought they might freeze on her cheeks.

"I know," her mother softly whispered back to her. The pets jumped on the bed to continue administering solace to their mistress. Karen opened the blanket enough to allow the cat to slip in, then wrapped them both up tightly together. Key-key's heated body warmed Sway and Daisy curled up close. The mist from their breaths was eerie, but Sway felt warmer by the moment, cozied up with her loving pets in the soft blanket. Her heart swelled with affection as she watched Karen fill her brother's backpack with the toys which she had gathered up for the games they would play – she tried to imagine what they may be. Sway obeyed without a peep when

Karen told her to stay there until she returned, and remained cuddled under the covers, the shivers diminishing with each second of warmth the animals provided. Soon, her mom returned with the backpack and packed lunches. Sway was happy to see her carrying Daisy's leash. Clasping it to the dog's collar, Karen told her it was time to go.

Sway's fear overrode the joy and had her once again in tears. "Mom, I don't feel good. It is so cold. Can't you see it?"

"I know Honey," her mother whispered, "but we must leave the house now. Trust me, you will feel better once we are outside," Karen promised, still in hushed tones. Sway watched her mother don the backpack, before reaching down and lifting her gently up off the bed. She clung tightly to Karen's neck, as the loss of warmth from her cozy nest under the blankets hit her like an icicle, escalating her shivers and whimpers.

"Hold Daisy's leash - don't let go," Karen instructed as she toted her from the bedroom. Daisy growled softly as they emerged into the cold, damp mist still eerily hanging in the hallway. Sway clutched Daisy's leash tightly and hid her face in her mother's neck as they made their way through it, past her parent's room and out the front door. Immediately upon leaving the house, Karen put her down gently and Sway drank in the welcome warmth of the outdoor air. Karen went back into the house and quickly returned with their shoes. The cat rushed out the door with her, just before it closed. Sway mused on how odd it felt to put their shoes on *after* they'd went outside. With immense relief, she dutifully followed Karen down the driveway and onto the sidewalk, feeling pretty much back to normal now. Karen led them back toward the school where they had just come from. Sway asked where they were headed.

"To the park," Karen glanced at her with a cheerful grin. Sway suddenly took note of the cat walking gracefully alongside her, and Daisy keeping pace with *them*, rather than setting her own pace – pretty much warp speed, as she did whenever she walked with Zac. Well, in truth, Daisy really took *him* for a walk.

"Mom," Sway called out, "Key-key got out of the house and is following us, should we take her back?" She felt concern that the cat may wander off too far away from home and not be able to find her way home.

"Oh, gracious no," her mother laughed, "it's a day in the park for all of us, especially Key-key - she has surely earned it with all the mothering she bestows upon you, don't you think?" Sway thought that comment a bit odd, but smiled softly at her furry pet, who was walking alongside her, as if it were the most natural event – a daily occurrence. Anyone watching would have never guessed this was Key-key's first time ever to go for a family walk – and without a leash!

"Yes, Key-key," she addressed affectionately, "you really do deserve a day in the park." Sway chose to set aside her reservations - certainly not voice them further, because the very last thing she would want, was to provide her mom with a sensible reason to return to the house. Sway felt a flicker of excitement as she noticed little kids, she figured to be below the age of five, eagerly and joyfully playing on the swings and other park equipment. Mother and daughter eagerly chose a bench to sit on and Daisy and Key-key served as a huge magnet for the little ones, who eagerly gathered around as Karen was busy drawing a Hopscotch game on the huge concrete slab. Sway was delighted to be learning this game from her mother, marveling at the sudden mental image of her as a little girl, playing one of her very favourite games. Karen had given Sway a special chain to use – one she'd never seen before. She smiled and swelled with pride when a child asked his mother why *she* hadn't taught him this game and the mother replied that she never knew about it.

Another mother politely asked to borrow the chalk to replicate the drawing for her and her own daughter. Key-key and Daisy patiently sprawled out in the grass watching their two mistresses play together. One child managed to sneak by her mother to kneel down to them. Karen gave permission for the children to pet them, as long as their moms were comfortable. Some of the smaller children hugged them gleefully and pulled on their ears. One of the mothers commented on how well-mannered the two animals were and inquired as to where they had gotten their training. Sway proudly piped up in reply, that it was from her and her brother.

"Mom, this is so much fun!" Sway was flushed with excitement. Hopscotch was a hit, and once they'd played several games, they moved to kicking the ball. The dog and cat tried to get in on that game which created a lot of riotous laughter. Sway and Karen then decided to kick the ball back and forth, with the pets in the middle, trying to keep them from grabbing it. Key-key was run over by the lightweight ball many times to her regal feline disgust, but Daisy took to it in no time. She would grab the ball with her paw, then, like an expert soccer player, nose it to one of them. Sway noticed her mother slowing down and looking a little peaked, so she mentioned it must be time for lunch.

"So it is," Karen replied, glancing at her watch. There were several picnic tables and benches in the park, and they picked the one closest to have their lunch. As Sway helped to put everything out, she was surprised to see there was food for both pets in the bag.

"Mom, how did you know Key-key was coming with us," Sway ventured?

"Oh," her mother laughed, "Key-key must have asked me, in her own feline way." Sway burst out laughing.

"Mom, I did not know Key-key could talk," Sway returned the joviality, thinking of the squirrel.

"Well of course," her mother replied, "doesn't she tell you when she is hungry or wants outside, or in your room?" Sway nodded thoughtfully. "So, this is no different," her mother concluded. Sway fed them and joined her mother, enthusiastically tackling a delicious lunch. Afterward, feeling sated and happy, they lay out on a flat stretch of grass beside their fur babies to enjoy the sun warmly kissing their faces. Sway did not ever want to leave the park, fervently wishing the afternoon to last forever, as she romped, played and rested with her mother and pets. She rolled over and put her head on Karen's shoulder, running her small hand back and forth across her mother's stomach. Key-key put her paws up onto Karen as if to imitate.

"I came from inside here," she informed Key-key, pointing to her mother's abdomen, continuing to trace the pathway. Karen smiled affectionately and reached down to take Sway's hand and place it on her heart.

"This is where I'll always keep you - in my heart." she whispered lovingly. Sway felt a rush of immense peace and love throughout and all around her – like a safe bubble. She prayed that this feeling would never go away!

As they relaxed on the grass after another round of fun, they took note of the older children stopping in the park. School was out, which meant Zac would be home soon and dinner would need to be ready – it was time to go. Sway's spirits fell a little, but she knew she would fiercely hold onto the memory of this day forever. Maybe they would even do it again soon!

"Mom, was Dad home when we were there?" Sway had been avoiding the question - was it safe to go home? At Karen's soft affirmative reply, she continued, "Is Dad OK?"

"Yes, your father is fine," her mother assured, but offered no further comment.

"The cold smoke that was in the house - it really scared me," Sway shivered a little, even though she was no longer cold. Karen bent down and took her face between her hands.

"It is nothing to be afraid of - just steam from your father's shower. When the water is warmer than the air it creates fog, or mist. Your father was having a hot shower when the house was cold. That is what created the steam," her mother explained.

"But why was the house so cold?" Sway reasoned.

"I am not sure, maybe a window open or something, maybe a draft from the basement, I will make certain that your father looks into it," Karen soothed. "Honey, please know that I will always protect you – you have nothing to be afraid of."

Daisy started barking and jumping up and down in excitement. Sway and her mother looked over to see Zac coming across the park with two friends. Sway noticed her mother give Daisy the nod and the big dog immediately bolted across the park to meet her master, barking and jumping all over Zac in her excitement to see him. Sway could not wait to tell her brother about her day, so she joyfully ran behind Daisy to greet him. She could barely contain her excitement as words poured from her mouth – sharing her happiness with Zac, the dog still yapping joyfully. Any bystander could easily discern the love that flowed from the pet to master, sister to brother, and Zac's love for them both. Karen smiled gently in witness, a single tear rolling down her cheek. All would be well.

"OK, OK, now," Zac laughed as he picked Sway up and swung her around while reaching out to pat Daisy. Sway hugged her brother's neck and couldn't contain the news as she blurted out the details of her afternoon with Mom - all the games they had played. Zac carried his sister over and dumped her at Karen's feet, in a puddle of tickles and giggles, and gave his mom a hug. "Sounds like a wonderful day," Zac replied to Sway's chatter. Karen smiled and asked after his day. "Good! I got another A in Math," Zac replied happily. This earned a high five from Sway.

"Amazing!" Karen beamed and squeezed her son extra hard. She took his hand as they walked together toward home, sending her gratitude upwards, that Zac had no hesitation to show affection to his mother and sister, even around his friends. She knew this was a huge positive factor for what was to come. Sway danced ahead of them with her two pets in tow - Daisy on her leash and Key-key prancing alongside her mistress. She slowed as they got closer to home, not wanting this time to end. If only every day could be like this with her mother - minus the cold and the intermittent waves of nausea. For some reason, she was grateful that they hadn't even discussed the schoolwork that was supposed to have been completed. Sway was certain, beyond a doubt, that this was her absolute best day ever!

Chapter 13

STEPPING OUT OF the shower, Tom could distinguish nothing through the thick steam. Deftly reaching for the towel on the rack, he tried to shake off the cold and the fear. Never before had he felt this level of dread. Something was terribly wrong in his home. It seemed to him that his life had morphed into a horror movie – weird fluctuating temperatures in the house, rogue pets and Karen's behavior – it was totally unnerving!

Tom shuffled to the closet, briskly drying himself and looking for something warm to wear. He called out to Karen – no answer. Out in the kitchen, he noted the sudden absence of chill – steam gone. God, he could use a drink right now, but Karen would definitely know something was up if she saw him with alcohol at this time of day. He *could* blame it on her - his worry for her, her lack of self-care. No - better he just settles for coffee. His brow furrowed with the intensity of this thoughts. If she questioned him on the odor, he would throw it right back at her – since when did she adopt this creepy habit of smelling his clothing? It was downright weird! Then he'd inform her in no uncertain terms that she had a very overactive imagination.

Feeling a little more in control, he smiled at the memory - hot sex with both Karen and Jean – all in less than a twenty-four-hour span. Yep – stud material right here! And to be honest, his libido was on maximum drive – almost like he'd realized his lustful fantasy of a threesome. Back and forth between them spurred an incredible turn-on! The confidence returned in his gait, as he deduced that the root of his fear was all with Karen - stress from the heart attacks being the main contributor. Ok, well maybe a little guilt from fooling around didn't help, but then he would never have even glanced elsewhere if Karen had looked after her health – if she'd been the same hot lover through their marriage as she'd been last night. Tom laughed at himself as he reflected on his crazy thoughts and fears - too many horror movies! He was back to being himself. Felt good.

Tom had poured himself a cup of coffee and was digging in the freezer for Karen's famous cookies when his phone rang. He glanced at the caller I.D. "Hi Jean, aching for some more of what I gave you this morning?" She could never resist his low sexy drawl.

"Don't come in to work today - I have told Doug that you are tied up at home with Karen's health issues." Sounding stressed and not at all affected by his seductive tactic, she instantly pissed him off.

"What the hell Jean? I was just about to head back to work. Karen is not even home for Christ sakes! I need the money, so I need to work."

"Shut the fuck up Tom!" She paused for a fraction of a second, and Tom was shocked speechless. "Doug just asked me to consider us selling the company - something about Karen's heart attack opening his eyes and we should sell everything, to finance a life change - traveling and quality time together."

Tom stopped in his tracks. "Wow, substantial change from Doug's pissed off demand that you get back to work. Are you sure there wasn't anything else bothering him?" Jean sighed and brought her tone back down to normal.

"No, I think just this. He apologized for his temper tantrum and then asked where *you* were. I was afraid he somehow knew about us, so my quick response was that you were gone for the day looking after Karen. That's when he hit me with the idea of selling the company and spending more time together." Tom felt a slight kick in his gut at the thought of Jean's absence from his life.

"I have more drama to add," Tom responded. "I think Karen may suspect something. I caught her smelling my clothes, when I was in the shower – she was staring at me. Then she threw them down and left." Tom added, "if looks could kill, I think I would be dead right now."

Jean heaved a sigh. "You shouldn't worry, your wife has the kindest, sweetest heart on the planet - probably worn out from all the goodness she gives everyone, including those who are not so kind to her. Look at those bitches at the church who cannot wait to snatch Karen's baked goodies but are the first to laugh behind her back about how fat she is becoming and what an asshole her husband is. Instead, they should be thankful and supportive of her." Tom felt an increasing annoyance at Jean's gushing admiration for his wife.

"One time, as I was standing beside Karen, I noticed she'd overheard them. I commented that they were all a bunch of bitches, and I was about to tell them so, but in true Karen goodness, she held me back – she said because the women had simply not been taught better. Can you imagine that?" The outrage in Jean's voice in support of Karen fueled Tom's discomfort. "Even if Karen finds out about us, which she better not because it would break her heart, she *will* forgive you – though you fucking don't deserve it. On the other hand, my husband won't ever forgive us," Jean concluded.

"You're right Jean, I do believe she would, but I am not taking any chances." He needed to exercise caution with both women now and wisely chose to keep his resentment in check. "What the hell will I do with this wasted day?" he mumbled sulkily.

"Maybe put those clothes in the wash along with some other laundry, so it looks like you are at least attempting to pitch in and take some of the workload – that would be novel," Jean suggested, then clipped, "I have to go. Take care of Karen, Tom." The phone went dead in his ear. Jean was right. There was more laundry than expected which was surprising as Karen was normally all over that. She knew he expected access to any item of clothing he wished to wear. Admittedly, she'd been on the wrong side of his bark, if it was not freshly cleaned, so over the years, she'd learned to make sure everything was washed on a daily basis. Well damn – she *was* home all day! A sudden dark flood of anger had him slamming the lid on the washer.

As he left the laundry room, the doorbell chimed throughout the empty house. Fuck! Karen probably forgot to take her house key – her absent-mindedness irked him beyond measure! His mood shifted instantly when he opened the door to find the delightfully attractive nurse that he had met at the hospital, standing on his doorstep, smiling up at him.

"Hi," she chirped, as she reached out to shake his hand. "My name is Hope - we met briefly at the hospital. I am here to meet with your wife Karen and your daughter Sway." Tom returned the greeting, his flirtatious impulse dampening a tad.

"They're out, and I am not sure when they will be back." Hope's smile widened and asked if he minded her waiting inside for their return. Before he could respond, she sauntered past him into the house, barely giving him a chance to move out of her way. He couldn't help but notice the seductive sway of her hips as she moved past him – off limits though!

"Oh, what a lovely home," Hope declared cheerfully as she swept through the living room and kitchen, taking obvious liberties in her surroundings. Spotting the freshly made pot of coffee, she peered up at him, making Tom keenly aware of his tall masculine stature in contrast to her petite very feminine frame.

"Do you mind?" She inquired politely, with the cup already in place to pour. Tom followed behind her, not sure how to gauge this woman's forwardness but enjoying her delightful spark of energy. Without inquiry, she grabbed a second cup and poured Tom one as well, placing them on the kitchen table, with obvious intent to sit down for a chat. Tom dutifully sat where she'd placed his coffee and committed to observe. Hope took a sip from her cup, closing her eyes for a moment as if savoring it before she drilled him with her incredible green-eyed gaze.

"Good coffee?" Tom inquired. He was becoming increasingly out of his element with this little vixen in control.

"Yes, delicious, thank you," Hope smiled pleasantly and resumed her silent regard. Tom sat back in his chair and took a swig from his own cup, watching her, envious – had he ever enjoyed a mug of coffee as this young woman seemed to?

"Why are you here to see my wife and daughter?" Tom opted for practicality, in an effort to gain control of the situation.

"Oh," Hope responded with the same pleasant expression, "yes, I don't imagine Karen has had time to explain my relevance. You may remember that I am a nurse and specialize in working with children with chronic illnesses. Karen has asked me to spend time with your daughter while your family is dealing with her heart issue." Tom's face instantly clouded over.

"I told Dr. Kerr that there is nothing wrong with my daughter!" he growled in anger, as he thought of the numerous times Karen had rushed Sway to emergency, with the same result. Tom startled as Hope reached over and touched his arm.

"Tom," she soothed, looking directly into his eyes, "your child has been in and out of emergency services without resolution. Now, with your wife's heart issues, your family is going through a very stressful time which will necessarily add further anxiety for Sway - I am here to help her with that." It was hard to stay angry around this young woman, which puzzled Tom, as being cranky with people was his specialty. "Of course, because of what your family is going through, your son, Zac, may also benefit from my help," Hope stated in a calming tone. "Tell me about your family, how are you all coping with Karen's illness?"

Tom's shoulders visibly slumped a bit – her caring demeanor sparked a vulnerable chord within. He was embarrassed to admit that he honestly did not know – as if he was an outsider in his own family. "I am not sure," he responded truthfully. Despite this, he felt a strange comfort with this woman – safe somehow.

"That is understandable," Hope assured him, "when there is a life-threatening condition it puts stress on everyone in the home as well as other family and friends. It can come out in so many ways - sadness, tears, anger, fear, which can result in varying behaviors from outbursts to isolation. Some of your family and friends will go overboard trying to help, where others will stay away because they feel helpless. All of that is normal," Hope explained.

"Thank you for saying that - I guess I have been mostly angry," Tom shared. "And isolated," It felt so good to have someone acknowledge his feelings – not all about Karen.

"I imagine there is a lot of fear there as well," Hope stated – she knew this to be the case.

"Yes, I am afraid for my wife and my kids," Tom held back tears and pushed back his chair from the table. Demonstrating this level of emotion was entirely out of the question and anger took over. "God damn Karen, God damn her heart! Why in the hell did she let herself get so fucking fat?" Tom ranted. "Too much fucking food and not enough exercise, right?" he turned in desperation to Hope, demanding her acknowledgment.

Hope remained calmly seated, her voice softer - quieter. "I wish it was that simple, Tom," she reasoned. "Many people dealing with serious obesity – well past Karen's situation, never develop heart issues. If it were that easy, Karen need only lose the weight rather than have her heart replaced. Truthfully, she is not significantly overweight. This is no one's fault Tom. Not yours, not your children's and certainly not your wife's." She paused to let that sink in. "Of course, in clinical analysis, we would most likely discover everything in our lives can be improved upon - coffee, eat, sleep, play, love better - be better people. My experience is that if people focus on what they can do now, right at this moment, rather than what they did not do in the past, the outcome for everyone is healthier and happier. I am sorry you and your family are going through this difficult period, and I will do my best to help you get through this. It is no accident that my mother named me Hope," she laughed, "because I have plenty of it and am more than happy to share."

Tom could not help but smile, "Yes, that is abundantly clear." You mentioned you work with children who are chronically ill. That must require a *hope*ful outlook," Tom joked, trying to lighten it up a little. Hope smiled indulgently. "Without a diagnosis, how will you be helping my daughter?" Tom queried.

"Well, we have already found your daughter to be extremely sensitive to others, so due to her intense level of empathy, her health can be negatively affected." At Tom's dubious look of skepticism, she continued. "I have helped other children like her come to terms with it, and the better she understands herself the stronger her coping skills will develop. This is only one of several ways we can support Sway."

Tom pondered over what Hope had just said, "Well, my daughter has been in and out of the hospital all her life. Doctors have never found anything wrong with her. Recently, they started focusing on Karen, thinking she may be one of those people who deliberately creates or fosters their child's illness in order to get attention. I started to wonder that, even myself. Sway *is* a sensitive little girl - I figured that is the way all little girls are, but all this stuff sounds far-fetched to me. Professional people are now putting labels on everything. Like ADHD - in my day a high-strung kid who had that excess energy just needed a task – work if off. Now they fill them with zombie drugs, so they'll be like the other calm and complacent kids in the classroom – avoid the issues - lazy teachers looking for an excuse to *not* do their jobs!" Tom's anger rekindled.

Hope intervened before Tom's emotions could escalate any further, "I imagine this has been frustrating and scary for you. Even more alarming, having your wife accused of making your child ill. I cannot profess to know what happened in the past with you and your family, but I am happy to do what I can with what is in front of us now. Does that sound reasonable – something you could work with?" Hope prodded.

Tom took another deep swallow of coffee and was starting to feel calm again. "Yes, thank you, I felt guilty even thinking Karen could harm our daughter. She is the most loving, caring person. I was talking to my boss's wife today and that is exactly how she described her - suggested that may be just what wore her heart out. To have anyone imagine for a second Karen would hurt another living being, never mind our child, is the most preposterous thing!" Tom stormed, missing the intense scrutiny evident in Hope's gaze.

"Your wife sounds like a wonderful person whom you must love very much. I can see how difficult all of this must be for you. Do you consider yourself a strong person Tom?" Hope asked. "The little I know of you has led me to believe you are a tenacious and capable man – you have the ability to ride this storm and steer your family into calm waters and better days. Am I right?" she nudged.

Tom was unfamiliar with this type of conversation and the emotions it was stirring up, but true to this young woman's name, in conversing with her,

Tom *was* feeling hopeful. Of course, there were other factors that could complicate things. "Yes, I will get our family through this." What else could he say to her? - so far, I've messed that up, because I was off screwing my boss's wife when my own wife had a heart attack; I am not a good man; I am a shitty father. None of this, could he confide to this young woman who had brought a light of energy into his home - describing him as the man he should be. He could not voice to her, that good men – good husbands - are pussy-whipped. It is better to be a man's man than a soft-hearted pussy. Good men do not fuck their friend's wives. So, he could only answer yes, he would get his family through this, although he still did not have a clue what this would entail. Would his wife get the transplant – was it possible for her to live through that? That was one of the pieces he was afraid to think about. Too many unknowns. Up until now, he could confidently predict what his next twenty years would entail. Now, would he have a wife, mistress - would he even have a job? The invasive fingers of fear again were creeping in.

Tom was immensely relieved when the conversation was interrupted by his family bursting through the door. He was not too sure who was more excited - the dog, or his daughter. They both seemed wound up. Daisy danced excitedly back and forth around the children while Sway's spirited laughter rang out through the house. Suddenly noticing Tom and Hope, they momentarily froze. Sway's surprise quickly turned to delight at the sight of the young nurse, and she rushed to give her a vigorous hug.

"How is your mom," Sway asked Hope? Then it hit Tom - this was one of the daughters of the old woman at the hospital who had warned him to go home and clean himself up from the smell of another woman. Was it possible Hope was also aware of his extramarital activities? A lump grew in his gut. He stood stunned as he watched Hope hug his daughter, and relay that her own mother was still sleeping, then give Karen a warm hug. The two women embraced for what seemed a long time. Hope stepped back and looked into Karen's eyes.

"How are you?" Karen responded that she was doing well and inquired in kind. Tom looked on as Hope pushed back tears.

"I am doing OK, just worried about my mother." Karen reassured the young woman that her mother would be fine.

Karen turned to him now. "Hope and I are going to go for a walk." Then - so unlike her, "Tom, since your home for the day, please help the children make dinner." His temper immediately began to boil.

"What a wonderful thing to do with your children!" At Hope's emphatic input, Tom choked down his angry rebuttal - no fucking way, Karen, get your ass in the kitchen and make dinner *now*! Sway had started bouncing again and said, "I want to help!" Zac quickly nodded his eagerness to do the same and Tom was effectively hooped. Hope and Karen disappeared, arm in arm out the door, without a backward glance.

Tom turned on his son and demanded, "How in the hell did that happen? You pathetic *pussy*! You agreed to make dinner? How many times have I told you - us men don't do women's work."

Zac started to laugh, "I'm no pussy Dad. I know where mom stashes all the emergency dishes for church functions. I am making Mom's famous lasagna right from the freezer." His eyebrows lifted in amusement, seeking his dad's acquiescence. "Sway loves making salad, so I guess, Dad, you will just have to look after the garlic bread. If you do it on the barbeque, that takes you from pussy to man again right?" Tom couldn't decide if he was outraged or impressed with his son's quick response. It certainly was gutsy, and he had to admit that the kid had listened and learned well. He tousled his son's hair.

"Now, aren't you the man's man?" Zac laughed at the praise - it felt good to be the catalyst that could alter his father's mood from blistering outrage to happiness. More amazingly - happy with *him*!

Sway seemed oblivious to the entire conversation. Zac went downstairs to the basement to find the lasagna while she and Tom started pulling the rest of dinner together. Sway started holding her stomach. "Dad, I don't feel well."

"OK, honey, go lay down, I will make the salad, your mom will be back in a moment," Tom said softly. He was in a generous mood now – more in control again. Tears rolled down Sways face.

"But dad, I want to make the salad." It was clear that she was invested in the three of them making dinner together.

"OK, OK," Tom responded, "I will help you, then you can go lay down." Tom quickly pulled the salad fixings out of the fridge and felt an immediate chill in the room. Sway started to shake, and Tom picked her up to rush her into the bedroom – the cat and dog right on their heels. He tucked her under her blankets and the pets went into the comforting protection mode that now seemed normal. For once, he was grateful for their devotion to his little girl. Hell, the salad could damn well wait! "Daddy is going to fix wherever the cold is coming from. Mommy will be here in a minute, then we will make the salad, OK?" She whispered a shaky agreement - her tears seemed to have subsided with the idea that the salad could wait for her. Zac came out from the basement just as Tom exited his daughters' room, closing the door to keep the chill out. "Is there a window open down there?" Tom asked Zac.

"No, I don't think so," Zac responded.

"Go put the lasagna in the oven, then come and help me find where this damn cold is coming from," Tom instructed his son.

"Sure Dad," Zac responded and disappeared to the kitchen. His pleasure escalated with his dad's request for his help – it made him feel important. Tom shivered, registering the cold seeping through to his bones, as he descended the basement stairs. Zac joined him and they stood rooted, thoroughly puzzled – they'd checked every window, both up and down. The house had warmed up again - the cold was simply and inexplicitly gone. "Dad come outside with me?" Zac implored.

"Why?" Tom responded. "We better get back to dinner Son."

"Let me show you something first," Zac pleaded. Tom reluctantly followed him outside – could this day get any weirder? Zac closed the door behind them. "Dad, I *don't* think the cold is coming from outside."

"Why, where in the hell else would it come from?" Tom snorted derisively.

Zac breathed deeply of the outside air and dramatically exhaled. "See Dad?"

"No, I don't see," Tom responded, getting a little annoyed." Get to the point, Son!"

"Dad, in the house, when the cold comes, we can see our breath but not outside - it isn't cold enough yet!" Tom thought this foolish, but the words caught at his sense of logic. He felt unrest sink back in, as he recognized Zac's line of reasoning – of course any cool air seeping in was simply not cold enough to cause that level of chill in the house. Then where the hell was it coming from?

Chapter 14

SWAY CURLED UP in her room, ardently wishing the pain in her tummy away. Key-key lay purring on the precise area of her belly pain – the radiating feline warmth comforting. Sway stroked her kitty's fur and scratched around Daisy's ear, just the way the pup loved it. Mom would be back soon, and everything would be all right again. She smiled at the memory of the awesome day she'd spent exclusively with her mother. What a wonderful time it had been! Daisy shifted and popped her head up to look towards the door. Moments later Zac entered to check in on her.

He quietly stepped nearer and sat on the edge of her bed. "How are you feeling?"

"I am a little better," Sway said. This reality had just occurred to her - the pain in her stomach vanishing at that exact moment, it seemed, just as it had so many times before. "I am good now," Sway quipped with welcome relief. She gently moved Key-key and sidled over to the other side of the bed.

Zac softly took his little sister's hand. "Fun day today, ay?"

"Yes," Sway's eyes sparkled with joy, "best ever! Mom and I had so much fun! Never played so many games in one day ever before – I've never seen Mom so...not serious." She couldn't quite find the words to describe her mother's carefree mood today.

"You are lucky," Zac said, as he reached up and tousled his little sister's hair. "I spent the entire day in school." Sway giggled at his exaggerated grimace. He smiled back affectionately. It was such a weight off his shoulders to see her feeling better again, and he patted Daisy's head in gratitude for her vigilance over Sway. Zac felt no envy or resentment at the time Sway had spent alone with his mom, though he admittedly yearned for that kind of time with her as well. He was worried too – couldn't put his finger on it. It was as though once she'd become ill, her attitude had changed towards him. He felt like she'd somehow pulled away. Pondering this and knowing his mother, he figured there had to be a reason! There was nothing she ever did that didn't involve the goal to make his world better or to protect him. Could she be trying to toughen him up? A worried frown marred his features.

Sway squeezed his hand. "Are you OK? You look kind of sad."

"I am OK," he made a point to mask his anxious expression, "just worrying about you and Mom."

"I think Mom is getting better," Sway chirped with excitement. "Look how much more energy she has! She has never been able to play or walk with me like she did today without running out of breath," Zac grinned at her obvious excitement, and figured perhaps he would do well to adopt his sister's positive view on their mother's situation.

"You're probably right," he nodded, not wishing to rain on his sister's happiness. "At that meeting with all those doctors, they talked about what we would have to do to support Mom for her new heart. Mom is working hard at everything they pointed out, and we are helping her – I'm proud of her, and of you!" Zac started to feel less worried. Yes, that made sense - she *was* doing everything in her power to improve her health, and to prepare them for what may be coming ahead. Mom knew that she could count on him to look after Sway and the family when it was needed. Her voice, in discussion with their dad, now drifted into Sway's room from the kitchen.

"Mom's home!" Sway spouted joyfully, jumping from the bed and bounding into the hallway. Zac chuckled and followed closely behind. "I'm ready to make the salad!" After grabbing her favourite salad bowl, with brightly colored hand painted garden vegetables, she chose a knife and began chopping up carrots and celery. Tom immediately cautioned her with the use of the sharp knife.

Karen laughed, "What's the worst she can do?" then quipped, "Sway honey, if you cut yourself, just make sure not to leave a trail of blood in the salad." Sway twittered – seemingly unperturbed by this out of character comment from her mom. Zac and Tom's jaws both dropped as they stared at Karen in shocked disbelief.

"Wow Mom," Zac found his voice, "what happened to miss worry wort? You always fuss about us not getting hurt." Karen grinned in her mirth.

"Well today is a new day," she responded lightly, offering no further insight.

"I, for one, like it," Tom smiled, "pleasant change and a lot less stress with you not worrying about all the trivial things." He cautiously touched her arm, unsure how she would respond after the clothing incident. His guts were churning, wondering if she suspected anything – had she detected the odor of lurid infidelity – as easily as the old lady had? This at least was a safe place to test it out because he knew she would not make a scene in front of the kids, but also figured that he'd be able to discern any cool rebuff if she *was* upset. Karen glanced at him with a pleasant smile. OK, maybe his imagination was running on overdrive – he heaved a visible sigh of relief. It could be that the odd expression on her face outside the shower, had been more questioning in nature – why was he not at work? Recalling Jean's words - Karen did not have a distrusting bone in her body - it seemed obvious that his inner guilt was messing with his mind. Tom grinned back at her amiably as he went over to give Sway a hand with the salad. He looked up at Zac and winked.

"We won't tell the boys at work about this," he mouthed to Zac, who responded with a, "man's man,"

"Yup," Tom parroted, "man's man."

"What does a man's man mean?" Sway queried; her brow furrowed in consternation.

"Oh, it's just guy stuff," Zac answered with a nonchalant shrug and a quick glance to his father, seeking validation.

"Hey," Karen laughed, "I, too, want to know what a man's man means." She lifted a brow, "exactly."

"Yeah," Sway responded, "us *girls* want to know."

"Well, to be a man's man, you're the type of guy that other guys look up to and aspire to be," Zac explained," then turned to his father, "right Dad?"

"Yup, that about sums it up, Son." Tom exchanged another conspiratorial wink with Zac.

"Well, I know a boy at school like that and I do not like him," Sway retorted with a disgruntled huff.

"Why?" Zac was curious as to who that might be.

"Because he is nothing but a big bully! That's why other boys follow him around and listen to him. He is loud and mean to people that do not do what he wants and pushes people around just because he can. He is especially mean to the kids who don't have many friends," Sway confirmed in an exasperated tone.

"I know you both have a lot of friends and sincerely hope you stay away from that guy," Tom advised his children. "That individual is *not* a man's man," he explained, "that boy is just exactly what you described – and bullies usually get their day in court!" he finished.

"Day in court?" Sway parroted - confusion evident on her sweet features.

"Yes, his controlling behavior will eventually catch up to him - his day in court is another way of saying that justice will be served." Tom gave Sway a squeeze and noticed Karen's thoughtful demeanor as she regarded him.

"Sounds complicated," Sway scowled. Tom, Karen, and Zac laughed aloud – sometimes she sounded like a little adult.

"Yes, it does, and it often *is*," was Tom's sage reply. Karen gazed at them with a soft expression.

Everyone chipped in with the setting and serving of the dinner. Karen commented the delicious lasagna and asked who made it. Zac guffawed, "I made it right out of the freezer Mom!"

"Oh, I see…" she nodded knowingly, "Zac's secret recipe, also known as mom's freezer stash," Karen grinned merrily, "wow, great cook!" There was a riotous round of laughter from all. As they feasted on the delicious meal, Zac noticed his mother's portions - small lasagna, generous salad and absent garlic bread. His heart melted a little - he knew how much his mother loved bread. Still an inward smile bubbled up - she was making great choices to ensure she'd be around for them. Everyone pitched in to clean up afterward and Tom headed straight for the easy chair.

"Hey, not so fast," Karen piped up, "we all have to walk the dog!" Daisy ears perked up with the cue – couldn't even fool her by spelling it out; "w-a-l-k" and was up and to the door in a flash, jumping and barking.

"Well, why the hell not?" Tom chortled at the dog's excitement. The kids scrambled to get their hoodies and headed for the door, Zac snapping on her leash before opening it. They all squeezed out one at a time - each one vying for the lead, or at least not left behind. "Hey, hey, hey," Tom called out behind them, "the cat got out!"

Sway smiled and looked back at her father, "Key-key likes to go for walks too, Dad."

"Since when?" Tom snorted, wondering how on earth he could miss out on all these developments.

"Since today," Sway giggled. "She's a good walker Dad, she doesn't even need a leash."

"Really?" Tom responded, a dubious frown on his face.

"Yup," Sway called back as she rushed to catch up to them all.

Hanging back, Karen slipped her arm into the crook of Tom's as they leisurely strolled behind their babies – human and fur variety alike, taking the opportunity to wave greetings to the neighbours that were also out enjoying the fresh evening air. To everyone's amusement a few stopped to comment on the cat out for a jaunt. Tom, in his usual form, was enjoying the attention but also appreciating this rare moment with his wife, and the happy chatter from the children. "Humm," Tom murmured thoughtfully.

"Humm, what?" Karen gazed up at him inquisitively.

"This is nice," Tom softly replied, returning her glance.

"Yes, it is," Karen replied, with an affirming squeeze to his arm.

"We should do this more often," Tom commented with a mirroring touch to her hand. Karen peered up at her husband but said no more. They both spotted Sharon Wilson, the curvy attractive wife of one of Tom's co-worker's, come hurrying out of her house, scooting down the long perfect asphalt driveway in an effort to catch up with them. Karen motioned to Tom that they should stop to wait up.

"Karen, so glad to see you mobile, how are you feeling?" Sharon gushed.

"I am doing well, thank you," Karen replied, "and how are you?"

"Busy as a bee," Sharon smiled broadly, "and I'm very happy to hear this." She cleared her throat purposefully. "I wanted to invite you both personally, to our house party next Friday night." She hurried on, "all of the gang from work will be there - I do hope you are feeling up to coming."

"Of course," Karen smiled, "we would love to come. Is it a party for the whole family or should we arrange a sitter for the kids?" Karen inquired.

Sharon seemed surprised at Karen's question, then laughed, "no young kids! But you *can* bring your big kid here along," she grinned at her own joke, motioning towards Tom. They all broke out in bantering laughter. Sharon pointed her finger in a final address, "Seven p.m. – potluck surprise, see you then!" With that their rather vivacious neighbor turned and rushed back into her house, as if perhaps she had something cooking on the stove that needed immediate tending to.

Tom looked down and pinned Karen with a questioning glance, "Wow, you usually ask me first," he prompted.

"Oh," Karen responded pleasantly, "well it is fine by me, if you do not want to go – you could stay and watch the kids." She couldn't quite resist a smug grin.

"Not bloody likely," Tom snorted, "we can ask Mrs. Jones when we get back to the house."

"Who?" Karen asked.

"Mrs. Jones, our next-door neighbour?" Tom stared at her – a bit taken aback.

"Oh, yes, of course" she continued softly, shaking her head, as if she'd been off in another world. The two continued their stroll behind their children and pets, watching in amusement at their enthusiastic antics. Before long they were back around to their home. Karen voiced her intention to go ask Mrs. Jones if she might be free to watch the children. The entire troupe, with the exception of Tom, followed Karen through the path - prolonging their last walk of the day.

Mrs. Jones was delighted to see Karen out and about, and more than happy to help out, promising that she'd bring over a treat for the children. Karen had always been so kind to her, never failing to bring over fresh baked biscuits and chicken soup when she was under the weather. Mrs. Jones felt grateful for the opportunity to be able to give back by minding the children from time to time - especially now that Karen had health issues of her own to endure. Karen offered her appreciation as they left for home, having agreed upon 6:45 p.m. on the following Friday.

The children and pets reluctantly followed Karen back into the house. It was hard to face the end to this wonderful day and no one really wanted to go to bed yet. There were many thoughts rolling around in their minds. Sway was reliving her wonderful day with her mother and was looking forward to perhaps more adventures in days to come, even with schoolwork - at least she'd be with her mom. She felt warm and fuzzy inside. Zac was preoccupied with the mystery chill that seemed only present inside the house – it was necessary to get to the bottom of it – of that, he was sure! Once inside, they headed to their rooms to begin the nighttime routine. The pets, as expected now, followed Sway into her room and Zac closed his bedroom door behind him without even giving a backward glance – it still bothered him a little, but Daisy still showered love on him too, so it wasn't so bad. Zac opened his computer and searched Google for causes of cold drafts in houses. The results brought up everything from the source of drafts to links for finding a building contractor. Hmm, this was going to take a while, Zac surmised as he started scouring through the list.

Karen and Tom lay side by side on the bed, both exhausted from their long day – Tom already in his pajamas under the blankets and Karen on top of the bed, still fully clothed. "It has been quite the day," he offered.

"Yes," Karen replied, "indeed." There was a pregnant pause – a feel of unfinished business in the air.

"You were pretty chummy today, with someone who came here with a specific agenda to investigate us and how we raise our children," Tom stated. Karen rolled to face him.

"If the investigation determines why our daughter keeps getting sick, then I welcome it," Karen answered quietly.

"You know that I don't like anyone sticking their nose in our business, but Hope does seem sincere," Tom stated as he tried to keep the conversation on Hope and away from the morning events that continued to feed that niggling fear in his gut.

"Yes, she is very nice," Karen agreed. "Not only has she reached out to support Sway and Zac through this challenging time, but she has also offered to take me to all my appointments, at least until the doctor signs off that I am physically fit to drive," Karen explained.

"Wow, that *is* good of her – quite a commitment," Tom responded genuinely. He was instantly relieved when Karen headed for the bathroom, informing him that she was going to have a long soak in the tub. He listened to the water run, shut off when the tub was full, registered the sloshing as Karen climbed in – sounds that should have been comfortingly familiar to him. Normally, the TV would be blaring as he'd verbally chastise about how often she bathed or showered. The last thought on his mind tonight was that nothing was normal in his house, and as he drifted off, welcomed the escape to oblivion.

Sometime during the night, he awoke to her groping hands intent on pulling down his pyjama bottoms - to just below his ass – fondling and playing with him until he had a full-blown erection which was instantaneous, to his amazement! Karen sensuously slid on top of him and sheathed him, humping and rubbing against him rhythmically and frantically - just long enough to satisfy them both with mind-blowing orgasms. He was mesmerized by the lusty pleasure evident in her hooded eyes, when she reached the crescendo of ecstasy, and he'd soon followed suit. She promptly rolled off him and went to sleep. Tom lay gazing at her in the moonlit room, wide awake, thoroughly enjoying the satiated aftermath of whatever had just happened. It was hot and messy – totally off schedule but incredibly erotic. If this were to keep up, he was truly not sure if he would have enough stamina to service both Karen and Jean. Chuckling, he supposed this is what Viagra was for – where there's a will, there's a way.

Tom pulled his pajamas the rest of the way up and climbed out of bed, regretting that she'd ended their session so soon. Man, now he was hungry! This wake-up sex had worked up an appetite. Tom headed for the kitchen for a light snack. There was still lasagna left in the fridge from supper that he could warm up. He smiled, reflecting upon his interaction with Zac as they'd prepared dinner earlier. Yes, his son just may become a proverbial chip off the old block, after all. Until recently Zac had always taken after his mother - kind and soft. Tom gave his head a shake, and his thoughts shifted to Karen – they had both changed of late. He guessed that is often what crisis brings, and this was a doozie!

He conceded that he was immensely proud of them - Karen embracing the lifestyle changes necessary to become strong and healthy enough for the heart transplant, and Zac gaining courage and strength to withstand the emotional turmoil that comes with the stress from the possibility of his mother dying. A momentary feeling of shame washed over him when he thought of his behavior, but as was necessary to his male ego, and the survival of his psyche – he quickly pushed that firmly away.

Tom popped the lasagna in the microwave and popped open a bottle of beer, chuckling to himself – a perfect post sex snack! He took his treat and sat at the kitchen table, savouring every bite and sip, sliding down his throat. Deciding it wouldn't hurt to wash the lasagna down with a second beer, he glanced at the clock as he popped the lid - 1:00 a.m. - time for bed. Clearing the evidence from his midnight snack, he headed for the bedroom and was taken aback when he noticed the sliver of light from under Zac's bedroom door. Thinking the boy had probably forgot to turn the lamp off before going to Sway, he went in to do just that, only to find Zac sitting at his desk staring intently at his computer. "A little late for homework, don't you think?" Tom snapped. Disobedience from the rules they laid out for the kids was something he could not abide by.

Zac jerked his head up as if in alarm. This response seemed over the edge to Tom. Did he have something to hide here? Thinking it was more pertinent to find out what he was up to, Tom changed his tone, "It's late - come on now put the homework away and get some sleep." Relief washed over Zac's features and Tom's concern grew. "Did I startle you when I came in?" he watched for a reaction. "I didn't mean to scare you, Son," Tom said softly.

"I was alarmed because I didn't know it was you, but I am OK now," Zac explained, clearly more relaxed.

"OK, who did you think it was?" His curiosity and need to get down to the bottom of this was increasing. Zac responded that he didn't really know. "Why are you up so late doing homework anyway?" Tom prodded.

"I wasn't doing homework," Zac heaved a resigned sigh, "I was researching where the cold may be coming from," he explained.

Tom bent over the desk and peered down at the computer. He could see an article, but not the heading. "What have you found so far?" Zac promptly handed his father a coiled notebook where he'd recorded some information.

"There is the usual stuff you'd expect on improper insulation, single paned windows, and lack of sealing around doors and windows that cause drafts and increased heating bills. There is also information on what type of building contractor to look for and the questions to ask," Zac explained.

Tom flipped through Zac's extensive notes then remembered how late it was. "Thanks Son," he reached over and ruffled his hair. "I think we both should get some sleep now and look at this again tomorrow, OK?" Tom prodded. Zac smiled up at him, relieved that his father wasn't angry.

"Tomorrow would be great Dad, and I *am* tired," Zac agreed. He hadn't even gotten ready for bed yet! He reached for his pajamas and headed for the bathroom to brush his teeth. Turning to Tom, he explained, "I am going to sleep on the floor again in Sway's room because I know it helps her sleep better." Tom smiled affectionately and thanked him for being such a good brother. Zac beamed with pride as he watched his father turn and go, with notebook in hand.

Tom attended to his own hygiene routine and wandered from the bedroom for one more check through the house. Doors were all locked and everything seemed like it was in its place. Still restless, he sank down on the couch to thumb through the notes Zac had recorded. Somewhere around the tenth page he drifted off to sleep, still sitting upright. He woke abruptly to the glare of the living room light and his teeth chattering from the cold. The notebook had fallen to the floor at his feet. He picked it up thoughtfully, his body and hands shaking violently, and headed for the bedroom, turning lights off along the way. Climbing into bed, he instantly cuddled up to Karen – seeking her blessed warmth. In alarm, he noticed the icy trails in the air from their breath. What the hell was going on in this house? In his haste to jump into bed he had taken Zac's notes with him, still clutched in his grip. Turning on his phone light for illumination, he placed the notebook onto his nightstand. The last page had fallen open and an ominous shiver assaulted him at the writing there – "ghosts". Tom felt an eeriness creep into his soul as he heard his wife whisper in her sleep, "not tonight, no, not tonight." Instantly the chill was gone, and they both fell into a deep sleep, still curled up against one another.

Chapter 15

ZAC WOKE-UP ABUPTLY to his father's hollering and Daisy bounding in to deliver a thorough face washing – where had she come from? Startled by his dad's loud declaration that the alarm did not go off, Zac realized that also meant he too, had overslept. Lying on Sway's bedroom floor, petting a panting Daisy and rubbing her ears, he peered up at the ceiling. The cold had been there again last night, and Zac pondered on the article he had read about ghosts. Was it possible they had ghosts in their house? His parents' voices drifted in – apparently his mom had taken Daisy on a two hour walk! Wow!

Zac waited until his father left for work before getting up. He did not want to go to school today and hoped earnestly to convince his mother to allow him stay home and spend the day with her and Sway. After all, it was Friday, and there was a movie planned for the afternoon in Social Studies, which he'd already watched with his family. If his father had any say, it would be a resounding no, so this was his best strategy for a positive outcome. He hung out in the kitchen alone as Daisy would not leave Sway's side. Did that have something to do with the ghosts? Was his dog protecting his sister from a ghost? Zac felt a little afraid. He had never really considered the possibility before – did they exist or was it all just nonsense?

His mother emerged freshly showered and dressed, after her morning outing. "What's up Zac?" Karen put her arm around his shoulder.

"Mom, do you know much about ghosts?" Zac inquired.

"Not particularly," she responded lightly, "why?"

"Well, you know how the house has been getting so cold that we can see our breath and it seems here one minute and gone the next?" After ascertaining he held her attention, he forged on, "I looked up some information on the internet, so I could help Dad find and fix the problem and the only thing I discovered that remotely describes what we have been experiencing is ghosts," Zac explained. He always felt better after talking to his mother about his concerns and the weight lifted just by sharing it with her. Before she could offer any insightful response, the doorbell rang.

"Just a minute Hun," Karen piped up, "that will be Hope - she is going to be driving me around today for appointments."

"Mom, can I spend the day with you?" Zac blurted out before she could reach the door. "Please?" Karen stopped and turned to study him for a moment. He wished he could read what was on her mind. It had now been more than a week since Sway had been doing her schoolwork at home with Mom, and Zac had been content to do his part – ensure he was not the cause for his mom's worry! Every night he'd been scouring the internet for more information on ghosts, but nothing new really came up. To his delight, his parents seemed to be happier and more affectionate than he'd ever remembered – it was awesome! Now this day with his mom would be the cherry on top!

"Yes, sure Hun, why not - go and phone the school and tell them you are having a family day and won't be in," Karen instructed, then turned back to answer the door. He heard them exchange warm greetings as Hope entered the house, fully taken aback at her directive – why didn't she call them? Shrugging, Zac found the number for the school and called, hearing a woman's voice pick up on the other end. Before he lost his nerve, he quickly repeated what his mother had said about having a family day and that he would be absent today. There was a short pause.

"Zac I will need to talk to your mother," was her firm reply.

Karen and Hope had just entered the living room, and Zac eagerly handed his mother the phone, "They need to talk to you Mom," he informed her. Karen took the phone and confirmed what Zac had told her. Zac anxiously watched his mother listen for a moment, then respond.

"Well then, that is exactly correct – family time - have good day and thank you." Zac expelled a huge breath he didn't realize he'd been holding and relaxed, excitement building, as his mother hung up and turned to Hope. "We have a very busy day ahead of us," she commented. Hope nodded in agreement. Zac stood for a moment, studying his mother. Was it his imagination? For a few seconds, his mother did not appear to be herself - she actually *looked* like someone else. Fear seeped through his body. He closed his eyes and then peered at her again - the image of another woman had passed! Zac gave his head a shake. Was his mind playing tricks on him? He had to admit to being out of his element of late - sleeping on Sway's floor; freezing at times; overall sleep deprivation, and then the ghost thing. All this, along with his mother's illness, Zac guessed, could give a kid an overactive imagination. Karen seemed not to notice his scrutiny - preoccupied with their visitor. She finally turned to Zac and asked him to go wake his sister while she made breakfast. Hope offered to go with him, and he led the way to Sway's room. Sway was still sound asleep with Key-key curled up to her hip. The cat began to purr as soon as they entered the room.

"Good morning," Hope greeted Sway cheerfully, "wakey, wakey - time for a new day of adventure." Sway slowly opened her eyes and peered up at them both drowsily, as if still in a dream. Slowly coming to a wakeful state, a huge smile lit up her features and she suddenly sat up.

"Hi Hope," she was clearly excited, "what are you doing in my bedroom?" Then quickly added, "it's Ok though, I am so happy to see you!" She promptly jumped out of bed and gave their visitor a huge hug.

"I am here to hang out with you and your family today and give your mom a ride to some of her appointments," Hope replied.

"Yay," Sway shouted with another monster hug. She decided to start her day with a shower and dashed off with a clean set of clothing. Zac smiled, so happy to be spending the day with his mom, that he didn't even mind sharing it with Hope and Sway. He and Hope wandered to the kitchen.

"Can I help with anything?" Hope offered.

"I think I got it," Karen smiled pleasantly at their guest. "I'm just going to make us all a smoothie, and we can have our choice of cereal or whole grain toast with peanut butter and or jam."

"I'm going for the smoothie and cereal," Zac said as he grabbed his favourite box from the cupboard. Hope and Karen chose whole grain toast with peanut butter. The fruit smoothies were whipped up in no time at all. Just as they were almost finished their breakfast, Sway joined them - all dressed and ready to start her day. She quickly noshed down her cereal and smoothie, while Hope and Karen went over the schedule for the day - bank, lawyer, lunch, and library.

"What are we going to the library for?" Zac asked. Karen smiled at him.

"I shared with Hope, your curiosity surrounding ghosts, so we thought maybe taking you to the library to research the subject would be a fun way to end our day." Zac gawked up at them both.

"Ghosts!" echoed Sway, "that sounds like so much fun! Are we going to go to a graveyard as well?" Her enthusiasm was infectious.

"No," Zac retorted, quite surprised that his mother would mention ghosts around his little sister, but he had to admit it was a great idea. "Thank you, Mom, that does sound cool, but no, Sway, I'm pretty sure we are not going to a graveyard."

"Well not today anyway," Hope whispered to Sway, loud enough for all ears, which earned another wide-eyed stare from Zac, and an exuberant giggle from Sway.

"The library sounds awesome – can we spend time together there while you are at the bank and lawyers?" Zac thought he'd rather visit the graveyard than those boring stops.

"No, I've decided that I need both of you there," Karen replied. At Zac's questioning stare she laughed cheerfully, "You'll see, it is a surprise!" Karen tweaked his nose and winked. They quickly put their tableware in the dishwasher and headed out the door.

The first stop was the bank. Once inside, Karen instructed them to sit in the waiting area as she and Hope conversed with the Account Manager.

As they idly thumbed through kids' magazines, they had one curious eye peeled on their mother, through the floor to ceiling glass wall in the office - she was completing some kind of paperwork. After what seemed like hours, she emerged and motioned them in. The young man, who they assumed to be the Account Manager, asked them politely to please sign their names, each on their own card.

"What is this?" Zac asked. He was feeling proud that he knew how to sign his name in cursive writing. Mrs. Blunt, his third-grade teacher, had insisted that her students practice this 'disappearing art', as she termed it.

"I am opening a bank account for you both," Karen explained. Zac and Sway each complied. Zac noted Hope's name was also on the card and pondered this at first. Then, the young man stated that he would witness the signatures, so Zac assumed his mother must have needed two witnesses – Hope being one of them. After all, his father was working and couldn't be there.

Once they finished their business at the bank, they drove over to a law office - an imposing brick building that looked old and important. Zac's mom had once told him that she used to work there before he was born, and he idly wondered if there might be ghosts in the aged building too. Zac and Sway were allowed to color and draw in another room while his mom and Hope talked to the people at the law office – no glass doors to peer into this time. By the time their business concluded, it was noon, and Zac was starving. Hope took them to a restaurant that he had never been to before. Her and his mom had a healthy salad with chicken for protein, Zac had a delicious hamburger with fries and Sway had chicken tenders with vegetable strips. The kids swapped fries and veggies and Zac decided that this was one of the best lunches ever – those vegetable strips were very tasty!

Though Zac acknowledged there had been boring moments up until now – it was all forgotten with the anticipation of the library visit! Feeling grateful, he glanced at his mom, thinking how cool she was. He sent up a silent prayer - God please don't let my mom die, please find her a heart - don't take my mom from me! Meeting Karen's eyes over the table, it felt like she could read his mind. Karen reached over and squeezed his shoulder ever so gently, then turned back to her conversation with Hope. He felt instant reassurance – everything was going to be OK!

Once at the library, Karen herded Sway to an age-appropriate book section, and Hope sauntered directly over to the library computer to search for books on ghosts, motioning for Zac to follow. The Terrace Public Library, on any day, was one of Zac's favourite haunts. He loved books – the feel, the smell, and the history in the air and between the pages. The building was particularly impressive, situated in the George Little Memorial Park. The grounds were beautiful and the shrubs and flowers well-tended. He figured it was pretty ancient as his mom told him it was built back in the 1960s.

"What, in particular, were you hoping to learn about ghosts?" Hope asked.

"I don't know - I am not sure if there is even a ghost in our house," Zac mused.

"Why do you think there may be a ghost in your house?" Her tone was curious but casual.

"Well, our house gets very cold for short periods of time - so cold that you can see your breath and then it is gone, in an instant. I looked it up on the internet to help my dad resolve the problem and none of the other searches could describe anything like we are experiencing, except ghosts."

"Oh, that's very interesting! Let's put into the search engine, 'phantom cold air and ghosts', and see what we get." Hope recommended. Zac's excitement was building. It was fun doing stuff like this with an adult. Most grown-ups would not take the time or even take a kid seriously about this kind of stuff. Hope was cool, Zac thought to himself – a lot like his mom.

Several books were flagged on the resource list from the key words Hope had input into the search bar. She retrieved a pen from her purse, grabbed a sticky note by the computer, and wrote down the names and library reference numbers - there were eight in total. All but one on the list was showing available. Hope said they would have to put that one on the waiting list and the library would call when the book arrived. Zac and Hope quite easily found and gathered up the seven books and sat down at an empty table to one side.

Hope read off each book's summary, and asked Zac if he felt any were applicable to what they were experiencing at his home – loud noises in the night; creaks as if someone were walking around; wailing sounds; things being knocked over for no reason; books flying off a shelf; lights flashing on and off randomly; seeing past loved ones in a mirror; taps turning on and off; history of a murder in your home; house built on a graveyard – an extensive list, but none of the summaries referred to and icy chill, so frigid that you could see your breath. The only thing that came close was a momentary fleeting cold feeling – the suggestion of a ghost passing through you.

Still, Zac and Hope scanned through the books for a couple of hours, until his mother came and announced it was time to go. "Did you find what you were looking for?" Karen wondered.

"Not exactly, but it was fun reading about it," Zac grinned and turned to Hope, "thank you for helping me."

"You're so very welcome - I have enjoyed today with you and have learned all kinds and sorts of things about ghosts," Hope commented and grinned back. "What did you learn about today, Miss Sway?" Hope pulled her in for a hip hug.

"Mommy and I read all about puppies!" Sway enthused.

Zac stopped at the front desk check out to put in a reservation request for the last book. Karen handed the library card over to the clerk. "I have one further quick stop," Karen said, "that is, if you don't mind."

"Not at all," Hope acquiesced, giving Karen a gentle hug, "where do you want to go?" Karen requested a stop at one of the local women's clothing shops. She assured it wouldn't take long as she knew exactly what she wanted.

"We are attending a party tonight and I want something that fits properly – it's been ages since I bought anything nice for myself. I hope it is still there," Karen blushed. Hope insisted it was no problem. Karen was in luck and in short order, they were headed home with the dress in tow. Everyone was voicing contentment with their day out together. Hope dropped them off at their house and gave Karen one more long embrace before getting in the car and driving away. Zac was sure he saw tears in the young nurse's eyes as they had separated. He guessed Hope was as worried about his mom as he was.

Back at the house Karen went into high gear, happily baking a cake to take to the party. She had Zac do a Google search for a chocolate cake and icing recipe and asked both of them to grab the ingredient items from the cupboards. Soon the delicious aroma was wafting out of the oven, delectably teasing the children's noses. Karen whipped up the icing to finish off, once the cake cooled. Glancing at the clock on the microwave, she announced it time to start dinner. Again, the children helped with the chopping, mixing, and setting the table - baked chicken breast, stir fried vegetables and wild rice. The children had grown to love this new way of eating. Zac pondered the reason she'd had him find the recipe – she was a master baker and was certain she already had a recipe for this cake. His young mind was astute enough to reason that it was part of her strategy to work together as a family – he smiled at this - he really loved it!

Dinner time rolled around - no Tom. Karen recommended they go ahead and eat, and that Tom could eat when he got home. Karen dished him up a plate and placed it in the microwave, ready to reheat when he arrived. Dinner over, dishes done, cake cooled and iced, Tom was still not home, and Karen headed for the shower. She carefully completed her hair and make-up and slipped into the new dress. It was low cut and revealing, the material soft and sensuous against her curves. Karen had never worn a dress like this before - she had always been very conservative, but not tonight.

When she emerged from the bedroom, both children gasped. "You look beautiful mom!" Zac said, then gave a low whistle. Karen laughed delightedly.

"Wow mom, you look amazing!" Sway chimed in. The doorbell rang - Mrs. Jones was right on time. The look on her face when she saw Karen was a statement in itself. "I would never have recognized you," she gushed. "You were always beautiful but, in that dress, you are an absolute knockout!"

"Why, thank you so much – all of you!" She kissed the top of the kids' heads. "Make yourself at home Mrs. Jones, you know where everything is," Karen offered generously. Mrs. Jones unloaded her bag along with the children's favourite peach cobbler.

"Oh, thank you," all three chimed in together at once. "Guess it's an all-out-dessert evening for you three - I also left a smaller version of the chocolate cake on the counter as a surprise – please help yourself Mrs. Jones – it's the kids' recipe!" Karen said with a laugh and picked up the phone to call Tom regarding the arrangements for them to meet at the party.

Zac and Sway watched their mother glide out the door with the cake in one hand and a bottle of wine in the other - rolling out instructions for Zac to pass onto his father. "Have fun Mom," he offered sincerely, as he closed the door behind her – pleased to see his mom looking so pretty and happy. Mrs. Jones took the children into the kitchen to start on their desert – having observed them practically drooling over it all. Zac cut a big piece of chocolate cake first, Sway wanted to start with the peach cobbler. Mrs. Jones chose a small piece of cake and both she and Zac took a bite at the same time. Zac instantly gagged and ran to spit the cake out in the sink. Mrs. Jones spat hers into a napkin and almost lost her teeth along with it. Sway was thoroughly shocked at the sour looks on their faces – her peach cobbler was absolutely delicious! Zac and Mrs. Jones stared at each other in confusion.

"Your mom made that?" Mrs. Jones asked. Zac nodded wondering what the heck had gone wrong. "Are you sure?" Mrs. Jones prodded further? Zac retrieved the recipe and they both scoured it for any strange ingredients. "Goodness, I never thought it possible for your mom to make anything less than superbly delicious - even boiled dish cloths I assume would taste yummy coming from her." All three were clearly bewildered. "And your mom has taken this cake to the party?" Both children bobbed their heads in assent. "Oh my," she murmured, and proceeded to cut Zac a big piece of peach cobbler, adding a large scoop of ice cream for good measure. He thanked her profusely and slowly savored each bite, as it served to replace the horrid taste from the cake.

Now Zac was truly worried about his mom. She never botched a recipe – in fact, rarely *used* a recipe. Zac thought back to when she was making the cake. His mother habitually tasted everything she made as she created it. But Zac did not remember her sampling this one. "That's it!" Zac shouted.

"What is?" Mrs. Jones asked

"Mom is trying to lose weight, so she never tasted her cake or icing, and she must have missed something," Zac concluded. Mrs. Jones nodded her head, but something told her it was more than that. Karen had not seemed herself – hard to describe, but there was something different in both looks and actions – even though very subtle. The heart attack had deprived oxygen to Karen's brain for a short time, and Mrs. Jones feared there was not only resulting damage to Karen's heart but also to her mind - perhaps her memory. But how on earth would she bring the subject up with her? Well, she figured after the cake was sampled at the party, she would not be the only one with concerns for her sweet natured neighbor.

Chapter 16

EARLIER THAT DAY Tom had woken abruptly to find he had slept in. As he'd frantically leapt from the bed, Karen was just returning with Daisy after their early run. "Good morning," she greeted him cheerfully as she headed for the shower.

"I slept in, why didn't you wake me?" Tom hollered grumpily at Karen.

"It was 6:00 a.m. when I went out - how was I to know you didn't set your alarm last night?" Karen called over her shoulder, her jovial mood seemingly not affected by his accusatory outburst. Tom grumbled and hastily grabbed a cup of coffee to go, a couple of apples and a snack bar to eat on the way to work. Shrugging resignedly, he followed her into the bathroom, watching as she dropped her clothing on the shiny tiled floor and stepped into the steamy shower. Well, they were all planning to eat healthier, right? "I am heading into work, see you tonight," Tom called out.

"Have a wonderful day and oh, don't forget we have a party to attend tonight," Karen replied.

"Oh, right," Tom responded with minimal enthusiasm, and headed out to the car. During the drive, he reflected on the evening to come. Parties of this sort were definitely not his thing, however, with all that was happening in his life at this time, he decided not to rock the boat - keep Karen happy! After all, she *was* giving her hundred and ten percent to healthy improvements. With a wide grin, he revisited recent events and mind-blowing changes with their sex life. Yup, he had nothing to complain about there. Give a little, take a lot.

Tom glued his attention to the speed limit today - three incidents with the police were more than enough for 10 years, never mind months. Damn, he still had that hefty fine to pay! Yes, he would talk to Jean about snagging some overtime hours so he could get ahead of the added expenses this month. Even though Tom had slept in he was still one of the first people to arrive to work. He headed straight to Jean's office to put in the overtime request.

She was seated back in her chair, feet up on her desk, studying a document when Tom knocked on her door. She put the document to one side but did not rise or move an inch in greeting. "Hi Tom, what can I do for you?" she inquired – her tone all business. He glanced over his shoulder and around the room to ascertain if anyone was watching, cautioned by the same impersonal tone she used when others were around. When they were alone, however, it was an entirely different story. Whatever! He was infinitely tired of trying to figure her motives and decided to get directly to the point.

"I've got a load of extra bills this month with Karen being sick so I would like to work some extra hours to get them paid down," Tom explained.

"I can't approve that for you right now," Jean replied sulkily. She went on to explain that Doug was calling a staff meeting to discuss the latest news, and they could revisit it afterward.

"What is it," Tom asked?

"I'm not at liberty to say," Jean replied - her tone cool, piercing him with a challenging stare.

"You can't say," Tom parroted, testily. He'd had enough of her wily manipulation.

"I *won't* say!" Jean snapped, finally exhibiting an emotional response, "you can damned well wait with everyone else to hear what Doug has to say!"

"Alright," Tom smiled smugly – at least he knew he could get under her skin. He wanted to ask if she was OK, but with her distant behavior and impersonal tone he thought best to wait until later for that enlightening discussion. Closing the office door behind him, he strolled to the staff room to await the meeting. It was not long before others were sauntering in – inquiring as to how Karen and the children were faring. "They are good," he offered in response. A few were fishing to see if anyone was aware of what this meeting was about. No one admitted to having a semblance of a clue. One fellow mechanic mentioned that he was concerned about Doug as he seemed not himself the past few days. Tom stayed silent, as he listened to the chatter. The vocal musings stopped abruptly as Jean and Doug entered the staff room, taking their customary spots at the head of the long conference table, which effectively doubled as a lunch venue. Jean held a stack of documents in her hand that she set down on the table in front of her. Doug thanked everyone for coming on such short notice. Of course, he was the boss and so their presence was fully expected – not by choice. Still, they all appreciated the respectful gesture. He was a great boss, and all shared the concern about the heavy stress that clearly was weighing him down – he was not himself at all!

"What I am about to tell you right now is confidential," Doug went around the table making eye contact with each one of them. "Jean and I expect all of you to keep this information to yourselves. Please do not even share it with your spouses." His stern demeanor left no room for argument. "We have made the difficult decision to sell the company and are going to offer it up to the employees first, for the opportunity to purchase. If one or maybe more of you submit a single or joint Offer to Purchase, we will give you one month from today to make arrangements with your financial institution, and submit it to us accordingly," Doug informed, "We will not entertain any offers that are subject to conditions," he clarified, "and if there is anything you may require such as company financial statements, business plans, etc., please feel free to come and see either Jean or myself."

A murmur went out within the group. Finally, one of the employees took the first step, "Why are you selling?"

"Good question," Doug responded jauntily. "I have taken a good look at our personal lives and have decided that it is time for us to go out and enjoy life - reap the benefits of what we have sown - before I, at least, am too old or crippled to enjoy the remainder of time left." Jean focused her gaze down at the table, her expression unreadable – uncharacteristically silent. All eyes had shifted to her, trying to gauge her reaction.

Doug went on to say, "if anyone here is interested in purchasing our company, Jean and I will be pleased to help you develop your business plan. We are committed to doing everything in our power to assist this company stay in the hands of one or more of you in this group as you are the only family Jean and I have. As you all know, we have prioritized our business before anything else in our lives, so have not been blessed with children. It is time for a shift - travel, see and do things we have not taken the opportunity to do."

Tom raised his hand and Doug nodded, motioning for him to speak. "What about our jobs - will there be any lay-offs?" Tom asked. Another rumbling murmur around the table – he had clearly voiced what they were all thinking.

"Honestly, I don't know," Doug sighed heavily, "once the company is sold it is up to the new owner or owners to determine how the staffing is structured. You have my word that each one of you will be provided with an excellent reference, should it be necessary. On the same token, if any of you decide to look elsewhere right now, we totally understand and hope you will afford us a two-week notice." Doug earnestly searched the faces of his employees and friends. "Again - please ensure all of this stays confidential until one month from today."

Doug stood up heavily, exhaustion evident on his features – Jean followed suit. Doug finished the meeting, "Have an enjoyable day everyone - try not to worry - you are all amazing workers and an asset to this company. Jean and I are available at any time to answer questions and help in any way we can to make this transition as painless as possible. Once more, we are hoping someone within this family will purchase this company because no one knows and values this business better than all of you. Thank you again for meeting with Jean and I - now let's get back to our busy schedule and take good care of our customers."

Doug left the staff room and headed straight to his office with Jean hot on his heels. Some followed suit while others hung back for a moment to absorb the information. Doug had closed his office door, but the staff could clearly hear raised voices – unmistakable arguing between the two - the words muffled and indiscernible. Jean abruptly flung open the door to leave Doug's office, and all could hear his sharp-toned parting words - "It's done Jean - no more discussion – let's just focus now on getting it sold." Jean slammed both doors forcefully as she retreated to her own space – leaving a resounding tremor of ominous finality echoing in the office hallway.

Everyone scurried off to their duties. It was obvious that now was not the time to seek a private discussion with either of them. Some of the staff was concerned about their jobs, others worried about Doug and Jean, a few contemplating on whether they possessed the skills and know-how necessary to buy and run this company successfully. There were those full of admiration for Doug - he had worked hard to build his empire and now it was his turn to relax. Common ground for all of them - they took Doug's words to heart on his praise for their excellent work ethic and his confidence in them to take care of their customers. History had proven that the business would take care of them in turn, and Doug never failed to credit his staff.

Tom tried to focus on the lengthy line of vehicles ahead of him for the day that needed service or repairs. Relief that there was enough to keep him busy and maybe justify the overtime he requested, kept him in high gear. Before he knew it, lunch was upon them. Remembering that he needed to scoot out and grab a lunch, he arranged his tools to one side and headed out the door. He had no sooner sat in the car when his cell rang - Jean.

"Where are you going," she demanded?

"I am going to grab lunch," Tom replied.

"Yes, I know that," Jean snapped irritably, "I want to know where?"

"I don't know," Tom snapped back, "probably a drive through – eat in the car."

"Good," Jean responded in a less sharp tone. "Grab me a cup of coffee when you order your lunch and meet me at the Mariner's Park". She ended the call without waiting for his response. Tom found it immensely irksome that she felt such unabridged entitlement to order him around as if he was a puppy, begging at her heels. He had a sudden urge to ignore her directive – but annoyingly adding to his indignation – he knew he was going to do exactly what she asked. Within ten minutes, he pulled up beside her car and she immediately exited and jumped into his. He glanced around nervously to see if anyone was watching – he was developing paranoia, and not at all accustomed to it. She reached for the coffee and took a long sip.

"Thank you," her tone exhibited gratitude, "just the way I like it - hot and black."

"You are welcome," He reached back to remove the contents of his take-out lunch and eyeballed her, "OK, now what is this all about?"

"I want you and I to buy the company!" Jean blurted out.

"Whoa," Tom put up his hand in a halting gesture, "There are all kinds and sorts of red flags popping up here. First off, I don't have that kind of money - I am just keeping up with my bills, never mind coming up with the level of investment needed for a down payment."

"Just listen," Jean coaxed. "I will already have half the funds, as I'm a co-owner now, so the down payment I can manage for us, but I do have to buy Doug out, and can't make this purchase alone!" As always, Tom was mesmerized by her power of influence over him. "Tom, I *can* manage this with you on board as my partner – we can do it together!"

"Well, what about Doug? Are the two of you splitting up, because I can't see him going anywhere without you," Tom stated logically.

"This is my life too - I helped build this company and I am not just lying down and letting him dictate what the next steps in *my* life will be. If he wants to do something else, he can damn well do it on his own because I sure as hell am not going with him!" Jean raved. She opened the car door in preparation to leave, and turned to him, softening her tone, "Think about this, Tom, please! You and I can pull this off - it is a win-win for us both." She glanced at his dash clock. "I better get back before he notices we are both gone. Do not come back to work for another twenty minutes – it will give me a head start to return before you," Jean instructed. Before Tom could respond she was out of the car and gone. He sat in a daze. How in the hell could he buy half of this company and enter a partnership with Jean? Hell, she would hold all the strings! Tom was not altogether comfortable with the implied inequities. She would provide the cash, and what was in it for her – what did she want from him?

Tom was back at work exactly to the minute that his lunch break ended. The rest of the day flew by and once he had completed the last order for the day, a glance at his watch told him it was 6:30 p.m. Two hours past his quitting time - overtime. This brought a smile, as he punched in his time card and headed out the door for home. He'd barely pulled out on the main road when the lights on the police car flashed behind him. Tom glanced at his speed – well within the limit. Really? He pulled over, confused on what could warrant this attention. Officer O'Reilly came up to the window and tapped quickly. Tom rolled it down, his driver's licence already in hand.

"I don't need that," he waved it away.

"What's going on?" Tom fought to keep his temper under wraps.

"Do you mind if I sit in your car with you and have a chat?" It was a direction more than a question, Tom was aware - his first inclination for a response was a firm 'no' – then he remembered how that would simply earn him a trip to the station. Well, he had done nothing wrong, hence had nothing to hide -nothing to lose. Tom nodded his assent and motioned for the policeman to hop in.

Jim O'Reilly immediately climbed in the passenger seat, his large frame quite effectively consuming the entire space. Tom reflected that this man would never be comfortable in a smaller car. "How can I help you, Officer?" Tom offered as politely as he could muster, stifling the urge to address the cop by his first name – after all, shouldn't they be at that point by now in their relationship?

"I noticed you were hanging at the Mariner's Park this afternoon - did you notice anything or anyone out of the ordinary there?"

"No," Tom stated, "why?"

"What were you doing there?"

"Eating my lunch in a quiet place and getting a break from work," Tom supplied, again with utmost of good manners, but his patience was beginning to wear. "May I ask why the questions?"

"Well, there have been some complaints of suspicious behavior in our local parks, so I am conducting some investigative work," O'Reilly threw him a casual smile.

"I am sure happy to help any way I can, but I wasn't paying any attention to what was going on in the park - my mind has been consumed with what is going on at home with my wife's illness," Tom explained.

At that precise moment, Tom's cell phone rang – Karen. "Hi Tom," her cheerful voice came over the speaker, "I guess you forgot about the party."

"Oh shoot! Yes, sorry honey, I had a full day and had to put in some overtime to get everything caught up. I am just on my way home now," Tom assured her, glancing over at the officer, who nodded his head in affirmation.

"OK," Karen said, "we are going to be late so how about I go ahead, and you just meet me there?"

"Sounds good!" He pressed the "end call" button on his steering wheel and turned his attention to Officer O'Reilly. "Listen I really want to help but am at a loss for anything I could contribute - I promised my wife I'd take her out tonight and I'm already late, so if there nothing further, I really need to get home."

"OK Tom, thank you for the chat, I will let you be on your way," Jim responded, then opened the door and extracted himself from the small space. He leaned back into the car, "I'll keep in touch," then closed the door and sauntered back to his cruiser. Tom sat there for a moment, wondering what he'd meant by those parting words. It couldn't be related to his recent speeding violations – must be something else. Tom slowly pulled back onto the roadway, noting with a glance in his rear-view mirror, the police car remained parked with the lights on. Tom wondered what in the world the man was up to.

His mind wandered to Karen's call and her plans on going to the party ahead of him. Why would she do that? Who cares if they are late, it is just a party, right? Not an important engagement, just a get together with friends - well maybe not exactly friends, more like acquaintances and coworkers. Tom had perfunctory relationships – a few work and poker buddies. Even then - none that he could call close friends. Karen was the social butterfly, with all the kids' activities and her church group. Come to think of it – aside from Karen, Jean was probably his closest friend. He supposed women naturally developed more intimate friendships. Jean was an entire other ball of wax - he figured they were two peas in a pod as he couldn't think of a single female that she hung out with. Perhaps he was her best friend too.

He arrived home to find everyone gathered in the kitchen, including the pets – he conceded that he'd lost that battle – one had to choose them wisely. Sway ran over to give him a hug, which he returned and headed to the kitchen with her following on his heels.

"Mom's gone to the party," Zac informed him, "and she wants you to meet her there. Dinner is in the microwave to warm up if you want it, and this part is from me not Mom – don't touch the cake Mom made, if you want desert, have some of Mrs. Jones peach cobbler." Tom figured that was a good bet – they all loved that treat.

"What kind of cake is it," Tom asked? "Something really special?"

"It's chocolate," Sway chimed in, "Mom made it for the party, but she left enough here for us to have some. Dad, I agree with Zac - you don't want any."

"Oh? Chocolate cake is one of my favourites."

"Not this chocolate cake," Zac replied, offering no further explanation.

Mrs. Jones laughed and added, "It is not as bad as they suggest - how about I warm up your dinner for you?" Tom nodded gratefully and grabbed a beer from the fridge, joining his kids at the table.

"So how have you been Mrs. Jones?" Tom politely inquired as he scoffed down his dinner, motioning to Zac to grab him second beer to wash the last of the meal down.

"I've been well, thank you for asking Tom," she cast him a friendly smile. Tom turned to Sway and requested her to grab him a slice of chocolate cake. She looked to Zac, who shrugged his shoulders, and commented, "we warned him." Sway came to the table with a teeny sliver of cake.

"What is this?" her father laughed, "it doesn't even qualify as a taste."

"I am giving you an itty-bitty piece dad because I love you. You can ask me for more if you like it," Sway reasoned in her big girl voice that effectively mimicked her mom. The adults both chuckled heartily. Taking the whole piece in one bite – he instantly wished fervently that he had listened to his kids. Tom hastily grabbed his beer and tried to wash the taste out of his mouth.

"I think I am going to need another one of these," he gasped. Mrs. Jones and the children burst out laughing. "Are you sure your mom made that?" Tom asked? Both children nodded, still giggling.

The kids replaced the ominous cake plate with a bowl of peach cobbler and ice cream. Tom took a tentative bite at first, eyeing them all dubiously, and smiled. "This is delicious," he complimented Mrs. Jones, who stood, beaming with pride. Tom finished his third brew while Mrs. Jones shared the local gossip. He then declared it was time to get ready and head to the party, or Karen may decide he had to eat the rest of the cake as punishment.

He was shocked to find that his clothes had not been laid out for him. Karen always preferred him to wear a complementing color to her own outfit – especially when the event was something she considered special – clearly this qualified. Even though he habitually grouched about her dictating what he should or should not wear, Tom usually would have been angry with Karen had she not laid out his clothes for an option, but tonight he found himself feeling an aching disappointment. Tom walked back into the kitchen and asked his children what their mother was wearing to the party.

"A blue dress," Sway quickly responded, "and she looks amazing!" Zac piped in. Tom smiled and thanked his kids as he headed back to take a quick shower before donning the black dress pants and blue shirt that he hoped would match Karen's dress. Breaking out in a wide smile, he realized that he was happy at that moment. As he walked out the door, his thoughts were on his wife and family - what a lucky guy he was! It was pleasant evening for the two-block stroll, and he was completely oblivious to the police cruiser that was parked nearby, watching his house.

Chapter 17

KAREN TOOK GREAT pleasure immersing in her surroundings - lush green lawns and colourful gardens – the sounds and smells of spring outdoor family activities, as she leisurely strolled the few blocks to the party. It was a gorgeous night, and she was quite happily anticipating an evening of stimulating socialization. Hurried footsteps told her someone was quickly approaching from behind.

"Hey," a man's voice called out. "Going to the Wilson's party too?" Karen stopped and turned to find a tall, quite attractive man hurrying to catch up with her. "I'm Greg Hubert," he flashed an inviting smile, reaching out to shake her hand before noticing the cake. "Here let me help you," he offered, taking the container easily in one hand.

"Karen Shorn,"

Greg stepped back. "No way, my God Karen, I did not recognize you!" Amazing what a new dress two sizes smaller can do, Karen thought inwardly. "Did you recognize me?" Greg asked a bit sheepishly. She nodded with a teasing twinkle in her eye. "Oh, you are so funny," he joined in the mirth. "Truly, I bet when we get to the party no one will recognize you," Greg wagered. "You look absolutely stunning – and that's not to say you were not already a knockout!" He eyed her dubiously, "OK, perhaps I should put my other foot in my mouth now? It's maybe the hair – the dress? There's something else too – a certain glow about you! Where is Tom?"

"He is running late, worked some overtime - he'll be along later," Karen responded good-naturedly.

"Hey, I have a stellar idea - how about we show up as a couple and see how long it takes for them to figure out your identity?"

"Hmmm…sounds like fun – albeit a little wicked – but sure," she grinned in agreement. Greg hooked his arm around her waist just as they were coming up to the front door to ring the doorbell. Their host greeted them enthusiastically in the foyer, talking incessantly and flitting around like she'd dangerously overdosed on caffeine. Snatching the cake from Greg, she placed it on a long impeccably decorated table, with several other mouth-watering potluck offerings.

"Great you could make it," Sharon gushed. "Greg, for goodness' sake, pour your girlfriend a glass of vino! What is your name dear?" Before Karen could response, the doorbell pulled Sharon's attention and she scurried to answer, calling over her shoulder, "Greg, introduce your girlfriend to the crew!" He and Karen twittered in amusement – this *was* a bit of a hoot!

Dutifully handing her a glass of wine, he pulled a mickey out of his jacket pocket and proposed a toast. "To a beautiful woman," Greg whispered and clinked the bottle against her crystal wine glass. They wandered amiably through the crowd of guests and sauntered out into the garden. Greg had a habit of bringing a new girl to every party, so they attracted very little attention. Karen took advantage of the opportunity to just relax and enjoy his refreshingly gregarious company. He commented on changes at work, in an effort to determine if Tom had mentioned anything to Karen about the sale of the company, but if she was in the know, she never took the bait. Greg figured Tom had honored the directive Doug had placed upon them. He also surmised that it would not take long for someone, with a few too many drinks under their belt, to let the cat out of the bag – it was shaping up to be an intriguing evening. "Now I am totally entranced by the new you," Karen laughed in response, keeping it light but enjoying this harmless flirt. "You would never guess that you've been ill – you look amazing!"

"Well thank you," Karen whispered back. "I think I better get a little closer to the door and keep an eye out for Tom," She found a comfortable vanilla cream leather loveseat within perfect viewing distance of any new arrivals. Greg trailed closely behind, grabbed the bottle of wine and liberally refilled her glass before settling down beside her. They chatted easily for about an hour before Karen noticed Tom's arrival. She watched their host greet him warmly.

"Where is Karen?" Sharon peered around him.

"Oh, she came ahead of me." Tom replied.

"That's strange - I haven't seen her," Sharon responded with a look of confusion. Tom slipped by her, searching the room. Greg noticed that he looked directly at Karen with no sign of recognition as he walked right past them. Karen began to rise, but Greg held her back with a gentle touch to her arm.

"Remember, this is fun," he whispered, "even Tom doesn't yet recognize you. Let's just wait this out and see how long it takes for him to figure it out." Karen sank back into the couch, accepting yet another glass of wine. It was harmless really – maybe for a bit longer. She watched Tom scour the party, searching for her – she assumed. People stopped him to inquire after her – he barely made it two feet before someone else pulled him aside. Though he wasn't always close enough for her to hear it all, a question arising from his co-workers piqued her interest - "what did you think of the meeting today?" Her curiosity grew at his response - "We'll just have to wait and see how if plays out." Tom eventually settled in to enjoy the attention he was receiving and mingled with his co-workers.

Greg's demeanor sobered as he brooked a glance at Karen and realized what he'd thought would be a fun and harmless prank was turning out to have a cruel element, affecting this beautiful lady who'd graced him all evening with her presence. "I am sorry," Greg whispered to Karen, "no woman should be invisible to her husband." Karen shook her head dismissively and continued to watch Tom. "Why are you still with him? Everyone knows he is an asshole and treats you like shit!" Greg growled, suddenly disgusted with the situation and feeling more than a little protective of her.

She took a sip of her wine and turned to look him square in the eye, "Greg, do you know what monogamous means?"

"Mana what?" Greg responded with a laugh.

"Monogamous means to mate for life," Karen continued. "Are you aware the variety of creatures on this planet that do this," Karen asked?

"Well, I've heard wolves do," Greg responded, not quite sure if he liked where this conversation was going.

Karen listed off other similar species, "gibbon apes, termites, sea horses, barn owls, beavers, bald eagles, golden eagles and the list goes on," He sat rather dumbfounded by all of this.

"Termites - really?" Greg commented, "who knows about this stuff?"

Karen went on, "Can you imagine a wolf's life? Out in the wild with food scarcity and an annual litter to feed. They must deal with pack politics. What do you think their lives are like in comparison to those animals that do not mate for life?"

"I think life in the wilderness would be much more difficult on one's own, willy-nilly, rather than having a life-mate in some ways, but the freedom that comes without that is also significant," Greg surmised.

"Yes, for the males that are out there just procreating and not taking any responsibility for their offspring I can see how that could be appealing," Karen paused to sip her wine, eyeing him over the rim of her glass. "With regard to the wolves, their offspring have a better chance of survival when they work in pairs and as a group. If there is a day where one is a little weaker, the other covers for them, resulting in a better chance for their survival and it is all in their genetics. Now on the other hand, do you think the odds of survival are greater for humans in a team, as opposed to the lone ranger?" Greg laughed out loud.

"You've certainly given me something to think about when I am sober," Greg jested as he raised his drink to her wine glass. "So, back to my question, why don't you leave Tom?"

"Well, this body and mind is genetically gifted or cursed – depending on your perspective, as a monogamous creature. Even if I wanted to leave him, I cannot - this body's genetics will not allow it."

"Wow," Greg whispered, "now that is fucked up." Then they both burst out laughing. "You are quite the lady," Greg reciprocated, "even if you are a fair bit off mark here!" Despite that, his admiration for her was growing by the minute – now here was a lady, if circumstances were different, who could likely tame his wandering soul. Greg took the conversation in a different direction, "I heard you were incredibly intelligent and ambitious – had plans to become a lawyer before you met Tom. I can deduce, just in the span of our short, yet remarkably lucrative drinking session, that you are one smart woman! I hope that man of yours appreciates you and proves the local gossip I hear to be errant. They say you have a heart of gold - next to sainthood, and that you are infinitely kind!"

Karen's attention returned to the room, seeking out Tom. Jean had just arrived, and it was obvious she'd already had her fair share to drink. Sharon created a big fuss over the presence of her husband's boss at her party. "Jean, come on in, what can I get you to drink? So happy you could make it!" Sharon prattled. Jean sauntered unsteadily over to the makeshift bar and mixed herself what appeared to be a good stiff drink as Sharon fussed alongside her.

"Where is the damn music, Sharon? Let's get this party going girl, turn on some good dancing tunes, I want to *move*!" Jean bellowed out to the group. The glassy sheen in her eyes betrayed the level of alcohol already prevalent in her system and Karen felt immediate concern for her. Sharon rushed over and turned the stereo on, eager to please, and avoid a scene. Jean's inebriated gaze found and glued on Tom.

"Tom, come on big guy, come and *dance* with me!" Jean sidled over to him, and grasped his hand firmly, moving provocatively to the music - creating her own private dance floor right where they stood. Tom's discomfort was clear as he glanced around, in search of Karen. Every fiber of his being urged him to extract himself from her clutches, and this volatile situation. Attention of this kind, especially from his thoroughly sloshed mistress, sent alarm bells clamoring in his brain! But he also knew Jean - If he did not play her game, there was no telling what might come out of her mouth. He was suddenly grateful that Karen was nowhere to be found!

Jean pressed lewdly against him as she turned and began rubbing her ass into his crotch, in rhythm with the throbbing music. Tom attempted to move back, but she followed and kept up the seduction. Turning around, she slithered down his body, undulating like a cobra – until her face was just an inch from his jewels. Tom reached down and not-so-gently pulled her up, in an effort to gain control of the situation. He took the lead, moving to the music and attempting to steer a safe distance away from the milling crowd by the food and drinks. She was having none of it and resumed the erotic grind – clearly intent on having her way with him.

"You dry humping my wife, Tom?" Doug's voice boomed behind him - calm and clear. "I know she is in heat right now but that does not give you licence to take advantage." The menace in his tone was clear and Tom tried to back away from Jean, who was intent on her purpose – seemingly oblivious to her husband's presence.

"It's not what you think," Tom strived to explain, in his own defense – he wasn't too sure he cared about Jean's outcome at this point – how could she do this? Jean was always so concerned about discretion – giving him hell whenever she thought he'd taken too much risk. People were obviously experiencing some discomfort with the situation as they began to disperse, making excuses and finding their way home from the party. Tom was well aware of his colleagues' reluctance to bear witness to their married bosses creating such a public spectacle. Sharon looked frantic – beside herself, not knowing what to do. Someone turned off the music – the silence was deafening.

Tom took charge, firm control in his tone, "Let go Jean!"

"If I don't? What will you do, big guy?" her throaty sexy laugh that normally would have him sporting an admirable boner, now grated on his senses. "Spank me?" she pinned him with a challenging leer, rubbing her ass suggestively. Tom could do nothing but appeal to Doug's sense of reason with an earnest plea – throwing up his hands in helplessness. Doug's thundering stare now focused on his wife, who maintained her onslaught mercilessly. Karen rose from the couch and approached Sharon.

"I suggest you do something about this situation," Karen advised quietly, "If you don't get a handle on it - as the hostess of this party - you'll find that no one will feel comfortable attending another one of your soirees."

"Oh my God, I know you're right!" Sharon whispered emphatically and rushed over to intervene. "Jean, that's enough! Sharon insisted. "Tom is my guest, and I don't care if you are everyone's boss at work - this is my home and you're not in charge here," Sharon asserted sternly. Jean seemed to snap out of her alcoholic, lust-crazed trance. She abruptly let go, lowering her head as she offered a mumbled apology and clumsily escaped to the bathroom.

Doug turned nastily on Tom. "This is your fault, if you would have had the decency to bring your wife, Jean would never have behaved in this manner - get a grip on your life Tom!" he growled. Karen quietly approached Doug from behind and gently placed her hand on his shoulder.

"I do not know what exactly is going on with Jean, but I did see everything that happened here tonight, and can attest that she clearly targeted Tom, with no provocation on his part. Quite the opposite – he was trying to de-escalate her embarrassment by gracefully accepting her offer to dance, rather than an all-out refusal. Doug, she was all over him, certainly not the other way around," Karen whispered softly in his ear. Although Doug hadn't seen her, he did know Karen's voice. Tom was standing agape – in total shock that he had not recognized Karen until she spoke.

"I am sorry Tom, I don't know what has gotten into me or my wife," Doug apologized and turned with his head bowed and spoke respectfully, "Thank you, Karen, you are a sweet soul, Tom does not deserve you." He then walked away slowly without a backward glance.

Tom reached out to take her hand, and though Karen didn't pull back, hers remained limp – effectively rejecting that physical bonding connection. Tom reluctantly turned to thank Sharon for everything.

"Karen?" Sharon stood in amazement. "You look so different - amazing really - I am truly sorry that I did not recognize you! When you came in with Greg, I assumed you were one of his many girlfriends." Sharon turned on Greg. "In fact, you did not introduce her at all!" her tone accusatory.

"Why would I feel the need? You have known Karen for years," Greg laughed. Sharon looked up at him with a helpless shrug of her shoulders.

"I am sorry Tom for your bearing the brunt of one of my guests' behaviors – I should have stepped in sooner, but to be honest – I was in shock!" Tom chuckled and hugged her briefly.

"Don't you worry about it; how could you possibly predict what your guests may do? To be honest right back – we all know that Jean is a force to be reckoned with! It *is* time for us to leave now." Tom glanced around and spied Karen's cake on the food table – flashing back to the awful taste he'd had to clear from his mouth. As they relayed their parting pleasantries, Tom felt that stab of dark jealousy – he didn't like the way Greg had looked at his wife. Diving into the pool of green goo, he called out.

"Hey Greg, mostly everyone is gone, and I am sure Sharon will appreciate you taking Karen's chocolate cake off her hands."

"Thanks Tom," Greg smiled – he did have a weakness for her baking.

"No worries, buddy," Tom patted him on the back, and couldn't resist taking immense satisfaction with the visual of Greg chomping into that godawful cake! Tom chucked to himself and turned to Karen, "Are we ready to leave yet?"

"I would like to go home," Karen replied and thanked Sharon for the evening. "You have a lovely home, and you are an amazing hostess!" She moved over to plant a chaste kiss on Greg's cheek. "Thanks for entertaining me until my husband arrived," Karen whispered.

"Any time," Greg smiled and returned the parting peck. Karen followed a glowering Tom out the door and down the walk. It was a lovely cool night, and the walk home was refreshing. Tom's expression was thoughtful as he wisely chose to ignore the urge to let his jealously take the lead.

"I am sorry for tonight," it was a genuine apology. "Especially that I didn't see you – I still can't believe that. You looked different tonight – your dress, hairstyle, makeup. Not that you aren't always beautiful but tonight you were over the top gorgeous." He squeezed her hand.

"Thank you," Karen smiled demurely. "I ran into Greg just before I got there - he didn't recognize me, so just for fun he suggested seeing who else may not." Karen's smile faded. "To be honest no one did. I expected at any moment, you would come and join me. I was right in front of you, but you looked right past me," Karen stated in an accusing tone.

"I am sorry," Tom said. "That must have been uncomfortable for you, and I am sure Greg got a big charge out of it."

"Yes, Greg thought it was quite entertaining," Karen confirmed with an amused grin. Tom snickered inwardly again as he thought of Greg eating the cake. They were home momentarily, and Karen thanked Mrs. Jones gratefully, giving her a warm hug as their ever-reliable neighbor prepared to head home.

"I'll pick up my peach cobbler pan when it is all finished – I hope you had a lovely night," Mrs. Jones threw over her shoulder with a smile.

"Yes, it was entertaining. Tom, would you please make sure Mrs. Jones reaches her door safely?" Karen generally walked with her, but Tom brooked no argument and did as he was bid. The house was noticeably quiet when he returned. "Are you hungry?" Tom assured her that he was fine. Karen reached out and placed her hand on his chest. "Tom, how could you possibly not recognize me?" Karen asked in a gentle query with an underlying sadness in her tone. He hated being the source of her pain!

"You are right, I was focused on myself, and I am sorry - it will not happen again," he promised, "I am guessing you share my exhaustion – should we shower and hit the bed?" Tom suggested and kissed the back of his wife's hand. Karen sighed her agreement.

Tom stood in the shower, allowing the hot water rivulets to take free reign over his body. His mind played over the events of the day - Jean with her wild idea to buy the business. Then later, the horribly distasteful spectacle she'd put on, embarrassing herself and everyone there. Going into work tomorrow was not going to be a cake walk - that was for certain. Tom remembered Karen saying she wanted a shower, so he cut his short, to save her hot water. He climbed into bed and instantly drifted off into sleep.

Heart pounding, he woke abruptly, to the sound of Zac yelling, "Mom, Mom!" Leaping out of bed, he noticed the house was once again freezing - his teeth chattered as he hastily followed the sound of his son's voice. In the kitchen, he was alarmed to see Zac shaking his mother as he continued to scream her name. He was further disturbed at the sight - Karen cramming cake into her face, without opening her mouth – it was everywhere! Tears were rolling down her cheeks. He felt completely helpless and immediately took it out on his son.

"What the hell are you doing?" Then he turned to Karen as Zac began to sob uncontrollably.

"I don't know what is wrong with Mom!" he wailed. Karen suddenly slumped over, lifeless. Tom took control, shaking her firmly.

"Karen, Karen, wake up!" Relief flooded him as she came back around, looking thoroughly dazed. She stared in confusion down at her hands, the cake, then Tom and Zac.

"How did I get here?" Karen moaned, a hint of hysteria in her voice, tears glimmering in her eyes. Tom asked what she meant. "How did I get here from the hospital?" Her befuddlement was obvious. They were all shivering violently now – their bodies' automatic response to preserve heat.

"Should I call an ambulance, are you OK?" Tom was more than a little concerned.

"No," Karen whispered just loud enough for Tom and Zac to hear, "I don't want to go back there." The tears streamed freely down her cheeks. "Help me Tom," Karen pleaded.

"OK, honey, it's OK," Tom soothed. "I'll get you cleaned and warmed up." He assured Zac that everything was under control and urged him back to bed. Zac was totally relieved as Tom took Karen by the hand and led her gently into the bedroom. He filled the jetted tub, closing the door to maximize on the heat from the hot steamy water. They were both shivering as he quickly helped her undress and get into the bubbly hot bath. The warmth from the water was effectively calming as her tears began to slow. Taking a cloth from the rack, he ever so gently washed all the cake from her hair and face, all the while soothing her with soft assurances. Tom realized that for the first time in their relationship, quite beyond his own control, he was following an intense compulsion – his only goal to protect her – to allay her fears and keep her safe. The inherent need to nurture and care for her was new and he wondered how much of it could be attributed to the fact that she truly needed him – that was a first as well! His heart swelled – it felt incredibly important to be needed by this remarkable woman!

Tom noticed his comfort level improve - the room was warm again, the steam dissipating. Karen was completely placid and starting to drift off. Not wishing to leave her alone, he helped her from the tub and wrapped her lovingly in a warm towel. He carried her to their bedroom – standing her before him as he gently dried her off. He grabbed a soft pair of pajamas from her drawer dressed her tenderly.

Alert once again, Karen just stood there – confused but somehow immensely comforted. She looked into his eyes with beseeching gratitude as he tucked her softly into bed and curled his body around her. Tom was exhausted but strangely content as he fell into an instant slumber. He did not hear his son come into the room or see the strange ritual that Zac preformed before laying down beside Karen on the floor of their bedroom.

Chapter 18

ZAC WAS PLEASED to see his parents go out for the evening - he loved his time with Mrs. Jones. She was like a grandmother figure, comforting and kind. That experience, he and Sway had missed out on as both sets of grandparents had passed before he was born. His mom had relayed that her parents had died in a car accident just after his parents' wedding, and that his dad had lost his parents when he was in his early twenties - one from a heart attack and the other from cancer. It made him wonder – why didn't his dad have more empathy for his mom's heart issues? But then, his dad never talked about his parents. It was like they never existed. Zac had a flash of memory – he was quite young when he'd first asked his mom about his grandparents. He smiled, remembering her wonderful stories about her childhood and how much she was certain that her mom and dad would have loved to be here with them, sharing in the awesome fun stuff that grandparents excel at! Mom had looked very sad after that, especially when she talked about his dad's parents. She knew very little about them and advised him that it was best not to ask his dad any questions. Zac thought that a little strange but trusted his mom completely. Still, he would have given his right arm to know what the story was behind it.

The whole day had been amazing! He'd been fortunate to hang out with his mom and sister – research ghosts - which was *so* cool! Hope was pretty swell too and although her and his mom had just met, they seemed like they were becoming good friends. Mrs. Jones, his sister, and he played a game of Go Fish – Sway's favorite! He had learned quickly from Mrs. Jones example, that if you win a game or two then let Sway win the next you could bank on her good mood, because it made her gleeful. So, he didn't miss the sitter's cue when she announced bedtime after this last game – Sway was the victor! Musing about it now, Zac had a feeling that his sister knew pretty much what they were about, but seeing the happy sparkle in her eyes warmed his heart, and after all, isn't that what big brothers are born to do?

Zac said good night and quickly dived into his research on the laptop. He was both a little shocked and duly impressed that his mom and Hope were so open to him researching ghosts – not weighing one way or the other concerning their own beliefs but allowing him the latitude to make his own decisions based on the research. Tonight, he decided to focus solely on "ghosts in your home" – infinitely more intriguing than reading up on drafty houses and structural issues. After an extensive play with words in the search bar, Zac found a write-up on unexplained temperature changes that clearly related to ethereal specters. OK, *now* he felt the excitement mount – could this possibly be the answer to their dilemma? Completely engrossed in the article, he read that not only could unexplained temperature changes be attributed to a ghost in residence, but there were other relevant possibilities. The author went on to describe some of these peculiarities and his heart raced as he realized that a couple of these very examples had actually occurred in their home. Zac had simply been unable to find a reasonable explanation – until maybe this point.

He was fully committed now to the entire meat of the article. It began with explaining that ghosts hang out in people's homes because they have unfinished business. It further suggested that the location of your home may be the reason - for example, built on an old grave site or battlefield. It could be that someone who lived in the house previously had passed away here and was not yet ready to move on. It went on to say that there was a ritual many believe can protect your home - put salt down in strategic locations – apparently ghosts cannot pass over the line. He felt a shiver at the possibilities this presented – did someone possibly die here under suspicious circumstances – perhaps gruesome, maybe even murder?

His excitement soared when it described how pets will often begin to act strangely out of character, because they reportedly can see ghostly figures, where humans cannot. Zac deduced that it was likely a sense they had rather than sight. Maybe that was why Daisy was now sleeping in Sway's room. Maybe that was the room that the ghost hung out in most often, so the cat and dog were there to protect Sway. Zac was jarred from his train of thought when he heard his parents come through the door. He was fairly bursting with the need to tell them about what he had learned. This was so cool! Dad would be relieved that they did not have to do any construction on the house. He listened intently to gain a sense his dad's mood – that would be critical. They were very quiet so he couldn't tell - maybe he would test it out with his mom first before talking to dad.

Once he heard him in the shower, he grabbed the opportunity to talk to her alone. He found her in the kitchen, seemingly dazed and confused. "Are you OK Mom?" He felt a lump of fear in his gut at her reply.

"How did I get here?"

"You walked," Zac replied.

"All the way from the hospital?" Zac was really concerned now. When had his mother gone back to the hospital?

"No Mom, from the party. Did something happen at the party? Did you get sick again?" Zac was more than a little frantic. She seemed confused – asking him which party. "The one you went to tonight at the Wilson's," he focused on staying calm. Her bewilderment was paramount and terrified him completely!

"I am hungry," she announced abruptly and moved to cut herself an enormous slice of cake. Zac did not know how to tell his mom that her cake tasted terrible and suggested she might enjoy some of Mrs. Jones' peach cobbler instead.

"Yes," Karen replied, throwing a grateful smile to Zac, "just as soon as I'm finished this cake." In panic mode now, Zac reminded her about her diet and staying away from too many sugary treats. It all fell on deaf ears as she smashed the cake up to her mouth – which stayed firmly shut. Though she made the motions of feeding herself, the cake never got past her closed lips – it was all over her face, mouth and chin, spilling down the front of her beautiful new dress, onto her lap then onto the floor. A sudden icy cold permeated the kitchen. Tears ran freely down her face, mingling with the dark chocolate – reminding him morbidly of the movie "Carrie" which he now fully understood why he was not supposed to have seen. Terror shot through Zac. What was wrong with her?

"Mom, stop! What are you doing?" Her only response was the look or horror on her face – tears streaming over the chocolate mess. He went over and desperately shook her – grabbing her upper arms– to no avail, "Mom, please stop this!"

"What the hell are you doing?" His father had raced into the room, and quickly turned his attention to Karen, who had slumped – lifeless – on the floor. Zac backed up, horrified that he may have hurt his mom. He watched his father take over to resume the shaking, pleading with her to wake up. She slowly came back around but was still disorientated - her eyes glassed over. She peered down at her hands, the cake, and raised her gaze to theirs, a wild-eyed silent plea for help. "How did I get here?" she moaned, trying to wipe the mess of tears from her sticky cheeks. They were all shaking violently in an effort to stay warm as his parents' conversation now parroted the talk that he'd just had with her. Tom told him not to worry and motioned him back to bed. Zac shivered from the cold as he made his way, and suddenly Sway popped into his mind. Fear clutched his innards once more as he rushed into his sister's room. Daisy's low growl registered in his brain as he entered her room. Both pets were on the bed with her, seemingly oblivious to the chill - he could see the moisture from every breath she took, curling into the air like the arms of a sinister demon. Zac quickly retrieved another blanket from his room and returned to lie down beside her on the bed, covering them both - Sway never stirred. He touched her cheek gently, shocked to find it warm amongst the God-awful chill. With a troubled sigh he settled closer under the blanket and allowed Daisy's warmth to provide comfort.

Zac knew he needed to be strong for his sister and mom but couldn't stop the tears rolling down his cheeks. He was deathly afraid for his mom – his family! What was going on? A glance at his sister's night table revealed two business cards – Hope and Faith. Reluctantly he left the warm shelter to grab the wireless phone from the kitchen – his parents nowhere in sight.

Ignoring the automatic chastising tone from the inner voice that warned him it was far too late in the evening, he dialed Hope's number - she was the only person other than his mom that he would dare talk to, and he sensed that she would understand. As he waited for Hope to pick up, he positioned himself on an easy chair at the far end of the living room - the farthest point from his parent's bedroom, the room temperature returned to normal. Relief flooded him at the sound of Hope's greeting, her voice suggesting she was wide awake, almost as if waiting.

"Sorry to phone you so late at night, Hope, but I did not know who else to call," Zac's anxiety was evident in his voice.

"That's OK," Hope assured, "what's wrong Zac, is everything OK?" she urged, and he instantly fell to pieces – wishing he could physically melt into her embrace.

"No, things are not OK," Zac whimpered through his tears, "something is wrong with my mom, and I think it has something to do with ghosts," he blurted out.

"What gives you that thought?" Hope asked gently.

"Well, my pets are acting funny, as if they are protecting Sway from something. Then there is my mom, she is acting different and tonight when she came back with my dad, she did not know how she got home. She mentioned being at the hospital, but I do not think she was there," Zac choked back a renewed onslaught of tears, feeling embarrassed and wishing he could gain control of his emotions.

"I can hear in your voice that you are very scared for your mom," Hope soothed in a soft empathetic tone. "I'm sorry that I'm unable to tell you why or what is going on with your mom, but I can recommend something that you can do to help her."

"What is it?" Zac was desperate for help - just hearing Hope's voice created a calming balm.

"I want you to go and get your blanket and sleep by your mom's bed just like you do for Sway," Hope encouraged.

"But Dad is there, and he won't like that," Zac trusted Hope but was more afraid of his father's wrath.

"Don't worry about your dad - your mom sounds very confused right now – that can be so scary - and having you there will help her. Just reassure her that everything is OK and if your dad wakes and minds you being there, then just explain how you just want to be by your mom to comfort her - I am sure he will understand," Hope assured Zac, who was trying to wrap his head around the situation. After a brief pause, she softly continued "I have to go now but you can call me at any time, no matter what time of day it is." Zac thanked her profusely and pressed the "end call" button, feeling less panicked and wondering what he would have done without her. Listening for any strange sounds in the now warm house, he guessed that the ghost must have gone to sleep or simply left – do ghosts need to sleep? Calmer now, he shuffled to the kitchen, hung up the phone and retrieved the box of salt from the pantry – he hoped that normal table salt was OK. Back in his sister's room, he began to spread a line of salt, starting at her doorway, then on to the windowsill. Deep in concentration, he finished with a ring around the entire bed.

In the hallway, he poked his head into his parents' room to find them both sound asleep. Zac heaved a huge sigh of relief as he padded off to get his pillow and blanket and quietly returned to lay it on the floor beside his mother. Then very quietly, so not to wake his father, he repeated the salt ritual and settled into his makeshift bed, the pillow and blanket inside the circle of salt. He reached up and gently took his mother's hand. As her eyes fluttered open, he whispered that everything was going to be OK.

Tears flowed down her cheeks. "I am scared," she whispered to her son. Zac knew his mother must be really afraid because she never expressed any concerns with her children. She used to tell Zac whenever he asked if anything was wrong, that everything was OK and if it was not, then it is the parent's job to worry. His job was to enjoy being a kid, and that there will be time enough for him to fret when he becomes an adult.

"It is OK Mom," Zac whispered back, giving her hand a little squeeze. Zac lifted himself up, so he was partially on the bed. His mother reached out and stroked his head. It felt so good and familiar.

"I don't know why I hurt all over," his mother whispered.

"It is because you have been working so hard to get better, it makes your muscles hurt," Zac explained in a whisper. His mother looked confused. Her tears continued to flow. Zac took the corner of the sheet on the bed and wiped his mother's tears away. His mother gave him a weak smile. Zac's father gave a little snort and Zac giggled. In the moonlight, he could see the corners of her lips lift in a smile, and it boosted his spirits.

"Your father must be worried about me," she whispered to Zac as she noticed Tom's arm around her.

"We are all worried mom, but we will beat this, you're going to get better."

"I feel a little lost and confused but I am sure it will pass." Karen offered another brave smile.

"Maybe I can help, what are you confused about?" Zac prompted.

"I don't want to worry you."

"I am already worried," Zac responded and gave his mother his best reassuring smile, "but you talking to me might help both of us, so we don't worry quite as much," Zac reasoned.

Karen pondered this. "How did I get home from the hospital - I don't remember anything since the doctor told me I had a heart attack."

"Probably because you have been overdoing it," Zac explained, but his heart thudded with uneasiness. "Dad said you were deprived of oxygen to your brain when you had the heart attack so you may act different or things may seem strange," Zac whispered.

"Oh," said his mother, still looking perplexed. "How did I get home?"

"We brought you home in our car weeks ago," Zac explained softly.

"Weeks ago?" Her eyes grew wide in alarm. Oh my God, where had she been since then? Why couldn't she remember?

"Yes, the doctors gave you a list of things you had to do to get ready for your new heart. That is why you hurt all over, you have been walking and running, eating different foods, cooking without tasting - which by the way, you may want to do a little more of. You are a much better cook when you try it first," Zac explained.

"Oh," his mother said in a questioning tone?

"Yes, good thing you didn't put your cake in your mouth, it tasted awful."

"Really?"

"Yes," Zac was really feeling badly for her now. "Why didn't you open your mouth when you were eating the cake?"

"I don't know what happened," she mused, in a hushed tone. "I was hungry, but when I tried to eat, I could not open my mouth, it was like something was holding it shut."

"That sounds scary," Zac validated.

"Yes, it was and is - not remembering anything is scary but I am sure my memory will come back."

"Yes, it will," Zac assured her. "Then you'll remember all the good things that happened these past weeks."

"There were lots of good things?" she asked.

"Yes, mom – for sure," Zac repeated, "and don't you worry anymore, everything will be OK," he was determined to provide some reassurance and kept his tone hushed, not wanting to wake his dad. Tom started to stir, and Zac slid back onto the floor outside of his father's range of vision. Both he and Karen remained absolutely still, as they listened to his dad's breathing. Once Zac was sure his father was once again sleeping soundly, he reached back up and held his mother's hand. "Close your eyes," he whispered, "I'll look after you, Mom."

"My little man," she murmured, then ran her fingers through his hair again. Zac held very still, enjoying being close to his mother and the sensation her touch was providing. When it stopped, and her breathing had changed, Zac knew she had fallen asleep. He was far from sleepy at this point. Pondering over the events of the evening, he reflected on the vibrant energy his mom had as she'd gone out to the party - dressed so beautifully and carrying herself with such grace. It was like she had a new lease on life, as if the heart attack had significantly altered her perspective on living.

Heck, even his parents were different together! Maybe that is what life and death situations create, new attitudes that help people make changes. There are some things that Zac liked about the changes in his home, yet other things he missed - Daisy sleeping in his bed; her total devotion to him. With a deep sigh he conceded that life was simply complicated – how was that for an oxymoron? Then there was the issue with the ghost – he was at a total loss on that one. Zac ran through his mind all he had read on the subject. He hoped the salt ritual would keep his family safe, but at the same time, other than the horrible chill and the pets acting strange, there was no real reason to be concerned for their safety. Maybe that was because the pets were keeping them safe, Zac thought to himself.

Hearing his dad stir again, he listened to his mother's breathing - sounded peaceful. He ever so gently pulled his hand from her grasp, took his pillow and blanket and snuck back into his sister's room. Zac put his blanket down beside Sway's bed, inside the circle of salt. Daisy moved and curled up to him and they both drifted off peacefully. No one noticed, as they slumbered, the ice that formed outside the salt borders that Zac had so carefully constructed.

Chapter 19

SWAY WOKE WITH a sleepy smile to Daisy jumping all over her. Karen and the pup had just returned from their morning jog. Her senses kicking in, she could hear the shower going in both bathrooms. Pushing her pets aside, she climbed out of bed and as her bare feet touched the carpeted floor, felt the shock from unmistakable dampness. She gave both of her pets the stink eye and voiced allowed that they better not have peed on her floor. As she surveyed the carpet, curiosity took over - a white fine-grained substance trailed all the way around her bed. Hearing her brother exit the bathroom, she madly dashed to take the space before anyone else got to it – lest she peed on the carpet herself – whew!

On her way back from the bathroom she noticed her brother seated at his bedroom desk reading his notebook. She took the liberty of going in to see what it was and to inform him of the mystery in her room. Zac looked up and greeted her with a smile. "I have white stuff on my floor, and my carpet is wet, what could have happened?" Sway asked.

"Yes, it's just salt that I put around your bed to protect you," Zac explained.

"Protect me from what?" Sway squeaked. Since his mother had already mentioned ghosts to her, Zac thought it was OK to share what he knew. Having things to accomplish before breakfast, he quickly showed his sister the pages on which he'd written notes where she could read up on the salt ritual. Sway too, was an avid reader – her literacy level far beyond her grade, and eagerly took her brother's place to peruse his suggestions. She surmised that Zac put salt on the floor because he believed that there may be a ghost in their house. If that was so, then who might it be? Could it be one of their grandparents or someone who lived in their house before? Sway was intrigued and took the book out to the kitchen table to continue, while she ate breakfast. As she glanced through more of the pages, she wished there were pictures – that always helped. Though Zac's printing was pretty neat – for a boy, there were some big adult words he'd copied that she was struggling a little with.

She sensed her mother's presence in the room, a split second before Karen asked her what she was reading, and Sway eagerly offered to share the book. Karen grabbed a cup of coffee, prepared scrambled eggs and a full breakfast plate for both kids, throwing two pieces of bread in the toaster before settling down at the table. She had no sooner set their plates down and started perusing the book, when Zac joined them. Karen got up to butter the toast and listened intently to Zac explain to Sway the reason he'd put the line of salt around her bed last night. Zac glanced at his mom, and she gave him the nod to go ahead and tell his sister – he'd already filled his mom in when he decided to join her on the morning run. "Well, you know when the house gets so cold that we can see our breath?" Zac began. Sway nodded. "That very thing happened last night while you all were sleeping. I had read in the online article, that salt keeps spirits away, so I put a circle of salt around yours and Mom and Dad's bed and I noticed it held the cold out. Daisy and I slept by your bed inside the circle of salt, and we all stayed warm," Zac explained.

Sway looked up and questioned, "Who do you think the ghost is, Mom?" Karen smiled affectionately.

"I am not sure that we have a ghost, but we can keep an eye out. Your brother tells me the research implies that the icy cold is only one indication and that there needs to be several other factors in play before we can assume it's likely a ghost."

"But what else could it be?" Sway mused.

"That's the million-dollar question - whatever it may be, I'm sure it is nothing to worry about," Karen soothed, "and Zac - fantastic job with the salt!" Zac beamed and continued to munch on his breakfast. The doorbell rang and Daisy barked a greeting as she romped eagerly to the door. Sway followed and returned to the table with Hope in tow. She *so* enjoyed being the little host and eagerly poured their guest a cup of coffee. Hope offered Zac a ride to school and said she was going to take Sway on a little outing as their mother had medical appointments to deal with. Though a part of him wished he could spend another day with them all, Zac swallowed his last bite of breakfast and went to get his things for school – he knew exactly what his mom needed from him.

Once the three of them were in the car, Hope glanced at the kids and quietly spoke. "Has anyone yet spoken to you about how to handle things if your mom were to have another heart attack?" Both children shook their heads negatively, wide-eyed. "I don't mean to raise any concerns or alarm you, but it's important that you are prepared for the off chance that it may occur. If your mother goes unconscious or complains of chest pains, remember to immediately call 911. She may become disoriented and not know where she is. Just reassure her and try and keep her lying down until help arrives." Hope looked over at their frightened expressions, and continued with a reassuring smile, "OK? Do you understand? It's going to be fine, as long as we all do what is necessary to keep her safe." Zac asked Hope what she meant by being disoriented. Hope clarified that it was common for people who have had heart attacks to lose short-term memory on what has happened in the past days - even months, "Do not worry if your mother is confused and does not remember things. Don't try to explain things to her, just tell her everything is fine, and that you have called 911. Keeping her calm is your job now."

Although Hope had urged them not to worry, it seemed an impossible feat. Zac then informed Hope all about what happened after he had gotten off the phone with her the night of the party - how his mother had lost track of time and could not remember things. Hope assured them that it was normal. Zac said his dad had mentioned that his mom should not be doing so much, like partaking in her morning runs. Hope repeated there was no need for alarm and that Karen's body would send messages, letting her know if she was doing too much. After dropping Zac off at school Hope drove straight to the hospital.

"Why are we here?" Sway queried. Hope explained that she was going to teach her some really cool and special techniques, as she led them into the hospital garden. They sat down on a bench under a big elm tree and Hope took both of Sway's hands in her own.

"Sweetie, do you ever wonder why you get sick as often as you do?" Sway nodded. "Have you ever heard of a person being called an empath," Hope asked? Sway shook her head. "Well, an empath is someone who can feel other people's feelings - like when they are not feeling well," Hope explained. Sway nodded her head. "You know what I am talking about, right?"

"Yes, but I didn't know what that was called," Sway explained that sometimes when she feels sick, she also feels it in other people around her, such as her classmates, her family and even strangers. "Doesn't everybody feel like I do? They don't all get sick like me." She mused. Hope squeezed her hand gently.

"No, very few people are like you, Sway. You have a gift and when used correctly you can help people tremendously, but you have had no one to teach you how to use this gift, and if it's not used properly, it can make you extremely sick."

Tears welled up in Sway's eyes as she said, "One of the nurses accused my mom of deliberately making me sick or making me pretend I was sick. It was making mommy so scared and sad that I was ill all the time. Is that what's wearing out her heart?" Sway burst out crying. Hope reached out and held the little girl close.

"Oh no, Sway, your mommy's heart condition is something she was born with – I promise. But I am sure many times that you have been sick, it was because your mom was not feeling well. Can you understand that now?" Hope leaned down to her ear and whispered, "I am going to teach you how to deal with the feelings that aren't your own – the ones that specifically come from others, and you will learn how *not* to take them into your own body. Does that sound like a good plan?" At Sway's fervent nod, Hope continued, "Now close your eyes and just try to relax – you are completely safe here with me," Sway did as she was bid. "Now concentrate on the feelings of the person closest to you, beyond where I am – physically." At first Sway could only feel pain in her leg which got worse the more she practiced and shared this aloud with Hope. "Which leg is it?" Hope asked.

"My right," Sway cried, in considerable pain, but relieved that it wasn't in her tummy as usual. Hope put her hands over Sway's leg, and the pain seemed to mysteriously disappear – Sway's eyes grew wide. Now she could feel – sense – the other person, "It's a man. I think he has broken his leg."

"Very good," Hope praised, "now pull your feelings back." She squeezed Sway's hand, "Keep your eyes closed, I want you to imagine a magnificent golden light - the colour of bright sunflowers. Now take that golden light and direct it ahead of your feelings, to the man with the hurt leg - feel that golden light all around him." It took Sway a little time but once she had created the practice of controlling her feelings the way Hope described – got the hang of it - she could actually *feel* the man and wrapped him in the golden light – this was seriously cool! Sway smiled, keeping her eyes closed.

"The man no longer feels any pain!" Sway was excited!

"Very good," Hope praised her again. "Now imagine that golden light flowing into the ground and going to sleep. Then pull your feelings back into yourself once you know the golden light is fast asleep." As Sway followed Hope's instructions she felt and imagined the pain of the man's injury going into the ground. As the golden light slept, she was able to let it go and pull her feelings back without bringing anything with it. Sway smiled. Sway heard Hope softly whisper, "Now you can open your eyes." Sway beamed with delight.

"That is so awesome!" she gushed joyously. "Can we do it again?" There was a distinct change of energy, and her cheeks were glowing rosy – Hope was encouraged by the healthy vibes coming off the little girl. She had caught onto this pretty quickly for her age – the power in this one is strong, Hope mused.

"Yes, we can practice a few more – it will be necessary in order to learn how to manage your fears, but we must be careful not to play you out. It is only when your energy reserves are high that it is possible to do this. It is like a flashlight with batteries as their light source. As you use up the power in the batteries the light goes dim until they are recharged. If the power in the batteries is completely diminished, then the light goes out. That can be extremely dangerous for you because the other's sickness or pain will stay with you," Hope explained. "Know that I will ensure you are with me at all times during this practice – tell me you will not do so unless I am here!" At Sway's buoyant nod, she continued, "Do not worry – soon it will become a part of your nature."

Sway closed her eyes and found another patient in the hospital - a little boy who had cancer. It amazed her how easily the knowledge flowed into her consciousness! She focused on wrapping him in the golden light and this time her body did not feel his pain and nausea, although she sensed and saw it -knew it was there. Sway stayed there with him for a while to help, enjoying the feel of his body relax, pain disappear, and her inherent insight that for the first time since his treatments, the young lad did not *feel* sick. Sway was aware that his mother was sitting with him. Sway could feel the hope well up inside of her as her young son asked for the fruit on his tray that he'd had no appetite for before. She cut an apple in small pieces and fed it to him, and Sway could feel his pleasure in the sweet taste of the apple. Hope's whispered words invaded her consciousness - remember your batteries. Holding on for just one more moment, she let the golden light sink into the hospital floor and lay asleep. Sway pulled her feelings back and opened her eyes.

"Just one more, please, this is so much fun and I *am* helping." Her excitement intensified the earnest plea.

"Yes, you are," Hope confirmed with a smile. This time Sway closed her eyes and searched for Hope's mother and was discouraged when she could not find her. Touching from one person to the next, she could feel exhaustion seeping in.

"OK, enough - time to come back." At Hope's directive, Sway pulled back, cold creeping into her bones. Hope saw the icy mist of her breath and felt her little body shaking, then enwrapped Sway into her arms - drawing the cold from the little one's body. Sway opened her eyes, a bit alarmed to see that Hope was now shivering – with the same conditions. Momentarily it simply passed as her favourite nurse opened her eyes and smiled.

"Now I need you to promise me something," Hope pulled back from Sway and looked directly into her eyes. "This is very serious - you will not do this unless I am with you. If you feel sick, I want you use the golden light to help you push the feeling into the ground and let it go - not look for where it is coming from, do you understand?" Hope demanded.

"But why," Sway asked? "I know I can help people now and can make sure my energy is not low."

"Until you have had enough practice and get much older, your gift has an immense power that can hurt you. I also need your word that you will not talk to *anyone* about this gift - you are to keep it between only us," Hope stated emphatically.

"Not even my mom and dad or my brother?" Sway beseeched.

"For now, not even them," Hope replied.

"But my mom said I am not to keep secrets from them," Sway cried, tears welling up in her eyes – she was especially fearful to disobey her parents.

"Sweetie, that is absolutely true for everything except this," Hope explained. "What do they say about gifts? This is a gift you need to keep secret. It is a gift you have for the world that needs to be nurtured and kept safe, like a baby kitty or puppy." Sway's tears stopped, and her face took on a beaming glow at the implications that she could actually make a difference in this world.

"I get it, when I have a gift for some one, I keep it a secret until they receive it, just like a birthday or Christmas!" Sway exclaimed.

"Something like that, yes," Hope confirmed, *"but even when you give the gift to someone like you did today, you still can't tell them."* At the little girl's look of confusion, she continued, *"I know this is hard to understand Sway, but you must trust me!"* Hope stood up, *"time to get you back home, I have faith in you - I know deep down you understand, and will keep this gift a secret,"* Hope smiled gently and reached down to take her hand as they walked back to her car. Sway felt a bubbling joy well up inside of her and was so glad that her mommy had made friends with Hope – she felt so happy and relaxed with her – somehow their secret added to it all. Sway was excited about her gift and looked forward to practicing with Hope again soon. It was

a short drive back and Sway skipped from the car to the house, hoping to snag another play day with her mom. That had been so much fun! Her mom and the pets were waiting.

"How was your outing with Hope?" Karen prompted.

"It was fun, but I can't tell you," Sway blurted out, knowing instinctively that it was the wrong thing to say and was immensely relieved when her mother only laughed.

"You don't have to worry about telling me about the things you do with Hope, but she is the absolute only exception, right?" Sway nodded emphatically; grateful she wasn't being forced to divulge the secret. Hope informed them that she had to visit her mother in the hospital, so Sway gave her a big hug and thanked her for the outing. Hope waved goodbye and left just as the phone rang. Sway could tell it was her father on the phone – something about the inflection in her mom's voice always gave it away.

After Karen hung up, she asked Sway if she could quickly go over to Mrs. Jones'. "Would it be OK if you hang out with her for a bit while I go meet with your dad?" Sway ran off and informed the sweet, kind lady of her mom's plans; Mrs. Jones was always delighted to have Sway's company, and instantly rang Karen to tell her it was fine. The elderly lady loved to paint – one of the many things they enjoyed doing together. She gathered up all the paint supplies and set Sway up at the kitchen table. The little girl's forehead furrowed in consternation as she contemplated the subject of her artistic endeavor – it had to be special, for a special day!

"What are you thinking about so seriously? Mrs. Jones asked curiously.

"I am not sure yet what to make," Sway mused.

"How about putting a group of colours together that show how your current emotions - like a feeling picture."

"That sounds like fun," Sway responded exuberantly. Mrs. Jones set to baking and for the next few hours Sway poured all her creativity into her picture. Once completed, she beamed with a sense of pride.

Ms. Jones came up from behind her. "Oh my, this is beautiful! Now tell me about your picture, Sway," Sway's heart swelled at the praise. "What does the red represent?" Mrs. Jones prodded the conversation.

"That represents my mommy's new heart," Sway explained, moving her finger along the creation. "The gold is the magic that makes her heart strong and better."

"What about the black?" Mrs. Jones encouraged. Sway's expression was thoughtful.

"The black is the sickness put back into the ground," Sway stated. Mrs. Jones chose not to inquire further, knowing this little girl had a lot on her plate right now. They both quietly admired every aspect of Sway's masterpiece, and Mrs. Jones then carefully placed it to one side to dry while they snacked on the scrumptious cookies she had just taken out of the oven. She nudged Sway to chat about Karen - was she was worried about her mother getting a new heart?

Sway smiled confidently, "No, my mom will get one soon." Mrs. Jones returned the smile - yes, she did believe too, that Karen would receive her donor heart in time. After all, she was an angel put into this world and it did not make sense why the Lord would take her home this soon, when Mrs. Jones was certain there was so much more for her to accomplish. Karen and her beautiful children had been a God send to a once very lonely old woman, she gratefully thought to herself. The gold inflections in Sway's picture reminded her of the light that this family had bestowed upon her. No, it did not make sense that Karen would die so young, Mrs. Jones reassured herself.

Stealing a glance now at Sway's beautiful picture, the kindly lady gasped. The black color had run all through the red and gold, creating an eerie foreboding spectacle. She distracted Sway for a moment, moving the picture strategically out of the little girl's sight, then bumped her coffee cup so it spilled over the paper to hide the change. "Oh, I am so sorry," her distress was genuine.

"It is OK," Sway offered generously, "I'll just paint another one." Mrs. Jones felt an icy cold permeate through to her bones, and the dread that she'd been feeling since Karen's heart attack, crept in again. What if she did not get her donor heart in time? What would become of Karen's beautiful children? She knew that their father was not in a position to provide emotional stability for such a loss. With a heavy heart, she gave Sway a gentle squeeze.

Chapter 20

WHEN TOM ROSE in the morning from a rare peaceful slumber, Karen had already left for her morning jog. He noticed the carpet was damp by the bed – what the hell? When he saw the water at the ensuite door, he reasonably summed it up as a result of Karen's bath the previous night – it had certainly been eventful! Unlike in Sway's room, the salt had dissolved into the water and carpet, so he was completely oblivious to Zac's protection ritual. Tom downed a quick cup of coffee and some toast before heading out the door. He was just about to get into his car when Hope pulled up. Waiting a moment to say hello, he instantly saw her distress - evident by the puffy redness in her eyes.

"Are you OK?" He felt genuine concern for this kind young nurse.

Yes, rough night – almost lost my mom," His compassion surfaced at the sight of fresh tears welling up.

"Oh, I am so sorry!" Hope smiled gratefully at his empathetic tone. "How is she feeling today – our family stuff can wait - go be with your mom."

"Thank you, I am spending every moment that I can with her."

"That is good," Tom assured, "so important!" He wished her the best outcome and headed out to get on with his day. Work was not his destination now though, as he headed straight to the hospital for a long overdue conversation with Karen's doctor. He needed to gain some understanding of what was going on with Karen's health and if there was anything that should be done to address it. The receptionist explained that since he had no appointment and was not a patient, he would have to wait until one of the doctors had a spare minute. "That is fine," Tom assured the receptionist - he would wait.

Hours later, he was finally granted an audience with a doctor and was ushered into the same room where the family consult had taken place. He could hear the resounding echo of their voices, laying out the recommended changes that would need to take place to ensure Karen's good health. Tom was immensely relieved to see Dr. Hamilton breeze in, reaching out to shake Tom's hand - clearly very busy. Dr. Hamilton quickly addressed the protocol whereby family meetings only occur with the patient present.

"Karen's present health condition dictates that she is mentally competent to make decisions for herself and I truly regret that I am, therefore, not at liberty to discuss the details of Karen's case without her written permission or her physical presence." Tom reflected for a moment before replying – he liked this man, finding him to be very genuine and to the point.

"What if I give you some pertinent information - then you can decide where we go from here, and I will respect your choice?" The doctor sighed and studied him, before nodding his agreement. Tom wasted no time in commencing a candid summary of the recent changes in Karen's behavior – totally out of character – morning runs, sudden interest in their sex life – forwardness and orgasms, cooking, odd behavior and physical changes – almost like a totally different person. Tom addressed his main concern that she may have suffered brain damage from her heart attacks and quickly summarized by describing the details of the previous night's incident; her attempt at stuffing food into her firmly closed mouth; the resulting mess and her ensuing confusion when she surfaced from what Tom deduced could only be described as some sort of medical episode.

The doctor glanced at his watch. "Where is Karen right now?"

"I believe at home," Tom responded.

"Well, why don't you go get her, and I will meet you both back here in one hour – I can examine her and if your wife agrees, I will share my findings with you both."

Thank you – this is much appreciated," Tom responded as he jumped from his seat to go pick Karen up. As soon as he exited the hospital doors, he called her - she picked up in just two rings. "Where are you?" he queried.

"At home," Karen answered. "Is everything OK?"

"I am calling to let you know the doctor wants to see you right now for a check-up," Tom blurted out hastily.

"Well, why did he not call *me*?" Karen pondered.

"Not sure," Tom fabricated, "but I am on my way to pick you up - be there in five minutes." He hung up the phone before there were any further questions, feeling the now familiar niggling guilt for yet another untruth that he admittedly was becoming entirely uncomfortable with. He reasoned that this time, at least, it was for her own well-being. By the time he arrived at the house, Karen had already sent Sway over to Mrs. Jones and left a note on the table for Zac letting him know where she'd be. It was a quick ride back to the hospital and although the doctor had said to come back in an hour, Karen was able to see Dr. Hamilton right away. Meanwhile, Tom had been given no choice but to wait in the Emergency room. He stopped by the vending machine to grab a coffee and paused - the exact spot where the old woman had caught him red-handed, with lipstick smeared on his face.

"Is everything OK Tom?" He turned to the welcome sound of Hope's familiar voice.

"Yes, just a follow up visit with the doctor."

Hope sighed in relief, "Thank goodness - when I saw you, I thought perhaps something was wrong with Karen or one of the kids."

"How is you mother?" Tom offered.

"Back in a coma," she replied. Tom's compassion reigned at the fresh flood of tears.

"Oh, I am sorry to hear that," Tom responded in an empathetic tone. Hope got herself a coffee from the vending machine as well. She took a seat just across from him, straightened and sighed.

"How are the children doing?"

"Very well," Tom assured, and Hope smiled.

"Yes, we had a lovely time together the other day and I learned significant information about ghosts from Zac on our expedition to the library."

"Oh? I did not know you spent time with Zac."

"Well not just Zac - I spent the day with your entire family, as I took Karen to her appointments, lunch and then the library," Hope explained. Tom refrained from asking any more questions. It explained the new dress Karen had worn last night, and a few other things he'd been missing, but he preferred that outsiders were not aware of anything that he might not have full knowledge or control over, when it concerned his family and household. Hope finished her coffee, bid Tom a good day and went back to spend time with her mother. Soon after a nurse came to escort him to the meeting room where Karen and Dr. Hamilton were waiting.

"Come in Tom," the doctor invited with a reassuring smile and motioned him to a chair beside his wife. "Karen has given me permission to provide you with enough information to ease your concerns. Most importantly, I have found the state of Karen's current health to be extraordinarily well in light of the situation – such improved, that I am reinstating her driving permit!" Tom was a little dumbfounded at Dr. Hamilton's conclusion, to say the least, and could only stare as he continued.

"Your wife has dropped an amazing amount of weight, with apparently no ill effects, which I understand is from diet and exercise. She has taken all our of recommendations literally to heart. I wish that all of our patients were as diligent with taking responsibility for their health. And her newfound interest in your marital sex life frankly lends much weight to her health and wellness, and I am sure you are enjoying those benefits, Mr. Shorn." He grinned at them both and patted Tom's shoulder. There was no arguing that reality and Tom nodded his head. With this Dr. Hamilton stood up, signalling the conclusion of their meeting and handed Karen the certificate declaring her medically fit to drive. Leaning in to take Karen's hand, he spoke quietly. "My great hope is that we will have a new heart for you soon." After turning to shake Tom's hand with a grin, he quickly exited the room. Tom had remained astoundingly quiet through the whole session.

"This is amazing!" Karen beamed as she peered down at the paper that would reinstate her independence. Tom was engulfed with instantaneous anger.

"Did you tell him about last night where you were confused – thought you should be at the hospital, and the cake you smeared all over your face and everywhere else?" He snapped testily.

"I am doing well Tom, why can't you just be happy with that?" Karen riled back as she rose abruptly and left the room, "I will get myself home, thank you." Tom sat for a moment, watching her march away, unsure of what to do. The doctor obviously had not paid any attention to what he'd said. Jean's words about lack of oxygen to the brain often causing irreversible damage made sense to him – why hadn't the doctor addressed this? They'd had to revive her two times when her heart stopped, for Christ's sake! But what did he know, he thought sarcastically? Recognizing his lack of influence on any of this, the helpless feeling prevailed and the only place he could think to go at this moment was back to work. He knew Karen would find her way home.

By the time he arrived at the dealership, it was almost quitting time. The receptionist advised him that Mrs. Thompson had requested to see him when and if he came in today. There was an emphasis on the *if*. Oh Lord, he'd forgotten to call in to advise that he would be arriving late today. He thanked her for the message and headed to Jean's office, wondering what was in store and feeling resentment at the 'walking on eggshells' effect Jean constantly held over him.

"Come on in Tom," Jean responded at his quick rap on the door. She motioned him in and asked that he close the door behind him to which he complied and took a seat in front of her desk.

"What's up?" He watched her closely as she took a deep breath.

"First, I want to apologize for my behavior at Sharon's party last night and please *do* pass my regrets to Karen." Tom put his hand up.

"No worries, we all get foolish sometimes when we are drinking." His tone was conciliatory, but Jean shook her head emphatically in disagreement.

"Let me finish," her tone quiet and controlled. "Now, I would like to discuss the partnership agreement between the two of us, and the terms with which we will buy Doug's share of the company." She paused to ascertain his total attention. "You and I will carry a fifty-fifty split - I can lend the funds to you for your share of the down payment." Tom squirmed in his chair, and keen to his discomfort, Jean hurried on, "You do not have to worry about anything - I will handle all the necessary bank negotiations." Tom's hand shot out to interrupt.

"Why are you doing this?" Alarm bells were ringing somewhere in his brain and his suspicious nature kicked into full gear. "Jean, you are aware that I know nothing about running a business. Karen is smart, yes – she may be able to shed light on the legal end of things, but has no business experience, nor does she hold any knowledge on selling or fixing cars."

Jean rose, came out from her side of her desk, grabbed a second chair, and sat down right beside him. She pointedly took his hand in a gentle and consoling manner. "Tom listen. I hate to be the one to bring this up to you, but everyone – you seemingly the exception - knows that the odds of Karen receiving a donor heart in time, are practically zero. The reality is that you are going to be a single parent soon and be solely responsible for raising your two children. How do you think you can do that on a mechanic's salary with daycare costs, etc.?" Her tone softened further, "Tom, I am not only bestowing a favour here - but I also truly believe we would forge a good partnership together and that fifty percent propriety in this business will afford you the opportunity to provide for your kids with ease, once Karen is gone."

Jean's words bit into his heart and soul, and he pushed back his chair to put distance between them. He did not want to hear what she was saying about Karen. Reflecting on this proposal, his first response had been of gratitude and flattery that Jean would even entertain him as a viable candidate for partnership in the business. Quickly though, his doubts had risen – what was her angle? Jean always had an agenda. Now, more than ever, Tom felt a foreboding sense of unease. For the moment, he set aside the angst from the possibility of losing Karen, to focus on the critical need for clarification. "Who would carry the loan?"

"Well, you would, of course, but the monthly profits provide more than enough cash flow to handle that payment, and more" Jean emphasized. Doug and I currently own this business outright. I will pay him my fifty percent through our agreement and yours he will receive from the funds you borrow from me – you will simply just pay me back, through the bank arrangement." Jean clarified.

"Why not just do this on your own? You do not need me," Tom reasoned.

"Yes, I do," her soft tone inferred sincerity, "As I said, I am firmly convinced that we will make great business partners, Tom, and this way I can avoid the restrictions and interest costs from a bank business loan for the full purchase price." she added. Tom was puzzled.

"But there *would* be a business loan," he argued, "what do you think the bank will want for collateral and assurance on the portion I am borrowing from you?" Jean stood up and sat on the edge of the desk and continued her conversation in a quiet empathetic manner.

"I told you, Tom, I will look after everything, but since you asked - I know this is very distasteful to say right now, but we need to accept and operate in the here and now - the real world, not fantasy." Jean shifted in her chair and straightened. "I took the liberty to investigate your wife's life insurance policy – Tom, it carries a one-million-dollar payout - Karen is a smart cookie because she set it up to ensure that you both had adequate coverage to land in a comfortable financial position, should one of you pass. Tom, when she dies - and she will soon – policy payout will be sufficient to pay off all your debts, *including this business loan*," Jean explained. "Hell, you will be able to send your kids to college – buy them homes and vehicles – set them up in life."

"For crying out loud!" Tom was enraged now, "What kind of heartless person are you?"

"Settle down, Tom," Jean instructed in a sterner tone, then she softened again. Wasn't she just a little too calm about this? How long had she been planning? "Listen Tom, I know this is hard for you to have to sort through. I cannot imagine what it is like to think about losing the mother of your children. But I did not conjure the idea to research the life insurance policies on my own steam," Jean provided. "To be honest, I overheard your coworkers commenting on the possibility of Karen's death – how they hoped you carried adequate insurance to handle raising your kids alone," Jean paused for effect, "now, do you honestly believe that is heartless? Tom, these are people who care about you – are worrying about you and your kids." Jean stopped to give Tom the opportunity to let it all sink in.

He got up and paced back and forth, dragging his hands through his hair in agitation - he felt a vice-grip headache coming on. He knew in his soul that the odds were against Karen's survival but did not want to face it – money be damned – it meant nothing! Jean sat in silence, watching him closely. Tom sat back down, focusing on his lap, deep in thought.

"I need you to decide soon," Jean stated, with finality. "I've already talked to the bank - I want you to go down and speak to this individual." Jean handed him a business card – he had noticed it on her desk earlier. Taking the card, he rose, thanked her, and departed her office – his expression unreadable. Inwardly, Tom felt nausea threatening, and his head was pounding unbearably. He glanced at his watch – a bit too early to go home. He headed out to his car and called the number on the card. A male voice answered instantly, commenting that he'd been expecting Tom's call and could see him, right away if he was free. Why not? What did he have to lose? It would give him the opportunity to deal with this once and for all. Pulling out, he noticed the police car parked just up the street from the dealership and made a firm mental note to himself to keep his speed in check.

The bank was just closing when he got there. The receptionist introduced him to Mr. Rice, the Business Loans Manager, and ushered him into a stark clean office. Mr. Rice offered Tom a drink and he deferred to a glass of water. The receptionist brought in the water, advising Mr. Rice that she was leaving - security was locking up and would let them both out when their meeting concluded. Mr. Rice thanked her politely and wished her a pleasant evening. Tom felt a nudge of apprehension with the confined isolation and felt the need to get to the point.

"I am not sure where to start, but perhaps you could provide some clarification on this arrangement." He noticed the bank employee presented as cool and confident, as he nodded his agreement.

"Taking on a business venture like this can feel a bit overwhelming but with Mrs. Thompson as your future business partner, I am certain this will come together to benefit you both." Tom noticed him reach for a file containing documentation that was clearly prepared for this very meeting. Tom suddenly wished in earnest that Karen was here with him. She was good with numbers - could always see the big picture and was totally detail-orientated, never missing the implications within the fine print. The realization hit him, that he'd never given her credit for any of this – always taking full control over their decisions, considering her input as dealing with minor details that he had no time for.

Mr. Rice made a point of informing Tom that Jean had done all the leg work which included a viable business plan. She'd provided the last five-year financials from the business, Tom's relative income, as well as an outline for the arrangement they would provide Tom for his share of the down payment and the structure for the repayment of the business loan. What Tom needed to provide was a statement, outlining his current assets and liabilities.

Tom glanced at the papers placed in front of him. "Listen, I would like to take all of this home and have my wife go through it with me." Mr. Rice looked a little surprised - perhaps uncomfortable? He quickly recovered.

"I am sorry, but as this is to be kept confidential – strictly between employees only, until the end of this month, you will not be at liberty to share it with your wife, at this point in time. I suggest that we get everything in order and once it is all approved you can then go over it with her." Tom was not comfortable with this.

"That does not make sense to me – my wife should be a part of any decision that I undertake – certainly signing of documentation. We are partners, first and foremost!"

Mr. Rice shifted in his chair. "I completely understand your position, Tom, but I want to explain that your wife will not be involved in this arrangement in any way - the sole proprietors of this business will be you and Mrs. Thompson. If anything should happen to either one of you, the share of proprietorship will automatically go to the other. Those are the conditions Mrs. Thompson has put into place."

Tom's discomfort increased. "Is this normal?" he queried? "That my wife would not receive any profits or benefits from my investment into this business, should I pass?"

"Yes, in business this is often the way it's set up," Mr. Rice confirmed. He then went on to say, "So, let us go over your assets and liabilities, and I already have your employment income verification from what Mrs. Thompson provided." Tom noticed him pull out another reference document which included information about their vehicle, their house, the RRSP files through work, and then a bold question mark in pen, beside the deposit account reference. While Tom was more than a little annoyed that Jean had felt entitled enough to provide his and Karen's personal asset information – he knew it was part of the leg work she had advised him she'd take care of - there was nothing overly private, and so reasoned that there was no harm in filling out a loan application. He provided an educated guess on the balances, then signed as he was directed to get the process going. Afterall, it was not a loan agreement at this point, and he'd perhaps see where this goes.

He was emotionally and physically drained - it had been an exhausting day. He thanked Mr. Rice and asked that he be advised as soon as the decision was in. Mr. Rice summoned the security guard to let Tom out of the bank and was on the phone before Tom was completely out of earshot. The banker's words were clear, "Hey Jean, it is done, yes all in the bag, drinks on me." Tom instinctively knew there was more to the story than what Jean or the business loan manager were divulging. He felt an urgent need to talk with Karen.

At the hospital Karen had gone to visit Susan. Both Faith and Hope were at their mother's side - Faith busy massaging her mother's arms and legs, alternating the positioning.

"How is everything going?" Karen's concern for Susan was evident in her tone and expression.

"Not well," Faith responded, "we can only do this for a limited amount of time before there are other complications. How did the visit to the doctor go with Tom?"

"He apparently has a lot of concerns regarding my behavior, but the doctor is so impressed with the weight loss and muscle gain he disregarded Tom's apprehension – I guess he felt some confusion is normal," Karen explained. Hope left her mother's bed and came over and gave Karen a warm hug.

"We are impressed with the changes you have made. Hopefully, you are buying enough time for the heart exchange." Karen smiled back at both Hope and Faith and stated, "mothers are invincible when they have their children working with and for them. We become an indestructible team."

"I couldn't do this without you!" Karen gave Faith a comforting embrace and watched fondly as Faith tearfully returned to massaging her mother's body.

"I won't let you down," Faith assured them, and Karen reluctantly left with Hope, who was driving her back home. There was much that needed their attention.

Chapter 21

WHEN TOM ARRIVED home, he found Zac busy with homework, and the rest of the family still out – seemed strange as it was past the normal time for dinner. When he asked Zac where they were, the boy was genuinely surprised that Karen was not with his dad, referring his father to the note his mother had left on the table. Tom thought back to Karen's emphatic insistence that she would get herself home, as she left the hospital. Perhaps she was still miffed at him, and this was a little rebellious punishment – for some undefined reason, he was OK with that.

"Well son, I suppose you and I are cooking tonight – any good ideas?" Zac was quite enthusiastic about the idea of the two of them making dinner and stated he would check out mom's secret stash in the freezer. Tom chuckled when Zac returned with a frozen shepherd's pie and a solid recommendation that they add a salad and garlic bread to the menu. Recalling how much Sway enjoyed making the salad, he picked up the phone.

"Hello, Mrs. Jones? Yes, thank you for taking care of Sway – please send her home for dinner now." Momentarily, Sway burst through the door, obviously excited about the day, her enthusiasm bubbling over, as she relayed her experience of painting a picture with Mrs. Jones, and how the poor woman had accidently spilled her coffee on it - but it was OK because Sway could simply paint another one on her next visit. Her excitement sky-rocketed when her dad put her in charge of making the salad. Pride swelled within Tom as he watched his two children interact with each other. Zac peered over at his dad, pulled a beer out of the fridge, opened it and handed it to Tom.

"Why thank you Son, that was very thoughtful."

"You're welcome, Dad – you earned that ice cold beer." Tom chuckled at Zac parroting of his own often spoken words. Maybe there was a little more of him in Zac than he had given credit for. Before Karen's heart attack Tom had only seen the reflection of Karen in his habits and gestures. Of late, he realized there was a lot of added depth to the boy than met the eye.

Dinner was on the table when Karen arrived home. Sway and Zac had put special effort into setting the table with cloth napkins and all the right cutlery, placed like you'd find at any fine dining restaurant. Karen waved, blew them a kiss and informed them she was heading for a quick shower – she'd be back in a flash. Tom pushed his normal derogatory comment firmly away, chiding himself that his wife deserved more respect than that. If Karen were on borrowed time, he would put forth his best effort to become the husband she deserved. The pets patiently waited for their family to settle in because that meant they would be eating soon as well. Karen came gliding into the kitchen.

"Oh my – everything smells so good! Wow – look at this display!" The kids glowed at her pleasure in their efforts. Tom walked over and gave his wife a warm embrace.

"Sweetheart, you look so beautiful!" He turned and pulled out Karen's chair and helped her take a seat at the table – she blushed becomingly. Both kids stared agape at this unusual display of gallantry from their father, but it made them feel warm inside. Zac and Tom placed the food on the table and Sway served up Daisy and Key-key's bowls and they all settled into a warm family dinner.

Tom contemplated the new routine in action. His children were becoming more independent, with no expectations that Karen dish up for them, or to cut Sway's meat. A deep realization that his actions and words to Karen this evening were genuine – she *was* beautiful – stirred an entire blend of emotions! Tom's heart fluttered as he remembered why he had fallen in love with this woman. She made it a point to know exactly what he needed and set out to selflessly provide that for him. She now did the same for the kids – hell, for every person she was in contact with. Somehow, she never got it wrong, always seeking to understand the needs of others. Cooking was her passion, and a resource. She had told him once that a satisfying meal or even a treat made with love, not only filled one's tummy but could also fill a need in their soul. Tom had scoffed at the time but now he realized the profound truth in what she had said. The epiphany for him in all of this? He now craved that quality for himself – wanted to give the same to her.

There wasn't a doubt in his mind that the children's newfound independence was a direct result of Karen's strategic plan to prepare them for a world without her. His thoughts flew to the insurance that she'd set up with his employer. Yes, she knew what they needed, and this again was proof of what an amazing, loving person she truly was. He felt a sudden rush of gratitude in his good fortune to call her his wife. He sat, enjoying the interaction as Karen prompted each one of them to share about their day, starting with Zac – it warmed Tom's heart to see his family so happy together. When it came his turn, he shared only the doctor's good news that Karen was doing exceptionally well and congratulated her on being able to drive again.

"Really?" Zac squealed his excitement, "that is awesome news mom!"

"Yes, it is," Karen replied with a warm smile.

"See dad?" Zac exclaimed, "us working as a team, like mom and the doctor said, is making mom better!"

"Yes, Tom agreed, "it *is* helping your mom get healthier." Fear seeped through every pore in his body. - his children's belief that their actions could actually save their mother – what permanent effects would they be assailed with if she died? The loss of their mother would be catastrophic enough without them harboring the notion that they did not do enough to save her. At that very moment Tom knew that the time for amends was now. He accepted that change would involve work - habits and selfless behaviors, but the beauty of it. He'd already achieved the paradigm shift and there was no time to waste in becoming the husband and father that his family deserved!

"Zac, Sway, come over here please." Sweeping them into his arms and onto his lap he planted a kiss on each of their foreheads. "I can't tell you how proud I am of the two of you, working together to help your mom with her goals, in preparing for a new heart. You have both taught me a lot about giving." As the kids returned to their seats, beaming from this rare praise from their father, he turned to Karen. "And you, my beautiful wife, are the most amazing woman alive – as I am the luckiest man!" Emotions were high with the love flowing around the family dinner table. Tom had always been aware that he was a lucky man, but today he faced the stark realization that his wonderful family, to this moment, had not been blessed with a deserving father and husband. Now, they all sat riveted, as tears welled up in his eyes. He continued, tone quiet and subdued. "I know my behavior at times has been shameful. There is no excuse for the way I have spoken to you all." Remorse flooded through him. Sway suddenly jumped up from the table and rushed to give him a hug.

"It's Ok Dad, everything is going to be Ok," spoken like a little caretaker – damn, he needed this, but struggled with accepting what he felt may be undeserved love – *unconditional* love, he realized now. "We forgive you Daddy," she murmured in a hushed tone. This was his undoing as Tom broke down in wrenching sobs. Through the snuffling tears and the catch in his voice, he promised them that he was changing - to be the husband and father his family deserved. He silently prayed to God above for mercy and help with this critical quest. Karen and Zac got up and put their arms around him – Zac echoing his sister's words – they were a team. Tom allowed his family's love to enwrap him completely! It felt wonderful and he knew this was an important piece to his transformation, but he recognized a discomfort within. He'd never allowed this depth with his feelings because to dive in – to give up that level of control - he was vulnerable to paralyzing pain. He knew it was all about trust and accepted that he had a lot of work ahead of him. Tom dredged up his inner strength and shook it off. He needed to get a handle on this situation - pull himself together, as he felt it clear through to his bones that harder times were ahead. He faced the high likelihood of losing Karen – his kids losing their mother. Indeed, the odds were against her.

Tom gently let go of his family's embrace and wiped the tears from his eyes. "I got this," he mouthed to Karen. Ruffling both of their kids' hair, he assured them, "No matter what lies ahead of us we are a team and together we'll rally to do our best!" The children smiled and nodded their agreement. "Now let us get these dishes cleaned up," Tom announced, in a cheerful tone. He could feel an inner change – his strength building. He stood tall and stowed his family's world up onto his shoulders. There was laughter and a playful banter between them as they cleared away the table. Tom's cell phone rang - it was Jean. He moved away to take the call. "Hi Jean, we are just finishing dinner and I'm a bit busy – can this wait until tomorrow?"

"No Tom, it cannot, I need you down at the office."

"At this hour?" he sputtered his objection. Good luck on that – I'm off the clock! "What's so important?"

"We can celebrate the beginning of this wonderful level-up to our relationship," Jean purred in a sultry tone.

"Sorry, that won't work for me," Tom replied, keeping his tone calm and professional. "As I said, I am busy with family at present and plan to spend a quiet evening with Karen and the kids."

There was a pause on the other end of the line. "What happened?" Jean demanded, her invitingly pleasant tone changing in an instant, "did Karen get news that they have found her a heart?"

"No, not yet, but we are confident we will hear soon," Tom assured.

"Something has changed," Tom could hear the wheels spinning in her head – how on earth could he have overlooked this less than attractive quality in this woman? "I can hear it in your voice."

"Yes," Tom stated, "*I* have changed – my priorities are now with my wife and children – as it should be. Work is still on my list, but secondary to them. I need to go Jean - have a good night." Tom hung up the phone before she had a chance to respond. Tom could almost feel the power of his strength escalating himself a little higher. The cell jingled again, and he chose not to answer, instead switching the phone off. He looked up to see smiles of approval on the faces of those so dear to him. "No work tonight – now, where were we?" Zac held up a towel with a lifted brow. "Yes, dishes," Tom confirmed and grabbed another to help dry. Leaning in toward Karen, he bestowed her a wicked grin and a suggestive wink. "How about a movie with the kids tonight and then a nice long bath?"

"I am in," Karen mirrored his flirtatious gesture and Tom felt a flush of longing – man, she knew how to turn a simple wink into something so sexy, his knees turned weak. They finished cleaning up from dinner and all climbed on the couch to watch one of Sway's favourite children's movies – it was her turn to choose. No one minded seeing it for the umpteenth time because it made her so happy. She was sound asleep when the show ended and Tom gently picked her up and carried her to bed with the cat, dog and her brother trailing behind. As Tom tucked her in, he didn't even lend a thought to the animals and Zac wandering in with what was now their normal routine. Nor did he notice the ring of salt around his daughter's bed.

"Good night, Buddy," he whispered to Zac and softly closed the bedroom door on his way out. Pride for Zac swelled in his heart. With a wistful sigh, he considered the fact that things may never be normal again in his home. Somehow instead of his usual angst, he felt a rush of determination – hope, was it? He smiled at the sound of the tub filling with water. Tom found his wife just stepping into the tub and sinking down into the bubbles. Karen's body had drastically altered since her heart attack – the results of all her hard work. Although Tom could not deny his pleasure in beholding the sight before him, he harbored a nagging feeling that Karen was pushing it too hard - was her heart vulnerable? He knew there needed to be a balance and wondered if the scales were dangerously tipped. Truth? His renewed attraction to his wife, even physically, was solid, without the weight loss and it floored him to realize that he was not so shallow after all!

Tom knelt by the tub, took a cloth, and started a gently rhythmic washing of her back. Karen breathed out a contented sigh. "That feels so good," she murmured softly.

"You are beautiful," Tom complimented, tenderness and desire evident in his eyes.

"Thank you, as are you," Karen smiled back at him. "Even more so to me, after what you did for our family tonight," Karen added, and Tom raised an inquiring eyebrow. "You provided your family with a sense of security - allowed your vulnerability to surface. You do know that this demonstrates strength, correct? The kids can feel that." Tom felt himself blush a little. "It also models that it's OK to *not* be perfect – tears and emotions do not equate to weakness."

"Was not easy," he admitted, swallowing a lump in his throat.

"I know that" Karen responded and rubbed his arms and chest in comfort and love. Tom continued the gentle administration to her body, and she leaned back, submitting to total relaxation, letting the warm water ease her aching body.

"I am worried about you and the kids," Tom confided, opening up to her in a way he never had before – sharing as opposed to accusatory or blaming.

"I know," Karen assured. "You're afraid that I may die and how it will affect the kids." Hearing this from her lips was like a punch to the gut, hard enough to take a man down.

"Yes," Tom conceded, "and I do not know what any of us will do without you!" Tears welled and Karen gently traced them down his cheeks with her fingertip. She was touched by this changed man sitting before her.

"Tom, you are not going to lose me, and your children are not going to lose their mother," Karen promised, reaching over to pull the plug. She faced him, slowly standing as the water drained under her. Tom took her hand and helped her out, then wrapped her in a towel. His arms firmly around her, he held her close for a moment and whispered in her ear.

"Do not leave me Karen, please!" She reached up to wrap herself around him. He picked her up and carried her to their bed – depositing her there like a precious gift, as he slowly and sensuously removed the towel. Tom gently massaged every inch of her body, bestowing tender kisses right down to her ten toes, leaving a blaze of warm desire in his wake. He made love to his woman all in - body and soul, allowing in the deep mind-bending, heart-wrenching emotion, that he had never dared to surface before. He took her to the highest peaks and back down, joining her in their shared ecstasy. Never before had the mix of carnal pleasure and emotional intimacy touched his existence and he knew it was the same for her – now he understood the true meaning of ultimate intimacy. They lay in each other's arms, content in listening to the pounding of shared heartbeats slow in tune to one another. "I need to tell you something." It had to be dealt with, and if trust was to be a part of their relationship – it had to start now.

"It's something to do with Jean?" Karen inquired, turning toward him. Tom took a deep breath and then let out a troubled sigh.

"Yes." God, he was terrified – what if she couldn't forgive? Forging on, he held her firmly in his arms and told her the entire story – the business put up for sale and Jean's proposal for them jointly buying the company; fifty-fifty split; the staff secrecy. Karen lay quietly and listened to it all - his plans of going into business, being coerced to do so without her knowledge and her husband's ugly confession of infidelity. Karen heard the authentic remorse in his voice and didn't respond for a heart-stopping moment.

"Ok, that was yesterday, what are your plans today?" Tom burst into tears of gratitude for her willingness to hear him out and at least to talk. He related his firm decision to steer clear of the business deal and echoed his words to the banker – Karen was his partner, first and foremost and he would do nothing without her.

"My promise to my family tonight is solid – I will say, act and do everything to honor it, from this moment forth!" He squeezed her in affirmation, "You three – and yes, complete with the pets are my absolute priority – your health and happiness."

Karen hugged tighter to Tom and whispered, "We will get through this." His relief at her continued commitment was so intense – it was almost painful. Jean had been right about Karen, although the woman deserved no accolades for that insight. Karen possessed a heart of gold. He could think of none other to equal the goodness inside of this incredible woman.

"Thank you," he whispered gratefully, "I will change - be the husband you *so* deserve," Tom promised her solemnly as they both drifted off to sleep in each other's arms. Tom slept so soundly that he did not feel his wife release his arms from around her and leave their bedroom. He woke abruptly to his son's raised voice.

"It is OK mom, it is OK." Oh God was this happening again? Tom bolted out of bed, aware of the icy cold permeating the room – seemingly reaching down to touch his soul. True to his fear, he found Karen in the kitchen - confused, in the same messy, food frenzied state as previously.

"What is wrong with me?" Karen pleaded, tears rolling down her face – the panic evident in her eyes. Tom was not quite sure what to say in reassurance, and Zac was waiting to see how his father was going to respond - all three of them shivering violently from the cold. He suddenly piped up.

"Mom, I think you're just walking in your sleep."

That seemed to calm Karen a bit. Through her tears she whispered, "I hurt from head to toe! What is wrong with me?" Tom went over and took her into a firm embrace.

"Come on honey, let's get you cleaned up and back to our warm bed. Zac is right - you are just sleep walking." With that he gently picked her up, shot Zac a grateful look and asked that he please clean up - then carried her to their bathroom. They were both still shaking, Tom ran the tub, removed her clothing and immersed her into the warm suds. Her hair and clothes were full of food – it was a formidable mess.

"Tom, what is going on," Karen cried?

"It is likely the side effects from your heart attack. Do not worry honey - I am here, and we will get through this. Remember that the doctor was not concerned about your behavioral changes." This did provide a measure of comfort and hope for him too! The warm steam-filled bathroom and soothing water seemed to calm her and the shaking abated. Tom pulled the plug and lifted Karen from the tub, wrapping her in a fluffy towel and gently guided her to their bed. He located a warm pair of pajamas and helped her into them. Tom climbed into bed and wrapped himself around her body – they needed warmth in this God awful inescapable deep freeze! Hearing a noise, he looked over to see Zac standing on his mother's side of the bed. "It's OK Son," Tom stated gently, "go back to bed."

"I need to be here to help Mom," Zac declared, not moving an inch.

"Zac, I got this - your mom will be fine." Zac left the room but then Tom heard him return, walking from one side of the bed to the next. Tom could instantly feel the cold vanish and the warmth seep in. Karen had stopped shaking. Zac then climbed into the bed on the other side of Karen and Tom refrained from voicing any objection. What could it hurt having the boy there? Karen seemed to be calming down, her breathing more even, and she had stopped crying. Whatever was going on in this house, Tom was increasingly cognizant of the fact that none of his family members were responsible, and any comfort to Karen now was vital – he needed to embrace team cooperation.

Zac wrapped his arms around his mother and whispered, "it is OK Mom, you can go to sleep now. Dad and I are here. We are not going anywhere. You're safe, Mom." Tom listened as she drifted off to sleep, held safely by both her husband and son.

He whispered to Zac, "Are you ok son?" At the affirmative reply, Tom reached over and squeezed his shoulder. "It will be OK."

"I want to believe that," Zac whispered, "but something is not right with Mom – we need to get to the bottom of it."

"We will talk about it tomorrow," Tom promised, in a hushed tone. "Your mom is safe and asleep right now," Tom reassured his son. "Thank you, Buddy, for taking care of her." Tom laid awake in the dark, comforted by the rhythmic sound of their breath. Neither father nor son surrendered to slumber until it was almost time to wake. They were roused suddenly, with Karen jumping out of bed.

"Come on, sleepy head!" She cheerfully addressed Zac, "if you are joining your mom for a run, you'd better get your rear in gear!" With that, she headed into the bathroom and re-emerged minutes later with a puzzled question on her face. "Why is all that food in the tub?" she directed her question to Tom. Zac and Tom looked at each other – at a loss to explain – Tom was not sure what to say. Karen only smiled, "Never mind, come on - let's get this show on the road." Tom waited until Zac left to get ready for the morning run. He slid his feet onto the floor and felt a grainy substance. Peering down at the salt around his bed, fingers of fear crawled their way into his soul. Everything in their world was turning upside down.

Chapter 22

"C'MON SLEEPHEAD, TIME to get up!" Sway allowed one lazy eye to open and focus on her brother's exuberant expression, but it was Daisy who brought her fully alert, and she quickly pulled the blanket over her head to dodge the dog's gooey kisses. Daisy bounded back out of the room after her brother and Sway laughed, reaching over to pet her kitty's head, who rewarded with a dramatic contented purr. Sway took a moment to reflect on everything that had transpired in the past day. Her gift – Hope had provided clarity and a name for it. Empath. I am an Empath, Sway said to herself. All the times she had been sick and those terrible trips to the hospital with the doctors saying nothing was wrong - well, she guessed they were right. There *was* nothing wrong with her! She had a gift that Hope was going to help her learn how to use. Excitement welled within. She wondered why Hope felt it so important for her to keep it a secret. Wouldn't people want to know about her gift – be happy that she could help them? There must be other people like her and Hope. Sway continued to stroke her cat's fur, lulled by the gentle purring. It felt so good just to lay there and enjoy the sounds of her family, the birds outside – the familiar melodies of life.

Her musing wandered to a ghost that may or may not be in their house. She wondered who it could be and really didn't know how to feel about that possibility. If there was a poor soul stuck here, she would feel sad for the ghost, but if it simply enjoyed hanging with them, causing no trouble, she'd be comforted by its freedom to be happy. Sway considered possible scenarios for a few moments and sighed - they were all just prospects after all - she would just stay open and curious. Both she and Key-key hopped out of bed at Zac's announcement that breakfast was ready – she decided to dress later. Once in the kitchen Sway fed the pets and joined her family at the table. Her curiosity rose at her parents' conversation.

"How are you feeling, honey?" Sway noticed her dad held fast to her mom's hand.

"I feel great!" Karen responded cheerfully. "Why do you ask?"

"I'm just a bit worried that you might be pushing yourself too hard," Tom held up his hand to stop her protest. "Honey, last night you scared both Zac and I a little." Karen seemed confused by this. Sway asked what had happened the night before. Zac chimed in and shared that their mother had been sleep walking.

"Oh, I know – that's when a person is still asleep while they are walking!" Sway declared, proudly.

"Yes Sway, that is correct." Karen smiled her concurrence. "Zac and Tom, I am really sorry I gave you both a fright, but really, I am fine – no need to worry!"

"OK, Sweetie, I just want you to promise me you won't overdo things, please – maybe a walk instead of a run?" Tom's pleading expression seemed to soften Karen a little and she squeezed his hand.

"Really, it's OK – you need to trust me on this." Karen laughed heartily, "besides, we need to get Zac and Daisy into shape and I'm not letting them off *that* easy!" Zac giggled and said he could barely keep up with her, so slowing down a pace would still do the trick *and* be a good thing. "Tom," Karen framed his face with her hands, "trust me, please – I will be just fine." Tom sighed, knowing that trust was something he needed to embrace – Karen was a smart lady and none of this was intentional on her part. He grinned, lightening up the morning mood. Sway was heartened by the family laugh and banter. She was accustomed to it always seeming so serious.

"Oh Honey, could you please pull the car out of the garage for me? I want to get groceries today." Tom knew the happiness that Karen derived from having her driver's licence reinstated and readily agreed, offering to drop

Zac off at school on his way to work. The bustle began as everyone cleaned up and left to prepare for the day. Sway stayed behind to take advantage of the opportunity to leisurely finish her breakfast – truly enjoying not being in such a rush.

Sway heard her father come back into the house and call to her mother that her car needed gas so they could switch today. He'd take hers and fill it up on his way back from work – his was ready for her to use. With that he was gone and quiet fell. Sway listened to the sounds within the house that were only discernable within this silence, enjoying the peace. She allowed relaxation to flood her body, absorbing the inner energy as she recharged and sighed her contentment. So, this was recharging – now that she had a name for it, like a recharging a battery. She vaguely wondered why everyone didn't know about this and choose to put it into practice.

Sway engaged in the process completely; not thinking; not feeling. She knew no sense of time - if it was minutes or hours that she held herself in this positive state of mindful, balanced energy. Her senses pulled her back to awareness when she felt a distinct presence in the room. Keeping her eyes closed, she moved her energy to this person, not quite sure on who or what - it was not familiar. Involuntarily her eyes shot open, and she was surprised to see her mother standing before her. She gasped aloud – something was not right here.

"Are you OK Sweetie?" Karen reached out. Sway jerked back from her mother's touch, unsure of what to say. She needed Hope right now. Karen pulled her hand back in surprise. "What's wrong honey, are you OK?"

"Yes, I am fine," Sway stammered. "Can we see Hope today?" Sway felt an inner desperate need to talk with her.

"I don't see why not," Karen replied gently. "Come on, let's go get our shopping finished and then see if Hope can meet us for lunch," Karen suggested cheerfully.

"Can I call her now?"

"Of course," her mother agreed. Sway grabbed the phone and dialed Hope's number, feeling a rush of relief when she picked up on the second ring.

"Are you OK?" Hope prompted at Sway's breathless voice.

"Yes," Sway replied, trying to calm herself, and asked if Hope could meet up with her and her mother at the Skeena Mall for lunch.

"Of course, I would love to," Hope replied. Sway heaved an audible sigh of relief.

"What is wrong?" Hope asked with a little more urgency in her voice.

"It is my mom," Sway whispered.

"What is up with your mom?" Hope asked her tone firmer.

"I don't think my mom is my mom," Sway whispered, as Karen summoned her to get ready to leave for shopping. "I have to go now, but please meet us at the mall restaurant at noon – Mom says it's OK." She quickly hung up the phone, brushed her hair and teeth, dressed and hurried to the car. Sway was not granted the opportunity to sit in the front seat very often - it was usually taken by her brother. At that moment she wished Zac was there so she would have an excuse to sit in the back – she needed time to sort out her feelings. It hurt Sway's heart to be dishonest and secretive with her mom, but something was urging her to keep these thoughts to herself. She didn't feel threatened exactly – but something was afoot. Securing her seatbelt, she took a couple of deep breaths – the way Hope had taught her, as her mom started the car and pulled out of the driveway. On route, Karen chatted away about the different stores they would visit in order to purchase all the items on her list. Listening to her mom prattle on, it felt almost as if they were in cahoots to avoid the emotional energy building up in the car – it was palpable. The constant chatter left no opportunity to ask questions so neither of them would need to address the heavy atmosphere. Karen turned to Sway and smiled before quickly turning back to watch the road. There was a steep hill with a two-way stop sign at the bottom. Karen had said many times how she hated that hill, and her focus now was clearly on safety. Sway felt her mom pump the brakes slowly a couple of times, then faster and frantically.

"Oh my God," Karen screamed, "the brakes are gone – the peddle is stuck to the floor!" The car picked up alarming speed as they raced down the hill toward the intersection at the bottom. Karen yelled at Sway to hang on. Sway's heart flew into her throat as the car flew through the stop sign and into the oncoming traffic. As if in slow motion, Sway felt an enormous impact to the side of the car that sent it spinning wildly – the force unbelievable, before it flipped into the air and rolled over into a ditch on the side of the road. Nausea overwhelmed her, followed by intense chest pain. From afar it seemed, she heard Karen screaming, "hang on, hang on!" The vehicle had landed upside down and Sway felt panic grip, still strapped in her seatbelt – the pressure from the blood-rush to her head pounding intensely into her brain. She whimpered, watching Karen frantically scramble to escape the airbag, undo her own seat belt, and fall heavily to the roof of the car. She immediately reached over to wrestle Sway's belt clasp loose and caught Sway in her arms as she fell. Karen kicked out the last bit of glass from the back window and dragged them both out of the vehicle, stumbling and crawling as far away as possible before collapsing on the grass – maintaining a fierce grip, and wrapping her body around Sway protectively.

"It's OK, it's OK," Sway repeated over and over – a prayer or mantra. The reverberation from the ensuing blast assaulted her entire body – the car had exploded! The ringing in her ears was painful and deafening! Karen had wrapped her body to cover Sway, shielding her from the impact of the blast that she had clearly anticipated, so although Sway could not physically feel any outward damage to her own body, her senses were keenly alert to the effect on her mother's. Karen fell limp and heavy atop her. Suddenly gasping for breath, Sway struggled to push her off, but she was firmly pinned down and fearful of hurting her mom. The intense heat from flames added to her growing hysteria – trapped in this nightmare, terror overwhelmed her, and she began to scream. At once, a man appeared and very gently moved her mother, asking if she was OK.

"My mom, my mom!" Sway cried out, "something bad has happened to my mom!"

"It is OK," the man reassured her kindly, "the ambulance and firemen are on their way." The man gently dragged her mother and Sway further from the flames of the car. It seemed like forever, but it was only minutes before the ambulance and fire trucks where there. They were quickly and efficiently hooked up to vital equipment, scooped up onto stretchers and secured inside separate ambulances. Sway had pleaded to go with her mother to help and comfort, but they informed her that there was not ample space. Sway's anxiety was suffocating - she had felt her mother's heart stop and not start again - everything had happened so fast. There had been no time to share her energy with her mom to see if she could start her heart. She was trying to sort it out in her mind and wasn't sure if there was something more she could have done – the fear for her mom's life was paralyzing.

As the attendants secured her mom first, Sway surveyed her surroundings and realized other people were injured as well - cars overturned and damaged. She heard people screaming in pain. Her first instincts were to try and help them with her healing energy, then clear as day, she heard Hope's warning words echo through her mind. "No, no! It's too dangerous and you need to save your energy to heal yourself." Taking in the utter chaos of the accident site, she observed the outline of a dark figure moving around and through the vehicles. A sudden inner chill set her to shivering and one paramedic hollered to the driver that they needed to hurry as this girl was going into shock. She felt an instant comfort from the warm blanket he gently tucked around her.

What seemed like a million questions were thrown at her as they loaded her into the ambulance and rushed to the hospital. Where did she feel pain? Her shoulder hurt. Sway was surprised when they cut her clothes off and examined her from head to toe. Asking her name, they kept up the barrage - did she know where she was, did she know what day of the week it was? Of course, Sway provided all the answers that a child her age would know. Minutes later, the paramedic explained to the nurse in Emergency that she had been in a roll over car accident – there had been an explosion and that they had only gotten one set of vitals and had not completed their customary physical exam – she displayed signs of shock. The nurse thanked them and took over.

"Where is my mom? I want to see my mom!" Sway pleaded. The ambulance ride had triggered her trauma from the previous ride with her mother, only this time, she had not been able to be with her.

"Once we examine you and make sure you are OK, I will find her for you," the nurse promised. "My name is Jenny," she pointed at her name tag, "I am going to be the nurse taking care of you. Now let's get a look at you and the doctor will be here to see you as well, very soon." Jenny hooked an intravenous line into the back of Sway's hand, and she jerked at the initial discomfort, which improved once the line was taped in place. Jenny hooked up a monitor to keep track of her heart and a clip on her finger, explaining that it was an oxygen monitor. Sway was grateful that there was no pain for either. A doctor came in – Sway was certain he was not one she'd seen before. He introduced himself as Doctor Crawley and asked how she was.

"I want to see my mom." Sway's distress was clear. The nurse provided details - the mother was driving the vehicle and was being treated for her injuries.

"Don't worry, your mother is being well cared for," the doctor touched her hand. "It is my job to make sure that *you* are properly cared for." Somehow his smile provided no comfort at all. "Now – back to your pain - I heard your shoulder hurts. Let's take a look," he gently pushed on her shoulder. Sway involuntarily jerked back from his touch - not from pain – rather from her intuitive senses signaling caution – something wasn't right. The feelings, the energy she was receiving from this man were not positive and indicated that this was not a man to be trusted. The doctor smiled at her, but it did not seem warm like those of the other doctors and nurses here. He turned and instructed the nurse to order an entire body scan and a full blood panel. Nurse Jenny seemed surprised by the request.

"What is it that concerns you? Her vitals are stable," she prompted in a hushed tone.

"I am not taking any chances," the doctor replied decisively, "this child has been in a roll-over accident, and the vehicle she was in exploded." The nurse seemed satisfied with his explanation and thanked him. Dr. Crawley smiled at her and turned back to Sway, who instinctively knew that his smile was phony. "All is fine young lady, just a few tests and you'll be back home in no time," he assured her. Sway thanked him because she was inherently taught good manners, but everything within her screamed that this doctor did not have her best interests at heart. Jenny informed him that she would call to book the test right away.

"Please take the child immediately to the lab – I will clear it." His tone brooked no argument. "We are not losing this little girl on my watch," he whispered to her. Jenny nodded solemnly and Sway was rolled down a long hallway into an elevator. The nurse pushed the button to take them to the third floor. The sign said radiology and lab. Upon arrival, they were quickly ushered in.

"What is the prime concern?" the radiologist inquired.

"Not sure," the nurse repeated the details of the accident and Sway's vitals. "I think he is worried about delayed symptoms and is opting for proactive treatment." The radiologist nodded thoughtfully. Sway was lifted onto the cold metal surface of a large machine where they placed earphones over her ears. She was instructed that there would be a knocking sound and she was to lay very still until it was finished.

At the hydraulic whine of the machine – ineffectively muffled – and the ominous motion sliding Sway into a narrow tube, she felt a mountain of apprehension building up within her. All her senses shrieked danger. "I feel sick," Sway said. I am going to puke."

"OK, just hang on," the radiologist replied, and the machine pulled her back out. Sway was gasping for air, trying to get her fears under control. But she knew instinctively that something about this wasn't right and hastily yanked the I.V. out of her hand and ripped off the other monitoring equipment.

"Hey little girl, don't do that!" the radiologist yelled, but it was too late. In seconds, Sway had freed herself from all devices and straps, rolled off the machine surface and landed on her feet, shouting at the top of her voice that she needed a bathroom. She was directed to a washroom just outside the room, ran in and firmly locked the door. Dropping her head into her hands, she dissolved in tears, feeling more alone than she ever had in her entire life, and wished more than anything that Hope was here - she'd know what to do! Sway stayed on the cold floor until she heard knocking at the door. As a stalling strategy, she flushed the toilet and ran water in the sink.

The radiologist asked through the door, if she was OK, and Sway replied that she had an upset tummy. Not knowing what else to do, she slowly opened the door – defiance was not a part of Sway's nature.

"Can I please call my aunt to be here with me?" Tears trickled down her cheeks. The radiologist hesitated then agreed, motioning to Jenny to guide her to a public phone on the wall, with instructions to dial 9, followed by the number she wanted to call. Sway stood for a moment. She did not know Hope's number off by heart, then she heard within her mind Hope telling her the number. Sway dialed and Hope picked up on the first ring.

"Sway, are you OK?" Hope implored when she heard the little girl's voice.

"I don't feel very well, Aunty Hope, can you come to the hospital and hold my hand when they are doing their tests on me?" Sway pleaded.

"Slow down Honey, what tests? Sway heard the urgency in her voice, "never mind - I am on my way, do you know where you are in the hospital?"

Sway looked at the sign on the wall, "Radiology, third floor," she stated, hoping she'd pronounced it properly.

"Hang on – I'll be right there!" As Hope hung up, Sway sighed in relief – everything would be OK now. But she needed to make sure they didn't put her back in that awful machine first! "My aunty is on her way over - I feel like I am going to puke again," Sway stated and ran for the bathroom, securely locking the door once more. She waited on the floor and soon heard voices outside the door, recognizing Nurse Jenny's, asking her if she could come in with her. "In a minute," Sway lied, "I am going to the bathroom." Just to be sure, she pulled down her pants and plunked herself on the toilet.

Jenny called out, "We can't let you be by yourself Honey, in case you have a bad injury and fall," she explained.

"I am OK, I am just upset about my mom," Sway called back through the door and was horrified when she heard a click of the lock and the door opened. "Do you mind?" Sway did her best to sound insulted, though fear was at the root of her angst, and tears filled her eyes. "I am going to the bathroom!" Thankfully she'd sat on the toilet!

235

"OK, Sweetie, but I'll stay right outside the door to wait – let me know when you are finished. You should not be wandering anywhere unassisted." Sway waited as long as she dared then flushed the toilet. She prayed Hope would get there soon, as she took her time washing her hands. The door swung open and Jenny rolled in a wheelchair, grabbing some paper towel from the dispenser for Sway to dry her hands. Jenny's expression softened - Sway's body language and face evidenced her inner fear and turmoil. "I know you don't understand this, but every minute we are here, the machine in there is not available to help other people who are at this moment, waiting for a scan." She looked into Sway's frightened wide eyes. "So please try to pull yourself together and let's get this done."

"OK, OK," Sway slowly sat in the wheelchair, without assistance. As they left the bathroom, the same dark figure from the accident site moved across the waiting area and into the radiology room. A familiar chill permeated her body.

"Who gave consent for tests to be done on my niece?" Hope demanded in a tone of authority?" Sway nearly fainted with relief, as Hope ran over.

"Who are you?" the nurse asked.

"I am Sway's guardian," Hope stated and handed the nurse a qualifying document. The nurse nodded and handed it back. Hope stepped behind the wheelchair and pushed Sway to the elevator and before anyone could utter another word, she closed the sliding doors and pressed the button to the main floor.

"I am scared," Sway hiccupped through her tears.

"I know," Hope soothed.

"First, I didn't think my mom was really my mom, and now I think she is dead," wailed Sway.

"I know, Sweetie, but trust me, your mother is not dead - I will explain later - right now we need to focus on getting you out of here." The permeating chill assaulted them both as the doors of the elevator slid open and Hope rushed Sway out of the hospital, like the very devil was on their tail.

Chapter 23

AS TOM DROVE his son to school, he took the opportunity to chat. "Zac buddy, when you go on your morning runs with your mom, do you think she pushes herself too hard?" He glanced over to check his reaction – not wishing to create unnecessary alarm.

"Well, she sure does go full steam," Zac responded," and faster every day. She says aloud to herself, "just a little more, just a little more." I ask her to slow down so I can keep up, but she now even plays Daisy out." His response confirmed Tom's suspicions.

"I won't lie Son, I am a little worried about your mom, but I'm unsure how to handle it," Tom confided.

"I know what you mean," Zac concurred, "I feel the same. There are times I could swear Mom is not even my mom. This heart thing is changing her. The only time she really seems like Mom, is when she has those horrible sleepwalking food attacks, and seems so confused – loses her memory for anything that's happened since her heart attacks." Tom's heart lurched, listening to his son. He instinctively knew though, that it was infinitely better for Zac to talk about it, than keep it bottled inside - a ticking time bomb. "Mom has always protected us from showing her own fears and troubles, so I know that this must be incredibly scary for her – enough that she couldn't hide it even if she tried."

For some strange reason hearing Zac describe Tom's exact fears provided a measure of comfort. He was beginning to feel like some crazed husband, his wild fears disregarded by Karen's own doctor, whom Tom truly did hold in high regard – it was confusing and complex. Pulling up in front of the school, Tom reached over to squeeze Zac's shoulder. "Do not worry Son, we will get through this as a family. As I promised, I am going to step up to figure this all out. Your mom is going through a rough time, but she will always be your mom, no matter what challenges or changes she must endure." Zac reached over and hugged his dad tightly and wiped his eyes, working to pull his emotions together before opening the car door. He addressed his father, looking him straight in the eye.

"I love you Dad, see you after school." Tom smiled affectionately – a monumental lump in this throat.

"Love you too Buddy, have an enjoyable day." Tom felt a pull on his heartstrings as he watched Zac walk into the school – the young boy had so much on his plate – he was one amazing kid! It was incredible, the way he'd shown up to calm his mother last night and joining her every morning on those relentless runs. He sighed in troubled reflection - he knew better than anyone the extent to which the changes in Karen had manifested in her persona; the loss of memory after the truly frightening episodes; increased energy and sensuality – even her physical appearance and mannerisms.

Arriving at work, his mind shifted to Jean. He was fully prepared for her wrath – only a fool would hang up on that vixen, not to mention his rejection of her physical charms. He chuckled inwardly – what was that phrase – laughing in the face of danger? Yes, he supposed it was true, but he was done with Jean in every manner, no matter what the cost. He had decided to forego partnership with her and sure as hell was not getting into that woman's bed or any other risky locale where she might decide to exercise her highly skilled seduction tactics – hell, he'd even forgotten about their weekly tryst. Tom felt incredibly veracious, liberated in fact. He squared his shoulders as he walked into the service entrance and headed straight over to the work board to check the queue for the day, feeling the weight of deception melt off his shoulders. Karen knew all - there were no more secrets. There was nothing Jean could do now to destroy his newfound dedication and love for Karen and his family. They were all that mattered. He was keenly aware of Jean's eyes on him and knew she was observing his every move, trying to figure him out. She now motioned with her head that he come into the office. His first instinct was to completely ignore her, but instead he adhered to a vital mental cue, reminding him that she *was* the boss. Therefore, he would fulfill his obligations accordingly, which now included responding to her royal summons. Creating the ensuing commotion that ignoring her would ascertain, could not serve any purpose other than rendering an already unpleasant situation even worse.

Jean sat down at her desk with her arms folded. "So, what is going on?" Her features were void of expression, making it difficult for Tom to predict where the conversation was headed. God, she was a skilled manipulator! This was fine – he'd stay cool. His newfound sense of self-worth and pride bolstered his confidence.

"I have decided to decline entering into this business venture with you," Tom announced. "My family needs my entire focus and dedication at this time." Tom further explained. "This undertaking would require time and energy that I am unable to commit, but I thank you for the offer, Jean." In conclusion, he turned to leave.

"Just a moment," Jean replied, her tone ice-cold, and Tom turned back to face her. "Do you really believe it's as easy as that?" she sneered. "You forfeited your choice to turn back on this deal when you signed the papers at the bank. So, you can bloody well forget about any notion of turning away now – you are frankly locked in, and the deal is sealed." Tom scrambled to remember exactly what the banker had inferred – he was sure it was simply a loan application, but a foreboding chill told him there may be more to it and he wisely stayed silent. "So, I suggest you now get your ass back to work! And Tom? The next time you hang up on me there will be hell to pay!" It was a viper's hiss and an icy shiver crawled up his spine. He turned without a word of reply and left Jean's office. A sudden nausea assaulted him. What the bloody hell had he signed at the bank? Or was Jean simply bluffing? Tom glanced at his first job on the board, hoping it would be one that did not require too much mental energy – his mind was on overdrive. At the sound of his name, he turned to find Constable O'Reilly standing a few feet away from him, confused at his presence. What reason would he have to show up at his place of work?

"Tom, I need you to come with me," Constable O'Reilly stated.

"Why?" Tom implored. "Can you please tell me what this is all about?"

"I will explain in the car - believe me, this is best," the police officer countered solemnly. Tom stood rooted to the spot, unsure whether to comply or stay. What could it be? Something must have happened with his family! Tom moved to accompany the policeman just as Jean emerged from her office.

"Officer O'Reilly, would you mind telling me what this is all about?" she drilled him with a demanding glare.

"It is a family matter," Jim replied curtly, seemingly unphased by her commanding attitude. Jean studied Tom – his confusion, blank stare and tentative move forward, and urged him onward. It was clear that he was experiencing shock, a state commonly onset by trauma or fear, like when a person is avoiding receiving unacceptable news. Jim O'Reilly took Tom's arm and guided him out to the cruiser.

Tom was in a daze. "Am I under arrest?" This he could manage! Something happening to his wife or family would not be something he could endure!

"No Tom," Jim responded calmly. "Should you be arrested?"

"Of course not," Tom replied instantly, "but you put me in the back seat of the car."

"Sorry, it's simply for your own protection." He leveled Tom with a measuring glance. "I have a lethal firearm up front, and we cannot predict how people will respond in a crisis."

"Is my wife dead?" Tom blurted out through choked tears – realizing he'd been on pins and needles expecting that last, fatal heart attack.

"Your wife and daughter were both in a serious car accident - they are at the hospital, and I do not yet know of their current condition. I decided it was prudent to pick you up and take you there myself. We both know how you drive when you are in a crisis and I would not want you or anyone else hurt today," Jim O'Reilly advised, the empathy and support in his tone effectively erasing any judgemental chastise that these words might suggest in any other situation.

"An accident – how?" Tom demanded.

"We do not know the details yet, but your wife went right through a stop sign at the bottom of Shoemaker Hill and right into oncoming traffic. She was struck by one or more vehicles. The car exploded but your wife and daughter managed to get out, beforehand. At this point in time, I have no further information." He checked Tom's profile in the rear-view mirror. They pulled up to the hospital parking lot. The officer escorted Tom inside and informed the front desk receptionist that they were there regarding the motor vehicle accident involving Karen and Sway.

"I'll ask that you please wait a moment," the receptionist replied, "As you are aware, Officer, we have multiple casualties brought here from that accident." Tom searched around the waiting room and saw numerous faces that he knew and was confused by their seeming unwillingness to meet his eyes.

"What is going on?" Tom beseeched. Jim requested a private space in which they could wait. The young lady nodded and directed them to a room that was familiar to the police officer. He had interviewed many victims and perpetrators alike, in this space. He now directed Tom to take a seat.

"Tom I am going to be straight up with you. We do not know what could have caused Karen to drive through that stop sign and into oncoming traffic – I know it is a risk that she would never normally take. The other victim's families are concerned that she may have experienced another heart attack. They are demanding to know why she was driving the vehicle. Tom sank his head into his hands, fighting wildly to quiet his mind. Then he looked back up at Constable O'Reilly.

"That is not of consequence right now to me - what matters at this moment, is whether or not my wife and daughter will survive this." Tears rolled down Tom's face. "Of course, I am concerned for the other victims as well." The officer agreed, placing a comforting hand on his back.

"You stay here, and I will find someone to come and fill you in on their condition. But remain in place, do *not* go anywhere without me, agreed?" Tom nodded and Jim exited the room, leaving him to his horrifying fears.

What had happened? The doctor had cleared Karen to drive. Did she have a heart attack?

Tom jumped as the door suddenly opened. He glanced up to see a man he recognized but didn't know personally. "Why did you let your wife drive?" the man demanded, anguish on his face.

"What?" Tom responded, confused by the question.

"You knew your wife had heart problems so why did you let her drive?"

"My wife does not ask or require my permission," Tom responded, blessed anger building to replace the paralyzing fright.

"What about your daughter?" the man grilled.

"What about my daughter, and how is she your business?" Tom felt the walls of panic closing in on him – it was all too much! His daughter may or may not even be alive at this moment.

"What makes your daughter so special that she gets priority over a life-saving MRI, with no medically compromising symptoms? Meanwhile, my son has a neck injury, and they cannot proceed with surgery until he has had an MRI," the man blurted out in anguish, his shoulders spasming with wracking sobs.

Tom approached the man, allowing space for the volatility of the situation. "Listen, I just arrived here – Constable O'Reilly brought me, and I have no idea if my wife and daughter are dead or alive. You apparently know a lot more about what is happening with my daughter than I do." Although he was still upset, the boy's father was listening. "Obviously by what you are saying, something significant must be going on, because they take people by medical priority, so if the doctors treated my daughter before your son, there has to be a medical reason." Sway was alive then?

"That is not what I heard!" the man yelled emphatically. "I clearly overheard the surgeon arguing with your daughter's doctor regarding the lack of medical evidence to warrant the MRI."

"I am sorry." None of this made any sense and Tom needed to know what was going on – now! He understood why this man was upset – hell, he'd feel the same! "Obviously, we are both very concerned for our families. Your anger is valid because you are scared – we both are! Let's try and stay calm and sort this all out," Tom suggested. "Do you know if your son has had the MRI yet?" The man confirmed that he was undergoing the procedure as they spoke. "Good – that's great!" Tom took a deep breath. The man broke down in tears and collapsed into a chair. "Where is your wife?"

"She is dead," It was an agonized whisper. Tom felt the cold go through him as nausea built in his gut. Would this nightmare ever end? He put a hand on the man's shoulder, knowing that it would not provide much comfort at this time. Amidst the well of compassion, with all his might, Tom prayed that Karen and Sway did not suffer the same fate.

Jim O'Reilly came back into the room and knew instantly that something was amiss. He turned to the man. "Can I help you sir?" A haunting loss was evident in the upturned tortured eyes before him – he'd seen it too many times.

"Can you bring my wife back from the dead - save my son? Can you keep him from being paralyzed for the rest of his life?" The man turned to Tom and said, "I heard your wife was an angel, but angels do not wreak this type of tragic horror, unless of course she is a fallen angel or a wolf in sheep's clothing." It was a cruel parting comment and was Tom's undoing - the grief and anger in the man's tone reverberated in his head as the man left the room, and though Tom knew in his heart that Karen would never have intentionally hurt anyone, there were so many questions rolling around in his mind.

"I am sorry that you were subjected to this," the officer imparted in a sympathetic tone. "He should not have been here."

"My wife *is* an angel," Tom declared. "She would sacrifice her own life before she would harm a fly, never mind another human being. If Karen did have a heart attack and drove into oncoming traffic that is the devil's work, not God's, and my wife absolutely had no part in it," Tom's defenses kicked into full gear now. "Where is my wife and daughter?"

"Your wife is currently in surgery. A nurse is coming here soon to explain the circumstances and your daughter has apparently left the hospital with someone who has guardianship over her."

"What?" Tom was truly alarmed now. "Who was she with?"

"The only information I have right now is that they were trying to run tests on your daughter, and she phoned someone who came with guardianship papers and left the hospital with her. Unfortunately, the nurse did not make a copy of the documentation, but she believes it is legal. In any case, it happened so quickly the nurse was unable to catch the name." Jim O'Reilly faced Tom squarely, "Tom, I will get to the bottom of this, I promise – I will find your daughter." Tom stood in silence, trying to sort out the myriad of thoughts crashing through his brain. Nothing in their lives had made sense since Karen's heart attacks. Intuition warned him that he needed to stay calm and quiet – to just listen. A nurse appeared to inform Tom that Karen was in surgery. The nurse smiled gently and relayed that an eyewitness had watched her save their daughter, by pulling her out of harm's way before collapsing.

"Mr. Shorn, your wife is a hero!" As she departed, the statement hung in the air. Heart surgery, here in Terrace? Not Vancouver as planned?

"The angels are working overtime today – both are alive, and your wife will have a new lease on life." The officer smiled gently.

"Yes, thank you!" Tom visibly drooped with relief. "Now we know that something else went wrong to cause the accident." Jim placed his hand on Tom's shoulder.

"I promise you that we will determine what happened!" Tom felt blessed in that moment, Karen and Sway were alive, and going to be OK. A doctor entered the room and Tom stood.

"You are not Karen's doctor," Tom stated, "Do you have information?"

"No, I am Dr. Crawley, the physician in charge of your daughter's care," the doctor replied. Something about the man seemed off. What about Dr. Kerr?

"What is wrong with her?" Tom asked.

"That is what I was trying to determine, but your appointed guardian took her out of the hospital before I could make a proper diagnosis." Again, Tom felt alarm bells go off within him. He took a deep calming breath – he needed all his faculties now. He had already deduced that it was likely Hope who took Sway – who else would she have called?

"You are the doctor who ordered an MRI on Sway," Tom was putting pieces together now. "I am sure my daughter is fine," he responded. "Now I want to talk to my wife's doctor."

"With all due respect, I will determine your daughter's state of health," Dr. Crawley challenged. "I am both curious and concerned as to why you have a guardian in place for her," the doctor's tone suggested arrogant superiority.

"For situations like this," Tom looked him dead in the eye, "where one or both of us cannot immediately be there for our children."

"Who is the woman?" the doctor challenged.

"That would not be any of your business," Tom sent a silent prayer of gratitude for Hope's timely intervention. His phone pinged and a glance confirmed that Sway was safe.

At that moment, Faith walked into the room. "Hello, what is going on here?" She directed her question to Dr. Crawley. Tom was significantly relieved to see her. "Dr. Crawley, I'm sure I don't need to remind you of our recent conversation – I remain the physician in charge of Sway's care." Dr. Crawley flushed with obvious outrage. "My sister Hope is Sway and Zac's guardian which was put in place recently in light of their mother's heart condition." She afforded Tom a gentle smile. "Karen needed someone to support the children and Tom and has put this in place permanently." She smiled sweetly at the intrusive doctor, "So, as you can surmise, we have no need of your services and will let you get on with your busy day." With that dismissal, she turned to Tom.

"Have you managed to speak with a doctor regarding Karen's condition?" At his helpless negative response, the nurse who had accompanied her volunteered to get an update as soon as possible. "Also, I would like to know the name of the surgeon who is performing the surgery," Faith chimed in,

245

then turned to doctor Crawley, who had refused to budge thus far, "As you have anything to do with this case, based on patient confidentiality I am recommending that you no longer have access to Karen or Sway's patient files." At Dr. Crawley's indignant objection, Tom intervened, firmly voicing his support of Dr. Kerr.

"I am the attending physician who took over your daughter's care when she was admitted today," he spouted obtrusively.

"Dr. Kerr is her doctor," Tom drilled him with an audacious glare, "and furthermore, the thought of you preventing another child from receiving vital care under the guise of insisting you are my daughter's doctor, when she clearly had no symptoms to justify the MRI procedure, sickens me!" Tom declared, "Be assured that I will be requesting a formal investigation." He stood tall and squared his shoulders, staring the doctor down.

The police officer strategically moved between them. "I believe Mr. Shorn has made his point clear. I suggest you leave while you are ahead," he advised. Assessing his lack of options, Dr. Crawley left the room abruptly, but his body language spoke of adamant disapproval. Faith stepped forward and shook Jim's hand.

"Hello, I am Dr. Faith Kerr - good to finally meet you."

"Finally?" He seemed a bit nonplussed at her comment.

"Yes," Faith clarified, "I recently reviewed the case notes on a child's file we are both working on."

"Oh yes," his features relaxed as understanding dawned.

"Nothing that we need to discuss right now," Faith added, as if to give the officer an out from the situation, and he promptly nodded his agreement.

"I am wondering what brought you here?" Faith inquired politely. The officer explained that he had brought Tom to the hospital when he learned of the accident and was just making sure that everyone was OK. Faith thanked him for his help and concern but assured him that she and her sister would look after Tom and the children now. Tom picked up on some tension between the two and wondered what that was about – the officer's responses had been rushed – almost defensive. Then Jim O'Reilly commented that there were questions he needed to ask of Tom, for clarification, and received Faith's nod of approval to continue.

"May I ask what is going on here?" Tom required illumination now, above all else.

"Tom, there are circumstances concerning Karen's accident that stand out immediately as suspicious. Witnesses confirm that the vehicle had not slowed at all, before running into the intersection. All possibilities must be investigated; did your wife have a medical episode; could it have been a suicide attempt; or much more likely, being that Sway was in the vehicle, something mechanically amiss with the car? When was the last time you had your wife's car serviced?"

"Our vehicles undergo routine maintenance without fail," Tom assured, "It's what I do for a living, but Karen was not driving her car – we had switched this morning, last minute."

"Then you were driving Karen's vehicle today?" At Tom's affirmative nod, he continued. "Now this is just a question I have to ask – can you think of anyone who might wish to harm your wife and daughter – your family?" Tom's heart dropped – the implications were horrifying but he too, had been pondering if the brakes had failed. He should have been the one driving the car this morning!

"It is impossible for anyone to have known my wife would be driving my car. It was a last-minute decision for me to take her car – it needed fuel." Tom pondered if the accident was meant for him. But who? His mind drew a blank. He had just replaced the brake pads on both vehicles less than 6 months ago…

Chapter 24

CONSTABLE JOM O'REILLY left the hospital with a furrowed brow, and more questions than answers. He held optimism that Karen could shed light on the issue, once she was safely out of surgery.

Jim O'Reilly did not believe in miracles, and too many coincidences were falling into play to be ignored. And what of the little girl? He reflected for a moment on the possibility that perhaps Faith had somehow found out that he had been following her. This was the third community he'd tailed her to. It had been easier in the big city to carry out his investigation undetected, but small communities, where everyone knows everyone, posed unique challenges.

He decided to head over to the Shorn home and instantly noticed the dark patch on the driveway – fluid? Had the vehicle Karen drove that morning been parked in that spot? Opening the trunk of the squad car, he reached in to retrieve his camera, gloves, and evidence bags. First, he took pictures of the pool of liquid in the driveway, then took samples. His keen eye spotted a small flake of what looked like rubber, which he put into a separate evidence bag. It was critical to be thorough. Multiple vehicle accidents involving injuries and fatalities required precise care with details – there were always plenty of questions and legalities to deal with.

Carefully placing the evidence in the car, he set out to retrace the probable route that Karen would have taken that morning. Arriving at Shoemaker Hill, his inner dialogue taunted him – how many times had he predicted that this intersection was a tragedy waiting to happen. Well, today the prophecy was fulfilled. As he slowed down to approach the stop sign, he noted remaining debris on the road from the accident that was yet to be cleared. An ominous chill snaked up his back. The tow-truck was loading the burned car onto the flat deck. Hopefully, there was enough of the vehicle left intact for forensics to work their magic so they could put more of the puzzle pieces in place. Experience taught him it was necessary to gain the full picture.

At the police station he handed the evidence over to the lab technician and filled out the required paperwork. "My gut feeling tells me exactly what you'll find." At the young lady's raised brow he continued, "brake fluid. The small speck in this bag? Brake line." Jim O'Reilly was confident in the outcome, guessing the reason that Karen was not able to stop at the bottom of Shoemaker Hill was because she simply had zero brakes. He reviewed his mental task list as he left the lab and recalled spotting Tom leaving the bank after hours – time for a strategic visit. Upon entering the bank, he smiled, tipped his hat to the receptionist and requested to speak to the Bank Manager. He was quickly ushered in and explained that as part of a routine investigation, he needed to know the nature of business Mr. Shorn had undertaken at their institution.

"I'm sorry Officer, but all client information is strictly confidential," the manager advised.

"I do understand this and respect your policy," Jim stated pleasantly, "however, this is part of a formal investigation that will eventually require your legal adherence to surrendering the records. I'd like to save the time and unnecessary red tape for both me and your bank, if possible," he regarded the Manager with a friendly grin, "so between us, may I ask only that you provide a general idea as to Mr. Shorn's business here, after hours?"

The banker hesitated a moment, before he sat at his desk to begin accessing computer records. "Mr. Shorn was applying for a loan for a business acquisition." Skimming through the documentation on the screen, he murmured, "This is very strange."

"Can you please elaborate?" Jim prompted.

"The terms of the agreement are highly unusual," the Bank Manager took measure of the policeman before him and decided to continue, "Upon the death of either Mr. or Mrs. Shorn, the loan is to be paid out in full from the proceeds of Mr. Shorn's employee life insurance policy. This goes against our normal policy for bank provided accidental death insurance, that only insures the individual indebted to us," the manager explained. Before leaving, he thanked him, and they both agreed to keep their conversation between the two of them at this time – off the record.

Jim O'Reilly had gained just enough information to guide the line of questioning for Tom. Back at the hospital, he found Tom in the same room where he'd left him earlier. Faith was no longer there. "Any news on your wife?"

"No, not yet, she is still in surgery – I've opted to wait here where it's quiet." Tom returned. Jim took note of his haggard profile – the man was under a load of stress.

"You are going through a lot, I hate to ask," Jim squeezed his arm. "Tom, is there any way possible that anyone could know that Karen would be driving your car this morning?"

"I can't see how - as I said, it was a last-minute switch, and we were both out the door first thing this morning."

"Are you aware of any financial benefit to anyone aside from yourselves, if either you or Karen should perish in an accident?"

"Well, my wife and I both have insurance," Tom replied, then added, "everything would be put into trust for the kids. Why do you ask?"

"Just routine questions," Jim waved it off. "You seemed a little surprised when Faith stated her sister Hope is your daughter's guardian," he commented.

"Yes, I suppose I was," Tom admitted, "but then it made sense. Karen has a legal background and just yesterday, my boss informed me that Karen had ensured the policy at work would be sufficient for our family needs if anything should happen to one or both of us, so it only stands to reason that she would include guardianship. Karen and the kids have become very close to Hope, and to be honest, I trust her."

"Tom, how would you have allocated the life insurance payout, should Karen have passed away in this car accident today?" Tom's anger reared, understandably – Jim reasoned.

"Do you seriously think I had anything to do with that crash? For God's sake man, I love my wife, not to mention that my daughter was also in that car!"

"Calm down Tom, that is not what I am implying. I'm merely trying to put all the pieces together to determine a possible motive. You are astute enough to know that we investigate every angle – these are necessary routine questions." he explained.

"What happened today was a tragic accident, nothing more," Tom stated.

"Tom, why were you at the bank the other day?" Jim chose another tactic.

"I was applying for a loan." Tom shook his head, trying to determine where this was going.

"A loan for what purpose?" Jim prompted.

"A business loan, to which I have signed a confidentiality agreement that is binding until the end of the month. Therefore, I am unable to disclose further details to you at this time," Tom explained.

"Just tell me this – who benefits from the associated business shares and profit margin, if something happened to you or to Karen?" Bells went off in Tom's head – he was beginning to understand where the police officer was headed with this line of questioning.

Tom froze, a wall of unease rolling in his guts. "If it were Karen to pass, then it would be shared between my business partner and I. Alternatively, if I were to pass, my business partner receives sole benefits to my portion," Tom replied slowly, "but I fail to understand the relevance of your question – Karen's accident was just that! Furthermore, I have already informed my potential partner that I am declining the partnership – please tell me where you are going with this."

Jim O'Reilly pulled out his phone and pulled up the picture he had uploaded showing the pool of liquid in the driveway. Handing the phone to Tom, he stated "I have not gotten confirmation yet, but I believe we might be looking at brake fluid. That is not all – I also found a piece of material that could very well be from the brake line." He surveyed Tom's shocked expression. "Believe me, I am hoping you are correct in your belief that it was a simple accident, but this evidence warrants an investigation concerning the possibility of the brake line being tampered with." Tom went white. "The car is under thorough scrutiny by forensics, so we are hoping to get a clearer picture of what happened. Aside from the criminal investigation outcome, this will grant insurance companies with necessary information, and provide closure for the victims' families," he concluded softly. "Tom, try to focus only on your wife right now and I will be back with hopefully more answers. Also, if anything comes to mind, please give me a shout - anything at all," he emphasized, before leaving Tom alone in the room once more. Almost back to the squad car, he saw Hope in her car with Sway in the passenger seat. Just as he was about to head over for a talk, Faith called out to him.

"Constable O'Reilly, how is your investigation going?"

"Not much to go on right now," he replied, with no intention of sharing his thoughts on the case with her. "How is the little girl doing?" he asked nodding towards Hope's car? "Her Dad is sure concerned about her."

"Worried about her mom, but physically she is fine - no injuries from the accident," Faith replied. Then she went on to say that it was a miracle that her mother pulled her from the car before it exploded. "From what she describes, her mother must have suffered another heart attack while she was protecting Sway from the impact of the explosion."

"I do not believe in miracles," Jim O'Reilly imparted.

Faith brushed his hand lightly for only a fraction of a second and breathed, "but you used to." He jerked his hand back as if branded by a hot iron, and pointedly chose to ignore that comment, firmly pushing down the well of unease that was creeping through his body.

"Speaking of Sway, I will need to talk with her," he stated and turned toward Hope's car. Faith stepped deftly between, effectively blocking his progress.

"Not at this moment," she implored quietly.

"Why not?" his tone was abrupt – masking his discomfort around this woman.

"They are praying for Sway's mom and all the other accident victims presently. How about I let Hope know that you want to speak to her after they finish?" Faith suggested softly.

"Oh," Jim stammered, taken back for a moment. "OK, I will wait in my car until they finish their business," he agreed. He supposed it wasn't his place to mess with divine intervention – not that he believed in it any longer.

"That's great! But I'm sure you won't want to subject her to questioning in the parking lot, or in the back of a scary squad car. It's also best to keep her away from the hospital, considering all she's been through today – at least until her mother is out of surgery so, it would seem sensible for us to bring Sway to you – would that be acceptable? Then, on the interim, you can get on with your routine police business, which I know is unending," Faith surmised, her tone sweetly sympathetic.

"OK, Dr. Kerr, that will be fine." You win this time little lady – this round, but you haven't seen the end of me, he promised silently. Faith asked for his number, and he provided her with a card from his wallet. She thanked him and stayed put until he got into his cruiser and took off. He begrudgingly conceded to a bona fide admiration for her, standing firm in protection of the little girl. One thing he knew for certain – Sway was in much better company with Faith and Hope, than with that slimy Dr. Crawley.

On the way to the station, his mind swirled around her comments and his knee-jerk reaction when she'd touched him. How would she know if he'd once believed in miracles? He also did not believe in coincidences. He was determined to put the pieces together on the cold case files where Faith's name kept coming up. His colleagues thought he was bat-shit crazy but there was something about this woman that threw his instincts into overdrive - telling him otherwise.

Once there, he checked in with the lab, confirming the liquid was brake fluid and that the tiny substance was indeed a piece of the brake line. He headed to forensics to pass on this information, who reported that there was little evidence left from the burned-out vehicle, but they had managed to salvage the brake line and the examiner believed it was cut. It seemed certain that someone had tampered with the brake line – seemingly with the intent to harm whoever would next drive the vehicle. Usually in these cases, the spouse would be one of the prime suspects – at the very least, to rule out. Tom had stated he had taken Karen's car to fuel it up. It sent shivers through him. Why would anyone be willing to sacrifice the life of a child in order to harm someone? Or perhaps was Tom the target? No matter which way he turned the information in his head, Tom just didn't fit the bill as the guilty party. Still, he needed to complete his investigation according to protocol. His next stop was Tom's place of employment. As luck would have it, he found Karen's car still in the parking lot, conveniently unlocked. He opened the door but knew that he would need the key in order to read the gas gauge. He entered the building and asked the receptionist if she had a key to Tom's vehicle.

"Maybe," she replied, "which one is it?" He gave her the make of the car and she went back into the office behind her and came out with a key. "You are taking Karen's car to Tom," she asked? He realized that anyone in the office now would easily know he'd taken the key and decided to play it safe by telling a half-truth.

"No, just grabbing something for Tom." Back in the car, he turned the key half-way in the ignition and the dash lit up. Wow, Tom had not been lying about the car being out of gas - barely reading on the fuel gauge. He pulled out his phone and took a picture, then went back to the key with a smile, just as Jean marched over.

"Excuse me, Constable O'Reilly," she challenged haughtily, "May I ask why you had the keys to Karen's car? I'm certain you realize that anything you may remove from the vehicle would not be admissible in a court of law, without a search warrant."

"Why would Tom or Karen, for that matter, be summoned to court, I wonder?" Jim maintained a cool demeanor.

"I did not say they would be." Jean spat. His cell phone rang - Faith advised that Sway was on her way over to meet with him. "Duty calls." Flashing a winning smile at Jean, he flipped the key to her and sauntered out the door. Jean had played the seductress when he'd first arrived in town, but he would not have any part of it. She was not a woman who took rejection well and so had always been a bitch whenever they crossed paths since. He had suspected Tom's arrangement with Jean when he'd spotted his car parked on a weekly basis, close to Jean's house. It was confirmed the time he had stopped him for speeding - the lipstick on his face, nervous behavior and overall disheveled appearance. Jim O'Reilly had little to no respect for cheaters.

Chapter 25

HOPE RUSHED SWAY out of the hospital and into her car. Sway was an emotional mess – traumatized, confused and thoroughly frightened.

"I did not help my mom," sobs wracked her little body.

"It is OK, your mom will be OK," Hope promised as she grabbed Sway and held her close. "Now I need you to listen to me," Hope stated, "we have very little time. You are now away from the crisis and sick people in the hospital, so you will be able to focus on my instructions." Sway sniffled but stopped crying.

"Am I going to help my mom?"

"No, you and I are going to help a little boy that was hurt in the crash you were in," Hope answered gently.

"But what about my mom?" Sway began to cry again.

"My mom is helping her now and she will be fine," Hope replied, with tears in her eyes, "now you and I need to focus on this little boy, OK? Can you do that with me?" Sway nodded. Hope placed her hands over Sway's ears and cradled her head, then looked into her eyes, "now take slow deep breaths and calm yourself – breathe with me, let's go," Hope guided the relaxation breath work. "Think of your most favorite thought that brings you joy," she instructed. As in the time before, Sway thought of her family making dinner together and her pets there with them - everyone laughing, love flowing through the space. "Now just breathe naturally – in and out," Hope whispered, "hold the thought, hold the feeling." Sway complied, feeling the absorption of positive energy as she filled her lungs.

"Now," Hope directed, "close your eyes and focus only on my instructions. It is important that you trust me and do everything I say." Sway acceded and just listened to Hope's breath and voice. "Feel the energy building in your lungs," Hope continued to whisper, "listen to my instructions, and do nothing until I say. Now, we are going take our energy to the Radiology room that we were in with the MRI machine. Here we will find a little boy. He has a broken bone in his neck – are you with me Sway?"

"Yes," Sway whispered, feeling almost as if she was in a trance.

"Great! You and I are going to visualize that bone repairing itself - the swelling around it gone; the pain completely diminished, and all the nerves in that area around the bone repaired like new. Once we have finished, you will feel me squeeze your hand twice. You will then take the black energy, sink it into the ground and gently come back to your body." She paused to allow her instructions to set in, then continued. "The color of energy we are going to use is teal. Picture the color teal. Yes, that is it," Hope whispered. "OK, now breath in and out slowly. Take the energy color of teal and let us go to this boy in the MRI room." Sway took the teal energy and went directly to the MRI room. There she sensed, more than saw, a little boy laying on the x-ray table – they were preparing to slide him into the drum. She could feel her and Hope's shared energy, surrounding the little boy, flowing through his body - focusing on his neck. Sway could see the broken bone, the swelling, and the severed nerves. She held her energy with Hope – she could see and feel in her mind, the teal energy at work – repairing the bone and nerves, and the swelling abating. She saw the black energy which looked and smelled horribly like sewage, thick and raunch. Hope squeezed her hand twice, and Sway adhered to the instructions, together with Hope, moving the black energy down into the ground. It was so heavy - Sway felt her own energy drain from her body and panicked momentarily. Hope immediately wrapped her in an orange light and brought her back into the car.

Sway was overcome with intense cold and exhaustion. Hope held her for a while, waiting for her warmth to return. "The boy will be OK," Sway stated – the certainty filled her mind and body.

"Yes, he will be OK," Hope confirmed, "good work, Sweetie!"

"So, you *are* like me," Sway marveled in the confidence and intuitive knowledge she felt flooding her senses. Hope had already imparted that to her, but now she felt it – had lived it!

"Yes, you and I have the same gift – now we have shared it together." Hope replied. "That is why I am here to teach and protect you," Hope confirmed, "I have been aware of my gift since I was very young.'

"I am glad we helped that boy," Sway said. "Can we make everyone in this hospital better?"

"Honey, I wish with all my heart that we could, but we only have so much energy to give, as I told you last time. If we give more than we have, then we die – it's that simple," Hope substantiated. Turning on the car heater to help warm them up, she continued, "just like this car - once out of fuel it no longer runs. Our energy is our fuel - we must never allow our tanks to empty because, unlike my car, there is no tow-truck to get us to the next gas station for a fill-up." Hope framed Sway's face, "I know I've told you this before and may sound like a broken record, but it's so important. Remember that you are just learning, so it is extremely dangerous for you to do this on your own - you must never do this without me. It is like trying to save a drowning person without your own life jacket - that person in their panic, will unknowingly and quite out of their control, take you with them as they perish. This is something you must follow no matter who it is, even your family. You just cannot do this alone!" Hope emphasised.

"OK, but it is so hard – I want to go to my mom. You said your mother was looking after her now, is she doing what we have been doing?" Sway requested.

"No, Sweetie," Hope replied, "my mother is doing so much more." Hope wrapped her arms around Sway. "I am going to tell you about my mother. Remember when you came to the hospital, and you first met us?" Hope appealed. Sway nodded. "Well, among other gifts, my mother has the powerful one of sight. When she first met you and took your hand, she was able to feel and see that you had the same gift as me," Hope explained.

"Really?" Sway squealed in amazement – this was such a wonderful learning journey, and she was excited to see where it would go.

"Yes," Hope chuckled at the exuberant expression on Sway's face. "Now you need to trust me," Hope stated. "Do you trust me Sway?"

"Yes, I do trust you," Sway firmly replied. "It's just that I am worried about my mom," Sway emphasized. "I want to be helping her," she broke into tears.

"I know Honey, I totally understand that. Just heed my words. Everything with your mother's healing needs time – it's a huge undertaking, and you must trust in the outcome. She is going to be fine," Hope assured her.

"But if I have this gift, why can't I give it to Mom?" Sway cried.

"Ok," Hope offered, "did you know that doctors are not allowed to look after their own family members?" Sway sniffed and shook her head. "Well, there is a reason behind that, and you need to believe me when I say you cannot be the one to help your mother," Hope emphasized.

"I have been feeling something strange about my mom. Like she is not my mom, but someone else." Sway's brow furrowed in thoughtfulness.

"You are learning all kinds of new things about yourself," Hope assured. "You need to be patient with yourself and accept all those feelings, trusting you will learn about it as you go along. In time you will understand everything, but for now - pace by pace. You will get tired of my saying this," Hope giggled, "but the key is patience – one day at a time." The two hugged warmly.

Faith tapped on the window, opened the back door and climbed in. "Everything OK,"

"Yes," Hope replied, the boy will be fine."

"Good!" Faith sighed and smiled warmly at Sway. "You are amazing, young lady! I think we should go in and give your dad support – he is beyond needing to see you - then that police officer wants to ask you some questions regarding the accident." She reached out and squeezed Sway's hand – it was clear she was distraught. "Don't worry, it will be fine."

"Where is Doctor Crawley?" Hope asked.

"Not here at this time so it's a great opportunity to see Tom," Faith added, and they headed to the entrance. Tom was still in the interview room, anxiously waiting to hear the outcome of Karen's surgery. Sway ran into his outstretched arms.

"It is going to be OK," she assured.

"Yes," Tom agreed through a veil of tears - your mom is getting a new heart as we speak!" Tom hugged her tight, and looked beseechingly at Hope, the gratitude written all over him, "Thank you for looking after her."

"That is my privilege," Hope responded. "How are you holding up?" she asked. Tom drew a shaky breath.

"I am OK, thank you," Tom confirmed.

"The police need to interview Sway on the accident details," Faith informed him.

"I cannot leave until I see Karen," Tom responded, anxious indecision evident in his eyes.

"We know that, so I will take her if that is OK with you," Hope offered in a gentle tone. "I promise I will not allow her to be exposed to further trauma." Tom agreed, then asked Sway if she was OK with first telling him what had happened.

"Mom was going down that long hill and when she tried to slow down, the brakes wouldn't work – I know because she yelled it out loud. Then the next thing I knew, there was a huge crash – we were trapped, but Mom got us out before the car exploded," Sway explained in an abbreviated version of the accident. Tom's heart lurched into his throat listening to his precious baby describe their brush with death.

"I am so sorry this happened to you and your mom," Tom soothed. "I promise, we will get some answers. I am ever grateful you are both alive." Tom broke down momentarily, overcome with emotion and Sway hugged him tight. "When you talk to the police officer, it is very important that you tell all the details that you can remember about the accident, so he can figure out how this all happened," Tom instructed.

"OK Dad," Sway replied and hugged him tighter. Returning the embrace, Tom was hit with the heat from several red flags burning in his mind

– could this have been intentional? So many elements seemed to be in question – the terms of the business loan somehow sparked his unease. Something wasn't right and though it may have nothing to do with the accident, Tom needed answers. He knew with a certainty that if it *was* intentional, he had been the target.

"I hate to impose any further, but I need someone to fetch my son from school," Tom appealed.

"I can do that," Faith replied, "I'm off shift." Tom thanked her and let go of Sway to phone the school. He explained to the receptionist that his wife was in an accident so he is at the hospital with her and he was hereby granting permission for their friend, Faith Kerr, to pick Zac up when the students were let out. The receptionist thanked him for letting them know and wished Karen a speedy recovery. Hope gave Tom's hand a squeeze and told him to hang in there - they would return once Sway had met with the police. The moment they walked out of the room, Sway was assaulted by an icy chill.

"Stay focused on yourself, not what is outside your body," Hope whispered encouragement. Sway saw a dark shadow move across the room in front of her, then another. "Do not pay any attention to them," Hope instructed, giving Sway's hand a tiny squeeze. As they walked past the waiting room, they heard crying from the little boy's father – Sway recognized him in the room while she and Hope had used their healing energy.

"So, you're saying my son Gabriel is going to be fine? There is nothing wrong with him?" Tears of joyous relief flowed down his face. Sway's heart swelled at the doctor's next words.

"His MRI results indicate no damage whatsoever - the lack of feeling and swelling in your son's neck was clearly temporary – the body's natural defense mechanism as it heals itself sometimes will kick in this way."

"My son can walk?" he cried out in joy.

"Yes, Gabriel has no impairment – he can walk, run, sprint to his heart's content," the doctor assured with a laugh. "The best news I have given today!"

Sway looked up at Hope and they shared a knowing smile. But the cold was still there. Sway saw yet another shadow move across the room. Hope held her hand a little tighter. Suddenly Doctor Crawley stepped into their path.

"There you are little lady, I have been looking everywhere for you," he droned – his tone masking a veiled threat. Sway instinctively scrambled behind Hope, still clutching her hand. "I am worried about this child - we need to run tests on her to make sure we've not missed anything – she's endured a horrific accident," Dr. Crawley flouted dramatically, sincerity absent in his demeanor.

"She has suffered no ill effects," Hope countered, loud and firm. "Now excuse us as we have somewhere to be."

"I will be left with no option but to call Child Services if you refuse to allow me to have this child's medical needs attended to, *nurse*" the doctor threatened.

"Please feel free to call Child Services," Hope snapped back, "and I, in turn, will have the Medical Board all over you, concerning the needless tests you have been ordering for several children, such as this little girl's MRI, with no symptoms to warrant it." Another doctor came out and asked what was going on, suggesting to a clearly agitated Doctor Crawley that he take this discussion somewhere private.

"With all due respect, we are not meeting Dr. Crawley anywhere," Hope relayed in a controlled tone. "He is not this child's doctor and we do not want him anywhere near her. Please check with Radiology in reference to an unwarranted MRI he ordered for this little girl earlier today." The mediating physician took Doctor Crawley's arm in an effort to steer him away from the child, until they could sort out the problem. Doctor Crawley instantly reacted with violence, grabbing the doctor's arm. The sound of his bone snapping – with a sick twist, was unmistakable and he screamed in pain. Sway's first instincts were to help the poor man – she was horrified! Hope squeezed her hand and whispered emphatically, "no." The injured physician backed away from Dr. Crawley in fear, intimidated by his cruel sneer – all masks were off – this was clearly a deranged man before them. Hope knew that the front desk receptionist would have immediately alerted Security.

Doctor Crawley turned back to Sway, who was still hidden behind Hope. Mercifully, two security guards moved in to secure the hostile doctor, who the injured physician had directed them toward. As Doctor Crawley's turned his raging attention to the security guards, Hope rushed Sway out of the hospital, into her car in the parking lot, and sped off, away from the hospital.

Hope took calming breaths and drove until she found a park. She quickly called Officer O'Reilly and left a message to let him know they were a little delayed – there'd been an altercation with Dr. Crawley at the hospital - but are on their way. "Come with me," Hope guided Sway over to the playground. They both took a swing and moved slowly, back and forth. "Breathe," Hope sighed, "just breathe." Sway did so, filling her lungs and her body with calming energy.

"Who was that crazy Doctor?" Sway finally inquired. She refrained from asking why they did not help the injured doctor - she knew the answer. "He scared me this morning too!"

"Dr. Crawley suspects that you have a special gift and is on a quest to find out what makes us different from other people. Children are easy targets in his position, and we can never afford him that opportunity. Do not worry - he will not be bothering us again," Hope promised. Although Sway couldn't imagine how Hope knew this, she implicitly trusted her.

"What were those shadows at the hospital? Are those ghosts?" Sway wondered.

"No, they are not ghosts, I will explain all of this to you when we are alone and have more time," Hope replied.

"Do other people see what we see?" Sway inquired. "I think I asked you this before, sorry."

"No worries, Sweetie, some people do," Hope responded, "but most people do not."

"Is that what is in my house? Those black shadows?" Sway asked.

"Yes," Hope replied, but we will talk about it later." Sway swung back and forth, deep in thought, pondering all that Hope had just shared. Hope waited patiently for Sway to process the information. "You sit here for a moment - I have to make a call," Hope relayed. Hope got up and just far enough to be out of Sway's earshot, yet close enough that she could still be by her side within a second. Soon she returned and sank back into the swing. "Are you ready to go tell the police about today?" Hope asked.

"I am really tired and want to go home," Sway professed, "but I just want to get this over with."

"Good thinking," Hope got up, took her by the hand and headed for the car. "You are such a brave and strong young lady!" As they pulled out of the park, Hope checked the rear-view mirror and spotted the unmistakable dark crazed glare from Doctor Crawley, as he pulled his vehicle up directly behind them. She peeled out and quickly made her way through the community with the doctor hot on her tail. Sway knew something was up as Hope sped and slowed erratically – it wasn't normal driving.

"Is everything OK?" Sway scrutinized the anxious look on Hope's face. Hope replied that everything was fine – just trust. She kept an eye on her rear-view mirror as the doctor tracked them, relentlessly. Soon, she swung into the police station, aware that the doctor had stopped and parked, maliciously watching them enter. Hope sent a silent prayer of gratitude that they had reached safety, feeling the clutching grasp of pure evil as they entered the building.

Chapter 26

HOPE RUSHED UP to the front desk, pleading to speak to a police officer as soon as possible, preferably Constable O'Reilly who had requested their presence to interview Sway – but urgency dictated immediate assistance. The receptionist asked the nature of the issue.

"Dr. Crawley from the local hospital, is in a rage. He is outside parked and is stalking us - followed me here from the hospital. He tried to assault me there and when another doctor stepped in to help, Dr. Crawley lost control and violently broke his arm," Hope was clearly desperate, anxiously scanning the door. "Please help us!" The front desk receptionist picked up the phone and quickly summarized Hope's description to a person on the other end.

"You said he followed you here?"

"Yes!" Hope confirmed. The receptionist repeated her words verbatim.

"What type of vehicle is he driving?" Hope described it the best that she could. A few other clarifying questions were answered. Hope nearly collapsed with relief when a female police officer emerged from another room and motioned for them to follow her to a room marked "Interview 2" above the door. They were ushered to sit on chairs surrounding a desk in the middle of the room. Hope pulled two of them together so she could maintain her protective hold on Sway, who was clearly exhausted and frightened. Sway leaned into Hope, who whispered a directive to close her eyes and rest.

The police officer introduced herself as Constable Jones and leveled Hope with a solemn look. "We were already made aware of the assault by Dr.

Crawley at the hospital and a unit was dispatched. However, by the time they arrived, he had fled the premises – clearly not too long ago." She paused for a few seconds. "A witness provided a detailed description and identified him, so if Dr. Crawley is outside this station, he will be arrested immediately. Otherwise, we will locate and apprehend him promptly." The officer assured them that they would be safe in here on the interim. "Thank you, by the way, for leading him to us," she imparted with a gentle smile of amusement. Hope returned the lighthearted grin and thanked her, requesting that she please let Officer O'Reilly know of their presence when he arrives. Hope tightened her firm grip on Sway and sighed deeply, releasing a mountain of tension.

"Sweetie, why don't you try to get a little sleep until Constable O'Reilly comes in – remember we need to recharge our bodies!" Her gentle whisper lulled Sway off to a relaxed slumber and Hope wrapped them both in a pale blue light, protecting Sway from hearing and feeling all the commotion and tension within the police station. As a result, Sway was not impacted by Dr. Crawley's enraged shouting when the police officers brought him into the station. Nor did she feel or sense the arresting officers' pain from the severe injuries inflicted upon them when trying to apprehend the man. She did not feel the effects of the taser gun that was used on the doctor to subdue him, nor hear the police officer reading Crawley his rights with the added conviction – "you are going away for a very long time, Doctor." Her only awareness was cocooned within the warm blue light surrounding, protecting, and helping to restore her energy, as well as providing her peace from the worries about her mother - a wonderful supportive pool of love and safety.

Sway was sound asleep when Jim O'Reilly burst into the room and stopped short. When he'd arrived at the police station paramedics were carrying police officers out of the building, into waiting ambulances. The perpetrator was restrained and in lock down. The one unscathed arresting officer had declined his offer to assist, assuring him everything was under control. It was important now, to attend to the accident witness. He could not overlook the possibility of vital connections. Hope gently woke Sway and told her that the police officer was there to ask her questions. Jim O'Reilly smiled gently at the little girl and asked her to start from the beginning, take her time and tell him everything she could remember. Sway took a deep breath and reached into her memories, still fresh, but painful.

"Well, my mom tried to slow down - she was stomping on the floor hard and yelled that we had no brakes. It would just not slow down," tears formed in Sway's eyes and Hope hugged her tight to her side. "Then things were crashing into us, and we flew around and landed in a ditch upside down. I was really scared but my mom got us both out of our seatbelts and out from the car, into the ditch before Daddy's car exploded. It was so loud!" Jim's heart melted, seeing the trauma reflected in her innocent wide-eyed stare. Mommy saved me – she was on top of me!"

"I know Sweetie – what she did was very brave! Now, I need you to concentrate hard. Did you notice anyone around your house before you left in the car that morning?" Sway's brow scrunched in consternation.

"Yes, there was a man on the street in a nice suit, just like the religious people who knock on our door, but Mom and Dad always say, no thank you."

"I think she has had enough for one day," Hope intervened softly. "If she thinks of anything else, we will call you - would that work out OK for you?" she concluded and rose to leave. Jim nodded and Sway stood up, promptly collapsing in Hope's arms. Jim O'Reilly immediately offered to carry the child out but Hope kindly refused, assuring him she had this.

"Let's go rest up, and then I'll take you to see your mother," Hope whispered softly." Jim traced their movements, his expression intense, as Hope carried the child out of the building. As he turned to make a path toward his desk, he deduced that the little girl had just confirmed the cause of the accident – failing brakes. The question that was burning a hole in his mind now – had this mystery man played a sinister role, or was he perhaps a door-to-door street vendor – end of that lead? Mulling it over, he figured that a criminal out to sabotage someone's vehicle, likely causing their death, would not be crawling under a car in a suit. Still, he wondered – great cover that could be. As he walked by Dispatch, Toby waved him over.

"What a crazy day and that little girl you just interviewed has been through more than any child should have to endure!" At Jim's affirmative nod, Toby decided it was as good a time as any to voice the issue that had been troubling him from the start. "Jim, there is a mystery with that 911 call that's been perplexing me and I haven't yet figured it out – can I run it by you?" The officer's interest was thoroughly piqued now as he invited him to do so. "I was hoping once her mother had healed, I could go over and talk to them about it," he paused, "but this new crisis in their family puts a halt to that plan. There's something strange going on though." At Jim's questioned brow, he let out a troubled sigh. "I think it's best if you just listen to the tape of the call." Toby led the way into a back room where they stored all the recordings and pulled the call from the computer files. Constable Reilly listened carefully to the call.

"Question – can I assume that the call originally placed by Karen Shorn requesting medical assistance for her daughter Sway, somehow changed to the daughter in question, advising that her mother required medical assistance?" Toby nodded his confirmation.

"The pets in the background are going nuts as well – very aggressive," Toby added. "Now let me pull up these other two sounds I managed to discern and isolate on the tape." Jim O'Reilly tuned into the sounds as Toby directed. There was a clear tapping sound, followed by a voice, calling Sway's name. Jim felt the hair on the back of his neck stand straight up and a chill travel up his spine.

"Scary shit, aye?" Toby stated.

"Yes, scary shit," Jim concurred, unable to ignore the foreboding in the pit of his stomach – no matter what his beliefs in the realm of strange occurrences, this one had him spooked. However, he needed to stick with facts that equated to evidence. "Who in the hell is trying to mess with this girl and her family?"

"Well, that's not all," Toby then handed Constable Reilly another 911 transcript. "I took the call today from the hospital reception, advising that a Dr. Crawley had violently assaulted one of the other physicians with enough strength to snap his arm clean through. During the call, they indicated that Crawley had just fled the scene, leaving the building." This confirmed some of what Jim had already pieced together. "We sent out a squad car to take the victim's statement – Dr. Styles, who stated that there was an altercation between Crawley and a woman – turned out to be Hope Newgard, the nurse who was just here with Sway. Dr. Crawley had been insistent that she place Sway in his care, in order to arrange for additional testing, even though other medical professionals had confirmed there were no warranting symptoms. Dr. Styles stepped in to assist and the rest you've just heard. Hope rushed out the doors with Sway as Security attempted to subdue Crawley. By the time the squad car that we originally dispatched to the hospital rerouted, Hope had called in to advise that he was tailing her as she drove to the station. The officers went outside to arrest the doctor and all hell broke loose."

Jim's mind went into overdrive. Hope was the sister to Dr. Faith Kerr, the woman he had been investigating regarding unsolved missing children/murders across the country. His police instincts told him that there was more to these two women other than biological sisterhood.

"What are you thinking?" Toby could almost see the wheels spinning in Jim O'Reilly's brain – this constable was well-known for his astute instincts and investigative prowess. Before Jim could respond, loud shouting erupted in the main part of the building. Both rushed out to investigate. Causing all the disruptive din, was a man claiming to be Dr. Crawley's lawyer. After some negotiation and a stern warning, the Staff Sergeant approved the lawyer's request to see his client. Jim immediately stepped forward to offer escorting him to Crawley's cell, hoping to gain some insight - intensely curious as to why the doctor was so interested in the little girl and Hope Burnett. The lawyer insisted on seeing his client in a private interview room, and the Sergeant reluctantly agreed – not wishing to compromise the perpetrator's rights, with a strict directive to another officer to ensure Crawley was thoroughly restrained, before bringing him to the room where the lawyer and Constable O'Reilly would await.

Jim had no sooner gotten the lawyer into the room, when shots were fired. He instructed the polished man to huddle under the desk and exited the room, pistol drawn, easing carefully out into the hallway. He quickly ducked back behind cover, after noting that Crawley had somehow managed to snag an officer's gun and was still waving it around in a menacing threat to continue the horrific barrage. The terrible sight of two bodies lying on the floor, unmoving – blood pooling around them, spurred him to automatic – all his training in the forefront. With heart pounding wildly, he figured that Crawley hadn't yet seen him. He cocked the trigger on his service revolver, stepped out and aimed, taking his first shot to Crawley's knee, effectively dropping him to the floor in a raging screaming heap. In accordance with protocol for the seriousness of the incident, his second shot rang and hit the now infamous Dr. Crawley, square between the eyes, eliminating the threat. All in that few seconds, the doctor had thrown his gun and put his hand over his head. Jim knew there would likely be an inquest – always was with these things, but he was confident that he had acted within protocol. Introspectively, had he had enough time to honor Crawley's surrender? Perhaps so, and he mulled it over – then why hadn't he? But the answer surfaced deep in his gut – there was so much more to Crawley than what went down today – a gut instinct moved him to seek an interview with the lawyer.

Toby suddenly ran to kick the gun on the floor to the dead doctor's body. "Area clear – the perpetrator is down; call an ambulance!" Jim stood in shock as the Sergeant barked orders, controlling the crime scene. It all whirled around in a confusing jumble in his mind. Moments later the paramedics where there working on the two victims shot by the doctor – the officer that had escorted and lost his gun to Crawley – pronounced dead on the scene, and the receptionist whose injuries were thankfully not fatal. Jim struggled to focus and handed his gun over to the crime scene investigative team before heading to the interview room where he had left the doctor's lawyer, with Toby following his lead. They found the interview room empty – the lawyer had clearly fled the scene. Toby groaned.

"Unfortunately, there were no cameras active in the investigation room, nor in the area when the lawyer first arrived, but entrance cameras will have recordings. You can get a clear picture of this lawyer and find out who he is." Toby paused, "just so you know, there is no footage of the shooting either – in the hallway or the main area."

Jim O'Reilly turned to Toby, "Do we know if the lawyer actually provided his name?" Toby shook his head – witnesses reported that he had not. Jim did not miss Toby's deliberate message that there had been no cameras as he'd fired his two shots. Momentarily Staff Sargent paged them both to be available for the internal investigative team. Toby patted Jim's arm and walked back out to the main area of the station.

"I saw the perpetrator aim the gun at Officer O'Reilly, who then shot the perpetrator in the knee, dropping him to the floor. The perpetrator then aimed again at Officer O'Reilly, who fired a second shot which hit the perpetrator in the forehead."

Another officer spoke up, "Officer O'Reilly saved lives today - there were four more shots in that gun - could have been four more victims without Jim's quick response. That doctor was clearly in a psychopathic state – crazed and dangerous – remember how many officers he took down without a weapon? Jim O'Reilly is a hero." Someone else chanted, "Here, here," and started a round of applause. The head of the investigating team held his hand up for quiet and informed Jim solemnly that they had enough information for today and would continue to follow up with the standard formal inquest. Everyone agreed that it had been one hell of a day at the Terrace precinct.

Jim's cell chimed. "Hello Dr. Kerr."

Chapter 27

KAREN WOKE EXTREEMLY groggy, to a nurse administering tiny droplets of water onto her lips - just enough to ease the intense dryness in her mouth. She cheerfully relayed to Karen that she was doing very well in Recovery. She fell in and out of consciousness as people came and went. At some point she looked up into the face of Dr. Edwards.

"How are you feeling young lady?" Dr. Edwards smiled and squeezed her hand. You can be proud of yourself for all the changes you embraced to prepare for this very moment." He patted her shoulder softly, "I have never met a patient more amazing than you. When you arrived, your heart had stopped from the impact of the explosion of the car. Upon arrival in the ambulance, we prepared you to be flown to Vancouver for heart surgery and I found your heart to be beating effectively. I ran more tests and found your heart to be perfectly fine. Your past surgery followed by all the changes you made in your life speaks volumes to what healthy choices can do. It is nothing short of a miracle, your heart is perfectly fine. As for why your heart stopped this time. Any heart including a perfect one could be stopped by an explosion.

Karen could only listen and try to absorb everything that was happening around her, then whisper thank you to the doctor. She understood she had been waiting for a heart transplant, remembered being in the hospital when she'd initially suffered cardiac arrests, and recalled being home and confused. She instinctively knew there were significant gaps in time missing in her recollection. Her mind played tapes – Tom bathing her, cleaning food out of her hair with gentle soothing; Zac lying beside the bed, telling her she was going to be OK and that her memory loss was normal. She drifted off - the confused jumble of images and emotions too exhausting to focus on, as she vaguely registered Dr. Edwards parting words, your bruised from head to toe with pulled muscles, you are probably feeling like you have been run over by a truck, but that will be managed with pain medication. I will be back to check on you again shortly.

One memory in particular stood out as vital, directly after her second heart attack, in the hospital. Karen had slid into a vivid nightmare - like a movie where she was helplessly watching herself, aware of lying in the hospital bed simultaneously. She and Sway were in a violent car accident. She was struggling to get out of her seatbelt, feeling intense panic – she needed to get to her daughter! They were upside down in the car, when it suddenly exploded with a huge blast. Karen watched in horror from afar as she and Sway burned inside the car, Sway screaming for her help. In that moment Susan appeared, from the neighboring hospital bed, taking her hand. The nightmare was horrific – so real that she could feel the flames, smell the gas, and hear screams all around her. Susan was reassuring and offered to take all the pain and terror away. Karen remembered granting her permission. The next thing she remembered was confusion and anxiety – at home with no recollection of how she'd gotten there. Her body was in extreme pain from head to toe, as if every muscle had been torn apart. She was ravenous without being able to open her mouth to eat, which did not make sense - she was able to speak with no issue.

Her last memory before emerging from the fog of and seeing Dr. Edwards, was lying on top of her daughter – the acrid smell of fuel; feeling of the grass beneath them; the explosion and scorching heat – the massive pain in her chest. As her conscious mind began to recognize her surroundings, her gut feeling told her it was no nightmare – rather a vivid horrific memory of her and Sway's narrow escape from death.

"Is my little girl, OK?" The nurse squeezed her hand in response to her croak and assured her that Sway was unhurt. Karen sank back and surrendered to her body's healing needs – it was a miracle! At the sound of Tom's voice calling her name, she looked toward the door – Tom tried to hide them, but tears were visible.

"You did it Honey, I am so proud of you!" The smile radiated. "The doctor's confirmed that all your hard work to improve your health was key. You would not have survived this otherwise – your heart is healthy now." Karen reached up and touched her chest, feeling her heart beating strong. "Sway – is she OK?" Karen whispered through a haze of tears.

Tom ever so gently wiped her cheeks and placed his lips on the back of her hand that was not encumbered by tubes and needles. "Sway is fine," Tom assured her. "Karen, somehow you managed to pull her from the car before it exploded. You are amazing! Neither of you would be here otherwise." Tom broke down and sobbed. Karen lifted her hand to run it through his hair in a sweet caress. He sunk into the pleasure of that feeling – eternally grateful she was still here.

"How is Zac – where are the kids now?" Karen inquired. Tom pulled himself back together.

"They are worried about you of course but doing well," he imparted with a reassuring smile. "They will be here to see you soon. Dr. Edwards insists that you not have more than one visitor at a time. You have no life-threatening injuries but the explosion from the car did a number on your muscles."

A nurse popped in to advise that the kids were waiting, anxious to see their mother. "We are going to move you to a private room. Rest is key though, so no more than ten minutes per visit, OK?" Karen nodded weakly, beyond excited to see them. "More rest – quicker you'll be home," the nurse affirmed positively. Karen was transferred to her own room, all set up and waiting for her. Once the monitors were all in place, Sway bounced into the room, her excited energy flowed straight to Karen's heart. She stopped to slowly approach the bed and leaned down to whisper in Karen's ear.

"I love you, Mom." Karen's insides melted, her sweet little girl's voice the tonic that made this journey worth every moment.

"I love you too, Sweetie." Karen replied as Sway placed her hand over her mother's heart.

"You have a beautiful heart, Mom." She kissed Karen's cheek, then remembering the nurses directions on just minutes for each visitor so smiled and said, "It is Zac's turn to see you now – I promise I'll come back after you rest." Sway bounced back out of the room.

Zac entered the room, tears flowing freely, as he hugged his mother gently.

"Mom, I was so afraid of losing you," through his hiccupping sobs, Karen could feel his pain and anguish.

"I know Sweetie," Karen empathized, running her fingers through his hair. "I have a strong healthy heart now, so time to quit worrying. Thank you for being there for me when I was lost and confused," she whispered. "With everything I've been through, the only time I felt safe, was with you. I was so confused, but you helped me through all of it – I don't know what I would have done without you," Karen whispered, still stroking her son's hair. Karen could feel her son's body start to relax. "Zac, I'm going to continue to lean on you if that's OK."

Zac sat back up so he could meet his mother's eyes, the sadness and fear left his mind, his mother needed him to be strong, "Absolutely Mom, you can count on me!" He paused, clearly in deep thought. "When you were going through those episodes it was scary, but it was the only times I felt like it was really you. The rest of the time, since your heart attacks, it seemed like you were almost someone else."

Karen laughed softly. "Well, I hope a better version of me."

"There is no better version of you," Zac declared adamantly, "you are my amazing mom!" Karen smiled and asked him if he felt better now. Nodding his head emphatically, he kissed her on the cheek as his sister had done moments earlier. The nurse came in to gently remind him it was time to let his mom rest but assured he could visit often.

"You have a beautiful family!" the nurse commented. Karen thanked her. Indeed, she was blessed! She drifted into a deep slumber, filled with vivid dreams - confusing, shifting, changing - repetitive circumstances but with different outcomes. The common theme involved the two women that she had first met when she brought Sway into the hospital. One was a doctor and the other a nurse. They offered to help solve the mystery of Sway's debilitating symptoms. When Susan appeared, she remembered their names - Hope and Faith. Karen woke abruptly to find them both standing by her bed. Was she still dreaming? When they spoke, she realized she was fully awake. Hope reached over and touched her arm.

"We are glad to see you are OK," she offered quietly with a bright smile. Hope re-introduced herself and her sister. "We understand that you will have lapses in your memory so we will be here to help you with your recovery. You might remember us, but you've been through a lot - we have become close friends with you and family," Hope explained. "Please know that you can trust us."

Karen pondered for a moment. "I do indeed remember you when I brought Sway into the hospital. There are other memories I'm trying to make sense of, but to be honest – I've also had some vivid dreams. Hope pulled up a chair and took Karen's free hand.

"I want you to understand that all of what you will be feeling and experiencing is normal. It will take time to sort out the dream from the reality and sometimes the two are intrinsically connected. Try not to stress yourself – just go with the flow. We will be right beside you, taking you through all this one small step at a time – it will make sense to you later.

Then Karen remembered they were investigating Sway's mysterious ongoing illnesses. She knew very well that some of the hospital staff were starting to suspect her of making Sway sick. Karen pulled her hand away from Hope. "Did you find out what is wrong with my daughter? Then added, you have been investigating me and my family. Surely you know now there is nothing going on in our home that would make Sway sick."

Hope reached back a touched Karen's arm, and spoke barely above a whisper, we know you would never harm Sway. Karen felt a warmth go through her before she experienced the anxiety and confusion melt away. Suddenly she was completely at ease with these two women, as if she'd known them her entire life - like sisters. Karen felt at peace and whispered, "thank you," as Hope gently removed her hand.

Faith walked over and gently brushed the side of Karen's cheek and said before her and Hope left the room, "now rest and heal. Do not worry about anything. We are here for you and your family."

Karen drifted in and out of haunting dreams, some normal and others completely terrifying. There were many wakeful moments over the next several days when she clung to Faith and Hope for solace – it was a blessing. Dr. Edwards popped in to see her often and relayed that the loss of memory maybe temporary, but he advised that he had deferred to another specialist to rule out any head injuries from the accident.

Dr. Edwards was a little worried about the mental health of his patient – physically, she was coming along great! All test results had come back normal, and the specialist speculated the loss of memory may be from oxygen deprivation when her heart had failed. They had met in consultation and Dr. Hamilton turned to Faith, whom he'd come to regard as a highly skilled phycologist. "Dr. Kerr, what are your thoughts on the matter?" "I only work with children and their families but trauma, such as an accident, or the heart failure, can cause memory loss," Faith echoed the other doctor's prognosis and agreed to monitor the mother as she worked with the child.

Karen transfer to a private room, was blessedly less frenzied – much quieter than having to share a room with four other patience. On the first day, she overheard the nurses discussing how fortunate she was - that apparently her medical insurance had recently been increased, covering all expenses, including the private room. She pondered on their musings about Dr. Kerr's presence – she is not Karen's physician – Dr. Kerr is a child psychologist - why did she have access to Karen's health files?

Karen's mind tuned into their finances which she's always managed – knew exactly how tight their budget was. How and when had Tom arranged to add the extended health benefits to their medical plan? It was such a blessing! Obviously, a lot had transpired since her health journey began, that she needed to catch up on.

Time slipped quickly by. Faith came regularly to administer physio care – muscle massage, and gentle manipulation of her limbs. Karen so enjoyed Faith's company and always felt at ease – looked forward to her daily visits. She reflected on the fact that Faith seemed to avoid personal questions and always maneuvered the conversation back to Karen. It seemed a bit odd, but she put it away for later.

The visits from her family filled her heart with joy – she lived for them. Karen found the time with each one of her children and husband, valuable to her recovery – filling the empty memory gaps. At the onset, the visiting restrictions provided her time to absorb their sharing; Zac running with her; his amazement with her commitment to health, and her lack of cooking skills. They had a good chuckle together when Zac described the hideous chocolate cake. She was pleasantly surprised to learn of the family stepping up to cook and clean. Zac solemnly shared his belief that she'd been preparing them for the possibility of a future without her.

She hungered to incorporate all these beautiful, shared stories into her memory. Geesh, Tom actually doing dishes – that one she could barely wait for! There was so much out of character for her, like keeping Sway home. Karen reflected on her priorities – the vital importance of attending school, for the educational value as well as the social piece. Karen would have considered her decision to keep Sway home with her as selfish, but Tom explained it had made sense as Sway was riddled with anxiety over the worry for her mom, as well as her own ailments. Tom relayed that it was intended only for a brief period of time and that Sway was back in school now - all was good. Karen was relieved to hear this.

Sway shared about their perfect days - going to the park, playing games together, errands and library. Karen fervently wished she could remember, confused by the role change. She self-defined as the perfect wife, mother and homemaker - the mediator who stood between her children and her husband's volatile mood swings. How had she become this strong person everyone kept telling her about? What on earth had happened with Tom? The adjustment she was facing seemed insurmountable without memory context, and Karen reclined on the bed, letting all the information run amok through her mind. So deep in thought, she did not hear Hope and Faith enter her room and was a bit startled with Hope's inquiry.

"How are you doing today? Sorry for the alarm – you seem deep in thought. Anything we can help you with?" Karen returned their amused grins.

"I am just trying to process everything." Karen sat up straighter. "The person you all are describing as "me" seems like a stranger - this super woman who has unlimited energy reserves; runs every day; keeps her daughter out of school to play games in the park and encourages her family to do all the house chores that I take so much pride and pleasure in doing myself."

Hope sat down and took Karen's hand – Faith hovered closely behind. Karen felt instant relaxation - both body and mind. "Well, my dear Karen, you are all those things and more. Each one of us holds incredible strength within us and given opportune circumstances and motivation, those strengths will come out. Didn't your doctors warn about the odds of qualifying for transplant surgery being low - you were far from being the perfect candidate? Then you incorporated drastic changes accordingly. At the same time, you were preparing your family to be able to stand on their own, in the event you might not be there to do all these things for them. Doesn't that sound like you?" Hope prompted. Karen mulled over her words. Yes, it did sound like her, when presented in that context! She reflected on her normal mode of operation - she did plan for everything - stocking the freezer with meals not only for family but for others who may be in need. Eons ago, when she'd thought to pursue a law career, her purpose included envisioning a bright future in helping others.

"Before you met Tom what had you dreamed for your future?" Karen smiled, thinking Faith must be a skilled mind reader.

"I was determined to become a lawyer and help those devoid of the means to help themselves." Karen anticipated what the next question would be, "I let those dreams go when I fell in love with Tom. After Zac was born, he made his wishes clear – my place was in the home." She'd accepted that her life would revolve around marriage and children.

"How would you advise your children if they were in your shoes?" Faith proposed.

"I would say go for their dreams." Her reply required no aforethought.

"Why is that?"

"Because it is their right to fulfill their destinies."

"And what of your dreams, your destiny?"

"I need to fulfill them," Karen slowly responded. "I always felt that my total dedication to my family was where I was meant to be, but now I see that I had accepted it – settled." Karen's face lit up. "Not that I would change it. I still feel this is the most important job I'll ever have!" It was a light bulb moment – she needed to rekindle the pursuit of that dream – it was her destiny, along with wife, mother, friend, and all the hats she would wear in her lifetime. "Now I know I can have both!" Faith breathed an outward sigh of relief, and Karen giggled, glancing over at the door in response to Tom's chipper entrance greeting.

"Hello ladies," he addressed them all with a wide grin. "How is my beautiful wife doing today?" Karen felt her heart flutter and smiled. Hope and Faith gracefully excused themselves and promised they would return later. Planting a lingering kiss on her lips, he inquired as to how she was feeling.

"Better every day!"

"That is awesome," Tom regarded her affectionately. "How was your visit with Hope and Faith?"

"It is always wonderful to see them," Karen responded.

"We are so fortunate to count them as our friends," Tom commented, and Karen nodded her solid agreement.

"How are the children?"

"Great," Tom smiled broadly. Zac is waiting on pins and needles to see you. Sway is going to hang out with Hope and asked me to tell you she'd visit later – afraid she'll tire you out!"

Karen smiled. Both of their children were so thoughtful. "So, what can you share today to jog my memory?"

"There's much I can say but I'm fearful to stress you out," Tom replied.

"Well, better I hear it from you than someone that's not able to answer my questions – no assumptions this way," Karen responded. Tom figured that made sense and decided to plunge in.

"Do you remember our conversation about Doug and Jean selling the business?" Karen shook her head. "Jean had proposed a 50/50 partnership between her and I to buy Doug out." He paused, assessing the wisdom of this conversation, and felt encouraged to carry on.

"Honey, I need to preface this with a heartfelt apology – for all that I've been up to this moment, and especially all that I haven't." Karen was deeply touched by the sincerity evident in his eyes and the tears he was fighting. "I promise you, my love, that every moment moving forward – I am a changed man, and I will be by your side every step of the way, for better or worse." With a shaky sigh, he went on to tell her the entire story once more – the company, his infidelity and his adamant vow that all of it was in their past now. Karen's response did not exactly mirror the bedroom experience, as he'd hoped. Tears rolled down her face when he confessed his infidelity – it was tearing his heart apart to witness the pain he'd caused, but she did not interrupt as he poured it all out – no more secrecy. Karen looked thoughtful as he explained the bank documents he'd signed and his decision to decline the company partnership. His heart careened between hope and desperation as she remained quiet for a few agonizing moments.

"Tom, I will ask that you please leave now – I need time to absorb it all." He reached over and kissed her forehead and asked if she was still up to seeing Zac. At her nod, he apologized once more and left the room. Pulling herself together, she bestowed a bright smile upon Zac as he came bounding in with the biggest grin plastered all over his sweet face.

"How are you mom?" he inquired. She assured Zac that she was recovering and getting stronger every day. "That great!" he enthused, "I knew you would, Mom," he loved his time with her – especially his role in sharing small lost pieces of her memory – confident that it would help her. Today he was looking forward to telling her all about the ghost in their home. He started off with the mystery chill in their home – his research and the library trip. Pride shone from his face as he relayed the salt ritual that he'd undertaken to protect them all. Before now, Karen would never have encouraged or condoned her child to research ghosts. She acknowledged the changes within – the old Karen would have wanted to protect her children from anything that may cause them fear. With a sense of acceptance, she realized that she was no longer that woman, and listening to her son regale the responsibility he had taken to help his family evoked a deep esteem for him, along with a well of gratitude. "Mom? Did this spark any memories?" With the hopeful look on Zac's face, Karen was relieved to relay that indeed, some memories were filtering in – her in the bathtub and the room overcome with steam, the temperature in the room icy cold.

"Did you come to sleep beside me on the floor? Or in our bed?" Zac's excitement was palpable as he confirmed that he had done both and hugged her warmly.

"Mom, it's working – I knew we could do it together! I must go now, Dad's waiting for me, and I think you need to sleep after this round!" Karen chuckled as she kissed and tousled his hair, and requested that he please send Dad back in.

Karen had asked Zac to wait for his father in the hallway because they needed a private chat. Tom gingerly approached her bedside, but she put her hand up to stop him. "I am tired Tom," she stated, "I just want to ask that you please bring a copy of the bank documents next visit." Tom hung his head, clearly crestfallen.

"I will do that," he apologized and left the room with a haunted, beseeching backward glance. Karen closed her eyes to rest - her body and heart were letting her know she would need it. As she drifted off, she affirmed that tomorrow was a new day, and vowed that she was not about to let anyone mess with her family. As she fell deeper, the room turned icy cold, and a shadow hovered over her bed.

Chapter 28

TOM DROPPED ZAC at home, then headed directly to the bank. Apprehension flooded him and a well of nausea rolled around in his stomach. He hoped in earnest that he hadn't plunged them into a pool of trouble. Karen did not deserve this – among other things. Parking the car, he took a deep steadying breath and headed in. As the Business Loans Manager that he'd original dealt with was away for the day, Tom requested to see the Bank Manager.

"I'm sorry Sir, but you will need an appointment." Tom's anxiety escalated several notches – he needed to deal with this issue – now!

"OK, please arrange an appointment today. I require a copy of the business loan application document I recently signed, and I will wait." Tom was accustomed to getting his way, his tone pleasant but firm.

"The soonest I can book you in will be the week after next," the receptionist regarded him calmly. Frustration reigned and Tom lost all control of his attempt to keep his cool.

"My business requires urgency, so I *will* sit here until I can speak with someone who can give me a copy of the document I recently signed," his sonorous tone was drawing attention from bank patrons. "I should have been provided a copy when I left."

"Is everything OK here?" Jim O'Reilly's voice further agitated his mood. Tom turned to face him.

"No, it is not, I require a copy of the document I signed, and am being told that I will have to wait more than a week."

Jim turned to the receptionist and appealed in a pleasant tone, "I think we can agree that Mr. Shorn has a right to request a copy of the document – would you be so kind to obtain this for him right now?" Other patrons of the bank where now glued to this interaction, and a few nodded their full agreement to the officer's reasonable request.

The receptionist curtly picked up the phone and rang the Bank Manager's extension. Moments later, he motioned both Tom and the constable into his office. Tom took a seat across from the Banker and Jim O'Reilly chose to remain by the door. Tom's entire focus was tuned to his goal and had no time to worry about the implications of the officer being present. Tom informed the manager of his previous business with the Business Loans Manager, and that he was not given a copy of the application he had signed. It was important that he have a copy now.

"Mr. Shorn," the Bank Manager stated, "this is quite out of the ordinary – I'm sure there's been a misunderstanding."

Jim O'Reilly abruptly chimed in, "It is my understanding that Tom has signed an application that he may not fully understand – I recommend that you take the time now to go over it with him."

"I'm sorry but I have other appointments…"

Officer O'Reilly interrupted "Mr. Shorn has recently endured more stress than any man deserves – his wife's heart surgery and she and their daughter were in a serious car accident in which other lives were lost. Surely you can at least take the time to provide him copies of the document before we leave. I'm certain you'd agree that a copy of the application should have been emailed to Tom by now." The manager surrendered with a sigh, nodded his agreement, pulled up Tom's file on the computer and quickly printed two copies of the signed document – handing one to each.

The manager went over with them, section by section. The application was straightforward until they reached the terms and conditions for pay-out. At this point, the manager stopped and explained that this section was not in accordance with normal banking practices – he pointed with his pen. Written clearly, was the stipulation that upon the death of Karen Shorn, the loan is to be paid from her insurance policy through Tom's employer.

Upon the death of Tom, the loan is paid through his death benefits and the sole beneficiary is Jean Thompson.

"I had asked the Business Loans Manager about this at the time I signed, and he assured me that this was quite often normal with business loans." Tom confirmed, and then went on to explain how all of this had come together – the details of their business partnership agreement. Jean had approached Tom, not ready to cut ties with the business that she and her husband Doug owned and proposed a 50/50 partnership to purchase the business. Initially Tom understood that the arrangement would provide him with the security he would need, as Jean reminded him of Karen's uncertain survival with her heart condition – he wanted to ensure his children were well provided for. Jean had met with the Business Loans Manager and put all the paperwork in place.

"However, I've since re-evaluated the viability of managing my commitments to both my family and an extremely busy dealership. When I approached Jean to advise her of my wish to decline the business venture, she informed me emphatically that I had signed a document that was final – and that I was legally bound to continue with this business arrangement, including this loan. The Bank Manager listened carefully and then offered his input.

"I'm afraid that I am not able to advise on your business agreement with Jean Thompson – my advice is that you seek legal counsel on this as soon as possible. However, with respect to the loan application, the bank's position is clear – you are not obligated until you sign the equivalent of a promissory note, and the funding has been transferred to you. In reviewing this document, I am confident you have signed only the application at this point." Tom thanked the manager and took the copies with him. Jim O' Reilly followed him out to his car.

"Are you OK?" Jim quietly solicited. "No concerns with speeding or anything?" he joked, lightening up an incredibly tense moment. Tom assured him that he was all right. "Jean Thompson seems like a piece of work."

"She absolutely is," Tom confirmed, with a troubled sigh.

"What are you going to do now?"

"Take this to Karen - she will help me sort it out," Tom replied.

"I do not imagine that will be easy," Jim offered sympathetically. Tom nodded his agreement. "Does your wife know about your affair with Jean?" Tom was taken aback at first - then remembered the lipstick fiasco when this good officer had pulled him over for speeding - what an idiot he'd been. Who had he thought he was fooling?

"Yes, I told her everything including the affair - twice."

"Twice?" Jim parroted.

"Yes," Tom scoffed, "an entire heartfelt bedroom sharing session – confessing it all!" his crestfallen expression shuffled something inside of Jim – compassion? Tom took a deep breath, "Karen's memory is not what it should be yet, but she will get there. It's a possible oxygen deprivation issue during her initial cardiac episodes," Tom related. Jim patted his shoulder and wished him luck, advising him to take it easy on the drive home. Back in the cruiser, the good officer watched him drive away, conceding that Tom Shorn had just earned a considerable measure of Jim O'Reilly's respect – sure as shit, Jim had gazed into the eyes of a changed man.

Home was not on Tom's agenda; he decided to take the documents to Karen right away. Unquestionably, the situation created unwarranted stress for her, but he was pretty sure that the longer it festered, the greater it would impact her – best to get it on the table! Karen was all about game plans, without her having the full picture she would not be able to assess their vulnerability in this mess. She was sound asleep when he entered her room, and the icy chill sent a tremor of fear through him – his heart raced, and he struggled for a breath. He ran to shake her awake, as gently as he dared. In seconds the temperature returned to normal, and Karen opened her eyes to the sheer terror on her husband's face.

"What is wrong?" Karen demanded, thoroughly alarmed. Tom instantly felt foolish – what the hell *was* wrong with him?

"Nothing, I was just worried about you," Tom sighed, affording a shaky smile. This new side of Tom was enlightening to Karen, but she couldn't shake the stab of guilt that surfaced when she reflected on the impact to her family from all of her health issues – to the point where Tom was terrified when she slept? On that note, she gloried in the benefits to so much sleep - Karen felt refreshed – as if she had slept for a week. Her energy levels were bolstering every day, and she voiced this when Tom inquired about how she was feeling.

In firm resignation, Tom pulled out the documents and handed them to Karen. He then imparted the details of his meeting with the bank manager. Karen listened intently. Once he concluded sharing the entire mess, he patiently sat back and waited for her response. Karen eyed him thoughtfully.

"This could not have been easy for you to disclose, Tom – not all of this information puts you in a good light," she gently remarked.

"Now you sound like a lawyer," Tom replied. Karen laughed. Yes, didn't she just? Tom reached out impulsively and kissed the palm of her hand.

"I am going to spend the rest of my life making up for the shit I have put you through," Tom whispered passionately. "I do not deserve to be forgiven and I do not deserve you, but I am determined to be the man that *you* deserve! I am so sorry," Tom choked back his tears.

"I know you are," Karen responded gently, returning the whisper kiss to both of his palms. "Just leave the documents here and I will go over them again. I'll track down a couple of my past colleagues from the law firm and get their take on our situation," Karen advised. Tom gently kissed her before leaving the hospital room. The expression he bestowed upon her was new to Karen – never before had he looked at her that way. It was beyond gratitude for her cookies and other things he appreciated from time to time; far removed from the usual post sex satisfaction, and infinitely infused with greater tenderness, respect and depth than he'd ever bestowed upon Jean – this she knew. Presently, her heart warmed and perhaps even skipped a beat. Karen certainly did not enjoy the ordeal they were going through, but she was thrilled with the emergence of this new man. She'd fallen in love with a little boy inside an extremely virile and attractive man, who had not yet experienced anything in life that he hadn't been able to control. Joy flooded her heart as she realized that the little boy was maturing – stepping up to the plate!

As Tom glanced back at Karen when he left her room, the love and tenderness on her face warmed his heart. Oh, he was under no illusion – there was a lot of work to do toward reconciliation and amends on his part, but he saw hope in her eyes. He always knew she loved him – never in doubt, and after all his bullshit, the cards were all out on the table now. What he saw in her eyes today, propelled him to greater heights and strengthened his resolve. Yes, with God's grace, obviously flowing freely through Karen, they would weather this together, and their future would unfold to incorporate the realization of their dreams. Tom had a spring in his step as he sauntered out the door – he was one hell of a lucky man!

Faith and Hope were at the house when he arrived. The four of them were sitting at the kitchen table playing cards, and he greeted them warmly as he passed through to wash up for dinner. Faith told him Chinese food would be arriving within the next hour. Tom thanked her for her generosity and paused in the hallway as he caught some of their conversation. Everything felt so natural and comfortable with these two new additions to their household. Obviously, Karen agreed and accepted them as family, or she would not have granted Hope power of attorney and guardianship over their children.

Tom grinned, hearing Zac joking with Sway that the pets were giving her all the luck and that was why she kept winning.

"But isn't it nice to have so many people and animals who love you and want to be near you?" Tom could feel his daughter's smile in her response to Faith that she was indeed very lucky. The next topic brought up by Hope made him catch his breath and go back to the kitchen.

"How did the ghost research go, Zac?"

"Really well," Zac stated, and eagerly described his protection ritual to put salt around their beds to keep his family safe.

"That is interesting," Faith observed, "did it work?"

"I think so, Zac replied, "I noticed it was not cold within the circle of salt, but the icy chill remained on the outside."

"Wow, that is amazing," Faith gushed with a look of wonder then looked pointedly at her sister, "I wonder if that would keep annoying people away."

"Now wouldn't that be nice," Hope burst out laughing but stopped when she saw the white pallor on Tom's face when he came back into the kitchen.

"What's wrong, Tom?" Hope inquired.

"I had a weird experience this evening when I went to visit Karen," Tom responded, "I do not know how to explain it." Tom added as he regarded their inquisitive gazes. Zac blurted out what was on everyone's mind.

"Dad, did you see a ghost?"

"I'm thinking not," Tom instantly replied. "But in her hospital room tonight, have experience the intense cold that has been occurring here in our home," he eyed them all in consternation, "I won't lie - it scared the hell out of me, I thought there was something wrong with Karen, the mist of her breath seemed ominous, but when I wake her up, it all instantly disappeared, and she is normal. I'm sure she thought I was losing my marbles – I must have looked terrified!" he concluded.

Sway reached over to touch Hope's arm and asked her if her mommy was OK. Hope assured her that all was good. Concerned for his little girl, Tom chimed in that Mom was perfectly fine and maybe he had just imagined it all.

"Sure Dad, so then we have been imagining the cold here at the house? The liquid turning to vapor – our breath; shower steam? Remember Mom in the bathtub?"

"I apologize - I am sure it is nothing. With everything going on at my work and Mom's health, I am clearly overthinking things."

"You could be right, Tom," Faith soothed, "your family has endured a significant host of events that you feel responsible to deal with. However, I have learned to trust what my gut tells me, "She smiled knowingly, "women call it intuition and men usually term it a gut feeling. Whichever resonates with you - trust that. If you feel a niggling in your gut, investigate a little more, or at the very least, keep your mind open."

Zac saw this as his opportunity to help his father, so he followed up on what Faith had said, "Yeah Dad, like I went to the library to read books and searched online to find out what makes a room cold. The thing that kept popping up concerned ghosts, and I do not know if we have a ghost in our house or not, but I followed through on the salt protection ritual that was suggested. Maybe there are ghosts in the hospital – that is where most people die, right?" Zac finished off, feeling a positive burst of energy.

Tom looked at his son and smiled, the color now returned to his face. "How did you get so smart?" Tom ruffled Zac's hair and gave him a hug.

"I take after mom," Zac quipped instantly, earning a huge burst of laughter around the kitchen.

"Yes, I believe you do," Tom chuckled. "I like to think you got the best of the both of us," Tom added affectionately.

"Me too!" Sway added her input, "I got the best of both of you too." Tom reached over to hold her close.

"Yes, you do Princess, yes you do!" The doorbell rang, breaking up the reverie - the Chinese food had arrived. It was perfect timing to pull everyone back to the here and now. They all sat and enjoyed the delicious fare and soon, Hope and Faith bid their adieus and departed. Sway tried to convince Hope to stay but Hope insisted everyone needed some normalcy and a good sleep, assuring her all was fine. Zac promised Sway that he would sleep in her room, and this seemed to satisfy her. Tom mused that the two women had seemed a bit rushed and wondered why.

As the two sisters were about to hop into their respective cars, Faith glanced over to see Constable O'Reilly parked up a little way up the street. Hope gave Faith the nod that she had seen him as well. Both were highly keen to their surroundings – life had taught them well.

I'll meet you at home," Hope confirmed. Faith paused and asked Hope if she was feeling sure about Karen being OK. Hope nodded in confirmation and commented.

"For now." Nodding towards the police car, she voiced what they both knew. "He is our main concern presently." Faith bobbed her head, then got into her car to follow her sister home. Jim followed at a distance and parked just up the street from their home. Both women knew of his presence but did not spare a backward glance. He sat in surveillance as the lights went on in the house and did not miss when they went out. Just minutes later, he received a call from dispatch and confirmed that he was on route. His pet project would have to wait. As he drove away, he did not see Hope and Faith get into Hope's car and head for the hospital.

Chapter 29

IT WAS LATE and Faith and Hope made their way to Karen's room unnoticed. She was awake and waiting for them.

"I saw you coming," Karen gave her head a bit of a shake, "I don't know how, but I did." Hope and Faith glanced at each other, grabbed chairs and pulled them up to the bed. Hope took Karen's hand.

"How are you feeling?"

"Better by each moment – it feels like warp speed recovery," Karen marveled, then queried in a puzzled tone, "we do not have a lot of time, do we?"

"No, we don't, that is why it is imperative that we catch you up on everything as soon as possible." Faith was extremely pleased with Karen's progress – it could have all gone another way.

Hope gently rubbed the back of Karen's hand, then asked "Is it OK for me to help you remember?" Karen nodded.

"I knew you would ask me that." Hope threw a glance at Faith before addressing Karen.

"What do you mean with those comments – you saw us coming and knew what I would ask?" Karen contemplated for a moment.

"I cannot explain it - I saw the vision in my mind of you coming to my room, and I heard an inner voice telling me what you were going to ask. It was a little eerie," Karen paused then added, "It sounds crazy, but I also know that you understand, and I trust you."

Faith interjected; it was time for transparency. "To us, it is *not* crazy and yes you can trust us - just as we know we can trust you." Hope continued to gently rub the back of Karen's hand and addressed her softly.

"I want you to close your eyes and listen to my voice as we take you back through time - to your second heart attack; to when you first met our mother, Susan." Karen closed her eyes as Hope had bid and felt her mind drifting through a pink cloud of warmth, back to when she was being returned to her room. She was in so much pain, her mind kept seeing over and over an accident where her and Sway had burned and perished in a car. It was horrible – the pain excruciating. Hope felt her pain and wrapped Karen in healing light, whispering reassurances.

"Karen, you are safe with us, I have removed the pain within the memories. Now, I will guide you through them - we need you to tell us all that you remember." As the pain dissipated, Karen felt a flood of blessed relief. She sighed and nodded her head, with eyes still closed.

"I am in the hospital room and your mother, Susan, is in the next bed to me. I am seeing my car burning with Sway and I inside. It is a dream but not a dream – more of a vision - just like when I saw the two of you walk into my room today. I am in so much pain and I am terrified. I can smell our burning flesh - can feel the scorching heat of the fire, and the horrific sound of screaming all around me. I can't get to Sway – I need to save her. During this vision, Susan came to me and offered to help me. I felt unquestionably safe with her, as I do with the two of you. I also knew that she had been waiting in this place, at that time to help me and my daughter Sway, but I had no idea why."

Karen took another deep breath and noticed she could smell and hear everything from her memory but the pain from before was absent – simply gone, affording her the strength to dive deeply. "Susan asked my permission to help, and I readily agreed." Karen went on to describe the feeling of her mind drifting off to sleep and Susan entering her body. "It was like dozing in and out of slumber while sitting in the passenger seat of my body with Susan driving."

Hope continued to keep Karen wrapped in the healing light and explained, "Karen I am now going to guide you through your memories and in particular the memories you have with our mother, Susan. You will see all that has happened between then and now." Karen again nodded and felt Faith place her hands on the souls of her feet. A gentle current moved through her. Hope and Faith directed their total energy to help Karen open her subconscious and in doing so, brought Karen and Susan's blended memories together. Karen began to see flashes - Susan telling Hope and Faith that they were to save the mother and child. Karen was aware that the mother and child Susan referred to was her and Sway. In technicolor, Karen's mind relived the memories - Susan taking Karen's body through a major physical work over each day and Hope following up with her healing and cleansing energy. Minus the pain, Karen could feel the muscles stretching and breaking with each work out, then gaining strength as they healed. She was able to focus on the flushing of toxins and fat from her system, with each drink of water Susan ingested. Karen was amazed – she could see all of this – feel it and understand it. It was like two people, merged into one.

Karen smiled and laughed through the memories of carefree playing with her daughter. Tears of empathy went out to her son as she witnessed his worry and despair. She blushed profusely through the sexual encounters with her husband. Wait – she could feel no pain from these memories as Hope had taken that away, but the pleasure was incredible. She reflected that a normal female would be jealous or angry with another woman taking over her body and glorying in hot sex with her husband, but Karen understood the intense sexual energy had healed her body quicker and made her stronger in each moment – she vowed to continue that healing journey! Besides, the memories were now hers too – Susan had given her that gift. The memory of the party both amused and saddened her. Karen knew that Jean was a tortured soul, and that her husband Doug, played an undefined role – she sensed it was not pleasant.

This journey through time had its moments of despair - Susan's memory of seeing Tom with lipstick on him, smelling like sex and another woman's perfume and Tom confessing his infidelity with Jean, causing both anger and sadness and a deep compassion for this man, having to endure the confession twice. When Karen came to the memory of the car accident, she gained a full appreciation for the brutal physical workouts Susan had put her through – it was the reason Karen was able to save Sway and get them both out of the car before it exploded – altering the nightmarish vision forever. Then, feeling her heart give out. Tears rolled down her face and she opened her eyes. Faith was still holding her feet and Hope gripped her hand. Both women were crying. Karen could feel their despair.

"I am so sorry," Karen offered softly, knowing something in this process had caused their anguish. "Thank you for all you have done for me and my daughter," Karen felt her own tears welling up. Faith moved from Karen's feet to hug her sister, then reached over and gave Karen a hug as well.

The two sisters pulled themselves together and Faith whispered softly, "As you said Karen, we do not have a lot of time - let's continue." Hope checked in on Karen's feelings – she was good to go.

"That is good," Faith stated, "we have a lot of ground to cover." Hope and Faith settled comfortably in their chairs by Karen's bed and Karen reclined slightly. "It's time to talk about Mom – Susan." The hitch in her voice clutched at Karen's heart. "Our mother is what we call a seer, or See-er, which means a person who is gifted with the ability to see things in the future, and some can also see both the future and the past. Our mother has been seeing you and Sway in the future. She did not tell us for how long or the details - a seer only shares when it is necessary." Faith took a deep breath and continued.

"Two years ago, our mother informed us that it was critical she be admitted into this hospital in this exact time period, so we moved here and sought employment in our present positions. We never question our mother's directives – for good reasons. All went according to plan, and we checked Susan into the hospital. While we waited for your and Sway's arrival, Susan disclosed to Hope and I that you and Sway would have a car accident. To ensure your survival, the three of us would have to help you become strong enough to save you both." Hope now continued the story.

"The three of us devised a plan to keep Susan's body alive, while she was helping you become healthy, lose weight and build muscle mass, through the process taking over your body.. Faith spent as much time as possible massaging and moving Susan's arms and legs while she was absent from her body. However, it's a complex and exhausting process and there were times that Susan had to come back to her own body to attend to the things Faith could not. Those were the moments that you regained full control over your body and could feel everything – eating compulsions, the torn muscles, extreme fatigue, and of course confusion."

As Karen sat and listened intently to everything that Faith and Hope had shared, her mind absorbed and pulled pieces together. It was an incredible event, and she was exhausted but knew a sense of completion – there was a reason she was here. She thanked them profusely for everything they had done for her and Sway and asked when she would be able to see Susan. Tears welled up again in Hope and Faith's eyes.

"Our mother made a choice, she is no longer with us," Faith explained. Karen felt intense grief as she now understood where their despair was coming from.

"My God, I am so sorry," she reached out to embrace them both, then pulled back, "If your mother knew about the accident, then why couldn't you have arranged to stop it?"

Faith went on to explain that every event in which a seer intervenes, changes the future, creating both negative and positive effects. "The seer has the heavy burden to weigh it out, then make the best decision with the least negative impact. It is an enormous responsibility. "The accident needed to happen," Faith imparted, "another person whose fate is to die in that accident would have lived, and consequently would perhaps been too great. A seer rarely sees all. Your heart was going to fail. Our mother put everything in place from her visions to ensure not just your survival but for you to move forward in your life with your family. She accomplished this without interfering with fate – this was her sacrifice. Only our two families were affected and yours with a positive outcome – she was guided to intervene."

Karen felt a wave of deep emotion flood her body as Hope reached out to take her hand. "Why did you give up your gift?" Hope coaxed.

"What gift?" Karen was duly shocked.

"We can only share a body of another who is like us." Hope paused to let that sink in, then wrapped Karen in golden light. Tears flowed from all three women's eyes as they shared each other's pain, then the golden light gently washed that pain away.

Hope lets go of Karen's hand and assured her, "I understand that all of this is overwhelming. If we had time, we would not be pushing your memories so fast, but to continue to keep us all safe, we need all the pieces of the puzzle. Remember that Sway, Zac and even Tom are part of this now. Our mother is no longer here to guide us with her visions, so we must rely on each other and our joint knowledge and expertise. I am a healer, your daughter Sway is also a healer, and Faith has the gift of working at a soul level by showing the person she is working with how their actions affect others. Someday another seer will find us – perhaps already has - and provide us with the missing pieces so that we can continue to carry out the work that our soul purpose has destined us to do."

"Why are we not safe?" Hope looked straight into Karen's eyes.

"Because there are others who covet our gifts, not for good, but for power. If it was solely for good, we would not have sacrificed every part of ourselves to stop the havoc that this foreign species has created. They lust for power and control, with an unquenchable thirst to devour all that is pure and good. They have brought imbalance to this planet."

"Who are they?" Karen felt a sudden drive for knowledge.

"You already know all these answers," Faith replied, "we now need to leave it to you to gain the rest of your memory. You have the full power to do so when you choose – when you are ready. We trust there is a good reason you remain unaware for now, so we leave it to you. Once you embrace full enlightenment, you will know the extent and power of your gift."

"If you can't tell me more about myself then can you divulge more about Sway?" Hope smiled widely.

"Of course – that is my pleasure! Your daughter is an amazing soul with the power to heal. She requires someone like me to teach her how to use her gift without harming herself. The way I explained it to Sway is that she is like a battery that needs to be recharged. It is important that she does not totally drain her energy before taking the necessary time to recharge. We do know that our mother saw Sway just after her birth and has been seeing her right up till now."

"Further, we all must be very careful with our gifts and to never use them in a manner that will draw suspicion. For example, if we did not put a plan in place, you would have had the enemy on your tail – placing you in dangerous vulnerability. A miracle healing is like putting blood in the water with sharks, they smell it for miles and experience a relentless drive toward it." Karen listened and absorbed all that she could. Most brought a feeling of familiarity, but she couldn't quite connect the dots.

Hope then went on to say their mother had been clear in her vision that Karen needed to get back on her path to pursue a law career as an attorney. This mirrored her recent epiphany that this was part of her destiny and a means of helping others like herself. Hope then went on to say, "Our mother marked out a path, for you to achieve your destiny without unnecessary added steps. You must forego the university degree and challenge the Bar. You *will* pass it and then set up your own practice."

"But how?" Karen challenged, "even skipping university, it will require funds that Tom and I do not have." Hope smiled indulgently.

"Do you now remember the meetings with the law office and the visits to the bank?" Karen felt memory surfacing. Of course, Susan had provided for Karen and each one of her children! "When Susan was in your body, she opened individual accounts for yourself, Zac, and Sway. She then transferred money into each of those accounts."

"I now remember," Karen murmured, "we opened the accounts in a different bank from where Tom and I deal. I have never maintained a separate account from him since we married. Tom has one of his own savings accounts, apart from our joint one." Karen then chuckled, "Susan was not impressed with how Tom and I managed our finances." Hope and Faith both smiled when Karen mentioned their mothers name. No, Susan had not been impressed at all with Tom. Suddenly Karen gasped, "that is lot of money!" Hope nodded.

"Yes, it is – the exact amount our mother saw in her vision that you would need to achieve your goal. Our mother also provided the stipulation that my signature is required for any withdrawals from all three accounts – strictly to avoid the possibility of someone manipulating your decisions. The money is there to secure Zac, Sway and your futures." Karen let out a sigh. Yes, she could see Susan's reasoning behind it – there was good cause for suspicion with Jean in the mix.

Hope and Faith could see that Karen was tiring. Hope gave Karen another healing hug, instructed her to get some sleep and they would see her in the morning. Faith gave Karen a hug whispered, "sleep well my sister," kissing her on the cheek. Karen surrendered to slumberland and as she drifted, smiling at the memory of Susan's altered opinion of Tom as she spent her days as Karen, his wife.

Karen's eyes teared as she thought of the ultimate sacrifice Susan had given for her and her family. Susan had given her life. The she heard Susan's voice in her mind, "yes, I gave my life and my heart, but this old girl got to have an amazing sexual holiday before leaving this body," then she heard Susan chuckle. Karen smiled.

Hope and Faith left Karen drifting off to sleep and quickly made their way down to the hospital morgue. They worked tirelessly – Susan's remains had been cremated, and they retrieved her ashes. Now they quickly accessed the medical software, to erase every trace of Susan's history from the system – anyone who might search her records now, would find absolutely nothing. It was imperative – an autopsy would have been out of the question, the coroner would have seen the repairs done to Karen's heart that now lay within their mother's chest, which would result in involving other medical personnel, making it harder to cover their tracks. They also effectively deleted Sway's test records and results, eradicating them from the system. Their involvement could not be detected. The preservation of their identities – their gifts, were vital to their survival and the that of the planet.

Unbeknownst to them a few hours before Dr. Gary Hamilton pulled a copy of the scans of Susan's and Karen's hearts. When Susan passed from heart failure, he noticed scars on Susan that where not there on his previous examinations. It was as if she had heart surgery. Then Dr. Edward's raved about how his patient Karen Shorn had healed her heart with lifestyle and dietary changes that are so miraculous her scars from her previous surgeries are nonexistent. Looking at the two scans he could swear there had been a change of heart.

It was nearly 8:00 a.m. by the time Hope and Faith completed all necessary tasks, and they were both thoroughly exhausted. There was no overnight shift at the morgue, so Faith and Hope needed only to ensure they were undetected by Security. That was a cakewalk – this wasn't their first rodeo! The morning shift was arriving as they made their way through the deserted basement passageways. They both startled at the sound of Hope's cell. Glancing down, she saw the Shorn residence flash on the display, and immediately picked up.

"Is Sway with you?" Fear welled up in Hope's throat at the sound of Tom's panicked voice.

"No, I am at the hospital now."

"She is gone, I went to wake her, and she is not here!" Tom screamed. In the background Hope could hear Zac crying and telling his father his sister was in her room when he left to take Daisy for her morning walk.

Hope forced a calm state within and instructed clearly, "Tom, hang up the phone and call 9-1-1 – do it now! I will call Officer O'Reilly." Tom did not even reply as he hung up to comply. Hope had no need to tell Faith what was happening as she dialed the policeman's number - this was what they had been preparing for in line with their mother's worst predictions – the one they had been trying to avoid at all costs.

To be continued in the next book: Change of Mind

ACKNOWLEDGEMENT

I HEREBY OFFER my heartfelt gratitude to those individuals in my life who've encouraged me to brush the cobwebs off the many manuscripts I have penned over the past four decades. Without you all, the expression of my passion would have lain dormant – I am forever blessed with your influence.

To my dear friend Karen Peddle who has inspired me from the first day I met her thirty-three years ago. This woman embraced courage and took on the world, fighting on behalf of those unable to do so for themselves. For the final ten years of her life, Karen fought a valiant personal battle with cancer, and has been the voice behind many survivors, urging them to never give up. No matter how grave her illness, she always made time for others and will forever be a guiding mentor and shining example for humanity.

Then the universe sent me the most amazing editor in Brenda Scatterty. My manuscripts would not have found the light without her incredible talents. Brenda embraces the gift of literacy, honing her skills with diverse educational, professional and freelance writing/editing, and our work together on this book has been a spiritual journey.

I would also like to acknowledge my grade three schoolteacher, Mrs. Stringfellow – another believer and mentor, as well as all my family and friends who encouraged me to embrace my worth and authenticity – to follow my dreams. Many of our experiences together are woven into my stories – as with my dear friend, Faith Brown and my beautiful granddaughter Sway Lattes, who inspires me every day – I love you.

A warm thank you to all the readers.

I am eternally thankful!

Printed in Canada